Glasgone

Glasgone

Nancy Bagato

Stilt Leg Press
2017

Text quotations:

Lewis Carroll, *Alice's Adventures in Wonderland*, (1865).

Lewis Carroll, *Through the Looking Glass*, (1871).

First Printing: 2017

ISBN 978-0-9985981-0-9

Stilt Leg Press
26 Kerr Street
Onancock, Virginia 23417
(540) 324-9512
www.lulu.com/spotlight/nancybagato

For my husband, Scott McGee,
who made sure I finished what I started.

"Ye Cannae Shove Yer Granny" is sung to the tune of
"She'll be Comin' Round the Mountain."

Contents

1: Let's Make a Deal

"He hasn't said more than two words together to me since he got here," the petite blonde whined into the phone. A Southern drawl smoothed her tone from grating to childish. "He won't answer my texts neither."

"He hasn't been in touch with me since graduation." The older woman frowned back down the line. She was old enough to be the younger woman's mother, and if her son got over his sudden moodiness, she'd become her mother-in-law. She had once looked much like this girl, but had overindulged in sun worship in her younger days and now had to soften the consequences with heavy makeup.

She offered up an explanation for her usually dutiful son. "He's trying to protect everyone. It would look bad for the research grant and the university to have the supervisor involved with an employee. I warned you about that."

This wasn't the first time they'd had this conversation. Her pale blue eyes hardened at the thought of spending the entire duration of the couple's engagement and married life soothing the girl's insecurities whenever her son followed his cultural roots of lads-at-the-pub neglect of his wife. The bitterness of personal experience tinted her voice. "And he's proud. Scots can be very macho at times. Being around women too long makes them uncomfortable. They need time alone with other men to reassure themselves that we can't live without them."

"But he acts like he doesn't even know me!" She punched the kilted teddy bear off her bed.

"Laura Beth. Has he asked for it back?" the older blonde snapped, a verbal slap to the face.

"No-oo." The younger woman drew out the answer into two syllables. She covered the claddagh ring protectively with her right hand. He'd promised to get her a diamond solitaire once he'd saved up the money. "Could you please talk to him?" she begged. "You can find him at that stupid Irish pub. He's in there all the time, watching soccer and drinking. Wearing a leather jacket! It's like he's trying to reinvent himself with some moronic bad-boy act. He even bought a motorcycle."

There was a long pause. "He's being careful. Something you need to do more of," Mary Booth said bluntly. "Is he acting professional?"

"I guess. He certainly isn't being personal."

"I mean with the job. Is he doing the job right?" Mary growled.

"Yes."

"Then stay out of it and follow his lead. His behavior doesn't put my work at risk. But yours does."

"But…"

The dial tone buzzed a curt dismissal in her ear.

"Why can't you just run a background check?" The dark-haired young woman hugged herself with the arm not holding the phone. "Doesn't your husband have the resources for that?"

"In America, yes. Not internationally. Not without justifiable cause." She had anticipated the questions and had plausible explanations. At least as plausible as necessary for the girl's perfunctory resistance. She was willing to play along, enough to keep the girl's guilt to a minor nagging doubt instead of a full outburst of actual conscience. Ray's clients all had one, somewhere deep down, over something; it was interesting what gave criminals pause.

"So if there's no cause, why investigate? Or have you gotten that paranoid?" Her hands trembled with nerves from daring to insult her benefactor. "Why does this guy matter to you anyway?"

"Ray's sponsoring him and wants to be sure there'll be no unpleasant surprises," she lied. "What does it matter to you, Alice? Unless you've got the rest of our money?" She paused to let the reminder sink in. They both knew how the game always ended. "You don't have much choice."

"What do you think I'm going to be able to do that a private investigator can't do better?" Alice paced the small apartment.

"I need details you can only get from personal contact. I think you'll be perfect. It's worth at least as much as we'd pay a detective.

More, even. Say, four thousand?" Mary Booth's mouth tightened downward into a smile. Money, the great motivator. She knew she had her on the hook. It was ridiculously more than the girl had been paid for any other task. More than waitressing private parties, housecleaning, paralegal research, or errands. It was a little over the balance of outstanding debt from the legal fees and the settlement loan. She loved when her husband took charity cases. This one had been good for seven years, and could be stretched out for another one, maybe two. Especially when she found fault with the job and rescinded some of the credit, as usual. Her own brand of community service.

"What kind of things am I supposed to find out, exactly?" Alice stopped in front of the battered dresser and picked up the plush rabbit with its once-white fur loved bare. *Here we go. Down the rabbit hole again, "wondering how she would ever get out again."* She blamed the running *Alice's Adventures in Wonderland* quotes on her father's nightly readings of the books to her throughout her childhood. He had even named her to coordinate with his home town. The long-dead amusement park Wonderland lived on in the name for the commuter rail stop in Revere, Massachusetts. Now that he was gone, the books remained like a guiding hand from beyond the grave. Not very useful, but it was all she had in the way of parental advice. Especially since her mother had disowned her in the wake of the trials.

"Things background checks don't turn up. Interests, habits, hobbies. Who is he? What are his favorite foods? What are his fondest childhood memories? What motivates him?"

It seemed a harmless enough request, though teetering on the edge of stalking. She hugged the rabbit tightly, leaving her mistress to stew in silence as she gauged the older woman's desperation and its leverage. "I want it in writing before I do anything," she said finally.

"Of course. Standard contract." The voice lilted with amusement, like a cat agreeing not to harm the mouse if it came out to play.

"No. Straight *quid pro quo*," she insisted, terrified by her own boldness. But after all, she was dealing with the cutthroat wife of her lawyer. "No qualifiers on quantity or quality of the results. I want half credited up front. That's standard contract for a private investigator. I have learned a little working for your husband. I'll put in two months."

"How do I know you'll do a satisfactory job?"

"Who else can you ask?" A long silence hung on the line. She pressed the rabbit to her forehead, eyes squeezed shut.

"Three thousand, then. And I want periodic reports, through Liam." Her mouth tightened into another inverted smile with anticipation.

Alice cursed under her breath, but knew she had pushed as far as possible. "Golden," she said sarcastically.

2: The Honey Trap Catches Too Many Flies

In his usual dim, sticky corner booth, Nick Kerr hunched up against the over-enthusiastic air conditioning and sipped his usual pint of wee heavy. He shifted his motorcycle helmet to the end of the table for more elbow room. Clicking the wall-mounted TV over to soccer, he turned on closed captioning so he could follow the score despite the pub's loud and inauthentic music. The establishment claimed to be an Irish pub, but the menu strayed and the decorations appeared left over from a Saint Patrick's Day party, all cheap shamrock cutouts and green glitter-covered hats. He would have been offended if he'd been Irish instead of Scots. At least the beverages included a spectrum of British imports, which was the main reason he was planted in the booth most evenings. Every other bar he'd tried only seemed to serve the cheap flavorless American lager college students drank in large quantities.

The usual suspects were present, holding down bar stools or huddled thick as thieves at tables. Rednecks waxed philosophical with country music lyrics. College alumni Peter Pans clung to the glory days of beer, babes, and bullshitting. Grad students or university staff hid from the fraternity-sponsored meat markets while trying to hook up in a more tasteful way. Small college towns were a uniquely American phenomenon that Nick still found foreign after three months in the thick of it. The culture was exaggerated by two colleges located only a few miles apart. He worked for Ag Tech, a large research institution with an all-male military past. Neighboring Sweet Thistle was a small former women's college, supposedly a great place for finding loose women. *A great pairing,* he supposed. *Like fish an' chips.*

"Gies yer blootered, yer blazin, yer steamin masses, mad wey it, yearnin tae furget," orated a second wiry Scotsman, flopping into the booth across from Nick. He tipped up a bottle of cheap American lager and eyed the unkempt version of himself.

"Shut it, Nicktoon. Ah've seen ye far enow," Nick growled back without much heat.

"Get tae fook. An' dain't ca' me tha' awfy nickname. Ye ken Ah hate it."

"Oniehin ye say, Nick Two."

"No' tha' wan neither."

"Wid ye raither Ah ca'ed ye Knickers?"

"Christ on a bike, ur an ersehole." He took an angry swill off his bottle. "An' ye thoat ye could lee me behind agin, Ah see. Nae chance, ya fookin bawheid."

Nick sneered at his friend's beverage. "Ye could at least huv the decency tae drink a local crafted lager instead ay tha' horse pish."

Nick Two jabbed him with a foot.

"Dain't gies a jag, ya wee diddy."

Nick Two waved off the mild insult and pointed. "Yer wee tottie at eleven o'clock."

He looked out across the room. She was in again tonight, for the fourth night in a row, by herself on the pool table as per usual, shooting erratically as per usual. He wondered how he'd missed her. Nicktoon's fault for certain. His mate had her classified as university staff, but enjoyed speculating on her particulars to needle him.

"Loner, iffy shot, toaff cue tae gude fur her shootin. Hoo dae ye cry it? Seen *The Color ay Money* tae many times, mibbe? Ah doot she's hustlin the pool. A wee hairy fishin fur a lumber?" He ran a hand over his perfect hair and straightened his shirt, an uptight button-down plaid that made skinny Nicktoon look like a tattie bogle fresh out of the cornfield for a night on the town.

"Ah've nivver seen her lee wey onieyin, no' tha' Ah'm keepin tabs an' that," Nick defended her half-heartedly, trying to disguise the true depth of his interest.

"Aye right. Scratch the wee hairy theory, then. On yer say-so."

He resisted punching his sarcastic mate right in his crooked, toothy grin. The lass wasn't hard on the eyes, but not a typical beauty either. Bedroom hair, dark curls falling halfway down her back. Not much in the way of tits, though.

"Ah, but seein as hoo ye nivver get onie tits, ye may as well like um aw, onie road," Nick Two commented philosophically as if he could read his mind, or at least follow his line of sight.

"Aye. Ur a philosopher an' a gennleman, mate." He refused to rise to the bait, instead continuing his train of thought. Her ass had an old-fashioned curviness that called to mind Marilyn Monroe and Christina Hendricks. She was neither heavy nor skinny. *No' tall either,* he added approvingly. A big plus for a fine-boned lad of average height, or slightly less, like himself.

"Like baith ay us," Nick Two interrupted with a competitive reminder.

She was about his age, or a handful of years one way or the other. There was something distant and guarded in her eyes and habits. Overall, the parts weren't everyone's cup of tea, but the whole package merited a second look. A long second look, in which both Nicks were currently indulging themselves.

"A fine bit ay gear, tha' yin," concluded one.

"Ah widnae mind gettin a grip ay her," agreed the other.

If it wasn't the package, maybe it was the way she moved with an absent-minded grace, unaware of her own effect. And maybe it was just the potent wee heavy.

"Aye, tha', an' mibbe ye huvnae been gettin yer nasties fur ages," Nick Two reminded him. "Ca' canny, chiefie."

Alice studied him from across the room. He looked like the photo she'd been given, but with a makeover to look less clean cut, more cologne-commercial unshaven-sexy. He was certainly studying her as much as she was studying him. And had been for several days. *Like Tweedledee and Tweedledum would say, "If you think I'm a waxwork, you ought to pay. Contrariwise, if you think I'm alive, you ought to speak."*

He noticed she was watching him watch her bend over the table. He self-consciously ran a hand over his medium-brown hair, slicking it back off his forehead even though it wouldn't stay there long. He typically avoided complicating his life with social contact, what with the Nicktoon popping up like a bad acid flashback, and due to the precarious nature of his immigration. But if he had been the type to go on the hunt for talent, this one was more appealing than most. And he'd never had a problem at home with relationships wearing out their welcome. He wondered if he should be concerned about his inability to commit.

"Ye been watchin tae mich American daytime telly, mate. A few mair months an' ye'll be drinkin this pish yerself."

"Shut it, ya eejit!" he said through his teeth. He raised his glass and flashed a grin, playing it bold as brass to test the slut theory.

The girl straightened with an audible snort. She heeled her cue and scooped the last ball into the pocket.

"Is she comin tae cuff ye intae mince?" Nick Two speculated eagerly. "Or gawn fur it wey the gennleman at the table? Namely, maself." He ran a hand over his well-behaved hair again and checked his breath in his palm.

Quarters clinked on the pool table, marking the challenge for a game. She turned toward the source, a smug, athletic-looking student.

"Wrang pub fur it, aye?" Nick Two noted. "Frat boy-lookin wanker an' that."

The girl shrugged and nodded. As the frat boy paid the table and the balls thundered loose, she gave Nick the international symbol for "I'm watching you," pointing two fingers at her eyes and then at him. Her lips curved into a Mona Lisa smile. A little competition for her attention was always a good play.

"Ye'd best strike whilst the irn is hoat, chiefie, afore tha' nyuck snags yer spare."

Nick turned back to the TV, doing his best to appear unmoved by his mate's urging. His pint was down to dregs. He waited for the commercials before heading toward the bar, past one more lost opportunity in a long history of them. He watched the girl lean in for a shot. Frat Boy sidled behind her, eyeing her rear, and gripped her hips while blethering about correcting her stance.

"Dead lame," sniffed Nick Two in his ear, making him jump. "Iven ye could dae be'er'n tha', ya big fanny. If ye iver got the boattle tae try."

Alice over-extended her backstroke with a hard jab, slamming Frat Boy in the gut with the heel of her cue. Both Nicks couldn't help wincing as the guy grunted and staggered back.

She met Nick's eyes. His stomach writhed with a cocktail of emotions, not sure what he saw in her look.

He felt a slap on the back. "Ye micht get a kick ay the baw wey tha' yin efter aw."

"Or she micht gies a kick in the baws fur tryin." He continued to the front room in a haze of schadenfreude, pleased the competition had gotten shot down on the first pass. He waited at the end of the bar for the gangly hipster bartender with heavy-rimmed glasses who was always suspiciously high on life.

"Another wee heavy, my man?" The bartender bounded away before he could answer.

As the pint thumped down, Nick tilted his head toward the pool table and added, "An' whitiver the hen is intae. An' quarters byraway. Ah'm feelin sponny, so Ah'm. Gawn tae try ma haun at this jeeked snooker yees huv got."

The bartender gave him a strange look and returned to the gantry with uncharacteristic slowness. Nick sipped the red ale to a safe transport level as he waited.

"Whit's wrang wey hum?" grumbled Nick Two with narrowed eyes.

Nick shrugged. "Ah reckon he disnae ken whit snooker is."

"Mair like, he disnae think ye kin get a click iven wey buyin the wee hen a beverage."

"An' he micht be dead right." Nick could feel his game face coming on: rising heart rate, quickening breath, tenseness in his wiry frame, stillness in his mind. He balanced the two glasses in one hand as he set the coins on the pool table rail.

"Please tell me urnae hustlin."

Nick gave him a dirty look over his shoulder. "Ah ken whit Ah'm daein."

"Dain't get onieyin malkied, mind," groused Nick Two.

"Fook ye. This isnae Glesga. It's the States," he growled back. "An' a pathetic wee toon at tha'."

"Oh aye. The States. So ye'll get someyin shot, then. Fantastic."

Frat Boy suddenly stepped back from the table, throwing out his arms in an exaggerated hip-hop gesture. Nick dodged, but stepped on the girl's foot with his heavy harness boot and spilled both drinks down his arm.

"Ach! Ah'm in ma oon road theday," he spluttered, setting the glasses on the nearest table and shaking ale off his hand. In the corner of his eye, he could see the Nicktoon face-palming in disgust. He looked at the girl through his hair. "Awright, hen?"

"I'm okay," she said. Her jaw was clenched in pain, irritation, or a combination of both.

"Dead sleekit, chiefie. Made a right coo's erse ay it, dinnae ye."

Nick pushed his hair out of the way and glared in the direction of his friend's heckling.

Alice leaned over the table, took her shot, and stepped back to him, favoring the trampled foot. *"The time has come, the Walrus said, to talk of many things..."* She tilted her head slightly as she studied him. "So, King of Physical Comedy, where are you from?"

"Maself? Ah belang tae Glesga, byraway."

"Dresden? You don't sound German."

He shook his head. She leaned in to hear better over the music, turning her ear toward him. He breathed in her scent, blooming heather in summer rain. It suited her. Her pale neck formed a long, smooth line from the curve of her throat, past the gently swinging chandelier earrings, to the soft swell of her small breasts. The beating of his heart drowned out the music.

"Scoatland, hen," he said to her neck.

Her eyes were as green as the pool table felt, with a halo of brown around the pupil. He awkwardly thrust out what was left of the drink he'd bought for her, spilling a little more on his arm. He made a stiff little bow as a desperate last-ditch attempt at sophistication. "Bartender said it wis whit ye wis huvin."

She gingerly took the wet glass from his hand. "Thank you," she said, fighting a laugh, and bobbed a curtsey. *"Tell me how you live and what it is you do,"* her internal commentary suggested. She opted for something more sane. "So, your lairdship, do the Blue Ridge Mountains really look like the Scottish Highlands?"

"Ah'm fae the Lullands, byraway." He hoped she could understand his rougher version of the Sean Connery burr, a thick, rollicking accent with the t's and l's dropped out like hiccups. "Baith ur mountains, mind. The Hielands, but. Broon an' smooth. Or purple wey the heather in bloom. Or bare stane, ken. 'S onerly green in the toaty wee bit ay summer we get. An' nae mich in the way ay trees. No' like err."

She stepped away reluctantly for a shot.

"Oh aye, the heather in bloom." Nick Two leaned in, fanning her scent up to his nostrils. "The wee tottie's pure eatin oot yer haun. Ye ken when a bird asks ye a pure stupit question, it means she likes ye. Or it means she's a fookin eejit like yerself."

"At least Ah'm no' shunted ootright," Nick snapped back. "Pish aff the noo an' lee me tae it." He turned back to continue his conversation with the girl. "Whaeiver telt ye they looked alike hud tae be pure marockulous."

"Miraculous?"

"Ye ken: wankered, steamin, blootered, full ay it, oot yer tights…" he tried.

She stepped away for another shot. "You realize I have no idea what any of that means," she said across the pool table to him, laughter in her voice. *This job might not be so bad after all.*

He jerked a thumb in the direction of a local who had peaked early and was now staggering for the exit. "Ye ken, stotting."

She barked a laugh. He exhaled, suddenly aware he'd been holding his breath. She leaned over the table, smiling at him between lining up her shot and taking it.

"Rinoo Ah could say, 'Ah'm gawn tae malky ye tae death, byraway,' an' she'd say, 'Ma bit or yers?' " gloated Nick to his mate.

"Ah bet she gaws fur onieyin wey an accent," said the Nicktoon dismissively. "Let me find oot."

Nick blocked him as the girl reached to pick up her drink from the high table behind him.

"I don't know who started it, but Sweet Thistle makes a big deal about it. I went there. You know, the Appalachians standing in for the Highlands, tartan school colors, a kilted caveman for a mascot, and a Scottish festival. It's a whole Highlands marketing extravaganza over there. I even tried out for the Highland dancing team. I wasn't very good at not stepping on the swords though." She looked up at him curiously.

"You're a Sweet Thistle girl?" hooted Frat Boy, reasserting his forgotten presence. "Hey, what does a Sweet Thistle girl do first thing in the morning?" He elbowed Nick. "Go home! Get it?"

Nick swiped at his hair, which for once didn't need straightening. "Tha's fookin unca'ed fur, mate."

"Har har. That old chestnut." Alice lined up a shot, her eyes angry. "Here's one for you: how many Ag Tech fraternity brothers does it take to screw in a light bulb?" she said coldly.

"Dunno. How many?" said Frat Boy with an anticipatory grin, looking like a Labrador retriever that thinks everything is a game, even the word *no*. Nick Two watched with predatory interest.

"Nobody knows. They haven't got it drunk enough yet," she said, and hit a hard cut to the side pocket. The ball clattered down.

"Good one." Frat Boy laughed loudly. "Hey, let *me* buy you a drink!"

The evening was going too fast in the wrong direction, sliding out of her control. At least she had only the eight ball left, giving her a quick out. She called the corner pocket with a curt gesture of her cue. She took aim, then adjusted her angle and dropped the cue's tail slightly. Nick opened his mouth to help her correct, knowing the equal and opposite reaction of what she'd just set up. With a fast, hard stroke, the eight ball dropped into the pocket, and the cue ball spun lazily after it.

She turned her back on the pool table and headed in the direction of the restrooms. *"It's a great huge game of chess that's being played,"* she reminded herself as she grabbed her cue case in passing.

Frat Boy turned his attention to the quarter tray. Nick sorted through the rack for a reasonably straight cue. The situation was recoverable. He could win quickly and get a match with her. Plus, a little showing off wouldn't hurt. He chalked up and took a long swallow of his drink. He eagerly waited for her return from the ladies' to continue their conversation.

"Whit the fook?" Nick Two said incredulously. "Yer bird's leein."

Nick's head snapped around like he'd been kicked. Light from the pub illuminated the dark-haired girl as she passed the large picture window. Frozen stupidly with a glass in one hand and a cue in the other, he inexplicably felt like she'd walked out in the middle of a right good shagging. "If it's fur ye it'll no' go by ye, aye?" he said hopefully.

"News flash, mate. It's fookin gawn by ye doon the fookin road. Ye huv a gift, ya tosser, a fookin gift." The Nicktoon grinned.

"Jen up, wisnae me! Ah dinnae dae nuchin," Nick protested. "Nuchin at aw."

"Heard tha' afore," Nick Two said flatly. "Ye huv the sore-faced look ay a dug whae jist realized tha' lovely trip in the motor cost hum his baws." He patted his mate's cheek consolingly. "The noo, cuff this wanker. Ur gude at tha' onie road."

3: Mr. Hyde and Dr. Jekyll

Alice Bonner kept to herself. She preferred to be taken for granted, invisible in the academic cycle. For a permanent resident in a transient town, life was a time-lapse movie of bars and apartments filling and emptying, cars flowing into town in the morning and back out at five. Students were replaced a fourth at a time by new warm bodies doing the same things as the ones that came before, complacent and self-involved, an unending loop of move-ins, youthful indiscretions, football seasons, and commencement ceremonies. Like a model of the solar system, faculty, staff, graduate students, and administrators were the outer planets moving at varied speeds from the general student body and each other, some hopping to different institutions every couple of years like career military under transfer orders, others settling in for the long haul in an increasingly myopic academic Neverland. Only Alice seemed to stay stationary on the edge like Pluto, distant, uninvolved, almost forgotten.

She was a pariah who knew her place, content with eyes sliding away and conversations falling silent as she passed. At this point, people went through the motions because everyone else did, without remembering the original reason. She was old news, faded to something vague, replaced many times over by the latest internet scandal. Her face was forgotten, her name recognized more and more infrequently. Like the homicidal hook-handed man who terrorized a mythical Lover's Lane, part of her was urban legend, the stuff of insensitive jokes and playful threats at student parties.

Alice didn't have any friends. She'd let them drift out of her life when Brad had drifted in. At first it had been because she'd been so infatuated with him that she'd had no time for anyone else. Then her friends had moved on, and she found herself tightly bound by a loveless marriage and controlled by mind games with no one to turn to.

Escape hadn't been impossible, but had come at a high price. She had traded one master for another, paying down the bill for legal services and the settlement loan with cash and odd jobs. She continued to do what she was told and when. All of it was on the right side of the law, the fine print in a contract. She was allowed plenty of rope between requests, and the jobs were little offers she could refuse. If she were completely honest with herself, she wasn't really looking beyond the indenture. It gave her life structure. To end the debt would mean an end to her twisted family: herself, a wicked stepmother, and a good but oblivious father figure.

She survived on the hollow interactions at work and around town. An observer, not a participant. A small ripple to indicate her path, to confirm her existence, like graffiti on a bathroom wall. She was reduced to a bit part of a handful of empty words. At best, she could achieve a moment of random kindness or a spark of connection that burned out as fast as it began. She stayed up above it, not down in it. She was an alley cat, feeding off the scraps of others, she who walks alone.

Until now. For the first time in years, an ordinary conversation felt real, felt like much more than empty words. *Of course it wasn't ordinary. I was paid to have it.* The words rang false as soon as she thought them, but they worked to shame the feeling into numbness.

"Morning, Dr. Kerr." The janitor nodded in greeting as he mopped the Commons floor.

"Moarnin, George. Awright?" Nick answered. His title still sounded odd to him, but it was a guilty pleasure hearing it.

"Getting antsy. Them activists don't go long without a fuss, you know. Been too quiet lately." He shook his head heavily.

"Aye, noo ye mention it." Nick held up crossed fingers, then slipped through the doorway and wound his way through the concrete hallways of the veterinary college complex. Except for the polished linoleum floor, everything—walls, doors, lockers—was painted institutional beige.

He stowed the helmet in his locker and pulled out a white lab coat, navy scrubs, and sneakers. After a quick change in the men's room, he hit the locker again, lifting a paper lunch sack out of his helmet and holding it in his teeth as he stashed his street clothes and boots. He smoothed his hair back in place, slammed the locker with one foot, and thumped open the stairwell door to enter the bowels of the building. In the piecework of several construction phases, corridors twisted, abruptly slanted uphill, or opened back on themselves. He navigated to the research labs with the absent-minded sureness of a rat running a familiar maze.

"Puttin the lab back intae labyrinth," quipped Nick Two.

"Dain't ye huv somehin ye should be daein, Nicktoon?"

"Nae, ye made sure ay tha', ye fookin tossbag." Nick Two leaned on the last set of stairwell doors and blew a kiss.

Nick went through waving a farewell victory sign, first two fingers spread wide and palm turned inward to make the gesture obscene. He tossed his lunch onto the break area table and nodded to the bleary-eyed graveyard-shift lab rat who was relieving the buttons of his white coat from their long shift restraining his protruding gut.

"Awright, Dave?" He self-consciously buttoned his own coat over his lean torso.

"Still kicking." Dave Barrows' moon face split into a grin. "I miss second shift. You're lucky you start next week. Get out right at prime time for the bars, when the ladies are one drink away from finding love, and you're still sharp and looking good." He waggled his eyebrows.

"Ah thoat ye wis pefter-efter the Third Wheel."

"Well, Laura Beth is a class act. She wouldn't want anyone to think she was compromising the grant project by dating one of us lowly lab techs."

"Nae doot." He eyeballed Dave's thinning hair, petrified with gel into a carefully tousled formation. *Whitiver hurts ye through the nicht, mate.*

Laura Beth was the project lead, a humorless blonde that Dave would have given his left nut to sleep with. He worked thanklessly toward that end by filling her substitution requests. Nick secretly called her Pavlov's Belle, due to the involuntary drooling she triggered in Dave. He couldn't understand the attraction. Although pretty in a fine-boned Southern belle way, her nose was too small for her face, a disparity he felt certain would only grow more pronounced with age until she was as noseless as Voldemort. Then there was the angry expectation for him to do or say something, but he hadn't the faintest clue what; he did the work as well as any of them. But most of all, she reminded him of his mother.

"He's got less chance ay a click wey her than wee fannybaws err wey his pool-playing doll," hissed a voice in his ear. He chose to ignore it and not even look around for the source, who hadn't pissed off as promised after all.

"Hey man, you should come out drinking with me sometime," Dave offered. "With that accent, those sorority girls at Champions would totally throw their panties at you."

"Tha' wis a fookin Welshman, ya numpty." Nick Two shook his head in disgust. "Bloody Tom Jones. Fookin eejits, thum Yanks. Dain't ken Welsh fae Scots fae Irish."

"Aye right. Jist whit Ah need, mair laundry," Nick joked, and herded his irate friend into the lab. "See ye later."

"Away an' fling shite at the moon, mate," catcalled Nick Two at the closed door. "We're getting fair exposure tae communicable disease right err."

Nick breathed in the pungent smell of ammonia and warm feathers. To him, it was comforting, the smell of summers on his grandparents' farm. He turned up the lights to daylight level and clucked to a sleepy pullet who perched nearest the lab door. He rubbed her crop where it hung over the perch like a fat man's gut over his belt. The chicken growled and stood slowly.

"Ur right crabbit theday, ma wee nippy sweetie," he crooned into the glaring orange eyes. The hen lifted her feathers and shook like a dog. With her ruff extended for a moment, she resembled a monstrous white dandelion before settling her plumage into a smooth slope and crooning back at him.

"At least ur pure aisy tae please. Unlike maist women." He frowned slightly, remembering the blazing green eyes. A small shiver rippled over his skin.

"It's no' thum hens ur supposed tae be gettin a click wey," sniped the Nicktoon. He turned his back on the birds, commandeered the lone chair, and propped his feet on the desk to surf the internet. "The least ye kin dae fur stealin ma joab is tae shut yer stupit gub an' get it done," he groused.

"If it's yer joab, hoo urnae ye daein it?" he retorted, going through the motions in the often-repeated exchange.

"Ah dain't mich care fur shovelin' shite."

"Oh aye. Tha's wahrk fur the likes ay me. Ye dain't need a degree fur this, ken."

Nick stepped into the aviary to begin his shift's work. The slatted ceiling rose nearly three feet above him. The space was divided into three tiers, each with separate manure conveyors and perches, with a communal scratching area and nest boxes. He tested moisture levels in the straw bedding. "Manky," he declared, and clicked his tongue in cheerful disgust. The birds clucked back. After mucking out, he shook out fresh straw, the rising dust making him sneeze. A hen breathed out a long, querulous note. He swung open the cage doors with a valet's flourish, and the hens crowded out into the Yard, as he called it. He watched fondly as the birds scratched with their yellow dinosaur feet, stepped back and peered around hopefully to see if they had won the chicken lottery, dug with their beaks a few times, and strutted forward to scratch again. After he filled feeders and checked the automatic waterers, he squatted in the sea of bobbing heads, jiggling wattles, and jerking tail feathers. The sharp yellow beaks clattered as they tasted his buttons, clipboard, and shoelaces.

Nick's thoughts drifted back to the Borderlands farm. Heavy rains rumbled on the barn roof. The strong earthy scent of wet dirt drifted through the open doors. Inside, surrounded by the dusty darkness, hay prickled his back as he lay half-dozing. Fat speckled hens pecked and scratched nearby. They chirped excitedly over the laces on his trainers, whiffling at them, then growled with disappointment when they couldn't be swallowed like the fat worms they impersonated.

He repeated the cleaning process in the second aviary. He stroked the lab hens' broad backs. He gently steered them around to check for pale wattles and shit-encrusted fluff, making brief notes on the clipboard. "Nae signs ay infection yet," he said hopefully.

"Ye still huv tae kill thum, an' carve oot their organs fur weighin an' that, then start over agin infectin the next clutch ay wee chicks," Nick Two said sharply. "Which ye should huv a degree fur, ken."

" 'S nae different fae the farm, but fur the scales and jags. Besides, they dain't ken aw tha'. See? They're dancin!" Nick seized a plump bird and broke into their favorite childhood song to break the Nicktoon's sour mood. He moved the plump body up, down, and around, while the small head stayed frozen in place as the neck rotated, expanded, and contracted. "Oh, ye cannae shove yer granny aff a bus. Aff a bus! Nae, ye cannae shove yer granny aff a bus."

Nick Two turned and stared in disdain. "Ur pure dead mental."

"Ye cannae shove yer granny, fur she's yer mammy's mammy..." A handful of other birds gathered, taking an aggressive stance toward the dancing chicken. He shooed them away, scolding affectionately, "Pish aff, yees. She's onerly at the dancin, no' takin the huff." He released the bird, which shook out her feathers before trotting after the rest of the flock. "Nivver gets auld. Cheers, doll."

An alarm shrieked through the building, muffled by the lab door. The hens cackled and craned their heads, wattles bobbing comically.

"No' agin," Nick groaned irritably. "George wis dead right, so he wis." He carefully waded through the birds. "Whit the hell is wrang wey people. Awyis stirrin up trouble." He gently pushed a few of the opportunistic hens back inside with his leg as he closed the aviary door, singing, "Push! Push!" Nick Two had already vacated the lab.

The piercing whoops of the emergency alarm engulfed him. He endured the pain to watch the birds through the door's glass pane until they returned to scratching and pecking. He smiled. Most likely it was another false alarm. Either way, it meant a long wait outside. He wasn't complaining on a day as beautiful as this one was forecast to be. With a quick squirt of hand sanitizer from the break area table, he pinched his lunch sack between elbow and ribs and took the stairs two at a time.

The early September sun seared his eyes as he stepped outside with a few other stragglers. He jogged across the recessed concrete patio and bounded up the few stairs to the parking lot and onto the expansive lawn that surrounded the complex. He fumbled into the sunglasses he kept on hand in the hopes of lunch outside, or an evacuation, on a nice day. A light breeze whispered with a few early fallen leaves, and he turned his face joyfully to the warmth and light, which even now was better than it ever got in a Glasgow summer.

Students settled under the huge oaks on the lawn or at picnic tables, some leaning over medical textbooks. On the far right side of the building, dogs on leads yipped excitedly from the small teaching hospital evacuation. He scanned the crowd for the Nicktoon. He weaved toward him through the lake of green and navy scrubs and stopped short when he recognized the mass of dark curls. His stomach lurched in the first long drop on a rollercoaster. His ears roared with white noise, and his shoulders tensed. The girl from the pub was facing away from him, allowing him to sneak a good look in bright light. Nick Two gave him a helpful shove in her direction. He bumped into her, causing her to stagger and nearly twist an ankle. He caught her above the elbow.

"Ach, sorry hen."

Her eyes shot up to his face. He released her arm and stepped back, searching for a way to disappear.

"The Lowlander! We've got to stop meeting like this." Alice's voice lilted with amusement and relief. She'd risked pulling the alarm to flush him out, but at least she'd thought to place a napkin between her fingerprints and the handle. Her long skirt swirled in the small space between them like a cartoon representation of her scent drifting over him. "You clean up nicely."

His eyes dropped to her feet in their strappy high-heeled sandals. He was relieved she didn't have a bruise in the shape of his boot. He tried surreptitiously to read her ID badge, but the side with the magnetic stripe was facing out. He could feel her studying him now, the green eyes running over his sharp nose, faint freckles, and sliding hair. He felt like he had as a small boy, all edges and out of sorts.

The sunlight confirmed her impression that Mary's photograph didn't really do him justice. "White coat. So you're either doing your residency, or you're in research?" She turned the observation into a question.

"Research," he muttered, his eyes behind the shades meeting hers for a moment and flicking away.

"Making me work for it. Okay, what are you researching? Or is it top secret, and if you tell me you have to kill me?"

"Nuchin tha' brilliant. Hepatitis E." He shuffled and searched the crowd for an excuse to evade her questions.

"Hepatitis E?"

"Aye. It's like Hepatitis A." He looked sideways at her and smoothed his hair back. She cocked an eyebrow at him.

"Christ on a bike. She's gawn tae need CPR tae get through this fookin conversation." Nick Two slapped him on the back of the head.

Nick's hair fell down into his face and he pushed it back out. The Nicktoon had a way of blending in so that he often went unnoticed; Nick hoped the dull drone of the alarm made his mate's comments unnoticeable as well.

"Pure uninterestin really. Seems tae be shooin up in mair species aw the time, an' they're no' sure hoo it transmits tae people. No' mich kent aboot it. 'E for enigma' is whit they say roond the lab. 'S no' ivven very serious as diseases go. Kin cause a thirty percent chance ay liver failure in pregnant women, but. Thus the research." His own internet research paid off for this conversation.

"So you work with…?"

"Chickens." He looked down at his sneakers, feeling a little foolish.

"That explains the straw."

He slapped at his clothes self-consciously.

"That wasn't so hard, was it." She grinned at him.

"Evidently it wis fur this nugwatt," the Nicktoon interjected.

"Right fittin, ken. 'The bird that nivver flew' an' that."

"Ye huv got tae be fookin kiddin me, mate. Ye soond like a dime bar the noo," Nick Two criticized, arms crossed, staring off into the blue sky as if hoping for a lightning bolt to put him out of his misery.

She looked like she was hoping the same thing.

"On account ay chickens no' bein the best fliers, an' me fae Glesga. 'The bird that nivver flew' is wan ay the miracles ay Saint Mungo. Ivry wean in Glesga kens it."

"For real? As in the Hospital for Magical Maladies? I don't remember reading about his miracles in any of the Harry Potter books."

"Nae, nae. Saint Mungo wis a real saint, the patron saint an' founder ay Glesga, wey four miracles. 'Erras the bird tha' nivver flew, erras the tree tha' nivver grew, erras the bell tha' nivver rang, erras the fish tha' nivver swam,' " he recited. "It's on the city seal byraway."

"An' the Uni ay Glesga seal. Ye should ken tha'," his friend muttered.

"An' the Uni ay Glesga seal. Ah'd explain in detail, ye'd fa' dead asleep but."

The alarm died suddenly. She nodded thoughtfully and the conversation stalled out into silence as other people talked about things that made more sense.

"So what made you go into research?" she asked finally.

"Ah awyis wanted tae be a veterinarian. Love animaws an' that."

Nick Two frowned. "Ye dinnae answer the question. Hoo did ye go intae research, eh? Ah'd pure fancy hearin," he asked pointedly.

"An' the animaws whit help find cures an' medicines in research need tae huv someyin love thum an' care fur thum tae, no' jist companion animaws."

The Nicktoon rolled his eyes, but at least she looked touched. Nick tried to concentrate on her to make his pal disappear.

"Aye, touched in the heid. Like yees. A match made in heaven."

Nick Two fluttered his hands under his chin like cherub wings. Nick restrained himself from punching him in the face, since that kind of Neanderthal behavior didn't go over well with the ladies. At least not with the non-psychotic ones.

"Ye ken James Herriot?"

"Are you kidding? I loved *All Creatures Great and Small* growing up." She crinkled her nose. "Except the whole arm-up-a-cow's-ass thing. I had such a crush on Christopher Timothy."

"Maself tae. Ah mean, Ah loved the program tae. An' the books." He felt his cheeks grow hot and fumbled ahead with a lie. "Tha's hoo Ah went intae veterinary science. The real James Herriot went tae Uni ay Glesga. Ma alma mater, byraway. Erras iven a library named efter hum an' that."

He thought back to the Herriot Christmas, as he called that first Christmas without his mother. The dense gray sky suffocated the sun into a dim lemon throat lozenge. A rare blizzard stilled the city, as if even the weather was off-kilter from his mother's disappearance. The sharp smell of his Da's holiday black bun, unfortunately and literally burnt black, choked out all the air until the windows had to be opened to let in the biting wind and damp cold. The mistletoe hung limply from the kitchen doorway. The presents he didn't feel like opening sat forlornly under a scraggly stick of a tree. He didn't even know why he hurt so much. Maybe because now even the illusion of winning her favor was gone. His wee brother pushed about the spilled contents of his stocking to eat the candy and leave the nuts and dried fruit. On the telly, the *All Creatures Great and Small Christmas Special* radiated love and warmth and a stable, happy family. Sure James and Helen quarreled, but Helen never screamed or threw tea mugs or disappeared for a fortnight at a time. And everything came out right in the end, except for the dog. He knew exactly what he wanted to be when he grew up, because everybody loved James Herriot.

"Apparently. Includin yer wee tottie. Whae is still staunin err lookin at yer stupit coupon waitin fur mair pearls ay wisdom, byraway," remarked Nick Two witheringly, bringing him back to the moment.

The all-clear siren blared and the crowd shifted toward the building in a mass.

"Noo or nivver." Nick Two gave him a jab in the ribs.

He pulled a slightly damp hand from his lab coat pocket and extended it formally. "Doactor Nick Kerr, byraway," he said in mock seriousness, "at yer service."

"Alice Bonner." She wrapped his long fingers firmly in her own and grinned. Maybe she wanted to know more about him for himself. It was a bonus that she was getting paid for it. "I think I like Lowlander better. Dr. Car?" She held her hands at ten and two on an imaginary steering wheel. "Like vroom-vroom? Sounds like an alias invented by a two year old," she criticized. No wonder the Booths were suspicious.

"Tha's a wee mich," he retorted, mildly offended. "Ah'm no' insultin ye, Alice in Wunnerland. An' it's spelt K-E-R-R, mind." He held up his badge on its lanyard.

"Nick Kerr." She repeated the name thoughtfully. "Nick-car...nickar. That must have been a bit awkward growing up, sounding a bit like 'knickers.'"

"Fook ye, ya fookin bint," snarled Nick Two in his ear.

He frowned and aimed a swift kick backwards at his mate which failed to land. He remembered all too well how unfunny that name had been, once their classmates had figured it out.

The spring after their mother's disappearance, her absence still tainted the space around the Kerr boys like a contagious disease. In the recess soccer matches, the older boy was always one of the goalies, a forgotten placeholder between the piles of jackets that served as goalposts. Most of the time, the other boys left him alone, but sometimes Billy Glennis would strut in front of the goal, faking strikes to make him jerk one way or another. Billy was a foot taller, an older boy who should have been in a higher grade and tended toward fat. He was good at the game because he trampled everyone in his way, or because they stood back in self-preservation to let him through unchallenged. Billy loved to make a hard strike at someone's head and then run off laughing.

One afternoon, the thrashing scrum of boys downfield looked for all the world like a brawl from an Andy Capp cartoon, a dust cloud with arms and legs protruding from it. They couldn't see what he could: his wee brother on the sidelines, flowing a piece of his mother's slip from hand to hand. It had been her nightclothes, and in the mornings when she had padded barefoot through the flat, the satin flowed over her beautiful pale skin just like water. He thought he'd gotten rid of that bloody thing. Typical for the sneaky wee shite to have it somehow.

While the tangled mass of boys struggled on, he headed purposefully downfield. His wee brother saw him coming and ran. He seized him and tried to bring him to ground, but the younger boy bucked and kicked with the precious memento held out of reach. At last the pink scrap jerked out of his hand, only to reappear high in the air at the end of Billy Glennis's loathsome thick arm.

"Whit's aw this then?" Billy boomed, imitating a Monty Python bobby. He fancied himself the comedian. As always, his two goons guffawed loudly. The rest of the exercise yard gathered in a circle around the two brothers and their tormentor.

"Gawnae no' dae tha'. Gies it back," yelled Nick with uncharacteristic ferocity.

"Hoo? Is it yer wee Sunday knickers? Right manky. An' poofty," taunted Billy. His thin lips curled in distaste. "Nae wonder yer maw left yees. Ur a manky wee poofter in girl's knickers, Nick Kerr." His piggy eyes lit up with inspiration. "Shoo us yer knickers, Knickers!"

Billy's lackeys took up the chant. The other boys looked askance at each other, some snickering nervously, some joining in to curry favor. The girls clumped together, giggling and smirking, whispering behind their hands to each other. Everyone was hoping that Billy would haul down Nick's pants. It would be the highlight of the school year.

As the wee boy looked from side to side for a place to break through the ring of faces, his brother's hands tightened into fists.

His heart thundered in his ears. His eyesight dimmed to pinpoints centered on Billy's swollen, gloating face. The flapping scrap of pink satin was like a red flag to a bull. He rushed in with an incoherent roar, his fists flailing wildly. The chants turned to shrieks as Billy's heavy team bolted. In less than a minute, the untouchable Billy Glennis was a whimpering fetus curled in the dirt, his face a smear of tears, mucus, and blood. A shocked teacher hauled away the berserker Kerr, who thrashed and kicked in midair like a crazed tomcat.

Da was called in to meet with the headmaster. His son sat outside the office on a hard chair for what felt like an eternity. The only evidence of his outburst was a ragged, angry-looking cut on his knuckles from knocking out two of Billy's teeth. He had punishment exercises for a fortnight after school, but he didn't care. He now knew his place in his small and broken world. He was the hard man who had to protect his brother all the way through secondary school, through all of his brother's stupid quirks, through the causes, protests, and petitions, through the lunchroom lecturing of bored and hostile peers, through all the Billy Glennises.

That night while Da and his brother slept, he sneaked into the tenement's community garden with the last piece of his mother's slip. He burned it, pissed on the smoldering, melted lump, and kicked dirt and grass over the blackened mud. All she had done was destroy their family, and he wanted no part of her left to taint their lives.

* * * * * * * *

"Knickers, tha' auld chestnut," he replied, trying to soften the bitterness in his voice. He rubbed the faint scar still visible on his knuckles from the schoolyard brawl that had redefined him once. He gestured toward the recessed courtyard. "Ye comin or plunkin it, Alice in Wunnerland?"

It was on the tip of her tongue to tell him about growing up in the real Wonderland. She swallowed it back. She wasn't ready to give anyone much of anything. Besides, it was her job to find out about him, not yammer on about herself. She pointed left toward the main entrance. "I have to return my pass. I was supposed to have a meeting with the café manager, but now it's too late. Lunch rush." She shifted from foot to foot, the skirt swirling around her legs like ocean eddies. The meeting had never existed, but it had served to get her in the building unescorted.

"Ah thoat ye wis wey the veterinary college. Explains hoo Ah huvnae seen ye roond afore the noo, but." He waved his bedraggled lunch sack. "Dinnae ken erras a café," he lied.

"Then obviously I suck at my job. I've got to go. I'll see you around, Doctor Kahhrrr," she purred and turned away, smiling over her shoulder at him.

"Ah like it when she says it like tha'. Ya dancer, Ah'm set up." He smoothed his hair back and grinned, his feline teeth flashing.

"Gob shite," argued Nick Two. "She aw but gnawed her oon leg aff tae get away fae ye."

"Ur talkin mince, ya cakey bastart. Did ye no' see the look she gied me? Ur ye blind the noo, as well as daft?"

"Ur fanny-struck." Nick Two gave him a playful shove and began singing their favorite childhood song with new words. "Oh Ah widnae shove tha' yin oot ma bed. Oot ma bed! Oh Ah widnae shove tha' yin oot ma bed..."

4: An Inconvenient Truth

Nick watched the entrance from his vantage point at the end of the bar. He still felt dead pleased with himself. Over the top of his pint, he spotted Frat Boy, an unwelcome reminder that he hadn't won the cup yet. Frat Boy still looked out of place and was now craning his head around the sparsely populated pub as he headed for the bar. Hutch the bartender bounded into action. Nick pretended to watch the TV while eavesdropping.

"Uh, I'm looking for this chick that was in here last night, bro," Frat Boy said, leaning over the counter.

"Yeah, we get a few of those every now and then," joked Hutch.

"This chick? She had, like, long black hair," Frat Boy blundered ahead.

"Brown, ya muppet," Nick muttered under his breath.

"And she shoots pool?" Frat Boy continued.

"She short, got a sweet black and white Lucasi cue, and an even sweeter ass?" The bartender illustrated with a curvy hand motion.

"Yeah, exactly," drooled Frat Boy. "So have you seen her or what? She was hot for me, but I got an emergency call from one of my bros and had to leave suddenly before I could get her number."

Nick stared at him, deciding whether or not to call bullshit.

Hutch leaned on the bar counter with a snort of derision. "Alice? My man, you have a death wish. Nobody in here will touch that. She's the *Black Widow*, man," he gloated.

"What bullshit is that?" scoffed Frat Boy.

"Aye, whit mince ur ye carryin on aboot?" demanded Nick Two, eyes narrowed.

"He's jist windin hum up," retorted Nick. "Ah wid tae, well."

"You don't know? It was all over the TV and newspapers and shit, about six or seven years ago. Her husband was the football coach's kid. Son of *the* Vic Taylor. You sure you haven't heard this?" Hutch stared as the clueless guy shrugged apologetically. "So anyway. One night she 'finds' him," the bartender waved finger quotes in the air, "overdosed under suspicious circumstances."

"No way, man," breathed Frat Boy.

"Way," insisted Hutch with an exaggerated Valley Girl inflection that was lost on its victim. "She must have had a damn good lawyer, because they dropped the murder charges. Had to pay the family a big settlement, though. Just like O.J. Simpson."

"That's some fucked-up shit," said Frat Boy, shaking his head.

"Nae doot."

"You said it, my man," agreed Hutch, pointing to them both for emphasis. "They looked like the perfect couple and everything. He was this Aryan god and shit. You know, like straight out of an Abercrombie and Fitch catalog."

Nick's eyebrows shot up. The Nicktoon nearly spit his lager all over the counter.

"An' ye thoat ye hud a chance?" he choked out.

"You gotta wonder," Hutch philosophized. "The papers said they had marriage problems, and she was leaving him. Maybe he tried to stop her and…wham!" He slammed a fist into his palm. "You got to watch those quiet ones." He looked askance at Nick. "No offense, man."

"None taken," he nodded back.

"Hey dude, I know you," blurted Frat Boy. "You were there last night when that Black Widow chick was stalking me."

Fookin gallus, urnae ye, ya wanker, Nick thought to himself.

"She was stalking both of us, dude." Frat Boy said magnanimously and shook his head in wonder.

"Away wey ye," he said modestly, realizing he was sadly deluded about his success that afternoon.

"Then this calls for a celebration," chirped Hutch. He dashed to the top rail and poured three shots of whiskey. "On the house."

Nick preferred his usual wee heavy, but free always tasted pretty good.

"To close calls," declared Hutch.

Several rounds later, Frat Boy tottered to his feet. "I'm outta here, bros. Off to chase some killer ass that doesn't, you know, like, actually kill," he slurred. He pointed a hand at Nick in a sideways gangster pistol gesture. "You watcha back, my man."

Nick nodded and waved vaguely. The Nicktoon had pissed off at some point, surely sulking because he hadn't been included in the free drinks. Nick aimed himself at his usual seat and navigated the rolling floor. He slumped wearily into the booth and fumbled with the TV remote. He managed to get it facing the right direction at last and settled into channel surfing.

"Black Widdy. Cannae be ersed wey tha'," he muttered.

He searched for a soccer match, but in his inebriated state, he was hypnotized by the lightning-fast chopping skills of an infomercial chef. A hand on his shoulder made him startle and nearly spill his pint. When her face came into focus, the green eyes were laughing at him.

"Jesusjohnny, wumman," he scolded. "Dain't creep up on a perr man oot his trolley."

"Well, hello to you too, doctor," Alice said, stifling a smile. "I'm guessing that means you know you're completely shit-faced."

"Aye, tha' Ah'm, byraway."

"I'm getting the sense that Scots are like Eskimos, except you have hundreds of words for drunkenness instead of snow."

She slid into the seat across from him. He tried not to stare at her cleavage, but the low-cut top and tendrils of dark hair framing it didn't help. Nor did shrugging the cue case off her shoulder.

"I was going to pick up where we left off last night, but it would be like shooting fish in a barrel in your current condition." She nodded toward the pool tables.

He straightened slightly and smoothed his hair back. "Ah'm Scoats, wumman. Whiskey's oor national drink," he said as soberly as he could.

"That's not whiskey." She pointed to his pint. "What is it, anyway?"

"Ah wis drinkin it airlier. *This* is wee heavy."

"Are you going to make me work for it again?" She raised an eyebrow and waited expectantly.

He thought blearily for a minute, then offered the best he could come up with under the circumstances. " 'S like a jeeked stout," he slurred.

"Thanks for clearing that up," she said sarcastically.

"Ah'm rerr useful, so Ah um." *So dain't marder me like ye did yer man.*

The Mona Lisa smile appeared. "All right. I promise to take it easy on you."

"Ah hope so. Ah wis hopin tae gie ma Da grandweans an' that."

Her smile stiffened. It occurred to her that "being perfect" for her latest task might mean she was expected to win his trust by sleeping with him. She wasn't opposed to the idea if it was a matter of chemistry, but a lack of free will created a new moral low, even for her. And a new level of manipulation for Mary Booth. "That's a bit presumptuous, isn't it? I only wanted to shoot a game of pool. I hardly know you. Don't go shopping for wee kilts just yet."

"Nae danger. Ah hardly ken ye neither," he growled. "The bonny Alice Bonner. The Black Widdy. Am Ah right, am Ah wrang?" The whiskey had apparently evaporated the firewall between his head and mouth. "Let me aff aisy las' nicht, dinnae ye? Whit's wrang? Ah'm no' gude-lookin enough? No' fit enough?" He slapped his chest angrily. His relief at being spared from death fought with a contrary vanity at not being good enough to be a victim.

Her knuckles went white from her grip on the table edge. *"Somebody killed something. That's clear at any rate."*

5: Flashback

Her rear was numb from the unpadded vinyl chair in the crowded hospital room. Her mother-in-law's hysterics hurt her ears. " 'The air seemed full of it, and it rang through and through her head until she felt quite deafened,' " she whispered to herself. She slumped spinelessly, no energy or will for the ladylike posture she usually assumed for her critical in-laws. Given the hospital's low thermostat setting and her lack of support undergarments, it wouldn't have been very ladylike anyway. Outside in the hall, an ER doctor talked quietly to a uniformed police officer. The cop nodded, called out to one of the EMTs readying the ambulance for a return to the station, and jogged out of sight, one hand bracing his belt. Ten years as head coach of the local football champions bought Victor Taylor a lot of pull. He was certain of the real cause of death and informed everyone in the entire emergency room, stabbing a finger at Alice's bent form with the same grandstanding that made fans go wild during games. She couldn't meet his eyes or speak against his accusations.

As he held court with one of his speeches about determination and teamwork, this time directed toward achieving justice instead of gridiron victory, Alice drifted from the room. Away from the body, the machines, the wailing and yelling, the accusations. " 'The well was very deep, or she fell very slowly, for she had plenty of time as she went down to look around her, and to wonder what would happen next,' " she singsonged. She passed into the hallway's eerie fluorescent glow and suffocating antiseptic smell, then glided like a ghost through the automatic doors to the parking lot.

The cold hit her in a wave. She was underdressed in thin flannel pajama pants and a thermal shirt. The weak afternoon light was fading rapidly. The day looked the same as when she had entered the hospital that morning, as if time had been suspended and might never move again. As if she were Lewis Carroll's Alice stuck in a mad tea party.

She fumbled through her purse to pay the taxi driver, giving him too many bills and not waiting for change. Crossing her arms high and tight to cover her nipples and tucking her hands into her armpits for warmth, she climbed the open concrete stairs to the third floor apartment. Neighbors craned to look down the hall with cell phones out, talking, taking pictures, or thumbs flying with text messages. Conversations dropped to whispers as she passed. The apartment door stood open. Orange rope sectioned her living room carpet into an orderly grid with uniformed officers in the squares. It reminded her of her namesake's chessboard adventure through the looking glass.

"Place is a clusterfuck," one cop groused. "She didn't exactly try to hide the evidence."

Another crouched in front of one of Brad's used syringe nests that she had refused to clean up. A forensics specialist, she guessed.

He snorted. "More like hidden in plain sight. Syringe in a haystack."

"Sheer genius," chuckled the first cop to a plainclothes detective who moved arduously through the room. He was focused on the doorway like a bird dog on point.

"I live here," she said to him in a daze, wanting to wake up from this nightmare.

The detective's eyes were locked on her as he called out instructions to the officers in the grid. "Lewis—" One man grunted acknowledgment. "Help Wilson bag and tag, or like the stand-up comedian said, we'll be here all week."

"God, give me a nice spatter pattern any day," Lewis groused. "We're not going to dust all this shit, are we, Sarge?"

The detective watched her carefully as he answered. "Yes. And we're going to dust all that shit in the bedroom. Don't forget to pull the trash in here and the dumpster." He stepped over to her. "Could I have the pleasure of your company for a moment?"

She nodded wordlessly, unable to meet his eyes. The detective wrapped his overcoat around her shoulders, and she thankfully overlapped it across her chest. He propelled her through the gauntlet of the neighbors' awed obscenities.

At the unmarked cruiser, she expected to have her head steered into the back seat, like in cop reality shows. Instead, the detective opened the passenger door, unhooked an organizer from the seat, and stood back for her to enter.

"Come on, get in. It's cold," he encouraged. He gently closed the door before storing the organizer in the back and getting behind the wheel. "Let's get some heat in here, huh? Ah, that's the stuff."

She was squeezed next to a laptop on a swing arm. Between her and a detective who resembled her dead father was a console housing a large radio and several banks of knobs and switches. She clasped her frigid hands between her pajama-clad thighs for warmth and tried to keep from touching anything in the cramped miniature office. Gradually her chill tremors calmed and her jaw unclenched.

"Feel better?" The detective loosened his tie, fiddled with a small pager-looking box on his belt, and sighed like he was releasing a long-held breath.

She nodded stiffly.

"Detective Sergeant John Albers." He offered his hand.

She took it gingerly in her ice-cold one. "Alice Taylor. Sorry about the popsicle fingers." She sneaked a look into the man's blue eyes. Crows' feet crinkled in the corners.

"Nice to meet you, Mrs. Taylor."

"Please call me just Alice, sir."

"Okay, Just Alice." The blue eyes twinkled at her. "And you don't have to call me sir. Sergeant Albers, or John, or Sarge."

She smiled weakly.

"Well, first off, Just Alice, I have to give you this." He held out a piece of paper.

She took it reluctantly and forced her eyes to focus on the words. She didn't make it past "search warrant," which seemed like the bleeding obvious, considering what she'd walked into. Matters could move fast in a small town if it concerned an important citizen.

"There is something you can do to help me out, Just Alice. It's going to be a little hard for you."

"What, sir? I mean, Sarge."

"Tell me what happened here, starting with yesterday evening."

She nodded, trembling. *"Begin at the beginning, and go on until you come to the end. Then stop."* The beginning: Brad angry over his high blood sugar, one of many times that day, that week, that year. Par for the course. Him taking another shot of insulin, she didn't know how much. Walking fast through the cold evening, bundled up, cold on the outside but sweating under the layers, her breath damp on her scarf, the cold freezing her nostrils shut, burning out all smells. Walking a long time, a few steps behind Brad's angry stride, a good, subservient wife. Brad stopping to test his blood sugar under the sickly orange hum of a streetlight, sucking the blood off his fingertip, the finger popping out of his tight, angry mouth. Staring up into the black sky, wishing herself away with the scudding specters of clouds. Wondering when she could make her move. Returning back to the apartment, avoiding him, keeping a safe distance. It was late. Ten-thirty, maybe? Time for her to go to sleep, she had to get up early for work. Work...

"Oh my God, I forgot to call in," she said in a panic.

"It's okay, Just Alice. I'll talk to your boss. You need to take some time off." Sarge's calm voice soothed her.

She took a long, ragged breath and nodded. Her accrued leave could keep her paychecks stable for a while.

"So you were telling me it was time for you to turn in. What happened next?"

"I put on my pajamas." She pulled at the thermal shirt's tail, the leg of her flannel pants, with a ghost of a smile. "Been wearing them all day."

Sarge cocked his head in a nonverbal nudge for her to continue.

"I went to sleep, but Brad stayed up to watch a movie. I got up at six-thirty, right before the alarm, and was headed for the shower when I saw the bedroom light was still on."

"Didn't you just come from the bedroom?" Sarge interjected casually, but leaned forward.

"The other bedroom." She wouldn't meet his eyes. She'd dodged Brad that night, locked herself in the second bedroom to avoid the usual: him angry and hard with high blood sugar, banging away at her, bruising her inside. She was especially glad of it now. Enough dirty laundry was getting aired without revealing everything. She pulled the drawstring of her pajama pants free from the weight of her small purse and wrapped it around a finger, let it spin free, wound it again. "We don't—didn't—sleep in the same room anymore."

The man's blue eyes turned sad, the crows' feet more prominent. "Tell me what happened this morning after you saw the bedroom light."

Alice nodded faintly and took a deep breath. The console's switches and knobs blurred.

She saw her hand push the bedroom door wide. The TV snowed at a low volume. Brad's sock feet splayed beneath his khakis. One hand hung over the edge of the bed, fingers slightly curled, index finger straighter, as if pointing at the scattered pile of used test strips and syringes on the carpet below. How many had been there yesterday? No one would notice any new ones in that mess. She moved slowly into the room. He was lolled sideways against both bed pillows. His eyes were open, dilated so that the brilliant blue was a thin ring around a black void. His polo shirt was soaked through with sweat. Two empty syringes stood upright, stabbed into the mattress like graveyard crosses. A third lay beside them, unused but filled to capacity. "Shit. Shit shit shit shit SHIT," Alice muttered frantically as she dug through his supply bag, scattering syringes and the large insulin vial onto the bed, finally fitting a test strip into the monitor with unsteady hands. The lancet pen punctured his cold fingertip with a clack that made her jump. She squeezed, her own fingers trembling as the dark drop wicked into the test strip. The monitor's screen blinked a countdown to a beep and spelled ERROR in digital block letters.

She dropped it and ran to the dresser. She yanked drawers open, shoving jumbled clothes roughly until she found the white foam box. She fumbled the kit open and pried the small vial of pale powder and a fat syringe of clear liquid from their molded compartments. She inserted the needle into the rubber lid and forced the liquid in. Shook until the powder was dissolved. Pulled the plunger back up, drawing out the cloudy liquid. She looked between the oversized syringe in her hand and the one waiting on the bed. "You know they'll blame me, you fucker. No matter what I do." She slapped his face hard. His head wobbled limply. It never worked to revive him from an episode, but it was a little payback. This time she didn't even feel any satisfaction.

*   *   *   *   *   *   *   *

She talked to the police cruiser's control panels. "He was lying there. The TV was all static. His eyes...they were open, but blank. Nobody home. I tested his blood sugar, but it wouldn't even register. I gave him the glucagon shot. It must have been old or something, because he didn't wake up, like he usually does. So I called 911. Then his breathing got loud, sort of gasping, like a fish out of water. And then he didn't breathe at all."

Sergeant Albers pushed a box of tissues at her, and she realized her face was wet.

"Can I drop you off somewhere, Just Alice?" Sarge asked very gently. "In town, that is. A friend's place? A hotel? I'm afraid you can't stay here tonight."

She shuddered. "Wouldn't want to," she said hoarsely. She gave him the address to the apartment she'd rented in secret. The apartment where most of her belongings waited, moved a few boxes at a time before work over the last two weeks, without Brad noticing. Or so she had thought.

"Can we reach you here?" asked Sarge.

She nodded.

"One more thing. I need your fingerprints."

"Do I have a choice?"

He shook his head.

She looked away. Cold air pushed aside the dry heat inside the cruiser. She felt the car bob from the trunk closing, and Sergeant Albers got back in with a tackle box. He gently pressed her fingers to the inkpad and rolled them onto a special form, one by one, one hand and then the other. He handed her another tissue and she attempted to wipe them clean.

Sarge held out a business card between his fingers. "Try not to smudge it so you can't make out my number. You can call any time you need to talk, or if you remember anything else you think I should know about this morning."

She took it gingerly by its edges and dropped it into her purse. He eyed it.

"Before you go, I need to examine the contents of your purse. I'll let you keep the essentials, but I need everything else."

She hesitated before handing it over, wondering about trace evidence. She didn't wait to watch what he did with it. She was glad she'd thought to find a sharps container at the hospital. Even if the police thought of that possibility, the containers would be emptied long before they got to them. Outside the car, the darkness was unexpected. Time had started again and spun away from her. She balled her ink-smudged hands into careful fists and shrugged off the overcoat that smelled faintly of Old Spice, an old man's cologne until the recent ad campaign. She stepped out of it into the cold air, leaving it slumped in the seat. It looked as though someone had evaporated out of it.

"One more thing, Just Alice. The warrant includes the clothes you're wearing, and your car." He gave her a little apologetic grimace that reminded her of her father taking away her privileges in high school.

She stared at him for a minute. "I won't want to wear them again anyway."

He handed her what looked like a plain brown grocery bag. "Please put them in this. Shoes too. I'll wait here, okay?"

She shuffled through a gap in the tall hedge that opened onto the subdivided house's back yard. Her shoelaces dragged along the brittle brown grass like pale worms. This wasn't at all how she had anticipated moving to her new place would be.

6: More Ghosts

Alice's eyes rose slowly to look into the near-blackness of Nick's. The TV's exuberant chef with the soon-to-expire deal on knives gushed idiotically. He felt his fine hair fall out of place, but he was paralyzed. Even through the alcohol, he realized he had gone too far.

"Yer tea's oot the noo. Whit kind ay eejit confronts the marderer weyoot bars between um? Dain't ye watch onie telly?" Nick Two whispered urgently over the top of the high booth back.

She spoke quietly, but her voice dripped with fury. "Some guy from *Glasgow* knows about this shit?" She leaned across the table.

His throat constricted and his mind was a complete blank.

"I was acquitted on the murder charges. I was in debt up to my eyeballs for the settlement and legal fees. I've been paying them off for years. I've paid out the fucking ass in more ways than you'll ever know, and I'm tired of this fucking shit. I don't owe you an explanation. I don't owe you a goddamn thing," she raged. "I don't even know you. Maybe I should interrogate you about your past." She fell silent, cheeks hot. *"Keep your temper,"* she belatedly scolded herself.

After a painful pause, she suddenly reached toward him. His arms flew up in front of his face in reflexive self-defense, but her hand closed around the pint glass and lifted it to her mouth. She drained the red ale and thumped the glass down heavily. Her eyes and hand stayed on the glass. She hadn't expected to be investigated in return.

Nick's muscles tightened. He knew too well what a pint glass wielded like brass knuckles could do to a skull. He remembered his last bar brawl like it was yesterday: his brother falling, tables overturning, ale splashing, glass shattering, people yelling, sharp pain, a sickening thud of glass on skull, a pair of angry, bloodshot eyes fading to dullness, his own hot blood soaking through his slashed shirt as he backed away.

She released the glass and jerked out of the booth, dragging her cue case behind her. It banged against the table, each clunk making him wince.

"Believe what you want. I don't need you or this shit. Screw you, Nick Kahhrrrr."

Even in her anger, she savored the sound of his name in a way that made him feel uncomfortably warm. He struggled to unstick his tongue from the roof of his mouth. A blossoming hangover threatened to split his skull.

"At least you had the balls to say something to my face, Lowlander," she said heavily, her anger already fading into sadness. Thank God she'd negotiated payment regardless of the results. She could walk away. "I'll see you around, but you'll act like you don't see me." She headed slowly across the room, trying to get a handle on her emotions. She wiped her eyes roughly. *"You won't make yourself a bit realer by crying,"* she reminded herself with an Alice in Wonderland quote.

"Let her go play tag wey the buses," growled Nick Two.

"She widnae be the first wumman tae lose the rag and gie her filla the big malky," Nick muttered in her defense.

"An' tha's supposed tae be a word in her favor, is it? Right efter she went aff on ye like a two-bob rocket. Suit yerself, ye bampot. It's yer funeral."

"Aye. Tha' it is."

The Nicktoon stared angrily, arms crossed.

"Dain't lee," Nick called after her. Through his hair, he saw her pause mid-step.

"What did you say?" she asked tensely.

Pushing his hair back decisively, he looked up at her. "Bide wey me. Stay. Please. Ah've got nae right tae judge ye."

She wished he hadn't called her back. Now it seemed that the reason she was perfect for the job was her criminal past. He was a liability that his own sponsors felt the need to investigate on the down-low. She thought she'd seen them all: a missionary hoping to save her, a playboy pursuing a dangerous trophy, a greedy journalist angling for an exclusive, an ex-con recruiting for a Hitchcockian murder switch. This one was supposed to be smart, talented. A researcher. Maybe he was an amateur psychologist on the side. She could use it to make this last a little longer, maybe. Long enough to get what she was contracted to get. Too bad she had actually liked him.

Served her right to want something for herself while still paying for her past. She'd had no right to let herself think there could ever be a future for her in this town. Especially not a relationship with ulterior motives as the catalyst. *"Sometimes I've believed as many as six impossible things before breakfast,"* she thought bleakly.

Her eye caught the bartender scurrying the length of the bar counter, stealing goggle-eyed looks back at them, and suddenly she knew it wasn't research that had clued in her mark. *Thanks a fuckload, Hutch, you prick.*

"Fae ma experience, some bastarts deserve tae die, aye?" he added hopefully.

I'll say. She turned around and said flatly, "Fine. What-the-fuck-ever. I'll shoot you."

She felt annoyance fight with laughter at the ridiculous expressions crossing his face. "You know, on the pool table? With cue sticks and balls. Even though you don't deserve another minute of my time, you asshole."

Nick strangled a nervous laugh so that it came out as a demented gargle.

"But if you so much as look at me cross-eyed, I'm done."

He nodded seriously, his head bobbling in an exaggerated motion, and she remembered how drunk he was. A perfect opportunity she'd almost lost. This could work out well. One confession for another. Perhaps she should thank Hutch after all.

She dropped the balls and racked them while he swayed in front of the cues. She joined him, watching silently for a while, before testing them herself and pulling out a decent one. She held it out but didn't let go, so that their hands clutched the stick like kids stacking hands up a baseball bat to determine who goes first.

"Do you need some water, or coffee, or a designated driver?" she asked pointedly.

"Ah could use a ginger," he admitted, then added sadly, "they huvnae got onie, but."

She let him take the cue and gestured for him to break, studying him carefully.

The crack of the balls hurt his head. He tried to disguise his wince of pain as one of disgruntlement with the ineffective break.

"They have ginger ale. It's a mixer. It's on the wand."

"Nut." He barely made a shot. "Ah mean Irn-Bru. The ither national drink ay Scoatland."

"What is it? Fermented liquid haggis with ginger?"

He gave her an appalled look before squinting carefully at the balls. "Ah dain't ken if tha's part ay the thirty-two secret flavors. It's a fruity, gingery, fizzy drink, but." He missed his target ball completely and swiped self-consciously at his hair. "Wee rusty."

"You or the iron soda?" she deadpanned.

"Ach, baith." He flashed his feline grin. "Right refreshing, byraway. Ma Da swears by it fur a bender mender." He watched her sink a shot. "Ye think tha's ferrlie, when Ah wis in wee school, ivrybody noshed Hedgehog Crisps."

"Fancy yerself Billy Connolly the noo, dae ye?" groused the Nicktoon. "Ye wey yer patter."

Another ball rattled down.

"I've had rabbit and deer and alligator, but that's…" She sized him up. "Pure bullshit," she finished with a tinge of annoyance. "You, my good sir, are 'full ay it' in more ways than one."

"Dain't get on her tits," warned Nick Two. Naturally, it made Nick's eyes drop to her chest at the very moment she leaned over the table, giving him a postcard view of her Highlands.

"They wis ordinary crisps," he admitted to her cleavage. "But they wis supposed tae taste like a hedgehog baked in clay over a gypsy campfire."

"Ur no' gawn tae blether aboot crisps, ur ye the noo? Whit kind ay patter merchant chats up a bird wey the history ay crisps? A fookin numpty, tha's whae."

She snorted. "That's oddly specific. Sounds like a Monty Python sketch: crunchy hedgehog."

Nick irrationally felt the need to defend the snack. "The packets hud tokens on thum, tae send in fur a donation tae hedgehog rescue an' rehab an' that. They get run over aw the time, byraway," he explained.

He had begged for Hedgehog Crisps every time he was going for the messages with Da, at every shop that might carry them. When the tally vans rolled by jingling tunes, he picked them over ice cream and sweeties every time. After Maw disappeared, everyone brought him the crisps. They became his comfort food, an unspoken language of caring in the inarticulate world of sentimental working-class men. Da's friends would drop by, having avoided fix-it projects with the point-winning excuse of "checkin hoo thum perr Kerr lads is hingin on," toting carrier bags stuffed with bottles of ale, jelly babies, and packets of his favorite crisps. He had carefully trimmed tokens from the crinkly bags, and licked the peppery, beefy flavor dust off them and his fingers. As he rode Da's bus after school until the shift ended, doing homework, reading comic books, or watching the city pass by, regulars would ruffle his hair and hand him hedgehog tokens like a second fare. He liked to look at the happy hedgehog face bursting from the seal in the tokens' centers like the overture to a Looney Tune, cartoon saliva drops spraying at the thought of its own tastiness. The wee creature was silly, even a bit mental, as it showed willing to go cannibal. Hedgehogs he would help, a score of tokens at a time. The other stuff, the stuff his mother had been so angry about, he couldn't care less.

"Ah sent in aboot two thoosand tokens in fiye years. Until ye couldnae find the crisps onie mair."

"That's very sweet," Alice said softly. She held his eyes for a long moment.

"Kin ye credit it? Erras hope fur ye yet. Should be usin it on better quality goods, but," griped Nick Two.

He was suddenly ashamed of the emotional ploy. "Ach, loads ay lads brought um fur play piece. Imagine aw those bags ay hedgehogs cheesin it. Wis the thing tae dae then," he said dismissively.

He realized the pool table was littered with striped balls. He fumbled in his pockets for change. She propped her cue in the crook of a high-backed stool, and touched his arm lightly.

"I've got it. Be right back."

She returned competently juggling three full glasses, two of them water glasses with lemon slices perched on the rims, the last a glass of dark reddish-orange liquid.

He perked up. *Ya dancer, she got a wee heavy tae replace whit she tanned.*

He tilted the glass for a long draft and noticed too late both Alice watching him expectantly and the ice. He choked down a mouthful that tasted of fizzy nothing.

"Is that close?" she asked.

"Close tae whit?" he countered, confused.

"You know, the other national drink of Scotland," she said eagerly. "I had Hutch mix almost everything on the wand: cola, orange, lemon-lime, ginger ale. I thought that might do it."

"Aye, uh…it's pure magic byraway," he faltered, trying not to offend.

She took a sip herself, then another. Her face fell. "All the flavors cancel each other out. It's like sweet seltzer. 'You didn't say it was good, you said there was nothing like it,' " she quoted Lewis Carroll. She belched, exaggerating the effect shamelessly. "At least the aftertaste is a little orangey and gingery," she said brightly, and burst out laughing.

He was surprised to hear his laugh join hers.

She paused her giggling long enough to choke out deliriously, "Seriously, it won't hurt my feelings if you don't drink it." She covered the glass with her hand as he made a comical lip-protruding attempt to slurp up more of the bland concoction, his lips so close to her fingers…

Hutch appeared at arm's length from their table and thrust a plastic basket and stack of napkins between them. Alice's laugh died abruptly and she pulled her arm back.

"Thank you, Hutch," she said soberly.

Nick noticed the bartender's ears darken to red as he pushed up the heavy-rimmed glasses that weren't out of place.

"Can I get you anything else?" Hutch asked obsequiously, while trying to catch Nick's eye for a meaningful bug-eyed stare.

The Mona Lisa smile played on Alice's lips. Nick met green eyes that glinted with mischief or malice. "I think we're all set for a very memorable evening."

"Cheers," Nick said with cavalier resignation.

Hutch left, shaking his head and staring intently as if memorizing details for a police statement.

"Help yourself." She pushed the basket toward Nick. "My personal 'bender mender.' Works every time. Except when it doesn't."

The smell of hot tortilla chips, spiced meat, melted cheddar, and pungent jalapeños made his stomach growl. He was glad the pub's menu was far from authentic as he settled onto one of the high-backed stools to get wellied in. Alice perched on the stool opposite, tucking her heels into the top rung to keep them from dangling. She rummaged in her bag and pulled out lip balm.

"Always be prepared," she said with a salute of the little tube, and slathered it on, caressing the curves and swells of her lips. They curled into a wicked smile.

He dropped his eyes back to the nachos and busied himself with selecting a chip with the perfect balance of toppings. She pried a chip out of the pile and set to work prying personal information out of him.

"Okay, Lowlander. It's only fair I get to ask you some questions." When he froze, she waved a chip at him and said, "Relax. I'll google you later for the boring stuff. I just want to know: what brings a Glasgow city boy here? Why this dot on the map? And do not say 'college football' or I will walk out."

"Ah hud tae find oot if the Blue Ridge Mountains look like the Hielands," he hedged.

Alice gave him a sharp look. "Oh, a wise guy, eh?"

"The veterinary college. It's kent internationally fur research," he answered apologetically. "Ah dinnae want tae bang on like a prospectus brochure, byraway."

"Okay. But you didn't sound that excited about your research. The Hepatitis E." They said it in synch. "And there are other top-notch veterinary research institutions around the globe," she continued. "University of Glasgow, for instance."

"Ye've been daein research ay yer oon, so ye huv."

She shrugged.

"Ah'm actually an American citizen," he admitted. "So it's like Ah'm comin hame."

"So you're not really a Scot, you're only faking it to pick up women?"

"Is it wahrkin?" He grinned. "Haun tae God, ma da's Scoats, an' Ah wis born in Glesga, lived aw ma life err," he defended himself. "Ma mither wis American, but. So dual citizenship. Best ay baith wirlds, byraway."

"Oh. Sorry for your loss," she said sheepishly.

"Whit loss?" he asked sharply.

"Your mom?" she said, her voice rising in confusion at the look of anger on his face. "You said 'was' so I thought she had passed on…" Her voice faded out.

"She *moved* on," Nick said finally. "Left when Ah wis six. Ah huvnae seen her since."

7: Glasgow, November, 1980s

Gray mist swirled in the early November afternoon, making a gloomy first day of school after term break. Rapidly fading sun loaned a pale golden light to the glowering sky. Damp cold air nipped at his chapped knees where they protruded from his school uniform. He tugged awkwardly at his thick navy knee socks, stretching them as high as they would go. They crawled back down his pale, skinny shins in a few steps. He pulled his matching hand-knitted scarf tighter. At least his heavy wool blazer and anorak kept the chill off his torso. His untied shoelaces slapped along the pavement. His fingers were too stiff from cold to fix them, and besides, the laces were as Scottish in their contrariness as he was, never staying tied for long. Maw would take a hairy about it when he got home, the unfairness of it an extra weight in his already queasy stomach. His wee brother was her favorite, always smirking from the shelter of their mother's lap, with her bright rose-scented hair swinging down around him as she tied *his* shoes, sing-songing about a rabbit running around a hole.

He alternated between dawdling with dread and walking faster to put distance between himself and his brother. He stretched out his stride like seven-league boots through soggy leaves that left brown tattoos on the sidewalk. Under his breath he chanted, "She loves me. She loves me no'," each step a petal pulled from the flower of his heart. He stopped on the pavement in front of the two-dancer tenement's old-fashioned split outer door, with its tiny twin knobs, inset glass panels, and bright pink paint. Beyond the door was a small close stinking of cat piss, with tumbleweeds of fur lurking in dark corners. Stairs led to their second-floor flat where his preoccupied mother painted protest signs and talked in heated voices with other activists. *Dae the steps coont?* He decided yes. With trembling legs, he climbed the stone steps leading to the pink doors, placing one foot beside the other, one stone step at a time. Right foot, left foot. *She loves me.* Right foot, left foot. *She loves me no'.* He tried to make the walk to the door come out right. He teetered on the lintel, triumphant. "She loves me!"

His small fingers, clumsy and red from cold despite the anorak pockets, wrapped around the right-hand doorknob. The door shoogled in its frame but held fast. In his worry, he had forgotten the door was kept locked now at Maw's insistence, to keep out drunks and delinquents that might hang about in the close sheltering from the rain, pissing in the corners, and letting her rescued cats out into the street to get run over. Maw would wait impatiently on the inner steps, stroking one of the half-wild beasts. Every evening, as soon as she hauled open the door with her usual sharp admonition to mind the cats, he would tumble upstairs ahead of her, dump his satchel, then stump back down with a marmalade sandwich and Wee Gonk to play in the dingy close until Da's expectant smile appeared in the dim glass. Sometimes he played keepyuppy with a worn ball. Sometimes the tamer cats kept him company, watching him with yellow eyes, tail tips twitching rhythmically.

"Oot ma road, ya eejit." He was shoved aside by his perfect wee brother. His hair stayed in place. His shoes stayed tied.

" 'S locked," he retorted.

"Nae shite. Dain't ye mind oniehin Maw tells us? Nae shocker ur awyis in trouble."

His cheeks turned red. "Shut it, ya tossbag, ye. She's no' on the steps. Whit the noo?"

"Ring the bell, ya muppet."

"Dae it yerself, since ur so smart."

"Ye dae it."

As usual, the younger boy got his way. The older boy stepped up onto the wall separating the front garden from the steps to the locked close. He tottered along its edge until he reached the building's rough sandstone side and pressed the top bell. He raised himself on tiptoe and leaned over to peer through the middle glass panel, watching for Maw to stomp down the stairs.

"Maw's right. Ye cannae dae oniehin right."

His brother stepped up on the ledge and shoved him again. He lost his balance and jerked his foot out to catch himself, but his shoelace was caught under his other foot. He crashed to the stone steps and rolled down to the sidewalk. The pink door blurred. He blinked fiercely. His hip throbbed and his knee stung terribly. He wiped his face roughly on his sleeve and struggled to his feet. A dark ribbon of blood trickled down his leg and was absorbed by his sock.

"Ye gawn tae greet the noo, granny's wean?"

He hobbled back up the steps, toward his wee brother. Both flats were dark and silent. He sat carefully on the wall, smiling shakily up at the glass panels and the warm close beyond. His knee burned. His brother pressed both buzzers at the same time, leaning into it.

In answer, the sky abruptly emptied its guts. The bickering dissolved in the glacial downpour. The boys climbed over the low railing into the garden, seeking the shelter of a sparse holly tree. He pulled up the hood of his anorak against the rain and biting cold and curled into a ball around his wee brother. He covered their heads as best as he could with his satchel.

He woke to darkness. The streetlight two tenements down cast a small pool of light that only made the early winter night feel darker and colder. The White Woman sighed and shivered in the branches above him. He felt her cold breath on his tingling hands. He squeezed his eyes tight to shut out her hypnotic beauty. Her long, sharp fingernails scraped across his satchel as she searched for bare skin to begin her feast, siphoning his lifeblood through her scarlet nails.

Footfalls clomped on pavement, muffled by puddles. The trudge of heavy boots could only mean a Red Cap goblin, brandishing his terrible pikestaff and wearing a blood-soaked cap of human skin. Their only hope was to run while the two fiends fought over them. He shook his brother awake, hand over the other boy's mouth, listening for the right moment. When the goblin rattled his pike, muttering curses, the boy vaulted over the wall. His cramped, half-frozen legs failed him. He staggered and collapsed like a slaughtered cow at the goblin's feet. The fresh scab on his knee tore open.

"Whit the hell!" Da's voice yelped in the dimness, followed by a clatter and crunching.

The boy peered up through the hair plastered to his face. "Da?" he whispered. His wee brother climbed out of the garden, for once not insulting his clumsiness.

Da stood in the fresh debris of Mrs. McGarry's potted plants, shaking soil off his uniform pants as he retrieved his bus conductor's cap from the next-door steps.

"Whir's yer Maw then? She dinnae let yees in?" Da asked, voice tense.

He shook his head and buried his face into Da's uniform, raggedly breathing in the pungent smell of wet wool mixed with petrol fumes and chip-shop grease. He shook with relief and cold.

"Dain't greet, wee man," Da crooned. He lifted the boy to his hip and turned so his body was between the boys and the close. He pulled his sleeve over his knuckles. The boy was jerked as glass shattered. Da shook shards off his coat sleeve and reached carefully through the hole, turning the lock from the inside and pulling it ajar. He kicked the door wide, his boots crunching on the glass as he stepped into the close and fumbled out his key ring. Yellow eyes gleamed in the dark. Da scooped up the second, drier boy and took the steep stairs at a run, then put him down to turn the lock and push through into the flat.

"Mary?" Da called. "Mary!" The word rumbled through the boy's chest where he was barnacled to Da. His father pushed straight past the bathroom's pebbled glass door. He turned the taps to full blast, and steam rose from the tub's deep belly.

"Perr weans," Da crooned. "Ur right drookit an' chitterin. Ah'll soon huv ye aw cosy. Aw cosy."

Hands tried to pry him loose from where he clung tightly like a wee monkey. He nestled deeper into Da's coat.

"Ach. Well, yer claes ur awready drookit."

He was tipped back and down. Warm water closed around his stiff body as he lay cradled in Da's arms in the bath. He relaxed at last and slipped deeper into the warm sea to settle against his brother like babes in the pale, hard womb of the bathtub. When he thawed enough to open his eyes, he saw Da's worried face, the sharp features more pinched and pale than usual. Da smiled and gently smoothed the wet hair out of his son's dark eyes, mirror images of his own.

"Ah'll gies dry claes. Back in two shakes ay a badger's tadger."

Da's footsteps pattered through the flat, his urgent whisper growing angrier each time he called for his missing wife. When he returned, stripped to his sleeveless undershirt, he held their matching blue flannel pajamas. He gently peeled off the coats and school uniforms layer by layer and slopped them in the sink basin as the boys lolled, thin limbs and hair moving with the sloshing water like they were jellyfish tentacles and seaweed.

Both boys were silent as they were lifted from the water and set on wrinkled feet, toweled, and dressed. Da placed them into the big bed and brought mugs of steaming beef tea for each of them and a box of oatcakes. The boys nestled against their father, one on each side in a Da sandwich.

"Da? Whir's Maw?" he asked timidly.

Da answered with false cheeriness. "She left us a wee note. She's gone doon tae London fur a right muckle protest at Parliament."

"Fur the perr wee animaws tha' the scientists torture?" asked his wee brother. "She telt me aw aboot it."

"Aye, Ah reckon so, wee man."

"When is she comin hame?" he asked.

"Her note said she wid be comin back on the train Saturday. We kin make a holiday outing of it, eh lads?"

8: Caged

Alice reached around the red plastic nacho basket, slipping her hand over Nick's. He couldn't meet her eyes. His thoughts were a sour taste in his mouth, his mind foggy with old wounds and too much alcohol. Every part of him felt like lead, his arms too heavy to move, his legs anchors scraping the floor. With great effort, he managed to move his millstone of a head feebly. For his trouble, blood pounded in his temples with a viselike squeeze. He pulled his hand away, not wanting pity.

"Ah've got tae go," he muttered thickly. He struggled into his motorcycle jacket, normally a soothing, protective weight, now a mantle of kryptonite.

"Nick?" She reached out to touch his face.

His hand moved of its own accord. His fist clutched her small wrist. They froze in a tableau of shock, eyes locked together, Nick as startled by his reaction as she was.

Her breathing was heavy, every muscle tight. This was how it had always started. Angry words. A hand tight on her wrist. A quick twist, and his chest hard on her back, her face pressed to a wall. His arm across her throat. His fingernails clawing her thigh, leaving long red lines as he yanked off her clothes. The pain as he shoved himself inside her. She couldn't fight him. He was too strong, and struggling only made it worse. He would only laugh and get rougher, pulling hair, tearing her clothes. If she bit him, he'd hit her or kick her. Never marks on the face, only where they could be covered. She had been glad when he was lying on the bed, unable to hurt her, eyes blank and dead. Worth every cent she had been ordered to pay his family. Priceless. Like the credit card ads.

Nick released her, appalled with himself and what he saw in her eyes. *Dain't greet, hen, please dain't greet.*

She blinked rapidly and tilted her chin with bravado. *"Consider anything, only don't cry,"* she coached herself. "Don't let me keep you, Lowlander," she said thickly. He didn't seem the type, but he had hurt her. She wanted to slap him hard and kiss him harder, and was ashamed by both urges.

Nick wanted to take it back, make it up to her somehow. He swayed indecisively and noticed they had attracted a small audience, some sneaking curious looks, others gaping openly.

"Ah'm away," he choked out and struggled toward the door as if against a strong wind.

Alice stood still, rubbing her wrist and listening through the crowd. When a motorcycle roared to life outside, she broke down her cue and slipped into the night. She wondered if this job was worth the risk.

Nick paced the circumference of his sparse efficiency apartment, pausing at various points to piddle about. Smooth the duvet. Straighten cabinets. Push in stools. Stare through the peephole into the distorted hallway. Take a sip of wee heavy. Repeat. He was angry with himself for the self-imposed house arrest. He'd scared her and made her pity him. He wasn't sure which was worse. He shouldn't have even been talking to her in the first place.

"Ur on middle shift, ken. Ye wullnae see the Black Widdy at wahrk or in the pub," Nick Two commented without looking up from the computer screen. "She makes an airly nicht ay it byraway."

"Dain't cry her tha'. Her name's Alice. Erras somehin between us," Nick retorted testily, hoping it were true.

"Tha' somehin will be ma fit up yer erse in a wee meenit, mate. Ah say ca' canny. Right daft, no' daft aboot ye, tha's hoo Ah cry it." Nick Two looked up from the screen and snapped, "Stoap stoatin aboot like a caged tiger! Nuchin's keepin ye in except yerself."

"Ah'm no' stoatin aboot," he said defensively. "An' dain't start it wey the fookin animaw rights soapbox. Tha's the exact shite whit ruined ma fookin childhood."

"The loss ay Calderpark Zoo ruined yer childhood?" he said sarcastically. "Place wis fookin questionable. If tha' wis the highlicht, ye wis a pathetic wee shite."

"Ye ken whit Ah mean, ye fookin wanker. Ye soonded like Maw, an' tha' is nae compliment." Nick remembered the last family trip to the zoo, a perfect day, no arguing, complaining, or snarky comments from anyone, his wee self even holding his mother's hand for a change, his wee brother holding Da's. It lasted all through the fun fair, even surviving the monkeys, reptiles, and aviary, a world record. Until the tiger. The huge orange beast paced the length of the zoo enclosure, back and forth, over and over. He was mesmerized by the rhythm of the tiger's steps, the flap of loose skin swinging on its belly, its rippling muscles, its strange vigil. Maw went off like a two-bob rocket, leaving them while she hunted down the management to complain. Her blonde hair glowed orange in the late afternoon sun over blue eyes with the same far-off wildness as the tiger's golden ones.

"Ach, tha's right, ur aw aboot breakin the law as lang as erras nae higher cause behind it," snapped Nick Two. "Jist like yer wide-o doll whae mardered a man. A fine pair ay rockets ye ur."

"Fook ye, Nicktoon!"

"Fook ye back harder, ya fookin eejit!"

Nick kicked the desk chair so hard it tipped over with the Nicktoon in it.

"Whit the fook's this?" Nick looked at the laptop's screen. "Ya sneaky wee shite! Ye googled her? Onieyin wid think ye hud a hit fur her yerself." He righted the chair and sat down to read the archived news articles filling the screen.

"Fur yer oon gude, ya thankless fook," Nick Two muttered, rotating his shoulder as Nick read. News briefs on Bradley Taylor's death. Interviews with the deceased's family and friends, full of allegations. Community sorrow and outrage. Charity drives for juvenile diabetes research. Ag Tech football fans in school colors for support of their coach and his loss. A makeshift shrine of flowers and school colors at the scene of the crime.

The accompanying photos were the same few repeated, revealing little. Bradley was ridiculously handsome and privileged and knew it, but his face was a mask of anger and dissatisfaction. Alice had the lost look he'd seen on plenty of wee wives in the housing schemes, old before their time, resigned to their lot, waiting for their men to come home full of whiskey and anger.

"Wis insulin, no' drugs," he called to his mate.

"Insulin's a fookin drug, ya non-educated delinquent," corrected Nick Two.

"Ah'm nae mair a 'ned' than ye ur."

"Whae has the uni degrees, then?"

He ignored the taunt, unable to look away from the screen. He skimmed a sidebar article of statistics on fatalities from extreme hypoglycemia versus long-term hyperglycemia, then on to archived articles of the police investigation and its inconclusive result. Neighbors recounted frequent arguments in the young couple's apartment. Speculation ran rampant on the ease of injecting insulin into a sleeping victim. Denied their pound of flesh by reasonable doubt, the family resorted to a civil suit for wrongful death. Their lawyer painted a portrait of a greedy young wife tired of her husband, wanting full possession of his inheritance and a hefty life insurance payout instead of whatever she could glean in a divorce settlement. It was enough to award all inheritance, insurance, and possessions to the parents, plus some.

"If it wis an accident, hoo let the Black Widdy thing ride?" Nick Two snorted sarcastically.

"She could dae hee-haw aboot it. Wanst ye got the name, ye cannae shake it. Ye ought tae ken tha', Knickers Two." Nick strode to the kitchen and pulled a wee heavy from the refrigerator. He flicked the cap at his mate where he propped up the bathroom doorframe.

Nick Two batted it away. It rang musically when it hit the floor. "Unless ye go mental on thum wan gude time. Tha' ends it. Ye ought tae ken tha', hard man."

"Telly news an' fish wrappers were pefter-efter her story, but, ya daftie."

The other man shrugged in acquiescence.

"Ah should look her up on the Facebook. Send her a friend request so Ah kin rummage aboot in her profile. Ah could look up her archived posts an' photies fae yonks ago. Look fur the wan where she updates her status tae 'finally offed ma man.' "

"Ye hud best no' be puttin onie shite on the Facebook," Nick Two growled.

"Ach. Ah furgot ur radically opposed tae keepin in touch."

"Dain't lecture me aboot keepin in touch, ya fookin tosser. 'S a two-way street, byraway."

"Ah've been stuck in this bog ay a town fur four months the noo an' no' iven wan fookin word fae onieyin back hame except Da," he groused. "Dead sad, tha' is."

"Whit aboot me?" his mate huffed.

"Tha' disnae coont! Ur right fookin err, unfortunately," Nick retorted. "An' whit aboot ye, ya fookin chancer? Ye think ma life wis a charity case, yers is pure dead boring, but. It's mair than flesh an' blood kin staun."

He sighed and took a long pull off the bottle of ale. "Hoo the fook ur we huvin this bloody kerfuffle onie road? This place mist be makin me pure mental."

"Ur lonely is aw. Cannae haunle the pace ay village life. No' tae mention yer guilty conscience. Next ye'll take tae washin yer hauns nonstop or somehin."

Nick rose and went to the window, spreading the mini-blind slats with two fingers to stare out at the parking lot. The afternoon sun felt warm on the glass. He watched college students toss a football, a pointed American one, the ball stumbling into parked cars with each fumble.

"Alice has been the onerly thing tae make it somewhit bearable. An' she's a fookin marderer," he said without turning around.

"Ur a hustler an' a thief, an' pure dead mental tae boot. An' then erras tha' questionable bit in the pub wey a pint mug."

"The mug wis self-defense. Mines an' yers," Nick murmured.

He returned to the desk and navigated away from the Black Widow to the Glasgow city webcam site. Tiny people appeared and disappeared with each interval capture, crossing the rain-soaked pavement of George Square. He pictured his father at the wheel of one of the tin-toy buses passing through the camera's eye, his hand lifted in an unseen salute.

He shut the laptop. What was the point? He was locked in for the duration of the grant.

9: The Hustler

Glasgow, 1980s

Uncle Malky visited with a big box that had fallen off a lorry and needed to sit in the flat for a few days. The boy remarked that boxes seemed to fall off a lot, and that if he were a lorry driver he'd make sure nothing did. Malky's girlfriend Maureen, the one with the stiff bubble of hair just like Princess Diana's, laughed, and Malky tapped the side of his nose, saying it was the last time for certain, her supervisor was getting wise. The boy asked Maureen if she was getting wise too at the makeup counter in Sauchiehall Street. She called him a funny wee man and asked Malky when he was going to give her a funny wee man of her own. Malky made haste to the sitting room to drink ale and talk quietly with the boy's father. The boy's mother went to check on supper, shadowed by the boy's wee brother. Maureen played with the boy in the nursery. The box was forgotten.

Until one Sunday morning. His parents were still in bed. Curiosity getting the best of him, the boy peeked into the box. It was full of expensive scents and the sorts of things ladies used to make their faces colorful. He tried it all out. Some of the scents got spilled when he opened them, which made the cats scratch at the door to be let out. He spiraled an entire can of mousse onto his head like a knickerbocker glory and molded his hair into a stiff cashew. He emptied several tiny hatboxes of pale powder on it, the closest he could get to white. It left a halo of color where he sat on the rug, which inspired a colorful miniature snowstorm he planned to play in later. He mixed face cream that cost more than two months' rent with pots of the compacted blue dust like Maureen wore on her eyelids. Powdery cakes of color were crushed into the rug in his eagerness to get the ones he wanted.

For his costume, he needed to borrow the curtain. He tugged sharply at the tail of it until the cheap rod flexed and bounced out of its brackets and thumped to the floor. He dragged the rod from the fabric, tapping the ceiling in the struggle. He wrapped the fabric around his waist and pushed the long tail over his shoulder. Assuming a heroic wide-legged stance, he swished the curtain rod awkwardly through the air. At that moment, his mother burst from the bedroom to find out what the kerfuffle was. Her blonde hair was mussed, cheeks bright pink, eyebrows compressed. She slapped at Da's hand that clutched the lace edging on her pink satin slip. Da stepped into the living room doorway behind her, shirtless, his hair nearly as peaked as his son's.

Maw took a trembling step toward the boy. He raised the curtain-rod sword in a salute that tapped the ceiling again. Her eyes widened as she took in his blue face, his pale, stiff hair, the smeared curtains, the rubble of ruined cosmetics. Her beautiful face, normally peaches and cream, burned bright scarlet and twisted nearly unrecognizable with rage and imminent tears.

The boy's voice sounded loud and strange in his own ears. "Ah'm Hielander Smurf," he explained tremulously. Da guffawed and quickly disguised it as a coughing fit.

"Animals died for that!" Maw turned sharply, her bare heel squeaking on the wood floor. She didn't seem to notice the popping noise of burst stitches where Da still held the lace of her slip. "And now we'll owe Malcolm for his cut, on top of not having it for the demonstrations." She slammed the bedroom door with a force that made the entire flat shiver.

"Cannae ye salvage the tins an' that fur yer protests? Urnae yees gawn tae dae jist whit he's done onie road?" Da's suggestion was met with stony silence.

He carefully scrubbed the expensive stolen cosmetics off his son and the flat. In the evening, he negotiated reparitions with Malky over ales while the boys hid in the nursery, ears to the door, hearing little and understanding less. Mary came out of the bedroom only to bang the front door shut as she left.

Nick slammed the door and stepped into the Saturday afternoon sunshine angling down the apartment building hallway. He didn't have to go far outside the town limits to find back roads for a proper ride. He relaxed into the rhythm of road and machine, leaning deep into curves, opening it wide on straight stretches, forgetting everything but the buffeting of brisk air and the stomach-dropping dips.

Backtracking carefully into town hours later, he pulled in beside the pub. He slung his helmet over the handlebar, not in the mood to be arsed with it inside. He paused inside the foyer to stow his sunglasses in a jacket pocket, but the room was so dim that he had to maneuver carefully through tables and chairs to his usual booth.

TV tuned to a soccer match, he leaned back and stretched his feet to the opposite bench to unkink after the long ride. His whole body kept up a phantom vibration as he sipped his pint. The afternoon sun faded, along with his ability to ignore both the thoughts buzzing around his head and the Nicktoon slouching in the seat opposite, looking expectant.

"Lang silence, aye?"

He wasn't in the mood to discuss it, especially not with him. "Isnae the first time Ah huvnae heard nuchin fae ma wee brither in ages."

"Las' time wis whit, four years?" Nick Two tried to draw him out.

Nick shot him stinkeye over his ale. "Four years an' seven months, tae be exact. Researchers need tae be exact."

"This is different, but. Ah feel it." He tried to make eye contact, but the other man wasn't having it.

"Oh, aye. Las' time ye wisnae aroond ridin ma erse. News flash, mate, ur no' real," he said tiredly.

"News flash, mate, the fookin Blue Fairy turned me intae a real boy an' ur stuck wey me the noo."

"Ah'm onerly haudin the jaikets. An' Ah huv nae idea hoo mich langer Ah kin fool aw the people aw the time. Somehin's gawn tae go wrang the langer this shite drags on."

"Like huvin tae live the porkpie 24-7 fur a bird ye fancy? Serves ye right."

He slammed his empty pint glass on the table and pointed a warning finger. "Shut it. Ah ken it's ma oon fault."

"Anither wee heavy, then?" Nick Two slipped out of the booth.

"Wid be dead nice tae be ma oon self agin, no' this haufway shite Ah get tae wedge in." He jerked angrily at the collar of his leather jacket. "Hell mend this uni toaff shite."

"Where've you been, Lowlander?" Alice rested her chin on her hands as she peered over the tall booth back where his mate had been sitting. Her floating face and wide grin reminded him eerily of the Cheshire Cat.

"Jesusjohnny, wumman." He startled, turning suddenly back to the TV to hide his hot cheeks. He wondered if she'd witnessed any of that, and realized the match had been replaced by an extended infomercial. He faked attentiveness to avoid her intense gaze. "Ye cannae keep creepin up on a man like tha'."

She sat down on the bench the Nicktoon had vacated, and good riddance. He shifted his boots to the floor, and she dropped her small bag and cue case on the table.

"Are you 'oot yer tights' again? Because for a people-watcher, you sure are easy to sneak up on."

He felt the green eyes examining him as if trying to read his mind. He pushed his fine brown hair off his forehead, trying to brush the thought away with it. From the corner of his eye, he saw her lean forward and twist awkwardly to peer up at the TV screen.

"Forgive my presumptuous insensitivity, but I doubt you need to talk to your doctor about erectile dysfunction just yet," she said drolly.

"Ah could be gawin doon the brae airly," he blustered.

She arched an eyebrow at him. "Are you sure you want to go there?"

"Ah'm fair affrontit by yer insinuation tha' Ah telt a porkpie," he ranted. "Ah could be mair auld an' doowally than Ah look." *Ah could be a lot mair ay a lot ay things than Ah look. Or a lot less.*

She ran her eyes up and down the parts of him that were visible above the tabletop and leaned closer. "Then prove it, Lowlander," she said fiercely. She jerked her head at the curtained coin-operated photo booth across the room. "In there, right now. We could even get souvenirs of the event."

He craned around the pub to see if anyone was watching. "Ur oot yer heid." He checked carefully around the photo booth squeezed between two video games. The room hadn't yet filled with the Saturday evening crowd. *Awfy exposed—ha—but noisy enough tae mibbe sneak in a wee shag...*

"Saw you consider it. I rest my case." Alice smirked. "You are a perfectly normal, red-blooded Scottish male. Except I think you have an unhealthy obsession with infomercials. You may want to consult your doctor about *that*."

"Shite. Ye wis onerly windin me up." He swept back hair that didn't need fixing. He stared at her, uncomfortable for looking like a sex addict.

Alice crossed her arms. "You were messing with me, so I was messing with you. You can't seriously think..." She slumped backwards, curling protectively into herself. "Are all Scotsmen completely insane?"

"We wear skirts, play bagpipes, chuck trees, an' nosh sheep guts," he answered solemnly. "It's ivrybody else tha's fookin mental."

She barked a laugh and relaxed, swinging her legs up onto the bench seat to sit sideways and lean her back against the wall. She flapped her bent knees in and out slowly, like a butterfly at rest. "So where have you been? Was there an infomercial marathon on TV or something?" she said with attempted nonchalance, avoiding his eyes.

Ah missed ye tae, so Ah did. "Second shift. Ah get loused at midnicht." He watched her out of the corner of his eye, hoping the other night's misstep would be written off as intoxication and subsequent memory loss.

"Oh," she said quietly, worried she'd revealed too much interest. "I didn't know you were on shifts. No wonder. I'm in bed by then." She blushed furiously and looked up at the TV.

He flicked it off and leaned across the table. He lowered his voice suggestively. "Hoo aboot it, well?" He shifted his glass to one side and caressed the wood tabletop. "Ye ken. On the table." Her knees snapped together. "Wey cue sticks an' baws," he teased.

She narrowed her eyes and watched the hair slip down his forehead. "Oh, you're on, Lowlander," she growled and inchwormed out of the booth, cue case in tow. "I'm gonna mop the floor with you."

Nick hummed "You Cannae Shove Yer Granny" to himself. Everything was all right again. *Better than awright. Pure dead brilliant.* His playing reflected his state of mind. His lag ball stopped gently a hair from the mark. He pocketed two solids on the break, and lined up shot after shot. He felt the green eyes running over his braced legs, across his curved back, around his shoulders, down his wiry arms in the pushed-up Henley sleeves. He smiled, conscious of himself, but not self-conscious. Himself again at long last, for a wee while at least.

After the fifth ball dropped into a pocket, Alice began to chant the *Jaws* theme softly, growing louder as he potted his next ball. He straightened and turned his back to the table, spun the cue dramatically, and aimed behind himself.

"You wouldn't," she growled. "You can't. There's no way. 'You might as well try to catch a bandersnatch.' "

"Care fur a wee wager, Alice in Wunnerland?" he said, flashing his feline grin. He didn't wait for an answer. The ball bounced off the pocket cushion, missing by a hair.

She puffed out her held breath. "Nice. Hustler turned veterinarian. Did you put yourself through school that way?"

"Practical exercises in geometry an' physics an' that. An' in readin jimmies an' gettin thum right where ye want thum."

"Did you get me right where you wanted?"

"No' yet," he grinned back, dodging a poke from her cue. "The photie booth's still waitin, but."

He watched her shoot, thinking of all his long afternoons and late nights in dim Glasgow pubs, at first watching the best billiard players, then practicing for hours on end before playing for money. He lost some, won more. In dark alleys stinking of piss, he got into rammies with drunk tossbags who were angry at being relieved of their cash. He had refined his game, his hustle, and his brawling, loving every moment of it. He earned the nickname "The Uni" because of the guise he used, an arrogant, clean-cut university student he copied from his academic brother. He even stole some of the wanker's preppy clothes for effect. It was catnip to the keelies in the local pubs dying to show up a uni chancer. But two years on the game had been pushing his luck. Drunks had remarkable memories for negative experiences, and new punters who found confidence in the bottom of a bottle became fewer and farther between. He burned out several lucrative locations, forcing him to venture outside the Maryhill locals into rougher Drumhill. Every night felt like it would be the one for some Buckfast Commando and a half-dozen of his mad-skull mates to teach him a lesson. Wise to his son's reputation, Da had pressured him gently to give it up, go to university in actuality. Instead, he had started an apprenticeship in a field as different from his brother's as night and day, but when opportunity knocked, he hadn't hesitated. He found out the hard way that the grass wasn't greener on the other side of the employment spectrum, nor the money either.

Now games of partners were starting up. A regular stacked quarters on their table to stake a claim for the next game. Alice eyed her options and the growing crowd. She settled into stance, fidgeting and adjusting her angles. She looked pleadingly up at Nick.

"A little help here, a handicap or something?"

He shrugged. "Ah'm no' so doowally Ah furgot whit happened tae the last jimmy whae gied ye a haun wey the shootin, ken."

She shrugged, unrepentant for Frat Boy's insult and injury. "But I had no idea you were Fast Eddie when you're not completely wasted."

He grinned impishly at her. "Lochs run deep."

"And have sea monsters in them," she countered.

The balls clicked together, wandering aimlessly around the table.

"Dammit. This is awful," she said, flustered. "Spectators make me nervous."

"Whit aboot the ither nicht? Ah wis watchin, mind."

"This is different. This is a crowd. And that asshole made me mad." She stepped back from the table.

"Wid ye like me tae drive ye mental?" he offered as he made his shot. "Sure an' Ah managed the ither day."

She gave him a guarded look.

Pure sleekit tae dig tha' up, ya tosser. He called and sank the eight. "Back in a wee meenit. Oh, an' please dain't dae us a dizzy like the ither nicht, byraway."

She gave a half-hearted salute and perched on a stool, fidgeting with the joint in her cue as he gripped the hand of his waiting opponent, a nerdy type with wire-rimmed glasses, an expensive cue, and a serious face.

"Awright? Ah'm Nick, byraway."

"John. I was watching your game. You should play league."

"Cheers, mate. Hayonya, will ye shoot partners instead?" Nick gestured at Alice. "Ah dain't want tae lose the bird, ken?"

John looked confused for a moment as he processed the accent. "You want to shoot partners with her against me? Hang on." He searched the crowd, then yelled across the room, "Alan!"

Nick checked to make sure Alice hadn't slipped out. She watched the second table, looking lost and uncomfortable. "She's gawn tae dae a bunk. Hurry up, wee man," he muttered.

A confident man with shoulder-length hair pushed through the crowd. His Hawaiian shirt bled into his full-sleeve tattoos. Alice shifted her knees as he squeezed past. He ogled her openly. Nick tensed for a square go, but the sideshow attraction brushed by him and leaned in to talk with the other player. After nodding and gesturing between them, John gave Nick a thumbs-up.

Alice watched anxiously as Nick returned. He leaned in, at that moment thankful of the crowd for requiring him to get intimately close to be heard.

"Awright hen?" he asked, his lips nearly touching her neck. She shrugged. He breathed in her scent. "Ye want tae be ma hauner?"

"Your what?" Her hair tickled his cheek.

"Ma hauner. Ma backup." He jerked a thumb at the pool table behind him and the two men fussily chalking everything in sight.

"You want to shoot partners with me?" She leaned back slightly to search his face. Her stomach exploded with butterflies. She could see each hair in the blue shadow of his stubble, all of his faint freckles, and the impossibly long eyelashes men seemed to be born with. His eyes didn't look black after all, but a very deep brown. "I'll just bring you down. You can beat everyone here, including those league guys."

He shrugged. "Whir's the joy in tha'? Boring an' gallus. Against us thegither, they huv a sporting chance, byraway. Ur ye right?"

"Uh, you're right," she faltered, not understanding the idiom. She hopped off the stool with renewed spirit. "It doesn't matter how shitty I am if you go first." She smiled slyly. "But I am the master of horrible leaves. Totally unintentional, of course."

"Aye, ay course. Ur ma heavy team." He grinned back.

10: Call Me, Maybe

The league shooters waited formally. Alice stepped forward and extended her hand. Nick didn't appreciate the carnivorous look the tattooed shooter was giving her, so he leaned into the middle of their handshake.

"This is Alice, byraway. These jimmies ur…"

"Alan." Her lip curled slightly. She removed her hand as if it were covered in slime. Nick watched through narrowed eyes. She reached across to the other player. "John. Nice to see you again." She leaned back to whisper to Nick, "Little hand says it's time to rock and roll."

He broke with a piercing crack heard over the rumble of the crowded pub, and was eyeing the table for strategy when she touched his sleeve.

"Use mine." She pushed her cue at him. It had been her father's, and out of character even for him. Which was probably why it had lived in the back of his closet, and her mother had been eager to be rid of it when he passed. He had never sold it, and she wouldn't either. It wouldn't have made much difference to her debt anyway.

"Ah dain't like tae share. It's dead distractin," he said, but eyed it longingly.

"It wasn't a question. I don't want to lose."

He took it and slid it through his fingers. The stick felt good in his hands. Perfect weight and balance. Not top of the line, but very nice. Almost as good as the one he'd left in Glasgow. "Ur ye sure ye widnae raither Ah make ye lose the rag?"

"Alan's got that covered." She stepped back, arms crossed high and tight, and watched him intently. "Go on. Do that magic that you do."

He made a four-ball run and threw the next shot out of habit as a stall. Alice shifted nervously as Alan also sank four.

"It's onerly a gemm. Gie it laldie, wee hen."

"Easy for you to say." Her shot bumped off the pocket, but the balls rolled to rest in a tight cluster. She returned to Nick's side and handed over the cue, leaning in to mutter miserably, "That sucked."

"Fur ye or thum? It's pure dead brilliant," he marveled. "Fain ye nivver did tha' tae me."

"Didn't get the chance." She elbowed him, fighting a grin.

John struggled to contact one of his team's balls. He cleared the jam enough for Nick to squeeze in two more shots before being locked out himself.

"Ah think ye overdid it a wee," he whispered in her ear.

"Totally unintentional," she reminded him.

Alan cleared a hard cut and moved in confidently to round up the stragglers. Alice stepped forward, reaching for a cue chalk on the table edge. The small blue cube skittered across the floor. Nick watched as she strode after it down the aisle between pool tables and bent over. After staring at her ass for a long moment, he realized she was taking an unusual amount of time to pick up the chalk. She finished adjusting her jeans cuffs over her boot tops and straightened slowly. She made a half-turn and stretched out her upper back, making a hell of a silhouette out of what she had before strolling back to him, hips rolling. Balls clicked and someone cursed. He pushed the hair off his forehead, uncomfortably hot and slightly dazed. The undulations stopped directly in front of him, very close. His breath stuck in his lungs. Her hand settled on the cue an inch from his own, the chalk twisting on the point in front of his eyes.

"It's my shot," she chided gently and pulled the cue from his damp hand. " 'It seems a shame, the Walrus said, to play them such a trick.' "

He looked from her laughing green eyes to the lay of the table. Alan had missed, leaving three stripes to their single solid. He felt a laugh choke out of his throat. "Whir were ye when Ah wis hustlin?"

She puckered her lips. He swayed toward her, but she put a finger to her lips in a shushing gesture instead of the kiss he'd hoped for. She easily picked off the last ball and called the eight. He tensed; he'd seen her scratch often, between erratic skill, nerves, and pure intent. But it dropped neatly, the cue ball rolled safely across the felt, and she broke into a wide smile. John rushed forward to shake hands. Alan stacked multiple piles of quarters on the table as another player loaded the coin tray.

They held the table the rest of the night. Nick hoped for more of the same from his partner to throw off Alan's shooting, if not a full frontal assault consisting of her making out with him to inspire jealous misses. He was more than willing to take one for the team. But Alice kept her distractions disappointingly hands-off, and intermittent enough to seem unintentional, at least to the eye of the inebriated beholder.

Hours later, the dim lights flickered and the music ended abruptly. Snatches of nervous laughter rippled through the pub.

"Last call, people!" Hutch bellowed.

Alice looked at her phone. "Shit. Seriously?"

"Ye got a magic neep instead ay a motor the noo?" Nick teased.

She looked at him strangely.

"Like Cinderella, ken," he added awkwardly. "Losin aw her magic shite at midnicht."

She smiled ruefully. "Nah, my fairy godmother pissed off long ago, and the prince turned out to be an asshole. I just don't like to close down the bar."

"Ach well, let's finish it an' get oot err. Let the bull see the coo." He stepped up and ran the table, finishing the match with swift precision.

" 'O oysters,' said the Carpenter, 'you've had a pleasant run,' " Alice gloated to herself.

They lined up for the closing formalities. John nodded brusquely without meeting Alice's eyes. Alan took her hand and addressed her cleavage.

"I like it when you play dirty. But you still owe me big-time," he leered.

"I owe you my foot up your ass," she answered briskly.

She pulled her hand away sharply and wiped the palm on the seat of her jeans, a dismissal and taunt in one. She broke down her cue as she waited for Nick. He shook hands with the league gents for the last time, squeezing Alan's tattooed knuckles a little harder than necessary.

"Watch that one, hot shot. She'll eat you alive," Alan warned with a baleful stare.

"Aye, Ah'm coontin on it." He leered back.

He rejoined Alice and leaned in close. "Ye pit oot his pipe, so ye did. Mibbe a wee harsh wey the patter, but?" he said, trying not to look as pleased as he felt.

She didn't look up from gathering her things. "Nope. He deserved it, 'sure as ferrets are ferrets.' " She headed brusquely for the door.

He grabbed his heavy jacket and followed.

"You don't have to go home, people, but you can't stay here!" Hutch hollered.

The overhead lights blasted on, causing small shrieks of pain and mass scurrying as human roaches scattered into the night.

As they passed the bar, Alice called, " 'Night, Hutch."

He nodded and looked back to his abundance of dirty glassware. He did a double take at Nick's low salute.

"Cheers, big man."

"Take care, man. Don't piss her off," Hutch replied with great emphasis and seriousness, his mouth hanging open slightly.

"Wheesht," Nick hissed back, putting a finger to his lips.

Outside, Alice shrank back against the building to be out of the main walkway. They faced each other in sudden awkwardness.

"Tha's us oot wey the sawdust." Nick shrugged into his jacket.

"That yours?" She nodded at the black motorcycle.

"Aye. Onerly looks bad erse. Ah got it on account ay it's cheap. An' so Ah cannae get muddled on whit side tae sit on byraway." He grinned. "Ah'd gie ye a buttie up the road tae yer bit, onerly the wan helmet, but." *Muppet.* He shrugged apologetically and pushed his hair back. "Kin Ah walk ye hame, but?"

"It's only a few blocks," she said to his feet.

"Nae bother. Least Ah kin dae fur ma heavy team." He pushed his hair back again and huddled into the protective shell of his coat.

She ran her eyes from his harness boots to his unruly hair, deeply conflicted. She needed him to think she was interested, but didn't want it to get physical. That would make the investigation too weird. And from a relationship standpoint, one night together this early would be the end of it. She was making good progress, but could get more, she was sure of it. More of what, exactly, and for whom, she didn't quite know anymore.

She thought about his hand tight on her wrist. She clutched the small key ring canister of pepper spray in her jacket pocket. It calmed her, even though she knew it was long out of date. She nodded. Silently they stepped side by side past the windows and around the corner. She felt Hutch's stare follow them out of sight.

She kept her eyes on the sidewalk. The last time she'd walked with a man, it had been long, driven marches with her husband. At all hours of the night, he had insisted she accompany him in his obsession to punish his recalcitrant body. If she had been reluctant to go, his rage had boiled over. She knew the high blood sugar had contributed to his temper, but it didn't excuse the escalating attacks. As they had walked in grim silence, he had plowed ahead, a fog of hatred and resentment in his wake. She had hung back to avoid being its target, looking in windows, open doors, and balconies at vignettes of normal life, as if hoping to be rescued. " 'Alice moving under skies, never seen by waking eyes,' " she had chanted to herself.

She looked askance at Nick's wiry frame. He was the antithesis of Brad. She let the pepper spray fall back to the bottom of her pocket. Her eyes met his. She couldn't tell where his pupil ended and the iris began.

He shoved his hands deep into his pockets so they wouldn't hang like useless meat or keep worrying his fringe, and attempted to diffuse the sudden awkwardness between them. "Ye did gude, between the shootin an' the shite leaves." He grinned crookedly. "An' the distraction. Perr Alan."

"I wasn't sure it would even work, but I was desperate," she admitted. "He's low-hanging fruit, though. I could be knuckle-deep picking my nose and he'd still be undressing me with his eyes." She shook her head in wonder.

"An' his hauns too, Ah'd wager, if ye wis close enow," he added.

"Eeew. No thank you." She grimaced, to his enjoyment. "Yes, the classic Elle Woods bend and snap. Liked that, did you?"

"Ach, awmoast tae mich."

"Oh, I'm sorry. Did I break your concentration?" She smirked.

"Aye. Awmoast threw aff ma gemm." He nudged her with his shoulder, sending her staggering. She punched him lightly on the arm.

"Ooyah," he feigned injury. "Wee collateral damage, tha's fair." He resisted the urge to put an arm around her waist.

"All's fair in love and war," she agreed.

"An' which is this, then?"

She blushed. His words hung between them for a long moment.

"I meant at the bar. Alan tried to screw me over several years back," she qualified belatedly and changed the subject. "You must have a pack of furries waiting up. All vets seem to."

"Widnae be me."

"Really?" She rubbed the sudden goosebumps on her arms.

He picked up on her unease and fabricated a hopefully plausible explanation. "It's a commitment, isnae it the noo? Ah like tae keep ma options open an' that."

"Okay." She tried hard not to sound disappointed and not to care.

"It widnae be right wey the shift rotation an' that. Ah dain't ken hoo lang Ah'll be in the States. When the research grant is up, tha's me in a bind." It was technically true. He realized too late that he'd missed an entire subtext which had nothing to do with animals. "An' ma flat is nae pets," he added lamely.

"Well, that will do it. You don't want to violate a no-pets clause in this town."

She stopped abruptly next to a high wall of hedge. "This is it."

"Ye live in a hedgerow?" he said incredulously. "Nae wonder ye fancied ma hedgehog patter."

"Around the back. The house is divided into apartments."

He noticed the dark gables rising behind the hedge, and a narrow gap in the leafy wall. "Oh, aye." He pulled his hands free of his pockets, waiting for her to invite him in, knock him back, anything.

She fidgeted with her cue case strap, a sourness rising in her chest. It didn't take much to suss out the usual asshole agendas, including Hutch's freakshow obsession with keeping her legend alive and Alan's intent to write a career-launching exclusive. But Nick remained elusive. Maybe he was just lonely. Maybe he didn't have any agenda at all, not even getting into her knickers.

She reached for his right hand, avoiding his eyes. He resisted slightly at first, but let her turn his handshake palm up and hold his hand cupped in her own. She bent over their joined hands so all he could see was her hair. He breathed in her scent, too wrong-footed to pay much mind to the pressure on his skin. She tossed her curls back and closed his fingers over his palm. As she parted her lips to speak, he leaned forward and kissed her. He felt the heat and softness of her mouth.

She pulled away reluctantly, eyes locked on his. Nick's heart thudded like a marathon runner's. He leaned in for another kiss, but she turned her head, and his lips met the side of her neck instead. She made a small noise that could have been dismay or pleasure, and widened the space between them.

"Whit is it wey ye? Ah thoat…" *Ah thoat ye fancied me.*

"Dis she fancy ye, or whae ur pretendin tae be?" Nick Two muttered.

His hands clenched involuntarily at the unwelcome reminder and its equally unwelcome source. She flinched and her hands brushed lightly along his skin like satin.

Satin. His mother's pink slip under his brother's side of the mattress like a scud book. Small wonder why his wee brother had so eagerly tackled the odious task of making the bed every morning. He'd stupidly thought it was all about the jelly babies he got for doing the chore. Only a wee bit of tell-tale lace had betrayed the hiding place. A tug and the satin had flowed out, a small bit going on and on like a magician's scarf. Still smelling of roses, shivering and slithering through his fingers, almost alive. Stiff but soft, holding its shape like a shed skin. An obscene thing, a poison, a waiting viper. He had chopped it to bits with his school safety scissors, a tedious task that had made his hand ache for a week, and had painstakingly gathered the scraps into the bin. He had volunteered to take the middens right away, earning a handful of jelly babies from Da and a suspicious, jealous look from his brother.

Alice dashed through the gap in the hedge before she could change her mind and regret sleeping with him instead. At least she knew he was attracted to her. On the other side, she half-turned. "Call me, Lowlander," she said from a safe distance, and disappeared into the dark yard.

"Away tae fuck! Ah dain't huv…" His outstretched hand shook as if he longed to slap some sense into her, and he noticed what she had done to it. He took a closer look at the ballpoint ink numerals and smiled wryly. "Yer phone number."

11: Taken for a Ride

Nick rolled the pint glass between his palms, absently watching the deep amber ale tremble with concentric ripples. To call or not to call, that was the question. He took a long drink and leaned back. He decided he wasn't ready to find out for certain which side of him she really fancied. *Let it go by me whether it's fur me or no'.* He immediately missed her. He shook his head, annoyed with himself.

Nick Two slipped into the booth. "Ye'll no' be rid ay me tha' aisily, chiefie."

He grunted in response and stared at the soccer match.

"Ye should find yer mither while ur err. Wis born an' raised a few blocks fae Sweet Thistle, ken." He took a drink from Nick's ale. "An' still bides in toon byraway. It's a wonder ye huvnae locked horns wey her. She'd pure fancy seein her lang-lost wean."

"Lost? Ah wis in the same place ma hool life."

He ignored the comment and drained Nick's glass. "Tha's no' hauf bad. Ah'd fancy anither. Isnae it yer bell?"

"Ah'm desperate." Never had the expression seemed more literal. Nick flew out of the booth and strode away before he had to listen to any more. He hid in a bathroom stall to buy some time. He punched the wooden door and cursed, shaking out his fist until the throbbing stopped. Someone clattered into the other stall, muttering urgently. A loud sigh signaled the waterfall of a long beer piss. Nick regretted his hiding place. He flushed the toilet with his foot, washed quickly, and left. He didn't stop until he was outside, leaning on the building like a tobacco addict. He pulled out his phone, dialed, and listened anxiously to it ring.

He suddenly realized it would be a bad idea, mixing her with a life he only half-understood himself. He couldn't explain what he'd gotten himself into, what he'd done. What would she think of him? He disconnected the call and darted back inside. He detoured to the bar and flagged down Hutch for a refill of the pint the Nicktoon had usurped. He glanced back. His mate was gone, but Pavlov's Belle had replaced him. He cursed under his breath. She must have come in when he was hiding in the loo. *Searchin me oot fur a substitution request? Aw she'll get is a run roond the table an' a kick at the cat.* Returning to the booth was definitely out. He added a shot to the pint.

Alice glided past the windows, face lifted to the cool evening breeze. He straightened and lifted a hand to wave her over. She hesitated in the doorway, looking toward his occupied booth, before seeing him. No doubt adding things up: the nearly empty pub, Pavlov's Belle in his usual booth, facing his usual seat, and him with two drinks. She stopped, an uncertain smile on her face, one stool down from where he sat. He was very aware of the space between them, the tumble of curls pulled back low on her neck, her familiar scent.

"You called. I thought you might be here and want some company."

"Nut." He shoved the hair out of his eyes. "Ah dinnae ca'." He should have just done a runner. Now he had three people he needed to swerve.

"Caller ID says otherwise." She jerked her head toward his corner booth. "But since you already have company, I guess you butt-dialed."

"It's hard tae explain. Ye'd nivver credit it."

"What, butt-dialing, or you being with her?" she said stiffly. "You could have just said you were seeing someone, instead of playing me."

"Ah'm no'."

"Not seeing someone, or not playing me?"

"Shite! Neither."

"What then? You're playing several at once, because you can get away with it on shifts and don't know how long you'll be in the States?" Her voice and eyes were hard. She didn't know why she cared. He was only a job. *"She means well, but she can't keep from saying foolish things,"* she scolded herself.

"Ye mean tha' yin?" He pointed a thumb at Pavlov's Belle. "Ah dinnae ask her tae come in err. 'S no' like tha' booth has ma name on it byraway. She kin sit whiriver she pleases."

"She certainly is giving you stinkeye."

"So ur ye, an' we're no' seein each ither neither. Ah huv tha' effect on women. She wahrks in the lab wey me. Maist likely tryin tae wheedle a shift substitution oot me. Ah awyis say 'nut' precisely on account ay it drives her pure mental. Thus the marderous look she nae doot has on her coupon this very meenit." He flashed her his ferrety grin. "Ah suppose this means ye fancy me?"

He was pleased she didn't protest that. He allowed himself a lingering sightseeing tour of her parted lips, exposed throat, and the soft swells of her breasts.

"Here you are." Laura Beth slipped razor blades into her buttery voice as she came up to them. "Oh. Who's this?" Her eyes ran up and down appraisingly, and her face indicated the verdict was less than complimentary.

"Alice," she offered. She switched on a bright smile and extended her hand, reaching past Nick.

He hurriedly added, "Alice, Pav—Laura Beth."

The fierce blonde narrowed her eyes to slits. Her delicate features turned blotchy, and her voice dripped with thinly veiled venom. "I've heard so much about you."

He shook his head almost imperceptibly and widened his eyes, mouthing, *No' fae me.*

"Sorry, Nick hasn't said much about you."

"Oh, I haven't heard about you from him." She gauged the effect of her words. "I think everyone knows about *you*."

"Yep," Alice said flatly, crossing her arms.

"She murdered her husband, you know." She tilted her head toward Nick, her eyes still locked on Alice's.

"Ah've heard somehin aboot tha', aye."

"How do you two know each other?" The blonde compressed her lips into a thin line and glared at Alice with such intensity that she stepped backward, tripping over his feet. He steadied her with a hand above the elbow and got a brain wave.

"Ah dae some wahrk on the side. Hoose ca's. Alice wis meetin me so Ah could huv a keek at her wee cat. He's feelin perrly, byraway."

Alice's face jerked toward him. He raised his eyebrows slightly and squeezed her arm, encouraging her to play along.

"I saw his notice in the vet school," she agreed, falling easily into the ruse. "He's cheaper than a regular vet. I have to pinch pennies where I can."

"Quality wahrk fur less." He flashed his ferret smile at Laura Beth, boldly looking her in the eyes to check if she was buying it. "Huv tae dash byraway," he said apologetically. "Veterinary oath an' that. 'Usin ma knowledge an' skills fur the benefit ay society,' ken." He started for the door before his qualifications could be questioned.

Alice called over her shoulder, "It was nice to meet you." Under her breath, she added, "Country club bitch."

"House call, my ass," the blonde hissed at their backs as the pub door closed behind them. "More like booty call. You didn't even study companion animals. What kind of fool do you take me for? Leather? Fur? *Her?* How could you do this to me? No wonder you won't answer my calls."

"Tha' yin's a right nyaff," Nick said to Alice as an apology. He loaded on the expressions, increasing in outlandishness. "Has a hit fur herself, tha' yin. Thinks she's big, but a wee coat fits her. If she wis choklit, she wid eat herself." Alice gave a small bark of amusement. He grinned crookedly. "Ah dain't crap it aff the likes ay her, byraway. Tha' yin hud it in fur me fae day wan." He handed Alice a plain black helmet and strapped on his own.

"You *were* expecting company, I see."

"Ah did ca' ye, haun tae God, an' then hung up afore ye answered."

"The truth comes out. That wasn't so hard."

She pulled on the helmet awkwardly, using her reflection in the pub window. She looked like a giant ant, and he couldn't help grinning. She gave him a long look.

"Laugh it up, Lowlander. I may look like the Great Gazoo in this thing, but I can still kick your ass."

"Oh aye? An' ye wid dae tha', whit wey me daein ye the favor ay a bargain-price hoose ca' fur yer wee cat?" He looked sideways at her.

She suspected he was after a bargain-price house call for something else. "Which I don't need and didn't ask for. I don't even have a cat. Why exactly did you make up that whopper?"

He straddled the motorcycle and faced the road, pulling on a pair of leather gloves. "Ah dinnae want tae say Ah met ye in a pub, whit wey the Sweet Thistle reputation an' that."

She snorted. "As if that's a worse reputation than murderer. 'I've heard nonsense, compared with which, that would be as sensible as a dictionary.' It's also not worse than liar, which you've now added to the list. I can't believe you had me lying for you."

Ah'd raither huv ye lyin on me. He clucked. "Ye dinnae miss a beat. Ur a natural at the deception. Ye've got me worried the noo."

"Thanks so much. Flattery will get you nowhere." She was glad he couldn't see her face. She rested a hand on his shoulder and swung up behind him. "You've got *me* worried. Your first instinct is to lie your face off, and you're a hustler," she said calmly. *No wonder the Booths want me to investigate you.* She placed her hands lightly on his narrow hips. "Bring the noise," she said over the loud beating of her heart.

The motorcycle roared to life. He eased it into the road and headed toward her apartment. He braced for the stiffness of an inexperienced passenger, but she was a natural. As the bike glided into the first turn, she clung to his waist and took the corner like an extension of his body. He hadn't expected that level of comfort from her, certainly not this early in the game, if ever. On the straightaway, he opened it up wide, enjoying her thighs clasped around his hips, her hands on his stomach. At every shift of the gears, her helmet tapped his in a watered-down Glasgow kiss. He barely heard her embarrassed apologies over the engine and buffeting wind.

As he passed the distinctive wall of shrubbery that marked her apartment, she turned with a jerk that made the motorcycle wobble.

She worked her hands under the waist-length tail of his jacket for warmth and relaxed against him, feeling the tilt of his hips between her thighs and the tightening of his stomach under her hands. She closed her eyes to focus on her senses, to shut out thought on anything but this moment with this man, to shut up any thoughts other than the ones normal girls had at a time like this. Things like, Where's he taking me? Is he good in bed? Is he boyfriend material? Instead, she had only complicated questions she couldn't begin to answer. *Why does he want to be around me? Why does he need a sponsor if he's got dual citizenship? Why would Mary lie about sponsorship? Or was Nick lying about citizenship? Does he owe them money too? If so, what did he do to need a high-priced attorney?*

She shivered hard, rattling against him. *"Curioser and curioser." Something is very wrong with the whole setup. But does it even matter as long as I get paid?* He turned his head back toward her slightly. She ducked deeper behind the shelter of his back to keep the wind from choking her, careful to keep her helmet tilted away from his. The night air raised goose bumps on her skin under her inadequate jacket. She breathed purposefully, willing her muscles to unknot one by one.

She shuddered again. He reached under the edge of his jacket and patted her hand. He slowed the motorcycle as he searched for a turnaround.

12: Bone Collector

Alice unlocked her arms from his waist as they passed through the gap in the hedge, half walking the motorcycle and half riding. She slipped off and staggered on stiff legs, leaving behind a damp chill on his skin in the shape of her body. Surreptitiously rubbing her sore buttocks, she struggled with the heavy helmet one-handed.

"Let me help ye wey tha'," he said gently, unzipping his heavy jacket.

She flashed a sharp look in his direction and slugged him on the arm. He patiently eased her helmet off and hooked it on the motorcycle, raising his eyebrows at her.

"Oh," she muttered.

"Ah kin help ye wey tha' ither thing tae, since Ah awready got skelped fur it."

She squatted abruptly and cooed, "Hello, Cheshire Cat."

He squinted at a pale shadow moving around her legs. A small gray cat leaned against her possessively. "Ye dae huv a cat." He crouched and rubbed his fingers together to call it. It glided over and rubbed against him. "Awright, wee man?" He scratched under the cat's chin. "He's thrumming."

"He likes everyone. Even vets, apparently." She barked a laugh. The cat shamelessly presented his soft white belly for Nick's hand, rumbling like the motorcycle. "But he's not mine. Appears and disappears mysteriously, when you least expect him. That's why I call him Cheshire. I suspect he belongs to somebody, but he visits everyone in the neighborhood."

He yanked his hand away as the cat started to bite. "Wee bastart. Jist like the devils ma mither used tae take in by the lorry-load."

"Your off-duty look must have only fooled him for a moment."

The pale cat rolled to his tiny feet and disappeared into the dimness. Alice crossed to the door. She entered, and a broad rectangle of light flooded the yard.

Once inside, she was nowhere to be seen. He hesitated just inside the apartment, taken aback by the jumble in the large main room.

Drawings and photographs ran floor to ceiling in a piecemeal wallpaper. Against one wall, a worn velvet sofa with threadbare seat cushions was covered with a fleece throw, the fabric tucked into the crevices like a military bunk. Across from the sofa was a small TV, flanked by shelves with a few DVDs and skulls in all sizes and shapes. In the back corner was a futon that obviously served as her bed. It had been hastily folded back into a seat, but was covered in sheets and held a bed pillow in a pillowcase. A worn dresser squatted beside it, its surface holding a cheap portable CD player, a plastic rack of CDs, and an elderly stuffed rabbit. The two small windows were crowded with potted plants as well as the clutter usually found on nightstands: candles in jars, a small lamp, a short stack of library books in cellophane dust jackets, a water glass. A multi-headed lamp with pink shades cast a warm light.

He perched awkwardly on the sofa and set his gloves beside him for want of anywhere else to put them. Hunched elbows to knees, he rubbed his hands together at a loss for what to do or say. Small noises echoed from an adjacent room, the kitchen maybe, or the bath. *Mibbe she's slippin intae somehin mair comfortable?*

The cat landed lightly beside him and climbed under the tent created by his arm.

"Whir did ye come fae, then? Ah dinnae see ye come through."

The small cat balanced along his narrow thigh and settled into a cat loaf. A clipped ear flicked against his jacket, making a ticking sound like a moth against a light bulb. He moved his arm and leaned back slightly. The cat blinked slowly and purred itself to sleep. He ran his hand down the cat's sharp spine to its jutting cow-like hips.

"Ach, ur a wee auldfaither, urnae ye," he muttered. "Used up aboot aw yer lives, aye? Ah ken hoo it is." He scooped the bony wee cat into his arms and crept closer to the morbid display of skulls, irrationally feeling a need for caution.

He recognized dog, cat, bird, hare, and deer from his late-night browsing of anatomy lab specimens when the graveyard shifts seemed interminable. The deer skulls were in various states of mutilation, some with antlers gnawed to stumps and green with old moss, others with crudely hacked holes where the trophy had been removed. The cat wriggled from his arms as he leaned in to examine a skull he couldn't identify. He held the jaw carefully in place and turned it over in his hands. Nearly primordial in appearance, it was long and flat with saber fangs and a tall ridge on the cranium.

"Sorry about the clutter. I turned the bedroom into a darkroom. It's usually a moot point. I don't have anyone over."

He straightened and looked over his shoulder. Alice stood in the kitchen doorway, a steaming mug in each hand. She was wrapped tightly in a frumpy white bathrobe, once lush, now stained at the cuffs and bare in patches like the stuffed rabbit. She eyed the skull in his hands. He hastily thrust it back into place.

"Virginia opossum," she said, and sipped from one of the mismatched mugs. She padded silently across the carpet and stopped next to him, holding out a mug emblazoned with a logo and advertising slogan. "I made tea."

"Cheers." He accepted the steaming mug gratefully.

She nodded at the collection. "I find dead things."

He gave her a startled look, but she didn't notice. She pointed at the hare and one of the cat skulls.

"Some are roadkill." She picked up a goat skull with a bullet hole between its eye sockets. "Some of them, I don't even want to know. Found this one in a creek." She replaced it carefully and gestured at a cluster of small songbird skulls. "These were gifts from Cheshire."

His imagination tumbled through gruesome images of skull extraction from little carcasses. "Hoo did ye get thum so clean? Or dae Ah no' want tae ken?"

"I find some of them like that. Others, I use fine gauge wire to sew the bodies into bags of window screen, wire them to a stake, and bury them in a shallow grave," she explained eagerly. "A few months later, I dig them up, and no muss, no fuss: perfectly clean inside and out." She grinned.

He wondered if he should be concerned about her enthusiasm for corpses in light of her criminal history. "Aw natural." He nodded in what he hoped was a knowledgeable way. He hesitated for a moment before drinking from his mug. The tea was strong and dark, hot but not scalding, probably not poisoned. Perfect.

"Fantastic collection, byraway," he said.

"Thanks. I use them in photographs."

"Ah kin see tha'." He gestured at the walls.

"I also work as a courtroom sketch artist, for some high-profile cases." At his raised eyebrows, she shrugged. "It's extra income. Though I don't generally like being in a courthouse if I can help it."

"Oh, aye," he said awkwardly. "Eh—sorry aboot ma cowahrker in the pub thenicht."

She studied the interior of her mug. "Once the Black Widow, always the Black Widow. I'm used to it. It's definitely better than it used to be." She made a small, angry noise.

His face fell, but it wasn't directed at him. She leaped across the room, seizing the gray cat by his scruff, and escorted him to the door like a bouncer with an unruly drunk. The small tom swiped at her with a sheathed paw before she hustled him through.

"Yeah, whatever, tough guy," she muttered.

Nick paced while Alice scrubbed at the sofa with a bottle of deodorizer. The furniture hardly seemed worth saving, which was about where this night was abruptly heading.

"Cannae ye train hum no' tae dae tha'?"

"He's not mine, and I don't let him in for just this reason. Do you have any suggestions?" she said irritably.

"Nae. Hoo should Ah?"

She paused her scrubbing and gave him a sharp look.

"Whit?" he said defensively.

She straightened. "You're a vet. Isn't animal behavior part of the deal?"

He froze. *Jesusjohnny. Yer tea's oot the noo, ya fuckwit.* He shoved a dog skull aside to place his half-empty mug on a shelf. "It's late. Ye mist be knackered." He zipped his jacket with finality and strode to the door. He couldn't look at her.

The night air closed around him like the cold dark sea around a drowning sailor. He settled onto the motorcycle and pulled on his helmet. Her silhouette cut into the rectangle of yellow light from the doorway. He could tell from the shadow that her arms were crossed.

Disnae matter onie road. Nae use gettin oniehin started when me bein over err is temporary.

As he walked the bike backwards, the dark shape disappeared, leaving a bright rectangle that lit the grass into tiny knife blades. Alice appeared beside the front wheel like a ghost. She thrust something at him. He stopped rolling the bike and looked at her hand, trying to decipher what she offered. His hands hurt from gripping the handlebars too tightly. She tapped his knuckles with whatever she held, and he snatched it from her. His gloves. He nodded brusque thanks, relieved that it spared him from having to face her again. He pulled them on, very aware of her still next to the wheel. *Huntin me like a snarky polis whae disnae huv grounds tae arrest, jist tae hassle.*

"Ah couldnae huv looked at the cat onie road." He tried out a partially true explanation. "See, Ah studied farm animaws. Tha's hoo Ah dain't ken aboot cats byraway. The hoose ca' wis jist somehin tha' came up ma humph."

"Right. The chicken research. Good thing I didn't really need your house call." She stepped back, arms at her sides.

He nodded, glad of the body swerve.

"Good night, Lowlander."

She waited while he resumed his backward crawl through the hedge and out into the street.

13: Calling Home

Two a.m., seven Glasgow time. He would call home as soon as he ran the gauntlet. An SUV packed as full as a clown car crept down the middle of Alice's street, giving the lines of parked cars on each side a suspiciously wide berth. Loud, clumsy drunks stumbled out of bars in disheveled packs. Some crowded onto the town bus under the tolerant eye of a fellow student behind the wheel. A couple, liplocked on the sidewalk, seemed oblivious to jostling and jeers. Pedestrians weaved from sidewalk to road, jaywalking freely as their balance faltered. He shook his head in wonder. It was like Hogmanay most nights of the week here.

Safely inside his apartment at last, Nick set both helmets on the kitchenette island and slung his jacket across the desk chair. He yanked off boots and socks, wiggling his toes on the soothing coolness of linoleum. Suddenly ravenous, he grabbed a jar of marmalade and a loaf of bread and settled onto a kitchen stool to call. The burring ringtone sounded distant, muffled. *C'moan, c'moan.* Nick worried he'd missed Da after all. He took a huge bite of jam sandwich, savoring the thick chunks of peel.

"Hullo?"

"Da," he said with relief, his voice muffled with sticky sandwich.

"Laddie?" Rabbie Kerr's smile could be heard across the ocean.

He choked down the mouthful. "Aye, Da. Awright?"

"Ye eatin an' bletherin at the same time agin, am Ah right?"

"Aye, ur right. Ah fund real Dundee marmalade," he reported with childlike pride as he filled a glass from the tap.

"Proof ur no' wastin away. Ye awyis did love a wee jeely piece, byraway." Rabbie artfully twisted the idle chat into a probe. "Ye kin find proper jeely, an' ye cannae find a joab or a lass, but?"

"Ah'm on holiday, Da. An' they dain't huv birds at the grocer's." He contemplated shrink-wrapped women lined up, ingredients listed on a tight T-shirt so you knew exactly what you were in for: bad temper, good in the sack; sweet, but needy; heavily armored, but worth the effort.

"Hoo dae the birds get the messages in the States then?" Rabbie asked with false innocence. "Ach, jist rattlin yer cage, son. Ur givin some wee tottie the sword ay the Lord, ur ye no'?"

"Da!" he spluttered, mortified. Even an ocean away, he wasn't safe from Da's unsubstantiated obsession with the possibility of grandweans. With Nick's track record, any affair was doomed to be brief, often not making it as far as the bedroom.

"Oh aye," his father said sagely. "A gennleman nivver tells."

"Nut! We huvnae got tha' far…" He realized he'd been played. "Ach! Ye sleekit wee stoater."

Da chuckled. "Whit's she like then, yer wee hen?"

"Pure mad skull," suggested the Nicktoon. "Next she'll be breengin in like the bawheidit Kool-Aid pitcher, destroyin oor sanctuary, providin mich-needed refreshment, but," he ranted with vigorous hand gestures.

"Whit the fook?" Nick stared at him. "She cannae decide if she iven fancies me. Nae chance ay her 'breengin in' an' playin hoose. Ur ye on the bevvy? Did ye tan aw ma wee heavy?" He checked his stash in the refrigerator.

"Get tae fook. Ah'm onerly speakin ma mind."

"Aye, whit toaty wee bit erras left ay it, ya fookin tube, ye." Nick sat back down.

"Huv a wee close-up keek fur yerself, ya cheeky bastart," Nick Two declared and gave his friend a Glasgow kiss that sent him sprawling off the stool.

He clutched his head. "Fook! Ah'm on the fookin phone, or Ah'd gie ye a right proper doin!"

"Son? Ur ye err?

Nick crawled to his feet, grabbed a bag of peas from the freezer, and pressed it to his throbbing forehead. He didn't even like peas; it was habit to have them on hand for this very purpose. "Ach, brain freeze," he groaned.

"Fae a jeely piece?" Rabbie asked incredulously.

"Ah hud ma ginger in the deep freeze tae chill an' it got a wee baltic," he lied.

"Ur ye actin it tae no' answer ma query aboot yer wee doll?" Rabbie said suspiciously.

"Fair enow." He resettled on the stool and gave his roommate the vicky. "Fit. Cheeky. Sleekit. Hud a rummle wey the law, but."

"Aye, an' whae hasnae hud a wee tango wey the polis kin lamp the first stane, kin he no'? She soonds pure dead brilliant."

"Onerly she's no' ma bird. Cat an' moose, mair like, an' Ah'm gettin the sharp end."

"Ach. Women. Sure an' they dain't expect us lads tae unnerstaun thum, onerly tae stick aroond an' let thum wind us up until they grace us wey a wee rummle in the sheets. Birds ur complicated, son. They huv the same urges as us lads. Erras some whit shoo ye right aff, yer pure slappers an' that. A pure brilliant lass widnae chance gettin cried the village bike, but. She has tae gies a dizzy wanst or twicet tae see hoo interested ye ur."

"Oh aye. A hustle, an' she's stallin an' that?"

"Somehin like tha'." He sighed. "Ach. Ah shouldnae huv tae be tellin ye aw this at yer stage ay life. Nae shocker Ah dain't huv grandweans!" he fussed. "Oh, an' fur the love ay God, be yerself. She'll onerly find oot in the end whae ye ur onie road, an' then tha's ye fooked." He switched from lecture to self-deprecating humor. "Rabbie Kerr's sermon on the fair sex, cauld kale het agin. Fur aw the gude it'll dae ye when the wee man stauns up wey a chorus ay hoochs."

"Cheers, Da."

"When ur ye comin hame fae yer wee holiday, laddie?" Rabbie asked pointedly, "Ye dain't huv tae stay, dae ye?"

"Ah'm jist haudin the jaikets wey the flat. Lease is over in May, ken. Chance ay a lifetime." So far the lie had held off too many questions.

"Oh, aye. If ye say so. Nivver hurts tae ask, but."

The older man changed the subject, knowing he couldn't sway a hard-headed son until he was ready for it. "Ye nivver ring so airly. Whit ur ye pefter-efter, lad? Ye gies a bell tae no' talk aboot a bird ur no' shaggin, or did ye find yer mither in her hame toon?"

"Nae, an' Ah dain't want tae. Hoo dinnae ye tell me she belanged tae err? Ah widnae huv come."

"Ah thoat tha' wis hoo ye went." Da added gently, "Yees wis onerly three-quarters an' six when she left byraway. Awfy wee. It's awright tae want tae see her."

"Whit happened back then, between ye an' Maw? Did ye gie her a doin?"

"Nut," Rabbie said emphatically. "Rare raised ma voice tae her. Mibbe Ah wis tempted when she wis sour on ye, but Ah nivver gied her a blow, hauns or words, Ah swear on ma Granda's grave, so Ah dae. She used tae gie ye a right leathering wey tha' tongue ay hers, but. Over wee things. Dinnae hauf go through ye."

"Ah remember," Nick murmured.

"Ah think she wis mair hamesick than she wanted tae admit, iven tae herself. Nivver did click wey the ither birds, dinnae huv troopettes or nuchin. Glesga wis a wee mair foreign fur her than she coonted on." Disapproval crept into Rabbie's voice. "Awyis correctin folks' accents, or nippin aboot words tha' mean somehin else in the States an' that." His words tumbled out, equal parts angry and sad. "She could be a right heidnipper, yer mither. Ah nivver thoat she meant it, no' really. When she wis in a huff, she went aff like a two-bob rocket at ivryhin, especially ye. God, she wis pure beautiful when she wis angry, awmoast electric. Wis aw a gemm wey her, takin the huff so we could make up later. Least at first. Ah've thoat it over a lot, so Ah huv. Efter a time, it wisnae a wind-up onie mair.

"Nivver could get a haunle on whit she wanted fae me. First it was the thrill ay petty crime, me an' Malky skimmin a bit fae the deliveries tae boost oor wages, ken? As yees lads got aulder, Ah wanted tae go straight. Wisnae worth the risk. When Ah telt her, Ah thoat she'd be over the moon. Isnae tha' whit the hens awyis want? Tae change ye? No' yer mither, but. She got involved wey thum Union fur the Abolition ay Vivisection nutters recruitin at the uni. Wis BUAV this, an' animaw rights tha'. She wanted us tae nick sairtain thingmies, thingmies wey a political agenda."

"Whit sort ay thingmies?" His fingers hurt from clutching the phone too hard.

"Luxury cosmetics, bloody furs. High-price items tha' wid send ye away fur a gude tick." Rabbie was incredulous even after the span of years. "Some thingmies we dinnae iven transport, so hoo wis we supposed tae nick thum? Iven animaws oot laboratories, which made nae fookin sense, since nae resetter wants thum. No' iven the dugs." His voice turned solemn. "Wis ma fault. Ah couldnae dae it. Ah gied her an ultimatum, see? Ah telt her it wis us lads or the bloody BUAV. So she did a runner. Left yees lads weyoot a way intae the flat while she went tae a protest in London wey her BUAV mates. Yees could huv caught yer death, locked oot in the dreich like tha'. It wis a sin, so it wis. Laboratory rats comin afore her oon lads."

His voice shook with emotion. "She left a note. She wis comin back on the train at week's end. So Ah took yees lads tae Queenie Station at the day an' time in her note. Tae huv her choose faimly an' come hame wey us, or choose the politics an' fook aff wey her activist mates. Ah tried tae make it a wee holiday ay sorts. A fistful ay sweeties each, a bag ay crisps, an' a boattle ay ginger. Ah suppose Ah expected it wid be a wee celebration. Hoo could she say nae tae yer wee faces?"

Nick remembered the trains gliding in on heart-quickening blasts of warm air as he searched the throng for a familiar gait or face, listening for her voice. His wee brother worked the crowd like a jakey for bevvy money, telling anyone that would listen that they were waiting for their mother. Over and over, "She's gone doon London tae help the animaws," until he wanted to give him a right kicking. Instead, he called the jelly babies by his brother's name and dismembered them one by one with small angry bites.

"Jelly baby?" Nick Two offered a bag of sweeties as a peace offering.

"Ya eejit, whae the fook dae ye think ye ur, fookin Doactor Who?" Nick griped, but set aside his bag of half-thawed peas and grabbed a handful. "Did ye order these wee bastarts aff the internet?"

"Ah huv ma sources," he replied mysteriously, his mouth full. He peered at the brightly colored tiny people, pushing them around with one long, thin finger. "Ye remember afore aw these different personalities? It's like the fookin Spice Girls in ma swedger the noo."

He sneered while he chewed, holding up orange and pink candies in turn. "Ginger. Baby Thingmy."

"Ah ken fookin tae well ye widnae mind eatin the Spice Girls." Nick lasciviously licked a candy before popping it in his mouth. He listed the jelly baby names while chewing, counting off on his fingers, "Baby Bonny, Bubbles, Brilliant, Bumper, Boofuls, Braveheart." He dodged a flying candy. "Bigheart," he corrected.

"Ya bawheid. Pits me right aff ma scran, so it dis." Nick Two tossed him the bag. "Onie road, wey aw the names an' special shapes an' that, it's near enow cannibalism."

"Tasty, tasty cannibalism." Nick bit off several heads in quick succession and chewed loudly with his mouth open.

"Fookin immature, pal."

"Hayonya, hoo aboot screamin jelly babies?" he suggested.

His mate stared at him for a moment, then grabbed the bag from Nick's hand. "Kill thum wey fire! Jist like science class wey Mr. Callan. Pure dead brilliant," he gloated. "Ah'm fur the aff. Hoo dinnae Ah go intae chemistry, onie road? Ah could be blowin up thingmies on a regular schedule."

Nick saluted as his pal rushed out the door, pleased with himself for getting rid of him so he could finish his conversation uninterrupted. "Aw we got wis a day ay trainspotting," he said to draw his father out of pained silence.

"Aye. Nivver saw horns nor tail ay yer mither byraway."

"Mibbe ye got the station wrang. Mibbe it wis wan ay thum misunderstandings tha' blows up an' yonks later, tha's ye reunited an' trippin aboot it."

"Onerly in the movies, laddie," Da said gently. "Right day, right time, right place an' that. If she hud iver planned on comin hame, somehin or someyin in London changed her mind. She stayed on in the city fur awhile, then went back tae the States."

"Hoo dae ye ken?"

"Ah asked aboot," Da answered vaguely.

"Asked aboot. Whae did ye ask?"

"The fookin BUAV youth organizer," Da answered with a flare of temper at his son's badgering.

"An' ye believed hum?"

"Oh aye. When ma fist wis done askin, he wid huv shopped his oon granny," Da snapped. "Ah'm nae stranger tae a rammie, son. Ah gied tha' Bearsden wanker a right doin, so Ah did. Mind ye, it dinnae take mich." Rabbie turned sentimental. "Ach, we'll awyis huv Glesga byraway."

"Fancy yerself the Scoats Bogart the noo, dae ye, auldjin?" his son teased.

"Wee, dark, an' leesome, tha's me. Birds cannae resist silent, wranged fillas. Listen an' lairn, laddie." Rabbie's voice rippled with mischief. "Speakin ay it, Ah huv a wee private do the nicht wey the fit Fiona."

"Isnae Fiona the yin wey a—hoo did ye cry it—'gub like a gator, bum like a pelmet'?"

"Ah, but she onerly blethers when overwhelmed by a dead healthy specimen ay Scoattish manhood like maself. An' Ah pure fancy a wee extra in ma curves byraway."

"Erras nivver a pick on Maw as Ah remember, but."

"Her jaws nivver wis gawn the right way. Ah hud high hopes but. She wis a wee smasher when she wis aw roonded oot wey yees. Couldnae keep ma hauns aff her. It's a shocker she dinnae gie birth tae a hale fitbaw team."

"Fur fook's sake! A son disnae want tae hear tha' shite fae his faither," he groaned in disgust.

"Ah'm lang in the horn, no' nudgin ma grave, lad," countered Rabbie.

"Talk tae ye later, Da. Ah'm gawn tae huey the noo."

"Talk tae ye soon, son."

"Bye ya."

14: Invitation

Nick woke later than usual, dazed and confused by both a late night spent on the violent, special-effects excesses of a cop movie marathon, and its aftermath, an especially vivid dream about making out with a snake-haired beauty on a bed of skulls, smack in the middle of the Queen Street Station upper deck while cars and bullets flew around them. He stood in the chill of the open refrigerator for a long moment, unable to remember what he was looking for.

"Ach," he scolded himself and grabbed the dog-eared egg carton he had refilled countless times with fresh eggs from the lab. They were supposed to be tested and discarded, but based on the typical results, he didn't mind taking his chances. He longed for a cold bottle of ginger as he pulled out his solitary skillet.

He focused on the immediate: cooking and eating the eggs, the satisfaction of cleaning the handful of dishes, the hot shower flattening his hair to his head. He shook his head like a dog and froze mid-shampoo, listening. He heard the last ring from his cell phone cut short and shrugged. *Lee a message, ring back, or pish aff.* Despite his nonchalant monologue, he hurried through the rest of his shower, anxious to check the phone.

He was vigorously toweling his hair into a thistle when it rang again. He wrapped the towel around his hips like a sarong, peered into the fogged mirror at himself with a snort at his own vanity and foolishness, muttering, "It's no' Skype, mate," and dashed for the phone on his desk. The caller ID registered one of the generic trunk numbers for a university line. He sighed, dreading a plea for shift substitution from Laura Beth, which he sussed was a particularly desperate attempt to make conversation with him.

"Whae is it?"

"Hi, Lowlander. It's Alice."

"Awright, hen?"

"Aye. I mean yeah," she stammered.

He was pleased. "Hayonya, did ye gies a bell a wee meenit ago?"

"Nope. Must have been your other 'hauner.' The truth is out. You really are starting a collection."

He let his grin be heard down the line. "Dae ye think Ah need mair than wan?"

"Quite possibly, between the hustling and your scary coworker."

"Scarier than an infamous marderer?"

"Nice. What does your choice of associates say about you, Dr. Kerr?" She feigned offense.

"Ah mist need some ay tha' therapy Ah've heard aboot."

"You're lucky we're on the phone, or else you'd be getting some physical therapy right now," she said with mock anger.

"Oh aye?" His voice rippled with laughter.

"With my fist. I meant with my fist. Get your mind out of the gutter." She was glad he couldn't see her hot cheeks. "So anyway, this Saturday is the Highland Festival at Sweet Thistle."

"Nae doot a load ay puddocks in kilts pitchin trees whilst bagpipes make yer lugholes bleed. Tha's hoo erras mair Scoats ootside ay Scoatland than in it," he ranted, then worried she'd think he was serious. It was a national pastime to heckle the pipes and heavy games while loving them. His native West End held a highland games festival that was a big draw, and watching heavyweight sports came in second only to football matches. A distant second, but all the same. As for bagpipes, Glasgow was home to a week-long bagpiping festival, complete with free concerts in the city center that culminated in a world championship. For a month, the city was overrun with tartans, pipers, drummers, and dancers from around the world. He could almost hear the skirling of the pipes echoing off the tall buildings of George Square and felt a sudden wave of homesickness.

"You can't have a Highland Festival without Scottish games and bagpipes. But there's also clan gatherings, food, and a ceilidh," she cajoled.

"Ah dain't ken," he said doubtfully.

"C'mon, Lowlander. A Scotsman fresh off the boat? You'll be a total rock star!" Her enthusiasm was infectious. "You can tell them what they've got wrong. That accent makes everything sound wicked good. You could insult everybody and no one would care."

"Naeb'dy wid unnerstaun, ye mean. Wey ma luck, Ah'll open ma gub an' ivrybody wull think Ah'm a wanker fakin the patter."

"I'll protect you. I'm your 'hauner,' remember? C'mon, Lowlander!" It seemed like a perfect test of authenticity. She needed him to go. She wheedled shamelessly, "Men in skirts throwing trees! Endless bagpipe jokes! I personally know a great one about an octopus, but I won't tell you unless you go. There might even be real Irn-Bru."

"Ye askin me oot?" he said slyly.

"Who is?" she countered.

"Whit?" he answered, confused.

"What?" she fired back.

"Ach." *Hard tae argue properly in a towel, byraway.* She'd left it for him to figure out her intentions.

"Wear a kilt," she ordered.

"Whit makes ye think Ah've got wan? On account ay me bein Scoats?" he said peevishly. "Next ye'll be askin efter ma golf gemm."

"Sorry, that was horrible of me to stereotype you like that. Forget the whole thing."

"Nae, Ah owe ye fur tha ither nicht, dain't Ah? Ye got ma erm up ma back." He dropped the bluff before he lost the opportunity entirely. "An' Ah dae huv a kilt. Dain't tell Billy Connolly, but."

"Who?"

"Nivver mind. But Ah'm no' wearin a Prince Charlie jaiket, a ghillie shirt, flashes, or ghillie brogues," he warned.

"I'm not sure what any of those are, but fair enough."

"An' nae motorcycle ride. Ye huv tae drive if Ah'm in a kilt."

"Okay! Jeez. You drive a hard bargain. How about ten at your place?"

"Aye. Tha'll dae."

"See you then, Lowlander."

"Directions," he blurted. "Ye dain't ken whir Ah live."

"Yes I do. We locals don't call the university directory 'Ag Tech Stalker' for nothing. You really need to change your privacy settings, Doctor Kahhrrr. Bye."

As he disconnected, he smiled and wondered if she really had called twice and wouldn't own up to it. He scrolled through the phone's log, past the switchboard number to a cell number he didn't recognize. There were no voicemail messages.

"Wrang number," suggested the Nicktoon. "Or anither bampot woman."

"Isnae mental fanny be'er than nae fanny at aw, but?" Nick countered. "Ah'll change the directory settings as soon as Ah get some claes on."

By the time he was dressed in a clean T-shirt and jeans, his friend was gone. He reached into the back corner of the closet for a dry cleaner's bag and checked to be sure all the pieces were as they should be: short black formal Prince Charlie jacket and vest, crisp white shirt, bold red and green Kerr clan kilt in traditional high-waisted cut. He had the Weegie disdain for the overused tartan, but his grandparents had saved up for years to get the full kit as a graduation present. Decked out in full regalia themselves at the commencement ceremony, they had beamed and pointed out their grandson to complete strangers, loudly and proudly claiming him. First of the immediate clan to graduate from uni, a doctor of sorts, and with honors. A good lad, a perfect catch for a fine lass. It was enough to make you shout huey and ralph, it made him that sick to his stomach.

During the summers spent on their Borderlands farm, Nanna had trained her grandsons in the traditions. Every evening was a ceilidh, accompanied by the radio or old tapes. He loved to watch his grandparents dance. There was a gentle electricity between them. Safe from urban scorn in the large farmhouse kitchen, guided by Nanna's fleshy arms, he had practiced with long-suffering patience to please her and to outshine his wee brother. She always told him it would pay off one day. It had paid instant dividends of extra cuddles and wedges of homemade shortbread, later in extra pocket money and privileges. Now he finally realized the opportunity for another payoff—to spark some electricity of his own.

"Bless ye, Nanna. Ah wid huv done it fur yer smile. This is pure dead brilliant, but."

15: Full Frontal Kilt

Nick had been ready half an hour early and was now at a loss for what to do with himself. Too early to have a drink, tempting as that was to take the edge off. He stepped into the bathroom for another check in the mirror mounted on the back of the door. Since it was one of the cheap four-footers that were standard issue in college apartments, he had to lean in to see his usual black leather harness boots and thick hiking socks. He pushed the socks inside the top of the boots, then decided they looked better showing above. He eyed his thin, pale legs with dissatisfaction. "Wee tattie bogle ye ur, wey thon sticks. Sure tae fearten aw kinds ay birds." He felt disproportionately exposed. "Nae wonder kilties wear tall socks." He straightened the claymore kilt pin, pleasing himself on the third attempt. "Ah dain't think a level an' T-square ur strictly required, mate," he said snarkily to his reflection.

The Nicktoon was mercifully absent and unaccounted for; he was able to denigrate himself just fine without the help. For the third time, he checked the long-haired sporran to be sure he had everything: keys, wallet, phone, shades. It all fit neatly with a wee room to spare. He would have preferred a plain leather day sporran, but beggars couldn't be choosers. He smoothed his plain black T-shirt, checking that the tail was neatly tucked in.

He gave his unruly hair a last go with the gel and grimaced to be sure there was nothing in his teeth. "The full kit wid huv been a gude distraction fae the rest ay ye," he informed his reflection.

His phone said 9:55. He crossed to the door and looked through the peephole, expecting to see the usual fish-eye view of empty hallway. Instead, he saw darkness, then a huge blue eye shrinking out to a sharp pale face. He grunted in surprise and spun to the side, pressing his back against the wall. He stared at the door as if expecting it to burst open. Pavlov's Belle knocked imperiously. He held his breath, feeling foolish, yet at the same time justified. After a pause, she called out his name, then knocked sharply again.

Whit the fook dis she want? Cannae be shift substitution, as onerly Mickey Patel wahrks the weekends. Hoo did she find oot whir Ah live? Alice wisnae kiddin aboot the privacy settings. Fookin Ag Tech Stalker is right.

He scanned the studio apartment for signs of occupancy that might be visible from the parking lot. The morning was bright and clear, so no lights were on. The TV was off, so he could be sure to hear Alice's knock. The blinds were open. He mouthed a curse. He knew the floorboards creaked but hadn't paid attention to exactly where. He checked the peephole again, this time getting unoccupied hallway, and dashed across the room and twisted the rod to shut the blinds. He fell onto the bed in relief.

A sudden stab of fear jerked him to his feet. He scrolled through his phone's memory to the strange number. Phone in hand, his thumb hovered over the call button. He felt like the mesmerized victim in a slasher film reaching to open the door that would reveal a psychopath with a bloody axe.

At another knock, he crammed his phone back into the sporran. He stepped in an exaggerated tiptoe to the wall, then creeped toward the door, staying close to the edge like a mouse. Leaning toward the peephole, he kept his feet at the doorjamb to prevent a telltale shadow in the chink of light under the door. He hoped the darkening of the lens wouldn't be noticed on the other side.

"Ach!" he declared, annoyed with his own melodrama. Remembering his knobby knees in time, he opened the door only a crack.

Alice's low-top Converse sneakers squeaked to a sudden stop. She backtracked, bent over and beeping like the reverse indicator on a delivery truck. He smiled at both the cartoon effect and the view of her backside.

"I thought you'd chickened out on me."

"Ye dinnae waste onie time tae lee," he challenged.

She shrugged. "I'm no stranger to rejection. I apologize for jumping the gun." She raised an eyebrow and eyed his floating head in the doorway. "You decent, Lowlander?" she asked warily.

"Tha's a matter ay opinion," he answered gravely. "Ye huv tae promise no' tae laugh."

"I promise." She tucked a dark bundle under her arm and covered her eyes with both hands. "Surprise me."

He yanked the door wide and stood aggressively self-conscious, hands limply at his sides, shoulders tensed. "Haw then."

She opened her hands like shutters. Her lips curved into an uncontrollable smile as her green eyes moved from his boots, over thin but well-defined legs, the crisp kilt, sporran, wide belt with its large silver stag's head buckle, flat stomach, sharp shoulders, defiantly tilted sharp chin, slightly crooked nose with boyish freckles, his worried eyes. She wolf-whistled softly.

" 'Large as life and twice as natural.' You've got more personalities than a comic book convention," she joked. "Nice man-purse you've got there."

"Tha's a sporran, hen," he said with dignity, trying not to laugh.

"I know. A 'wee badger handbag.' I looked up Billy Connolly's standup comedy. Nearly peed myself laughing."

"Ye could unnerstaun hum?"

"I turned on the subtitles."

"Some bastart subtitled the Big Yin?" he asked indignantly.

"No. I was kidding. Seriously, Lowlander, I understand you. Wait, let me rephrase: I understand the words coming out of your mouth." She gestured at the tartan. "It's a bit more…Christmasy than I expected."

"Kerr Modern," he said proudly, posing heroically in a Superman stance, hands on hips, profile looking out over an imaginary Metropolis or Highlands. His eyes flicked askance toward her. "Nae, ye cannae see whit's worn underneath."

"Never occurred to me." She flashed him a devilish grin. "Until now." She remembered the bundle under her arm and thrust it toward him. "I found it at the thrift store. Thought you'd like it. It's nothing, really." She wasn't sure why she'd bought it, but it couldn't hurt.

The bundle unfolded in his hands into a T-shirt, sharp store creases intact.

"I find lots of wicked good stuff there, some with the original price tags still on, like that shirt," she rambled nervously. "Gotta love college towns."

Aye right. He turned the shirt over and read the bold red alphabet-soup letters on the front: *With a shirt this awesome, who needs pants.* "Pure dead brilliant. Cheers, hen," he said with a crooked grin. "It's pairfect. Ah'll wear it the noo."

He eagerly pulled out the tail of his plain shirt. He stopped mid-yank, the jersey tented out between his fingers. He gave her a reprimanding look, releasing the distorted fabric to twirl his finger at the ground. "Turn roond. Nae free shoos theday."

She cocked a foot forward and crossed her arms, framing the slogan on her own navy shirt. It read: *Beam me up, Scotty.* "What's the admission fee, then?"

He made a tsk-ing noise, pretending to be affronted, and turned his back to her.

"I was married, remember? I've seen man titties before," she argued as he hunched self-consciously and pulled off the plain shirt and dropped it to the floor.

She stared at his long, pale back, feeling overwhelmed by the small waist and surprisingly broad shoulders, the muscles shifting beneath the skin, the peppering of freckles. It had been a while since she'd seen that much naked man. He pushed his head into the new shirt and unfurled the tail, cutting off her view. The loose fabric camouflaged his build, making him appear scrawnier than he was.

He turned to face her, a little flustered himself, and smoothed his hair back into place. "No' like these, ye huvnae. Ah'm jist tryin tae protect ye fae their effects." He tucked the new shirt into the high-waisted kilt, sucking in his stomach to make it easier.

She snorted and looked away, fighting a sudden urge to help, and moved past him farther into the apartment. She tried to focus on the purpose of the day: a look around his apartment, a test of his authenticity. At least that's what she told herself it was about.

Not many personal items were visible. A laptop sat on a drafting table, a modest TV perched on a battered coffee table, and an open sofa bed was shoved into a corner. Not much of anything, just as expected from an expatriate in an efficiency apartment. Her eyes fell on the single framed photograph next to the computer. She crossed to the makeshift desk and picked it up for a good look. A family group posed against a dramatic indigo-smeared sky. Nick posed stiffly with a dark commencement robe open to show the kilt and black jacket beneath, his face frozen in a tight smile as if his patience were worn thin. Face slightly blurred in motion, another young man laughed openly, his arm flung around the other's neck, hair falling into his eyes. He wore a leather motorcycle jacket with jeans, and a mortarboard rested tipsily askew on his head. Except for the clothes, expressions, and body language, they were two peas from the same pod. On the left, a short older woman clung possessively to Nick's arm, the plump cheeks of her wide, proud smile nearly obscuring her eyes. Beside her, a rail-thin older man hovered, his formal wear hanging loosely, his grin a spark of life in an otherwise cadaverous face.

"Vet school commencement wey ma faimly," he lilted.

"They look wicked proud."

"Aye. First tae graduate uni, a doactor an' that."

"Is that your brother? It's blurry, but it looks like you could pass for twins."

"Aye, tha' we could." He grimaced.

"He looks like a real character. And you look less than pleased," she said with a smile in her voice.

"Ye huv nae idea," he said fondly. "Jealous bastart, tha' yin. He wid crash uni parties pretendin tae be me. An' then in class, birds wid gie me the eye, jimmies wid talk tae me like we wis best mates, trippin aboot ma pure funny patter." He smiled wryly. "Thoat Ah wis gawin bammy. Ah've nivver been so blootered Ah couldnae mind whir Ah'd been, but it hud me wonderin, so it did."

"Why would he do that?" she asked.

"Telt me it jist came up his humph." His voice turned melancholy. "Jen up, Ah think it wis because Ah dinnae need hum onie mair. Ah treated hum like an embarrassment, an' he wanted tae shoo me Ah wisnae onie be'er than hum. He dinnae actually say he wis me, but. They jist assumed, ken. Proved the point."

"No one noticed?"

"Wid ye huv?" He gave her a searching look.

She shrugged. "I guess it would depend on how well someone knew you. And what they were expecting."

"Naeb'dy noticed, no' iven ma best mates, until the nicht we shooed up at the same hoose. Efter tha', they jist invited hum. Life ay the party, byraway."

"That must have been terrible," she empathized.

"Wis dead awfy. Ah looked a right muppet. Wisnae fun fur hum onie mair neither, efter tha'." He shook his head. "Stopped gawn, said he hud tae wahrk nichts."

That was when he had started working on his hustle, leaving the flat empty-handed with a mumbled "aff tae the Uni."

"Aye right. The uni ay hard knocks, mibbe," Da had said pointedly one morning.

His son had stopped in the doorway, shamed and angry like a schoolboy caught skipping school.

"Son," Rabbie had said, altering a quote from his favorite American western, "Erras two kinds ay people in the wirld, those wey uni degrees an' those whae get chibbed."

"Da, tha's no' hoo the line goes. An' urnae Clint Eastwood. Clint Easterhoose, mair like."

He hated that Da had been right. It had taken a slash to the ribs in a back alley brawl to get him off the game. Too late, it turned out; like the Black Widow, the Uni had not been quickly forgotten.

"We should go, byraway," Nick said brusquely, taking the photo from her hand and putting it back on the desk. He wondered why that photo had been the only one packed in his suitcase.

16: Bad Bagpipe Jokes

"I have an idea," Alice said slyly, pointing at his silver claymore pin. "If you use that to pin the front to the back, we could take the bike."

"Pin ma kilt intae troosers? Ah'd look a right eejit byraway," Nick lilted indignantly.

"A man in a kilt on a motorcycle. Your argument is invalid," she countered.

"Soonds like the start ay a dirty joke. Ah still say eejit," he said stubbornly.

"Think of it as a safety valve," she reassured him. "Just enough dorky to offset the Axe body spray effect of kilts combined with motorcycles, so you can safely venture outside."

"Ah'm scoobied." He shrugged.

"You've never seen those commercials?" she asked. "A guy sprays on this cheesy sleazy cologne, and hot chicks pop out of the woodwork, pawing him and moaning."

"Ach, whir kin Ah get some ay tha'?"

She punched him on the arm. "He gets buried under a pile of grabbing, fighting people. More zombie apocalypse than sex appeal, if you ask me."

"Women awyis says they're efter me fur ma brains." He grinned down at her. "Then ye could pit ma lovely cleaned-oot skull in yer collection."

"What if I'm one of the feasting horde that loses all personality to the zombie virus? Your noble sacrifice would be wasted."

"Ah like it when ye talk nerdy tae me." He grinned and braced for another one of her punches.

"Science geeks." She rolled her eyes. "My shirt must be a smash hit, then." She stretched the navy fabric out away from her breasts, looking down as if to read the Star Trek slogan printed on it. "Sadly, it's the most Scottish thing I have, without getting all rah-rah Sweet Thistle school spirit or going with some random plaid," she said, suddenly self-conscious. "I didn't want to accidentally declare myself part of someone's clan. You can't go wrong with pop culture, though. Too bad I don't have a band shirt for Simple Minds or Belle and Sebastian."

"Nae bother. Scoats ur kent fur their sense ay humor an' that," he reassured her, running his hand over the cheeky slogan on his own shirt. "Did ye ken tha' the lead singer ay Simple Minds no' onerly belangs tae Glesga, he is awso a Kerr? No relation, but. Jist a wee fun fact," he added awkwardly, afraid he was putting her off.

"Small world," she remarked.

"Nae. Sma' country," he quipped.

He wondered what sort of crowd the festival would attract: hard-core traditionalists ranting about tartan tat and low-hanging sporrans, or opportunists declaring everyone Scottish for the day to make a buck.

"So are we taking the bike?" she pushed.

He shook his head. "Nut. An' tha's ma final offer. Ither kilt an' motor, or troosers an' motorbike. Ah dain't want tae be groond intae mince if Ah huv tae drap the motorbike doon."

Her face fell. "I never thought of that. Yeah, let's definitely take the car."

He tried to cheer her up. "Ah belang tae Glesga, hen. If yer motor's no' on fire, it's pure posh."

She smiled. "Well, in that case, your chariot awaits."

" 'Moan then." He held out his bent elbow, and she hooked her arm through it.

She led him to a pale blue Ford Escort at least a dozen years past its showroom date, its paint powdery with age. Small dents bled rust.

"I have to move some junk," she apologized, pulling away.

She leaned in the passenger side and began clearing the seat. Nick held the door from closing on her legs, since the supporting spring had long since rusted through. It afforded him a fine view, until she'd finished gathering an unruly sunshade, two umbrellas, and several reusable shopping bags. Her cheeks blazed and she avoided his eyes, so he politely turned his attention elsewhere as she flipped the seat forward to move the clutter to the back seat. He scanned the three-story apartment building with its unimaginative block shape and open-air main stairwell.

"Sorry about the mess. Thought I could get out of cleaning with the kilt pin trick." Alice stepped out of the car and brushed her hands together.

"Nae luck," he said wryly.

"Can't blame a girl for trying." She grinned at him, standing very close for several heartbeats with only the car door between them. Her eyes dropped and she hurried around to the driver's side.

He tucked the kilt under carefully as he sat down. As they turned onto the street, he cranked down the window and hung an elbow out.

"You're in for a treat, Lowlander," she said, eyes on the road.

"Oh aye?"

"Mmm-hmm. You'd better buckle up. I'm going to take you on my favorite road." She grinned. "You'll like it. When the signs say 15 miles per hour, they mean it."

He raised his eyebrows. "Right curvy, is it?"

"Among other things. I'm all about the *fahrvergnügen*."

"The whit?"

"Does no one besides me remember those Volkswagen ads?" she sighed. "The love of driving, the joy of the open road."

"Oh aye. Dinnae ken erras a word fur it."

"Well, not really. It was invented for the ad campaign by slapping two German words together." She glanced over at him and added apologetically, "According to a German exchange student I met."

"Ach. Ferrvugnugget." He felt a stab of jealousy and suspicion, wondering if she'd taken the German exchange student to an Oktoberfest and had a sexual passport going. He tried to relax into the *fahrvergnügen* and the perfect fall day.

As they moved through town traffic, he noticed in the side mirror the unmistakable dome of a black Volkswagen beetle. He thought he glimpsed pale hair before other vehicles filled in the space. He pushed his hair back, a futile gesture with the air buffeting in the window, and rubbed his damp hands along his tartan-covered thighs. He longed for pockets.

Mist huv been her ca'ing, before shooing up. Tailing us the noo.

"Ay course, ya muppet." A familiar voice sneered from the back seat. "Yer secret admirer."

He looked back to see the Nicktoon stretched out, covered with the sunshade and reusable bags so that only his head was visible. He batted his eyelashes in a way that would have earned him a fist to the face if Nick hadn't been afraid of startling Alice and making her wreck. Especially since her driving was halfway there on its own.

"Whit the fook? Ur ye pure mental? Dain't ye huv a fookin life? Cannae ye no' tag alang tae, Nicktoon?" he snapped under his breath.

Alice sneaked a fast glance at him. The small car swooped downhill into a long, hard curve over a deep ravine at a speed that threatened to break traction. He gripped the dashboard with both hands.

"Jesusjohnny, wumman!" cursed the stowaway.

The car passed the nadir and barreled into a steep climb that gutted momentum from less aggressive drivers. She downshifted and crested the hill, then cruised into the slalom-like serpentine that signaled the road winding down to a four-way intersection. The comparatively sedate pace did nothing to loosen Nick's white-knuckle grip on the dash.

"While ur err, ye should pay a wee visit to yer mither byraway," nagged Nick Two.

"Shite. Ur oot yer fookin heid. Ye huv tae be thick as mince tae no' huv some idea hoo Ah widnae want tae see her," hissed Nick over his shoulder, trying to look like he was merely looking out the window.

"She thinks ur somehin else, but, ya eejit," retorted his friend. "An' speak fur yerself. At least she has conviction."

"Needs convicting, ye mean," Nick grumbled. Alice's hand tensed on the gearshift.

"Erras nae need tae spit oot yer dummy, ye big granny's wean. Ye kin jist walk away."

"Ye ken it's no' tha' aisy. An' the noo Pavlov's Belle is on oor heels tryin tae be oor best pal."

Alice frowned. "Everything okay over there, Lowlander?"

He looked over at her and smiled reassuringly. He made a concentrated effort to ignore the intruder in the back seat and relax. He peeled his stiff hands off the dash and dropped them to his lap in what he hoped was a casual pose as the car slowed to a crawl in the backlogged traffic at the light.

"So tha' wis ferrvugnugget, wis it the noo?"

She checked the rear-view mirror out of habit. Several cars back was a VW Beetle she could have sworn had been behind them through town. *Speaking of fahrvergnügen.* It had been years since the press or other predators had tailed her, and the road served as a major artery between the two campuses. She wrote it off as coincidence.

"Hope I didn't scare you too much."

"Widnae be me."

"Good." Her mouth curled into a wicked grin. "Because the real *fahrvergnügen* hasn't started yet." She turned her attention to the cars filing through the intersection ahead of them.

Most of the traffic turned right toward Sweet Thistle, and the rest turned left toward the shopping district shared by both campuses. The Escort surged straight through, bounding over the hump of the intersection and dropping down sharply onto a narrow track. Nick's stomach flew up as if riding a rollercoaster. Alice whooped, laughing as they rose and fell over more rapid hills, the car body lifting off the chassis with each swoop.

"Ach! Ferrvugnugget, ma erse. Ur a wee maddy, byraway." He felt a grin split his face. "Huv tae try this on ma motorbike." In the side mirror, he spotted flashes of the Beetle between the rolling gray waves of road. He stole a look at Alice, wondering if he should mention it.

"Ah wonder hoo she fund oot aboot this wee track. Hoo it's her favorite road. First thing a Sweet Thistle bird dis in the moarnin is heid hame, mind," Nick Two remarked.

"Shut it."

"Onerly sayin whit ye wis thinkin, mate."

Her grin was gone, replaced by narrow-eyed focus. Her left foot engaged the clutch as she braked hard, hauled the wheel to the right, and downshifted. The little car darted down the only offshoot that wasn't a gravel driveway. He grabbed the door handle to keep from getting slung into her lap. A thump and muffled cursing came from the backseat. She coasted, watching the rearview mirror. He looked back over his shoulder in time to see the dark dome of the Beetle flash past.

Alice executed a u-turn, arcing from one shallow grassy culvert to the other, the steering column groaning angrily. The Ford rolled sedately back to the road entrance. She took the car out of gear and rested both feet on the floor, letting it idle in place at the stop sign. She rattled the gearshift, her hand inches from his leg.

"I think someone was following us." She watched his face for a reaction. "Or I could just be really paranoid. Old habits die hard."

He pushed his hair back from where it had fallen during the evasive maneuvers. "Ye want ma opinion?" he asked cautiously.

She nodded.

"Wid be a shame tae come this far an' stoap." He left it vague enough to include the entire relationship. "Especially as ye huvnae telt me yer bagpipe joke."

She gave him a long look. "Okay then. This man with a pet octopus walks into a bar, and he says, 'I bet a hundred dollars my octopus can play any musical instrument.' So people run home and come back with all kinds of instruments: guitar, flute, banjo, clarinet, violin, and they slap down their Benjamins. The octopus plays every single one, and he doesn't just squawk out some sour notes, he's good. Really good. Then a Scotsman brings in a bagpipe and puts it on the bar with his hundred bucks. The octopus studies it, then turns it this way and that. The Scotsman laughs, grabs the money, and says to the octopus, 'Ha! Ah knew ye couldnae play it!' And the octopus says, 'Play it? If I can get its pajamas off, I'm going to fuck it.' " She waited for a laugh.

"Wis be'er than a slap in the face wey a wet haddie, Ah'll gie ye tha'," he said apologetically.

"Guess it's all in the delivery." She put the car in gear. "I'll work on it. Do you think I should say 'make love' instead of 'fuck'?"

"Ah suppose tha' depends on yer audience," he answered, taken aback.

"I've got another one. Why does a piper walk when he's playing?"

"Tae get away fae the soond. The noo we've got tha' oot the way, ur we headin back or gawn tae the festival?"

In answer, the old car leaped forward onto the main road. Nick clutched the door handle. She was a strange one, even as the difficult-to-fathom fair sex went. They hurtled between a deep ravine and a steep hillside that crowded the hairpin curve, blocking out light and warmth. He wondered if she had a death wish.

"Or mibbe she's ontae ye an' is tryin tae scare the truth oot yer malinky erse," hissed his mate through clenched teeth.

They zigzagged through the gloom and emerged in an open valley. The Ford jostled across twin railroad tracks, cut a sharp left, and bumped over narrow planks bridging a creek. She downshifted, and the car leaped into another ascent through a dense thicket. At the top of the mountain, the trees stepped back from the road, blinding them with sudden sunlight over cornfields. Like a rollercoaster winding down to the loading platform, the lane straightened before ending abruptly at a T-intersection.

He released the door handle and hung his elbow out the window again, trying to hide a long, slow exhale. "Ach. So tha's yer favorite road, is it?"

Alice flashed him a devilish look as she merged onto the wider thoroughfare leading through the outlying small-town sprawl. "What did you think?"

"Be'er than the bagpipe joke. Ither ay thum." She punched him lightly on the arm. "Next time Ah ride in yer motor, Ah'll be sportin full protective gear, but."

"Wuss." She chuckled. "That road gets pretty weird sometimes. One night I saw floating white fangs coming up the road straight at the car."

Nick thought of the *cù-sìth*, the huge black dog of Scottish myth that foretold death and carried off the souls of the newly deceased. He wondered if she'd seen it just before her husband died. It was a childish thought.

"A stupit thought, mair like, since she mardered hum. An' this isnae hame."

She sneaked a quick glance at the man frowning to himself out the window. "We can take a different route back."

"Nae bother. Ah dain't mind." His adrenalin rush was fading. "It's awmoast like ridin, byraway."

"Less touchy-feely though."

"Oh aye." He raised his eyebrows. He heard gagging sounds from the back. "Is this the toon, then?" He gestured out the window.

"The outskirts. Historic downtown's west of campus. West End's pretty posh, on the uphill part at any rate, not along the tracks. Lots of really nice big homes."

A clutter of scattered run-down storefronts, a half-hearted fill-dirt quarry, and a series of grim used car lots disappeared behind them to be replaced by woodland and the entrance to a high-end subdivision. The road curved to avoid a jutting steep hillside. The looming raw brown rock weeped spring water, and tufts of fern clung to crevices like hair in an old man's ears. Railroad tracks echoed the road, at first uncomfortably close, then dropping deeper into a ravine and distancing themselves from asphalt as more rail lines sprouted from the wasteland nearer campus and the town's center. The transience of the railway permeated the earth, heavy and stifling like the rank smell of railroad ties in hot sun, echoed by the transience of the university population. The melancholy weight of the town reminded him of wild stretches of Highlands. He could almost hear the high lonesome sound of bagpipes.

17: Phenomenal

As the old Ford pulled into a lot marked for festival parking, the unmistakable and very real sound of bagpipes greeted them. Sugar maples flamed orange against a deep blue autumn sky, reminding Nick of the Irn-Bru label.

"Ach, it's hoat." Although the thermometer hovered around 70 degrees, he was sweltering in what would have been a summer heat wave in Glasgow.

"Do you want me to put up the sunshade?" Alice reached to tilt the driver's seat forward to reach it.

He froze. "Dain't bother yer shirt aboot it. Ah'm pefter-efter the games," he said to distract her from the surprise in the back seat. He wasn't taking any chances.

"You sure? I guess it will cool off before we're ready to go back." She pulled a small bag from under the driver's seat and stowed her keys in it.

"Aye." He shoved on his sunglasses and started moving away from the car.

"Lowlander."

He turned expectantly. She held a tiny digital camera.

"Whit, ye dain't huv wan ay thum camera phones like ivryyin else?"

"Nope. Can't afford it. I've got pay-as-you-go. Do you have one?"

He shrugged evasively in answer. "Nuchin tae take photies ay onie road."

"We'll have to fix that. Say 'haggis.' "

He pushed his hair back and posed stoically with hands on hips. The camera cheeped softly.

"You looked underwhelmed."

"Ah wis gawn fur majestic: Monarch ay the Glen," he said, slightly hurt.

"The 'monarch of the glen' is a stag."

She slipped the credit-card sized camera into the tiny bag she wore across her body. The strap nestled between her breasts in a very distracting way.

He didn't want to explain the convoluted plot of the British TV saga about a Highland estate and its lairds. *Which Ah onerly watched wanst or twicet tae rip the pish oot ay, when err wis nuchin else on the telly. Haun tae God.*

"Aye, Ah dinnae ken ye kent it but."

"That is the busiest painting in advertising. Pear's soap, Glenfiddich, Hartford Insurance," she rattled off as she passed him.

"An' ivry biscuit tin iver made tae haud shortbread," he added.

"Even busier than I thought." She looked back at him with her Mona Lisa smile. "You did look very majestic though, even without antlers."

He strode after her. Without pockets, he wasn't sure what to do with his hands. A good breeze up his kilt cooled things off nicely to make up for it. He thought of Alice in the apartment hallway, slavering over his big reveal. That made up for it as well.

They turned the corner of a dormitory and were engulfed in the sound of bagpipes. She laughed at the intensity of unearthly sound. He grinned back. She placed a fist on her hip with the other hand overhead, wrist turned in, thumb and forefinger pinched together into a hand-shadow stag. She hopped on one foot, snapping the other alternately behind and in front of her calf with each hop.

Nick raised his eyebrows. "Gawn yerself!"

She tossed the tiny camera to him at her next quarter turn. He snapped her laughing at him, mid leap, her hair flying out around her in a wild mane. At the next turn she stopped.

"Enough of that. C'mon. Let's find the games." She had to get at least one of herself on the memory card to throw him off from her real purpose for the photos. Not that she minded having them for herself. She stowed the camera and pushed forward into the ring of tent awnings surrounding the events field.

"Ach, it's pure hoachin wey kilties an' tartan tat," he exclaimed, bemused. "Looks like Edinburrah during festival season."

"You know you love it." She led him to the orange net fence bordering the competition field.

A burly athlete in kilt, T-shirt, and cleats spun while holding a long-handled hammer. As he heaved it, he roared and the kilt flared, revealing a flash of spandex shorts on oversized, bulging muscles. Alice was disappointed that the secret of the kilt was bicycle shorts.

Nick made it through the hammer throw before his thirst won out. "Ah need a ginger, byraway."

"A real one?" She smiled at him. "You know one of the vendors is bound to have it."

"Ah hope so. It's the onerly reason Ah let ye talk me intae this."

He craned around for the distinctive orange and blue, honed in on a large display, and made a beeline through the crowd. Alice followed, catching up in time to see him pull two bottles from a bin of ice. She took a picture of him displaying them proudly like freshly caught trout.

"The second national drink ay Scoatland, hen," he announced, handing one over with great decorum. "Ah'm dead chuffed byraway."

"It's wicked orange." She eyed the soda warily.

"Gawn yerself." He upturned the bottle and drank blissfully.

She took a cautious sip and looked incredulous. "Oh my God."

He grinned broadly at her. " 'Phenomenal,' aye?" he asked, quoting the soda's ad campaign.

She took another sip and burst into giggles. He raised his eyebrows, waiting for her to explain.

"It tastes like Juicy Fruit. A kid's chewing gum," she choked out. "When it tastes like anything at all." She laughed long and hard.

"Mair fur me, then. In fact, Ah'm gawn tae stock up," he said gleefully. He handed the vendor several bills and hefted a case of soda to his hip.

"I definitely need a picture of this," she declared, wiping away tears of laughter.

He flashed his feline grin, hugging the case and lifting his open bottle in a salute.

"Looks like you have a drinking problem." She turned to the vendor. "Could you take a picture of us?"

The big barrel-chested man cheerfully stepped around his display. He was fitted out in a pirate-style ghillie shirt and Black Watch kilt. His thick beard was liberally streaked with gray.

"Ye don't have one of those camera phones that everyone's got?" the Irn-Bru man asked.

They answered in unison, grinning like madmen. Alice showed him which button to press. Nick placed the heavy case of drinks on the grass at his feet as she joined him. He posed like a Captain Morgan's ad, one foot propped up on the drinks. He slipped an arm around her waist, feeling fly for sneaking it in when she would be unlikely to protest. To his surprise, she leaned into him and rested her hand on his hip.

"Cheers," she said softly, and tapped her vibrant bottle to his.

The soda vendor handed the camera back with a knowing smile. "Got a couple of nice ones there."

"Golden. Thank you so much." She looked through the images, tilting the screen so Nick could see. "We can send these to your dad."

He craned to see the small preview images through the glare. "Da wull be chuffed, so he wull."

"Where ur ye two from?" the barrel-chested man asked intently.

Nick looked uncomfortable. "We came over from Ag Tech," he enunciated stiffly.

Alice gave him a meaningful stare. "I'm from Revere Beach in Massachusetts, originally. I'm Portuguese and English, not Scottish at all, unless you count alumna status." She gestured at the surrounding buildings.

"At the games, we're all a wee Scottish," he flirted, still waiting expectantly for Nick's answer.

"I'll drink to that!" She smiled and raised her bottle.

The two men echoed her gesture, still giving each other the eye.

"*Slàinte*," toasted Nick.

"To honest men and bonnie lassies," the soda vendor countered with another traditional toast.

Nick narrowed his eyes, wondering if the man was trying to dig him up.

"Nice shirt," the vendor said. "Where'd ye get it?"

Nick pegged it as a transparent attempt to draw his accent out into the open, and felt disagreeably like a performing monkey. He nodded at Alice.

"A lass with a good sense of humor. Hold on to that one, laddie."

"Thanks again," she said sweetly. "We'd better go stash this so we can enjoy the rest of the festival."

Nick hefted his soda and nodded curtly as he hurried out of the vendor's line of sight. He lengthened his stride to catch up to Alice. As they reached the parking lot, she rounded on him indignantly.

"Really?"

"Whit?" he panted, nearly tripping over her.

"Your accent. Or should I say, the lack of it."

He shrugged guiltily. "Ah dinnae want hum tae think Ah wis anither wanker fakin a Scoattish accent."

"So you were an asshole faking an American accent?" She frowned fiercely.

"Well…aye," he answered simply.

She raised an eyebrow. "Only a real Scot would want an entire case of liquid Juicy Fruit. Just relax and be yourself, Nick. Okay?"

He nodded, wondering if she was on to him. He brushed at his hair with the back of the hand holding his open drink.

She gave him the Mona Lisa smile. "I like your hair better down."

"Ah look like a Hieland coo wey it doon," he argued. When she turned back toward the parking lot, he shook his head so the hair fell down over his forehead again. *Hairy coo it is then.*

18: Authenticity

"Hot dogs? Barbecue? I was hoping for something Scottish to go with this." Alice waved her drink sadly at the food vendors they passed.

"An' Boab's yer uncle." Nick pointed out the red lion flag flapping in front of a tent. He rubbed his hands briskly in anticipation. "Ah wonder whit thull huv? Fried Mars bar, fried pizza, fried red pudding, fried black pudding, fish an'chips…"

"Fried pizza? Fried candy bars?" She gave him a horrified look. "Don't let my boss hear about it. He'll put a fried food truck outside your building. Then I'll have to do menus and signs for it and try to spin it as nutritious. How do you even fry pudding?"

"In batter." At her confused look, he added, "Red an' black pudding ur sausages, ken."

"I'm not sure which is worse, frying actual pudding or battered sausages. Though I guess it's no different than a corn dog," she conceded.

"Used tae drive ma mither hauf mad when Da cooked a little fry-up," he offered.

"Why? Because of the fat?"

"Nae. On account ay the meat."

She ran her eyes over his lean frame. "How do you stay thin eating stuff like that anyway?"

"Chitterin oor erses aff whilst walkin aw aboot. Haun tae God, Ah nivver noshed it aften." He rubbed his hand across his flat stomach. "Aw this bletherin on aboot it is makin me dead ravenous byraway."

She leaned out around the line. "Can you see what they have?"

He craned to see the menu. "Bridies, meat pies, haggis pockets…" he read.

"Seeing how I'm clueless and you're ravenous, want to get one of everything and split it?"

"Tha's fine. Ah could go oniehin."

At the front of the line, he thrust some bills at the vendor and gestured for Alice to order. She clutched the tubular bridie in its crimped hotdog paper, grease already leaking through. He stacked the haggis's foam plate on top of the pie's sturdy crust.

"Gies some ay tha' HP sauce, wull ye?" He nodded at the huge pump bottle of brown sauce.

She loaded up an empty chips paper. "What's it taste like?"

"Jist try it," he urged.

She poked her pinkie in and licked it. "Sort of like steak sauce. Is that the Scottish way? You put it on all this stuff?"

"Aye. Dead gude on eggs awso."

She looked dubiously at the sauce. "If you say so."

Loaded down, they climbed into the stands in time for the final rounds of men's stone toss. She carefully pried everything in half with a plastic fork.

"Nothing like eating something stunningly bad for you while watching someone else exercise," she said cheerfully.

"We whae ur aboot tae die ay coronary artery disease salute yees." He was pleased he'd remembered to use the five-quid words for authenticity.

He used technical terms like a med student should, she noted.

He tucked in, scattering greasy flakes of puff pastry everywhere. She looked down at the mess covering her own front.

"Didn't know I'd end up wearing it." She took a bite of the haggis in puff pastry, chewed a couple of times and grimaced. She washed the bite down with soda and pushed the rest of her half at Nick. "That's all you, Lowlander."

He brushed hair out of his eyes, leaving flecks of pastry behind. "Ah wis gawn tae warn ye. 'S mair fun tae watch ye lairn the hard way but," he said cheerfully. "Rite ay passage."

She slugged him on the arm. "Nice one, Lowlander. The rest is wicked good though." She swatted crumbs off her cleavage and lap, drawing his eyes.

"Haw, let me get tha' fur ye," muttered a voice behind them.

Thankfully it was drowned out by a loudspeaker announcing the March of the Clans. Droning "Scotland the Brave," a pipe band took the field. The first clan followed them, banners held high.

"If they're in the same clan, how come they're not wearing the same colors?" Alice leaned in to be heard over the bagpipes.

"Aw the same sett, but," he explained. "It's no' so mich the exact colors, it's the pattern." He stopped short of wiping his greasy, pastry-flecked hands on his own tartan. He looked around to find their napkins under the stands waving mockingly in the light breeze. "Like mines. Kerr sett in Modern colors. Erras awso the same weave wey a peel variation, ca'ed Kerr Ancient. Tae look faded like an auld faimly heirloom, Ah suppose. An' a blue wan, the hunting tartan."

She stretched out a leg, pressing it against his thigh. He swallowed hard.

"Go ahead, help yourself," she encouraged, gesturing for him to rub his hands on the denim. "I already wiped mine on them."

He hesitantly placed his hands on her jeans. He could feel the curve and warmth of her through the fabric. He rubbed gingerly, sneaking a look at her through his hair. She seemed preoccupied with the parade. He was unable to resist a long, slow stroke along the length of her leg, his fingers tingling. Under his caress, the muscle tightened.

He froze guiltily, but she was still concentrating on the field. He looked out and his stomach flipped treacherously. The third group paraded in red and white fabric with a grid of thin lines of blue, yellow and forest green forming the sett and traditional hues of the MacAlister tartan. His mother's clan.

"Shite," he breathed.

Alice cursed mentally. Of course Mary would have guessed that she would bring him here as a test. She hoped she wouldn't be expected to report her findings here, of all places. She wanted time with Nick without having to think about the ulterior motive for bringing him here. Better make herself hard to find and keep him close. The MacAlisters wouldn't dare approach as long as she and Nick were together.

"This is boring. Let's look around." She slumped into the riser floorboard behind her and hauled Nick backwards by the belt.

"Ooyah," he griped as his tailbone and elbow crashed into the metal. He struggled to gather the kilt fabric around his legs and regain his seat.

"Come on," Alice urged. She slipped her sneakers through the gap in the risers. Clutching the seat she had just vacated, she swung through and dropped to the ground.

Worried she'd get a keek up his kilt, he followed without protest, hanging one-handed like a monkey before dropping down beside her. He felt a breeze on his backside as the pleats billowed out. She scuttled beneath the spectators, and he loped after. She cursed and doubled back. She jumped for a riser footboard, pulled herself up enough to wedge an elbow on the metal platform, and made a couple of fast, clumsy grabs before slipping back down. She staggered backward into him. He caught her, and she rested against his chest for a long exhale, enough time to remind him of an excellent use for the underside of risers. She pushed off suddenly and darted the length of the stands and out the side, a half-empty soda bottle in each hand. She headed toward the tent awnings at a fast walk. He jogged to catch up.

"Ye ken we could huv walked doon thum, no' drapped oot the bottom, aye?"

She shrugged. "Didn't want to block anybody's view." *Or draw anybody's attention.* "It's called consideration."

She thumped his arm half-heartedly with a plastic bottle before handing it over and changing the subject.

"Look! The petting zoo. You can reunite with all your old buddies from vet school. Like those cows. They're so wee! They look like Shetland ponies with horns and emo haircuts."

"Emo? Ye mean thum wee nyaffs aw in black? Schemebos?" huffed Nick Two, his back to them. "Word ay advice, mate. Nae rummle in the sheets is worth this abuse."

"Ye've ca'ed me mich worse, an' Ah got hee-haw," Nick shot back, knowing the jessie remark would drive his mate away. "They're Hieland coos, hen." He pushed his hair out of his face self-consciously.

"Ahhh, I see the resemblance," she teased, pulling out her little camera.

He crossed his arms. "Nut."

"Oh yes," she insisted. She stepped in very close and gently smoothed the last crumbs of pastry from his hair, teasing it back over his forehead in the process.

He surrendered, stooping to hold the halter so they posed head to head. The cow peered through its own long forelock and lowed.

Alice rushed over to the cow and stroked its soft bangs. "You're so cute," she cooed. "If American cows looked like you, I'd stop eating them."

Nick basked in the indirect compliment. "We dae eat thum in Scoatland, but. An' they're mair tender an' lean than ither beef. Nae fat layer under the skin, ken. They insulate wey dead thick hair instead."

"Get tha' aff the animaw biscuits packet?" Nick Two resurfaced.

Nick jabbed him in the ribs with his elbow. "Shut it!" he hissed through clenched teeth.

She looked sideways at him. "And do *you* eat them?"

He looked confused. "Aye. Ah huv. Hoo widnae Ah?"

Nick Two silently shook his head.

"Most vets are vegetarians. At least now I can stop feeling guilty about the meat in the nachos the other night. And I can feel better about the meat industry." She gave him a long look. "Or maybe I should just really wonder about you."

"Whit did ye think wis in the haggis an' the meat pie byraway? Ah studied farm animaws which ur raised fur meat. Whit did ye expect?"

"Gude swerve," Nick Two admitted grudgingly.

She shrugged and turned back to the animals. He had a good point. "Now what the h-e-double hockeysticks is this one? You look like a devil from medieval paintings," she said to a black sheep that stared her down.

"Hebridean ram. They kin huv mair horns than tha' byraway." He gave it a scratch between its four uneven black horns. "She dinnae mean it, big man."

"Yes I did," she retorted jovially. "Counting sheep like that would give me nightmares. Got any fun facts on this guy?"

"Gie the bint a fun fact. Bints love fun facts," Nick Two heckled.

"Ach, well. They're descended fae Viking sheep. Used tae huv different colors, were bred fur the black, on account ay black hooves ur resistant tae rot, an' thus pairfect fur Scoattish boglands. Oh, an' the meat has less cholesterol than ither sheep breeds."

"Ye lairnt tha' fae Granda, ya tossbag."

"Whit dis it matter whae Ah learned it fae, uni professor or faimly?"

"Everything comes back to food with you. Watch this guy," she warned the ram, pointing a thumb at Nick. "He's probably got a knife and fork in that sporran." She moved on to the next pen. "These rare livestock breeds are amazing. They're as well-adapted to their habitat as native wildlife. No wonder you chose farm animals." She stroked a rotund Shetland pony. "Of course, these little guys are Scottish. But what is up with the Budweiser Clydesdale?"

"Wumman, tha' is *the* horse ay Glesga, born an' bred tae haul alang tha river Clyde. Ah'm deeply affrontit." He rubbed the draft horse's huge head. "A true Scot. Erras mair ay thum ootside Scoatland than in it."

She squinted up at him. "I do see a family resemblance." She took his picture with the gentle giant.

"The noo ur rippin the pish." He pretended to stay offended, but grinned to himself as they washed at the portable sink.

"Wid ye credit it?" Nick Two muttered, in line behind him. "Dinnae think ye could pull it aff." Nick ignored him.

Leaving the exotic livestock behind, they headed directly for the Celtic bakery booth like two kids with allowance money burning holes in their pockets.

"Pure magic. Ah'll huv wannyose, an' wannyose, an' wannyose…" Nick gathered up pastries one by one.

"Let's split everything again," Alice suggested.

"Hooch aye," he protested. "Aw ye'll get is a run roond the table an' a kick at the cat." He hugged his selections tightly.

She looked dubiously at the armload of baked goods. "You'll burst your kilt if you eat all that by yourself."

"Nae. Tha's hoo it has an' adjustable fit an' that. Da awyis says Ah kin horse intae some scran."

"We call that a hollow leg." She smiled ruefully. "I, however, have expanding thighs, so I'll settle for a wee bite of your stash, if you don't mind."

"Ah dae mind, byraway." He eyed her for a moment, especially the so-called expanding hindquarters, which looked fine to him.

She raised an eyebrow and handed the vendor several bills. "Ha. Now you don't have a choice," she said with satisfaction. "You can have what's left of *my* pastries when *I'm* done with them."

"Ach. Think ur pure sleekit, dain't ye jist. Ah'm fly fur ye, byraway. An' Ah'm nae midgie-raker, hoovering up efter ye." He glowered, still clutching the pastries. "Ah'll pay ye back. When Ah kin reach ma dosh."

The vendor handed over her change and offered a large white paper sack. With a nod of thanks, Alice took them and stalked up to Nick with a determined look. She shook the bag like a trick-or-treater with an entitlement issue. He sighed and loosened his grip so she could unburden him. When the pastries were safely in the bulging sack, she thrust it into his arms.

"Ah'm yer bleedin cuddy the noo?" he complained.

"If you say so."

The Nicktoon quietly sang "Beast of Burden," emphasizing each "never" with very rude hip thrusts and sticking out his lips in a Mick Jagger impression. Nick guided the oblivious Alice away, using the bag as incentive.

She reached in with childlike glee, pulling out a pastry with a slitted top crust. She broke off a chunk, exposing the dark filling "So what's this one?"

"Eccles cake."

He waited until she popped it in her mouth to add nonchalantly, "Awso kent as fly's cemetery. A proper wan's made ay champit midges, byraway."

She paused mid-chew.

"Scoatland's pure hoachin wey thum. We huv a wee sayin: 'When life gies ye midges, make a fly's cemetery.' "

"Wicked good. Squashed bugs." She gave him a bored look. " 'Something interesting is sure to happen whenever I eat or drink anything.' You know what would be great with this bug paste? Carbonated, rusty Scottish sewer water." She took a long drink of her Irn-Bru. "Ahhh. Golden."

He looked crestfallen. "Dinnae spoil yer appetite, did Ah no'." He peered into the pastry bag with such a forlorn look that she barked a laugh.

She fed him the rest of the cake, wiped her hands on her jeans, and said briskly, "So what am I trying next?"

19: Close Encounters of the Unpleasant Kind

A slab of shortbread, an empire biscuit, and three kinds of scones later, they had browsed the clan displays, the genealogist had guessed Nick's tartan on the third try, Alice had eyed the Celtic jewelry for ages and bought nothing (declaring she would feel like a wanker impersonating a Scot), and the ceilidh had begun. A few brave couples danced in front of the stage, rapidly acquiring an audience, while others waited in indecisive clumps.

Nick was reluctant to become the entertainment. "Ah'm desperate an' gantin fur a ginger, byraway. Meet ye back err in a wee meenit?" he stalled.

"Behave yourself." She watched him disappear into the crowd before searching the other faces anxiously. She had a short time to find Mary or Liam and make a preemptive strike.

Nick detoured to the jewelry booth, checking over his shoulder to be sure Alice didn't see what he was up to. He disqualified rings as too meaningful and bracelets too twee. The necklaces were so expensive she would think strings were attached. Which left earrings.

A set of miniature claymores caught his eye. He worried they were too Goth, but decided the cheeky reference to his kilt pin would outweigh the potential negative. He stashed the jewelry box in his sporran and steeled himself for the drink vendor.

He waited anxiously for the group in front to wind up their empty chat, cringing at the Irn-Bru man's faked accent. As they drifted off, he stepped forward with two bottles in one hand and cash in the other. The vendor took his money with a salesman's smile, raising Nick's hopes that he was forgotten in the blur of kilted customers. He nodded thanks and turned for a fast getaway, pleased he had managed without a word.

"Two more for the laddie with the clever shirt and amnesia." The broad man placed his hands on his hips. The thick beard crawled up his cheeks in a toothy grin.

Nick froze.

"You can't remember where ye're from or whit accent to use," the man called to his back. "I hope ye didn't forget about the bonnie lassie you were with, or I'll go find her for maself."

Nick spun around, the burning surge of his own anger taking him by surprise. "Get tae fook, ya fookin big bastart ye, ye an' yer pish-perr Hieland gaff. Ye hud best furget aboot the bonnie lassie fookin rinoo or it's a square go!"

The big man boomed out a laugh. Nick bared his teeth, more animal snarl than grin, eyeing the man's loose-fitting ghillie shirt for any clues of a punch about to be thrown.

"You're definitely a true Scot," roared the big man. He held out a thick hand and dropped the fake accent. "Jimmy Campbell. I'm from Pennsylvania, but I've got family in Stirling that I visit as often as I can."

"Nick Kerr. Ah belang tae Glesga, byraway." He shifted the sweating bottles to his left hand and wiped the condensation on his shirt before gripping the man's hand.

"I thought so." The smile disappeared into the beard as he gave the smaller man a sharp look. "Rangers or Celtic?"

He named the two Glasgow Old Firm football clubs that maintained a fierce rivalry. To declare loyalty to one was to declare war on the other, as well as revealing one's religious affiliation. Catholics cheered for Celtic, Protestants for Rangers. Kerrs were fans of the Maryhill local club, Thistle. "Dead aisy tae cheer fur winners, wee man," Da would say, grinning and passing a mug of beef tea and a Scotch pie at modest Firhill Stadium. "It's these sorry punters tha' need yer erse in the seats, but."

"Partick Thistle," Nick answered with conviction.

The beard split into another booming laugh. "Jags. That explains everything. All Jaggies are wee eccentrics. What kind of season are you having?"

"Pure shite, as awyis." He grinned broadly back, relaxing into the familiar and safe language of soccer. He quoted a team chant, " 'We dain't fear oniehin, oniewhir, onietime.' Especially no' losin a match."

"You managed to score one on Stirling, though."

"Aye, an' yer two goals cuffed us tae the bottom ay the league. So mich fur a brilliant second-hauf opener."

"Well, it was a hell of a match." The big man clapped him on the shoulder. "You'd better get back to your girl before some enterprising lad sees an opening."

"Aye," Nick agreed. "An' me weyoot a *sgian dubh* in ma sock." He nodded farewell and worked his way back to the ceilidh stage.

Ironically, Liam and Mary were nowhere to be seen when Alice was trying to find them. She gave up and turned back toward the central festival ground. Taking a quick detour into an academic building's restroom, she looked herself over in the mirror as she dried her hands. Someone came up beside her, too close for comfort. She sidestepped to give the space invader access to the paper towel dispenser, but the woman made no move for it. Instead, she leaned against the neighboring sink and crossed her arms. Alice glanced over quickly and did a double take. Nick's coworker, the mean blonde, stared daggers, her delicate features blotchy with anger.

"I did a summer abroad at the University of Glasgow. That's where we met. Where did you meet him?" she challenged. "Definitely not BUAV. PETA? The local animal shelter? I know damn well it wasn't a house call. I never saw any fliers. Besides, it's a conflict of interest, which is against his employment contract. And he didn't study companion animals."

Alice gave her a long look, deciding against acting clueless. "It's none of your damn business." They faced each other, eyes blazing.

"I have the ring," Laura Beth said finally.

Alice raised an eyebrow, deciding this one had a screw loose. "Um, okay, Gollum. I won't touch your Precious."

A pair of women came in, chattering and laughing loudly. Alice took advantage of the distraction to escape through the door. She hurried through the building and into the safety of the festival crowd.

* * * * * * * *

Spotting the distinctive mass of curls, Nick crept closer until he stood behind Alice. He eased the drinks to the ground and pushed the sunglasses to the top of his head. He carefully removed the earrings from their box, one in each hand.

"Nieve nieve knick knack," he chanted. He straightened his arms so they hovered above her shoulders, his fists where she could see them.

She glanced sideways at each and turned to face him, eyes laughing. "What are you up to, Lowlander?"

"Which haun wull ye tak." He lowered his closed hands to waist level.

Her hand shot out and tapped his left lightly before retreating to her chest. He unfolded his hand, palm up, to reveal one of the silver earrings. She looked from it to him questioningly. He opened his other hand to reveal its mate.

"A wee minder, hen."

"Thank you. I love them," she said simply, but felt like she was about to cry or run. She felt a pang of guilt. She choked it down, reminding herself that she had wanted to spend the day with him for her own reasons, not just for the payoff. She had even managed to forget the assignment most of the time, when she wasn't hiding from, or looking for, her employers.

"Ach. Friendzoned. Tha's a pure dead shame." Nick Two wasted no time turning the knife.

She busied herself with removing her other earrings, buying time to regain composure. She dropped the simple studs into her bag and carefully lifted the tiny swords from his damp palms. *What did I do to deserve this? Maybe I'm too perfect for the assignment. Or horribly wrong for it. It's getting too personal.* Maybe she could continue this once the job was over, as if it hadn't started as one of Mary's schemes. He wouldn't have to know. She smiled uncertainly as she slipped the wires into her ears.

"Should huv gawn wey a necklace so ye could huv fastened it on," Nick Two sneered behind him. "Nae, be'er yet, should huv gawn wey a ring an' thrown yerself doon on wan knee so she could kick ye in the teeth fur the fookin nugwatt ye ur."

"Ah couldnae find a dead funny shirt fur ye. Ah kent ye hud yer eye on the jewelry, but. An' ye liked ma kilt pin," he babbled, wrong-footed by her reaction.

Her focus shifted to his chest, and she realized it was reciprocation for the shirt she'd given him a few hours ago. He was not so forward after all. She'd started it. She was relieved and disappointed. "And I thought you went to get yourself another Irn-Bru."

He scooped the bright orange drinks off the grass and held one out to her.

She narrowed her eyes. "Wait, did you get these as yourself or as your evil American twin?"

Nick Two jabbed him with a bony elbow. *Jist an expression,* Nick reassured himself. They were safely back to ripping the piss. His specialty.

"As a proud native son ay the finest country on airth…" At the lift of her eyebrows, he added, "Scoatland, ay course."

"I'm wicked proud of you." She smiled. "Feel better?"

"Aye. Hud a dead nice wee blether aboot the fitbaw."

"Men."

He shrugged. "Turns oot he's heard ay ma team."

"Which is?"

"Partick Thistle."

"Funny name."

"Aye. Ye should see their playin. It's iven funnier."

She poked him with her drink. "Are they on TV?"

He snorted. "Definitely no' over err." He stashed his sunglasses in the sporran and gestured at the dancing couples with his bottle. "Ur ye ready tae jine the dancin?"

She hesitated, watching the twirling couples go through complicated steps. *"Will you, won't you, will you, won't you, will you join the dance?"*

"Will my feet be safe?"

"Ah'm dead gude at the dancin. Ah onerly step on a fit in the pub tae meet birds." He grinned when her fist hit his arm. "It's no' as hard as it looks, byraway. If ma nanna could teach a seven-year-auld wean wey two left feet, Ah kin teach ye. 'Moan then." He gently took the drink from her hand and tossed both bottles to the grass.

"Hieland Scoattische," he announced. "Standard bawroom haud. Yer right erm oot, an' take ma haun," he coached, gathering her lightly in his arm.

She felt a flutter in her stomach at his touch.

"Rest yer erm on mines. It's like the stag dance the noo. Tap, point, tap. Nae, yer right. Aye. Ither side the noo. Repeat." He stifled a laugh at her flustered look and the awkwardness that seemed so unlikely on someone who moved the way she did simply crossing a room. "An' polka!"

His kilt flicked against the back of his thighs as he spun her into the dance field, giving him a niggling of doubt about going traditional to a dance. She laughed and finally looked up from her feet.

"You're full of surprises." She relaxed into the rhythm of the repeating dance steps.

"Aye, tha' Ah'm."

The band transitioned into another melody and the lead fiddle called for a Highland Barn Dance. Nick lifted her hand from where it rested on his arm, shifted underneath hers, and replaced her hand so they stood side by side. He held her waist and led her into the pattern of forward and backward steps and hops. He felt sweat beading on his forehead, and was again thankful for the breeze up his kilt.

"Split away sideyways two steps an' chap."

She struggled gamely to translate and follow, ending up a beat behind.

"Come on back the noo, hen. Same way."

When she returned to his side, he swept her into another ballroom hold.

"And polka!" she exclaimed gleefully along with him, swirling a full circle.

She glided her arm along his shoulders and resumed the original tandem position.

"I feel like a chicken trying to keep up with a swan," she puffed before skipping away sideways and clapping.

When she returned to his arms, he reassured her, "Ye look hee-haw like a chicken, hen."

She barked out a laugh, and he joined in, realizing how it sounded. "Ur gettin on gude style fur a first time at the dancin."

"Oh yeah. Golden," she laughed.

The band transitioned to a new tune and called Gay Gordons. Nick led Alice in a slow twirl, catching her free hand in front and shifting his upper arm to hover above her shoulders.

"Four steps furrad, clockwise hauf-turn. Four steps back, baw change, four furrad, hauf-turn, four back," he coached.

"What? Oh God," she wailed.

"Jist folley whit ma body tells ye."

He winced, realizing how suggestive it sounded, but her fists were safely out of commission. She closed her eyes and relaxed into his lead, following the gentle pressure of his hands.

"Four lovely walkin spins the noo," he said softly as he released her left hand.

The Mona Lisa smile appeared as she pirouetted from his fingers like a sleepwalking ballerina. Dark curls flew out from her shoulders. At the end of the fourth turn, he let her slip from his fingertips in preparation for the shift to ballroom hold. Her eyes flew open. His arm circled her waist and he took her hand. She rested her fingertips lightly on the bare skin of his neck, the silver earrings swinging at her throat. Her green eyes burned into his. His heart thumped wildly.

"You make this wicked easy," she said wonderingly.

"Ye make this pure dead brilliant. Ah'm used tae ma nanna wailin aboot her bursitis by noo."

She laughed. They resumed the side-by-side position of the dance's first movement, faces turned to each other with the intensity of a tango.

They were oblivious to the rest of the field until the last half-turn, when they came face to face with a handsome man standing in military at-ease stance with a confident smile. She faltered, then scurried to catch up with the reverse steps as if making a hasty retreat. The plain black tie, Prince Charlie vest, Glengarry cap, and MacFarlane kilt declared him a member of the university pipe band; the patches on his crisp white shirt and a wide red sash distinguished him as its drum sergeant. He followed alongside as they walked through the spins, his words lost as Nick struggled to place the déjà-vu familiar face and decipher the Southern accent. When he released Alice for the switch, the gray-eyed drummer stepped forward, flashing his perfect movie-star smile, and clasped her fingertips like a prince escorting a princess from an enchanted carriage. Nick watched dumbfounded, his hand still outstretched, as the stranger swept her away.

"Fookin bastart! Tha's no iven proper bawroom haud," Nick Two remarked indignantly.

The handsome drum sergeant held her too close. She blushed. The green eyes met Nick's before the flow of the dance swept her away.

"Ur fooked." Nick Two sounded downright cheerful.

"Dead helpful, ye ur," Nick crossed his arms and glared *sgian dubhs* as Alice allowed the competition to pull her hand around his neck and clasp the other against his chest.

"I knew you wouldn't miss this. Interesting choice of companion." A blonde sidled next to him.

She had been beautiful once, but age was taking its toll. Her scalp gleamed pinkly through carefully styled hair, and the roots showed a combination of silver and the mousy brown many blondes turn in adulthood. Her cheeks slumped into the beginnings of soft jowls. The thinning lips tightened into a downward smile. "Aren't you going to give me a proper greeting?"

He noticed the MacAlister tartan sash across her shoulder. He pushed his hair back with a shaking hand and shrugged, stalling for time. "Whit d'ye want me tae dae, burst oot in fairy lights?"

She chuckled. "You look just like your father when he was about that age. How is your father, by the way?"

He hoped his hair hid the shock in his eyes. He exhaled a long breath to calm himself while he studied the strange mannequin that was the mother he hadn't seen in twenty-odd years. He tried to do a lost-persons retrofit to reconcile this face with his memories of her. A curtain of shining hair, satin on perfect skin, the scent of roses, blue eyes bright with passion over her latest cause. They were scattered puzzle pieces found when moving house, the puzzle itself long ago discarded. He closed his eyes to help the memory sharpen, but it was no use. He could no longer remember his mother's face. He opened his eyes in panic. The woman's mouth twisted into another of the convulsions that passed for a smile. When had she begun fighting that expression of happiness? She had smiled so rarely at him that he couldn't recall ever having seen it.

He worked hard to keep the anger and hurt from showing, glad of the discipline hustling had given him. He would rather have a hedgehog shoved up his erse than play nice, but he was only a placeholder.

"Da's awright," he answered noncommittally.

"And your brother?" Her blue eyes seemed to bore into him. "Not prison time, I hope?"

He fought back another flash of anger. "Nut. Stayin oot trouble. Awyis the underachiever. Wid bring a tear tae a glass eye, so it wid." He grinned and wished he could be saved by an alarm here. "Got his lorry driver's license, byraway."

"Let's hope the shipments get to their destination in full." She either smiled, or frowned, or whatever it was her face did, and changed the subject to someone she cared about. "You've been here for months and didn't get in touch. You made me track you down."

He flared his hands in an apologetic gesture. He hadn't known she was here, or he would have stayed put in Glasgow, in his underachieving life. He wondered how he'd managed to pull this off. He must have been a natural for the part. He wasn't sure if that made him feel better or worse about it.

"Whitiver hurts ye through the nicht, pal," Nick Two sneered in his ear.

"Gawnae no' quote Glasvegas tae me," Nick muttered. "Ah thoat ye dinnae fancy their music onie road."

She laid a hand on his arm. The red-tipped nails could have belonged to the White Woman of the Highlands. He stared at them. The fewer words, the better. Be a blank screen for her to project what she wanted to see. Besides, the only things he had to say to her were far from kind.

As if she could read his mind, she said, "You know I didn't want to leave you boys, but I couldn't get your father on board. He wanted me to give up activism, afraid it could put you boys at risk for being put in a foster home." She looked away to control her emotions, or at least give that impression. "Once he got a scare, he was afraid of the world. But he was strong in his own way. He went straight, gave up his old ways, struggled to make ends meet honestly. I knew you would be all right without me. He's a good man, in his way. Not everyone can fight the good fight."

The good fight. As if taking care of one's weans was the wrong thing to do. He gritted his teeth so he wouldn't release an angry tirade, and crossed his arms tightly to keep from strangling her. *Keep the heid, mate.*

"But you knew that already. We talked about it ages ago." She watched him carefully.

Liam and Alice completed a half-turn towards them. Mary waggled her fingers in a wave, and the drummer flashed his perfect smile and nodded. "Your cousin Liam. My brother Paul's son. I was hoping we could all get together. Liam, Paul, your stepfather…"

Nick only half-listened, too busy watching his lovely day go down in flames. His focus on the dancing couple wasn't lost on his mother. She shifted the topic of conversation.

"Your stepfather is a lawyer and has been a great help to me in my work. Most of his cases are dull as dirt. Run-of-the-mill redneck crap." She shrugged dismissively. "But every now and then he gets a client that makes the news. Have you heard of Raphael Booth, Nick?"

"Mibbe," he said slowly, drawing out the word. The name was vaguely familiar, but he couldn't remember why. "Wisnae he wan a thum mutant ninja turtles?" he said cheekily.

"He was defense attorney for the Black Widow trials."

Too many coincidences, too many landmines. "Ach. Wid ye credit it?" he said, projecting the cheerful ignorance of the village idiot, but revealing he already knew Alice's secret. At least the one all over the internet.

20: Checkpoint Bonnie Prince Charlie

"What the fuck, Liam? Could you be a little less obvious?" Alice scolded, glancing over at Nick and seeing Mary sidle up to him. She must be running interference by way of social chitchat with her sponsoree.

"I had no idea you were so good at ceilidh dancing." He flashed his annoyingly perfect smile and pulled one of her hands around his neck and clasped the other to his chest.

"Nick's a good teacher." She felt Nick's eyes on her, and her cheeks grew hot. "You're risking my cover," she snapped.

He raised his eyebrows. "Is this not a good time for you to check in? I'm trying to do you a favor. I'm pretty tied up most of the day."

She broke away for the spins, and hesitated to reconnect for the next steps.

"He won't realize anything. There's nothing unusual about asking a pretty woman to dance."

She reversed, ball changed, stepped, and half-turned before answering. "Not here. Not *now*."

"But we're both here. Right now. Here and now is perfect. No one can hear us."

She knew he was right, but couldn't help feeling irritated by the interruption. Liam had been trying to get into her pants for years, and she knew that any whiff of another guy on the playing field for her affections would only bring out his competitive streak full force. Best to get the report over with. "Fine. He knows a lot about Scottish heritage farm breeds. He knows his Scots foods and drinks, and likes them. And he's not a vegetarian, which is a little odd, but then he's British and works on food animals. He's hooked on some Scottish soda that is really hard to find here. His favorite soccer team is something Glaswegian and obscure. Partick Thistle, that's it. I'll have to send you all my notes later."

"Are they in your back pocket?" His hand dropped to her butt and caressed it. She turned away into the walking spins early, neatly stepping on his foot.

"He's engaged, you know," he said when she came back. His gray eyes studied her expression.

"You're full of shit," she snarled. "You don't know him. I haven't seen any indication of that at all. No photographs, nothing. Not that I care."

"Really." He laughed. "Some private eye you are."

"Well, it's not my day job. I've found out plenty, without knowing exactly what I'm supposed to look for. Or why she hired me to do it." She gave him a sharp look. "Do you know?"

"I just do what I'm told," he said, avoiding a direct answer. "But you should check his family tree."

"Why? There might be murderers and criminals in it?" She squinted angrily at him. "I know he's from a working class background, not some laird with a castle. And his mother left him when he was six. Who would do that?"

He shook his head. He'd tried to warn her. The shock would certainly pop the bubble of infatuation she'd developed for his cousin, and then the field and his conscience would be clear to make his move.

The music wound to an end. She tried to pull away, but he held her hand and lifted it to his lips. "Caledonian Society's masquerade ball is coming up. Would you like to be my date? I could probably even work out some kind of compensation for you with my aunt."

"I'll send you the report."

He held out a business card. "My address and cell number. Call me any time."

She crumpled the card and shoved it deep into her purse.

Mary watched her son's reaction to the dancing couple. "Are you having cold feet?" Her face tightened into her unnatural smile again.

"Whit the fook ur ye bangin on aboot?" he blurted before realizing he should keep his mouth shut. He tried to swallow, but his throat was too dry. He couldn't breathe. He shouldn't have come to the States. He was in way over his head. He wanted to confess, but then his mother would have proof he was as worthless as she'd always treated him.

The dance ended. The gray-eyed tartan prince released his princess reluctantly, holding her fingers to prevent her from leaving his side just yet. He lifted her hand to his lips. She took the piece of paper he offered.

"Ach," Nick grunted. "Fookin hell."

"I can give you a ride home, honey. We can spend some time together like you promised we would. That was one reason you took the Ag Tech job, remember?"

He couldn't bring himself to be around Mary for another moment, especially without knowing what his treacherous idiot wanker of a brother had been up to in the past four years. Like making promises to their long-gone mother. There was also the case of drinks in Alice's car. He wasn't giving those up, regardless of the sudden complications. Besides, riding home with Alice would ensure she wasn't going home with dear cousin Liam.

"Ah'd raither shag a sheep," he retorted crudely and strode across the makeshift dance floor with a complete disregard for personal space and safety.

He unflinchingly absorbed every flying elbow, body check, and toe trampling. Alice hurried toward him in alarm. She seized him by the oversized belt buckle and towed him to the sidelines. He followed dully, aware of the symbolism of being led around by his hips. After her antics with Alan in the pub, she couldn't possibly remain unaware of the effect she had on men. He didn't fancy a tease jerking his chain.

"Whir's yer lovely new filla?" he lilted with false joviality, roughly shoving the hair out of his face.

"He's not my new anything." She held his eyes. "We just danced together, remember?"

"Ah'm no' daft. Ah saw hum gie ye hus phone number. Ye could jist say ye wisnae intae me an' huv done wey it."

Her stomach twisted. She couldn't tell him why she'd taken the card, but she didn't want Nick to think she was planning to ditch him for Liam. "I didn't want his number. I wadded it up, but I'm not going to litter. And I could have done without the hand spit. What a creep."

"Aye, right," he said bitterly. Dear cousin Liam looked like exactly her type.

She tried to sound casual as she redirected the conversation. "What were you and that woman talking about?" She didn't know what Mary was up to, but hoped he wouldn't hold back about their conversation. She felt like she'd been set up.

He glared at her, but let her change the subject anyway. He was making enough of a fool of himself already. "She wis jist pointin oot some ay ma kinfolks an' that," he prevaricated.

She was taken aback. "But you can tell that yourself." She gestured at her thigh as if showing off a kilt. "And she's not wearing your tartan. At least I don't think it's the same set or whatever you call it," she blustered.

"Aye, no' clan Kerr tartan. MacAlister." He resisted being pleased that she'd distinguished between them. "Ma mither is a MacAlister."

So Mary was some kind of distant relative, using Alice to check up on him to prevent offending the family with direct inquiries. "Oh. But how did that woman know?"

"On account ay she *is* ma mither. Mary MacAlister Booth. Huv ye met?" he asked pointedly.

Her heart missed a beat, and her knees tried to buckle. She managed to ask, "Why would we?"

He narrowed his eyes. "On account ay she's marrit ontae yer lawyer, Raphael Booth." A nearby couple do-si-doed briskly, so close that the breeze of their passing swayed his kilt.

She dropped her eyes, then forced herself to raise them again. "It's not like I see my lawyer socially." It was technically true. She saw him for business, for payments, or on the opposite side of a serving tray at his parties. She felt queasy. *Her son? Why is Mary having me investigate her own son? Because of the estrangement? This job is getting weirder by the minute.* It was an improbable coincidence for him to emigrate unaware that his mother lived here, regardless of the proximity of an internationally known research institution. Was this actually about finding a long-lost son? Why have Alice investigate, only to approach him herself before she got the report? *"It takes all the running you can do to keep in the same place. If you want to get somewhere else, you must run at least twice as fast as that!"* She felt a headache coming on. *"Fan her head! She'll be feverish after so much thinking!"*

"So ye dinnae ken ye wis flirtin wey ma cousin Liam. Bonnie Prince Charming," he muttered sullenly. He jerked a thumb in the direction of the pipe band milling around the main stage. He thought he saw the drum sergeant looking in their direction. He addressed the slogan on her shirt, wishing someone would beam him up to boldly go where no wee bastard Liam had gone before. "Dinnae ken Ah iven hud a fookin cousin Liam tae move in on ma bird."

"You let him cut in," she snapped. She felt light-headed.

"Ah dinnae huv a choice, did Ah? Hud tae thole through wanst he got his hauns aw over ye." He waved his own hands in agitation. "Ah couldnae iven unnerstaun hauf the words comin oot his gub."

She snorted despite herself at the irony.

He stared at her, hands on hips. Mary had inadvertently reminded him of an important point. He was surely fouling up whatever the hell was supposed to be going on in the life of Dr. Nick Kerr, veterinary research assistant. Maybe he could disentangle the parts he wanted from this life and discard the rest. He was disgusted by the selfish thought. Better to destroy this before it went any farther. The perfect opportunity to nip things in the bud, pleasant as they may have been, had presented itself: Alice was showing signs of being the village bike.

"Ye dinnae huv tae fancy it so mich."

"I never said I did," she barked.

"Dinnae huv tae. Wis bleedin obvious."

"Then you weren't paying attention! Why are you so jealous? Are we on a date? Because as I recall, I had to beg you to come with me. And you walked out on me the other night." The little swords flashed angrily at him. "Do you two have some kind of thing going?" she demanded.

"The fook ur ye on aboot?" he said, horrified. "Ah dain't iven ken tha' wanker."

"Some kind of Saturday-night-dance-fight-for-the-girl thing," she retorted. "I will not be treated like a goddamn carnival prize."

"Nut," he said emphatically. "Ah telt ye. Ah dinnae iven ken he existed until a wee meenit ago. Ah cannae speak tae hoo he sees ye, but tae me, ur pure…" He stopped short before baring his heart.

"Don't you dare say any Scots words you think I won't know," she growled.

He regretted the outburst. He'd almost given everything away instead of chasing her off. He shoved his hair back and crossed his arms tightly. *She dinnae protest the 'ma bird' bit,* he realized.

She stuffed her hands in her pockets and watched other couples whirl past. She sighed. She did like him, and wasn't ready to give up on him or the mystery behind the job. *"There was nothing else to do, so Alice soon began talking again."*

"It's getting late. I'm hungry. I want to get something to eat." She kept her voice neutral, as close to making an apology as she was going to get right then.

"Tha's fine," he grunted, as close to an apology as he ever got. He hated apologies. He was pretty sure he was allergic to them. " 'Moan then." He stomped off toward the food tents.

"You're going the wrong way."

He stopped short. He closed his eyes in exasperation and stomped back, hands on hips. He stopped toe to toe with her. "The scran is maist definitely over err," he said with strained patience.

"I want to go somewhere else. I'm all puff-pastried out."

"They hud ither scran, mind. Whir else is err tae go?" he growled.

"Downtown. It's just a few blocks." She pointed.

He sighed loudly. Now he understood why kilties wore the ghillie brogues. His feet were hot and sore and it looked far, especially without comfortable shoes, pleasant company, or proper apologies from those who could make them without going into anaphylactic shock. "Kin we drive?"

"It takes just as long to get from here to the car as it does to get from here to downtown." She cocked her head, studying him.

"Twicet as far back, but," he argued.

"You said Glaswegians walk everywhere," she challenged.

"Nae, we ride the bus byraway."

A red-faced man trotted over to Alice and bowed. "I'd be delighted to dance with you, darling, since he won't." He wore a dress Gordon kilt and a leer.

"Get tae fook ya prick or Ah'll punch fook oot ye the noo!" Nick snarled back at him, full up with tartan-clad chancers making passes at her.

The man's face fell and he trotted away in double time. *Agin wey the jealous bit.* Nick needed to get Alice away from the dance floor before he started a fight and got arrested. Or she left him here with his mother. He fought to compose himself and turned toward her.

The stress must have been too much. Tears streamed down her face. Her body shook with convulsions. She staggered and doubled over, clutching her stomach.

She dinnae iven apologize, but, he thought dimly.

21: Cheeky Knickers

"Jesusjohnny, whit dae Ah dae? Alice! Ur ye awright? Whit's wrang? Fook! Ah dain't want tae lose ye. No' like this. No' tae ither ay thum wankers neither, but fook!"

His outburst only made the seizure worse. He twisted to look into her face, clumsily feeling for a pulse in her neck while fumbling the wallet out of his sporran and poking it at her mouth. She thrashed about, blocking the wallet sandwich and clutching the front of his shirt. Eyes wild, face contorted, she dissolved into another body-shaking attack of silent laughter.

He straightened, and she tipped over on her backside. He was disgusted with himself for wearing his heart on his sleeve and irritated she'd gotten it out of him. He looked angrily around at the crowd, who glanced away. "Ur ye done?"

She nodded, wiping tears of laughter from her eyes as she wheezed to a stop. He reached down and helped her to her feet.

"That escalated quickly," she said, choking back giggles. "I haven't laughed like that in forever. One of these days I'm going to die laughing, and it will be your fault. Thanks for trying to save my life."

His face twitched as he remembered his last effort at life-saving.

Alice stepped away from the dance, and he followed. She scooped up the forgotten drinks and wiggled her eyebrows at him. "That's one reason I like you, Lowlander. You're as fucked up as I am."

"Ur a wee maddy, ken." He grinned despite his dark thoughts. He couldn't believe how well it had turned out despite his outbursts. Or maybe because of them.

The half-hour ride back was wreathed in silence, the rushing air providing an ocean hum. Alice was lost in thought, wobbling under the speed limit, then accelerating erratically for a while, only to drift slower again, which was only marginally less stressful than her balls-to-the-wall driving on the trip over.

Nick struggled with his own thoughts. When he had boarded the plane for the States, he hadn't thought about the details. He hadn't thought he'd meet someone he wanted to keep in his life. He hadn't been thinking at all.

The old Ford bumped into the apartment parking lot. He pointed to the second reserved spot for his unit. Now was the moment to end it or confess. Before he could make a move, Alice turned off the engine and jumped out. He scrambled out of the passenger side as she rounded the back corner of the car. He stood awkwardly, using the car door as a shield, still trying to choose. He liked where all of this was going, but it couldn't last as the precarious house of cards it was. She stopped at the back of the car and opened the hatch. *The Irn-Bru. Ya eejit.*

He hurried around and lifted out the case of drinks. He steeled himself for the moment and turned, holding the drinks protectively in front, but Alice was already halfway to the building. The squeaking of her sneakers echoed loudly as she raced through the open stairwell. She paused on the stair landing and leaned out.

"Hurry up, Lowlander."

"Haud the bus!" he called back, flustered.

She barked a laugh. "Okay, but not for long." She burred in a Weegie impersonation, "Ah'm desperate fur a pish!"

"The best laid plans ay mice an' men gang aft agley, mate," sighed the Nicktoon behind him.

"Shut it. Dain't Rabbie Burns me, ya bloody dime bar," Nick snapped. "Go an' play tag wey the buses, awright?"

"Huv it yer way."

When he emerged onto the upper hallway, she was squeaking out a comical little tight-kneed dance, her sneakers loud on the slick concrete. He shifted the case of drinks to one hip as he rummaged through his sporran for the keys. With Alice clipping at his heels, he pushed through and wordlessly pointed out the bathroom door.

He thumped the drinks onto the kitchen island and broke the case open. He filled the refrigerator door with bright orange bottles while racking his brain for a way to ease into the truth. A full confession would likely drive her away, making it pointless to come clean, except to say he had and hope she could get over it. But a lie told often enough could become the truth. Why couldn't he be what everyone believed him to be? He bent to stow the overflow bottles onto one of the island's shelves. He was nearly done with his task, but no closer to a solution, when she came out.

"Aw better, hen?" He kept his eyes on his work as she leaned against the counter behind him.

"Oh yeah. Golden. Thanks," she muttered absently.

He felt a shift in the fabric of his kilt and heard a sharp inhale. The tartan swooshed against the back of his thighs.

"Is 'flashes' Scottish for underwear?" she said in a strangled voice.

He turned with slow dignity and leaned back against the island, crossing his arms loosely under the "who needs pants" slogan on his shirt. Her face was bright red.

"You went commando?" she asked, stifling laughter.

"Ah went traditional, byraway," he corrected her. "Ye ken the secret the noo."

"I expected boxers covered with little blue Braveheart smiley faces or Scottish flags. Or anything besides freeballing."

He shifted onto a stool and hooked his heels up, letting his knees fall open. He revealed nothing, but her eyes dropped down as if hypnotized.

"Nice girls wear panties under *their* skirts, you know."

He smiled placidly, waiting for it.

Her eyebrows compressed in dismay. "Does everybody…"

"Nae. Maist dae, but. Tha's hoo it's cried traditional."

Her eyes looked haunted as she rewound through the entire day of kilted men. "I may be scarred for life."

"Ma bahookie wis dead awfy, eh?" he said sharply.

She looked up from his knees, startled. "No! You have a wicked nice—"

The feline grin creeping across his face stopped her. He caught her flying fist and made an easy decision to simply enjoy this while it lasted. The green eyes widened as he guided her arm around his neck, causing her to slide between his knees.

"Is that a sporran or are you happy to see me?" she whispered.

"Baith." He kissed her hungrily. "Ah've wanted ye iver since ye chibbed tha' punter in the gut wey yer cue, byraway," he confessed.

"I've wanted you ever since you called me a hen," she said with a breathy laugh.

She leaned into him. Her free hand found his bare thigh. He unclipped the sporran from its chain and dropped it to the floor.

Tossing aside her little shoulder bag, she pulled off her shirt and set to work on his. The claymore earrings swung gently, tapping the side of her throat. He ducked his head through the shirt and cringed at the spectacle of his bare chest.

"I giveth and I taketh away," she crooned as she tossed his shirt aside.

Her warm hand traced his collarbone and down the faint midline of chest hair, detouring along the pair of scars across his ribs. He'd had a hard go of it, that much was plain. She felt a flash of guilt about how they'd met, about why she'd pursued him at first. She shrugged it off, along with her bra straps. This was not part of the job. It was her choice.

As their lips met again, his hands glided up her body of their own accord. The satin of her bra brushed his arm on its way to the floor. He cupped her small breasts. Her fingers rasped against the stubble on his cheeks as she pulled him in for another kiss. She fumbled with the stag belt buckle, and he felt the broad leather belt slither from around his waist. It clattered to the floor. His hand moved to the waistband of her jeans. He wrestled the button undone and tugged down the zipper to reveal a triangle of plaid cotton.

"So what clan am I in?" she whispered.

"The clan ay the MacCheeky Knickers," he retorted, and peeled the layers of fabric away from her round ass.

"Yes, you are cheeky, Nick Kerr," she chuckled.

She helped him push the denim down her legs. Steadying herself with an arm around his neck, she kicked off her sneakers and pants. She picked feverishly at the side buckles of his kilt. His fingers moved between hers, unfastening the straps for her. As she felt along the top of the kilt searching for a way in, he unfastened the last buckle and let the kilt fall open.

Her hands rested on his shoulders as she stepped onto the stool rungs and swung her leg over to mount him where he sat. She eased him inside her, and he grabbed her hips. The only truth on his mind was how good she felt, how right, how unlike any other time. He felt orgasm building too quickly and tried to hold her back, but he was unable to slow her undulations. He gave in with a quiet curse. She cried out and melted into him. He slid his arms tight around her and held her close, the hard edge of the kitchen island biting into his back. Her body shivered against his, her legs trembling.

The realization of how badly it would end now was creeping in to ruin the moment. He was disgusted with himself for not coming clean before going this far. He released her and stood up suddenly. She hung around his waist with her arms looped around his neck and their skin glued together from perspiration. She slowly unfolded her legs and leaned full-length against him. Her forehead pressed into his neck. He grimaced with a surge of nerves and shame.

"Liked tha', did ye?" he said gruffly.

She reared back slowly and speared his dark eyes with her green ones. He couldn't look away. She clasped his face and pulled it toward her. Her lips met his in a deep, gentle kiss, and he felt himself reciprocating. She released him, smiling languidly as her hands traced his neck, along his chest, and over the gently rolling hills of his abdomen, her touch parting their bodies like a zipper pull.

She felt calm, content. It had been years since she'd made love to anyone. She had forgotten how good it could be. She searched her mind for a glimmer of guilt or shame, but found none. She was off the clock, as it were, as if the investigation job didn't exist. And for once, she'd found someone who was okay with who she was without having a weird agenda.

She pushed off from his hips and padded across the apartment. Her skin glowed like a full moon. He felt like he was in way over his head with no clear way out.

22: Hot Fuzz

Alice pulled the duvet up over her nakedness, leaving only head, shoulders, and hands exposed.

"Show's over. Your turn." She grinned like a madwoman. "You can't hide back there all night."

He flicked off the light, plunging the apartment into twilight darkness and effectively hiding his reddening cheeks.

"Ye dinnae tell her," scolded Nick Two's disembodied voice.

"Pervy wanker! Were ye err the hale time?"

"Nae, an' Ah'm still no' err, ya eejit. Ye should tell her the truth, rinoo," his mate whispered urgently in the darkness. "Itherwise, she'll hate ye fur lyin tae her when she finds oot on her oon. She'll likely hate ye nae matter whit ye dae the noo ye've pegged her."

"Aye, Ah shouldnae huv," he muttered. "No' tha' it wisnae pure dead brilliant, or Ah'm no' fain tae huv anither go."

"Don't be shy. I've already had my hands and et cetera all over you," Alice drawled.

He fumbled the TV on and straightened so its flickering glow played over his nakedness. The uneven light allowed him to see her reaction clearly. Her eyebrows pulsed once and her mouth twitched. He latched onto the tiny encouragement.

"Awright then, feast yer eyes if ye think ye kin haunle it." He broke into a nervous sweat and fought the urge to cover himself. He didn't understand the attraction. He had the short, thin build, pale skin, and sharp features common in residents of Glasgow's subsidized housing, literally and figuratively an ocean away from the beauty, athletic form, and privilege of Bradley Taylor and the American MacAlisters. All of which left him wondering if she was the village bike after all. Or simply felt sorry for him.

"Mibbe she has an angle. Has she asked tae see yer place ay employment yet? Mibbe she's wan ay thum animaw rights nutters like maself," whispered Nick Two.

Alice's eyes shifted down and back up to his face. She smiled and held the covers open for him.

"Shut it. She kin get intae the building on her oon. An' she's no' vegetarian, like they awyis is. Ur jealous, jist. No' yer best feature."

He crossed the distance in two strides and climbed in. She fell back beside him so they lay face to face. He pushed the hair off his forehead. She smoothed it back down.

"I thought only women were that self-loathing."

"Aye well, Ah'm nuchin like yer dead husband. Or..." he gestured vaguely, "Yer las' dance partner."

"Lowlander!" She punched him on the arm. "Stop being jealous over nothing."

"Ah widnae cry ye nuchin."

She rolled her eyes. "Relax. I'm sober, I just made love to you, and I'm not going anywhere. You're too hard on yourself."

He placed a hand under one swinging claymore earring on her lovely neck and gently pulled her lips to his. "Mibbe aye, mibbe hooch aye," he mumbled. His hand moved along her soft skin to cradle her breast.

"Are you up to something?" she murmured.

He pulled away sharply. He lifted the edge of the sheet and pretended to inspect himself. "No' yet."

She giggled. "Too bad."

"Mibbe later, aye?"

"Maybe," she purred and propped herself up on one elbow. "Does this mean we're going to watch infomercials now?"

He shrugged. "Aw Ah've got is coancil telly. Nae cable or nuchin."

"Me neither. But no one can survive on four local channels. So where are the DVDs?"

He pointed at the coffee table where the TV sat.

"I knew you had to have some stuff," she chirped. "You can tell a lot about someone by the movies they own. Especially when they seem to live out of a suitcase." She gathered the blanket around herself and scrambled off the end of the bed, leaving him exposed in her wake. He grabbed her pillow and covered his groin.

"Some ay thum's no' mines," he said nervously.

"Nice ass-covering." She grinned over her shoulder. He turned the pillow to cover more. She raised an eyebrow. "In more ways than one." She turned her attention back to the stack of music and movies. "Glasvegas?" she asked, holding up a CD.

He shrugged. "Local talent fae home. Tha' is mines."

"I'd like to listen to that later." She loaded a disk into the player and walked back up the bed, stopping beside him. "You done with that?" She pointed to the strategically placed pillow.

He shook his head and held it tight. "No' until ye gies back the blanket."

Alice dropped suddenly, lunging for his face with one hand, her fingers hooked into claws.

"Jesusjohnny!" he yelped, shielding his head with an arm, stopping himself short from grabbing her wrist. A blast of cool air struck his crotch as she reclaimed the pillow.

"Ya sleekit wee stoater," he said with grudging admiration.

The pillow hit him full in the face.

"Jings, wumman!" he yelped. "Whit wis tha' fur?"

She straightened and began beating him in earnest in a one-way pillow fight. He cowered comically in a defensive curl, periodically yelling "ach" and "ooyah" to make her laugh. When she reared back for a big swing, he found his moment to snatch the blanket. Despite flaunting her nudity not long before, she squealed and clutched the pillow tight against her naked body. He grinned and reached slowly for his own pillow.

"Truce?" she panted.

Nick gathered the cushion into attack position. Alice backed herself against the wall and cringed for impact.

"Ah'm keys," he agreed, raising his thumbs around the pillow, then fluffing it fussily.

"I take it that means yes?" She considered renewing hostilities just for the fake-out, but the DVD player tired of waiting for a command and started the movie. She sat down sulkily, hiding behind her pillow, while he took his time arranging the bedding. With a final flourish, he tossed the blanket over her head and settled back. She pushed it aside, replaced her pillow, and crossed her arms to hold the blanket in place on her chest.

Eyes intent on the screen, she sniffed, "If I didn't like *Hot Fuzz* so much, I would kick your ass right now, truce or no truce." As if underlining her point, Nicolas Angel in bicycle safety gear skidded into the camera, sneering as if he had veins clenched in his teeth while "Goody Two-Shoes" blared. She added prudishly, "And just so you know, I do not go to the movies to make out. I go to watch."

Nick choked on a laugh.

"That came out wrong. Especially with that song playing."

"Aye. Subtle innuendo an' that." His voice quivered with amusement. "Aye, it did."

She sneaked a sidelong look at his shit-eating grin. "I am very serious about films," she insisted haughtily before dissolving into giggles.

"Ach, Ah huv a confession tae make as well," he said, his voice suddenly serious.

Her giggling stopped abruptly, cautious eyes on his. Her stomach plunged.

"Ah wis hopin fur wan ay thum 'bad romances' yees Americans are awyis bangin on aboot."

She made a noise somewhere between a gasp, a growl, and a snort of laughter, and smashed him in the face with her pillow. "I'll see what I can do."

Nick's cell phone rang insistently from the discarded sporran on the kitchen floor. He sat up and stuck one bare leg out of the covers, but stopped indecisively. With a wicked smile, Alice pressed back into her pillow and gripped the edge of the covers tightly, still looking straight ahead at the TV. He sighed. As he got up, he placed his pillow over his bare buttocks like a censorship block. Safely behind the island, he flopped the cushion on the countertop and sat on the kilt-draped stool.

"Hullo?" he answered hesitantly, wishing he'd thought to check the number first.

"Awright, son? Ah wis jist thinkin aboot ye, lad." His father's voice staggered down the line like the drunk Weegie it came from, jovial and thick with whiskey.

Ach. Poker nicht wey the lads. "Da. Ur pure blazin."

"Aye. Tha' Ah'm, son, tha' Ah'm," Rabbie Kerr answered philosophically. "Hayonya, ye hud onie contact wey yer mither?"

"Cannae talk rinoo, Da." He glanced at Alice, who cackled loudly at the TV screen.

"Whit? Hoo no'? Someb'dy err?" Rabbie's voice turned sly. "Ach. Wisnae theday the festival ye telt me aboot?"

"Aye, Da. Haun tae God, Ah got tae go. Talk tae ye later, aye?"

"Ye got the bird wey ye, dain't ye? Ya jammy bastart. She a goer?"

"Aye," he strangled out, answering both questions at once. He felt his face reddening. He stole another glance at Alice, who grinned widely back and flashed her tits.

"You're missing a really good part," she taunted.

"Ah'm no' missin it when ye dae tha'," he called back, startled by his own cheekiness.

"Ur ma onerly hope fur grandweans, ken. Make sure ye get her up the stick, son, so she wullnae lee ye," the elder Kerr slurred.

"Da! Tha' dinnae wahrk oot so well fur ye, ya daftie," he retorted, distracted by the possibility of more nudity. "An' ye need tae be givin ma brither some grief."

"Gob shite it dinnae," Rabbie declared indignantly. "Ah hud yer mither fur nearly eight years instead ay a fortnight."

"Ur talkin mince, auldjin," he said fondly, turning his eyes from the bed with great effort. "Stack up a few zeds, aye? Ring ye themorra." He hung up, shaking his head in wonder at the crazy shit parents say.

Alice smiled as he started around the island. His eyes narrowed.

"Dain't act it," he warned.

Her smile widened as her eyes dropped and flicked back up to his.

He looked down. "Ach."

He snatched the modesty pillow and held it high as he ran. "Freebawin!" he shouted joyously, and threw it at her as he dove under the covers.

She shielded her head and barked a laugh as the pillow bounced off. "That's streaking, silly."

He caught it and stuffed it behind his back before she had a chance to start another pillow fight. She smiled fondly at him and settled back into the movie. She was oblivious as he watched her. Her facial expressions. Her enjoyment of the movie. Her hair tumbling across the pillow in heather-scented tendrils. Her smooth skin.

His mind wandered to his father's warped advice and his own lack of planning, least of all on contraception. He had to admit the entire subject made him uncomfortable on many levels. "Hoo'd ye get marrit, then?" he blurted. It came out with more edge than he intended.

" 'How' as in 'why'?"

He nodded in reply. She shifted uneasily, with a flicker of a smile.

"I don't know. Too many fairy tales about happily ever after? All my friends were getting their 'MRS. Degrees'? I thought I was in love?" She smiled sadly at a thread in the blanket that she was worrying. "Seemed like a good idea at the time. The Taylors are like royalty around here. I was flattered and naïve." She sighed heavily. "I think the real question is, why did he ask me to marry him?" Her eyes met his and fell away at his expression of disbelief. "I've asked myself that question a million times, with no good answer. He was Catholic, but he wasn't religious. Never went to mass or confession. He could have slept with anyone and everyone, and tried to. So why marry me? Like my grandmother says, 'Why buy the cow when you can get the milk for free'?"

"Ach. Tha's a mercy. Fain Ah dain't huv tae roond up some dosh," he joked awkwardly. Her hurt look stopped him cold.

She turned back to the movie, cheeks blazing, shamed by the fact that money was changing hands over him. She should have confessed to the assignment before letting it go this far. The line had been crossed, regardless of what the road to hell had been paved with, and there was no undoing it. But she could enjoy this until it blew up into the bad romance he'd joked about.

He lay stiffly beside her, hoping for a change in her mood.

23: Morning After

Television static lit the room with a dull glow, accompanied by a quiet fizzing. Nick was pleasantly surprised that Alice was still there, despite falling asleep on watch. Long after her silence had been transformed into sleep by the plummy English accents on the local PBS station, he'd lain awake to make sure she couldn't leave without telling him where he stood.

He was curled around her hot, still body like spoons in a drawer. His arm rested across her waist, his erection pressed against the roundness of her ass. Moved by the moment, he kissed her bare shoulder.

She made a soft noise, then startled awake suddenly like a half-wild cat, banging into the wall in her blind rush to get away from his touch. He raised his hands in surrender like a burglar caught in a floodlight. He was thankful the hair in his eyes shielded him from the intensity of her stare.

Her disorientation and terror faded to embarrassment. She curled around her pillow, keeping it between them, fighting tears until her eyes gradually closed. He exhaled a long breath and moved to the far edge of the bed. He stared at the ceiling, seeing her face from the news photos and wondering what he'd done to make her look exactly like that.

At least she hadn't taken her clothes and run.

Outside in the parking lot, a Volkswagen circled, the headlights raking across the residents' cars. The apartments were dark and quiet as football fans slept off a victory celebration. Inside the building, there was no reaction to the crumpling beer can sound of American-made quarter panel collapsing under German bumper. The dark bubble of metal maneuvered out of the lot without further incident and glided down the street unharmed.

The black Volkswagen slowed down as it passed the arch of hedges and hesitated before turning down the adjacent alley. It reversed into the parking area of another rental house, positioned so that the yard and door were visible through a gap in the hedge. The engine and lights shut off to wait for the walk of shame.

Laura Beth was glad she had thought to bring her laptop. She could make the most of her time by researching possibilities for the next research project, one she would get into without an inside connection. She skimmed grant application listings, press releases from research institutions, abstracts. Enough to put nearly anyone out cold, but not her. Insomnia was a side effect of shift rotation, and when sleep finally called, she listened, regardless of how many shift substitutions she had to beg. Tonight she was wide awake.

As night paled to dawn, she saw motion in the yard. Something small. She craned forward to see an ugly gray cat cross the grass and squeeze under the hedge. She rolled down the window and called softly. The cat changed direction and trotted over, tail high. She opened the car door and leaned out. It squinted at the sudden light and sat back on its haunches. She stroked it absently, out of habit. Her mind rolled over what she would say and do when the other woman came home.

She looked down at the cat's clipped ear and was seized with an idea. She stepped out, careful not to startle the animal, and opened the front trunk. The live trap and pet carrier were there where she always kept them in case she ran across feral animals. She scooped up the cat, shoved it inside the carrier, and secured the door. With a satisfied smile, she closed the trunk and settled back into the driver's seat. The black Volkswagen eased into the alley. She'd make his little chippie come onto her turf, on her own terms.

Mid-morning sun lent the room a golden glow, but Nick wasn't willing to open his eyes and start the day just yet. The TV was silent. He sprawled flat on his back with Alice's scent surrounding him. He stretched his left arm in a slow sweep over the place she'd been last. He rolled onto his side and continued searching until his fingers brushed the cool wall. His eyes flew open to confirm the empty bed.

He raised himself on one elbow and stared numbly at the empty mattress. Well and truly gone. So it came down to a hit and run after all. He tried to take grim satisfaction in Dr. Nick Kerr's failure as some sort of dim hope that he would have had more success as himself, and might yet, if some miracle got it sorted. "Keep calm an' carry on," he murmured. He rolled from the warm nest of covers to face a joyless day.

He staggered in and out of the bathroom, then beelined for the consolation prize of his favorite soda. He stopped short. Alice perched on one of the tall stools, elbows on the countertop, heels up on the rungs. Her wet hair, surprisingly long from the water weight, brushed the formica and created a damp patch on her T-shirt. She held an open bottle of Irn-Bru.

She was poised, clean, and dressed. She looked more amazing than ever, and dangerous with it. He was acutely aware of his naked body, sticky with sweat and fanny batter from their lovemaking. She'd washed the traces of him off her skin, but he was covered in hers. He sidestepped to put the island between them. He wasn't sure what was supposed to come next. He desperately needed some caffeine. His eyes followed the bottle longingly as she sipped from her drink. When she rested it on the countertop, he noticed the neat pile of carefully folded shirt, coiled belt, and sporran. He had a brief churning of fear that she'd gone through the contacts in his phone, then remembered there weren't any incriminating numbers in it anyway. He was relieved and disappointed that his secret was safe.

She shifted the belt and sporran aside and lobbed the folded T-shirt at his chest. He snatched it and waited for more.

"Jings, wumman. See ye over err aw decent an' that. See maself over err in the bare scud. Tha's aw Ah get?"

"You're a doctor. Deal with it," she answered impudently, quoting last night's movie.

"Ah thoat ye hud gone hame."

"Not disappointed, I hope."

"Nae. Surprised, but."

"Why?"

"Isnae tha' hoo it's done?" He directed his full attention to wrapping the shirt into a makeshift kilt.

"How what's done?" She sat very still.

He shrugged, avoiding her eyes.

"Oh, you mean a one-night stand?" Her voice was conversational. "Usually the person who doesn't live at the scene of the crime leaves during the night while the other person is asleep. Sometimes he or she stays for breakfast if they're heavily in denial, but that just gets awkward."

"Awkward isnae in it," he agreed. "Ur ye stayin fur brekwist or no'?"

"Do you not want me to? Should I go?" She gestured at the door.

"Suit yerself," he said noncommittally.

"Based on the contents of your fridge, I'd say I'm already having the breakfast of champions around here anyway." She gestured with her bottle.

"Gies a ginger, then, eh hen?" he groused.

"Come and get it," she lilted. "I was just leaving." She stepped down from the stool.

He rounded the island, one hand clutching the shirt to his hips. Despite the confined space, he ignored her and hoped she couldn't reach anything sharp. He jerked a bottle of soda from the refrigerator and slammed the door with an elbow. Without releasing his grip on the shirt, he squeezed the bottle between arm and side to open the cap. He scowled from the cold chill on his skin. He looked so aggrieved that she struggled not to laugh.

"You're going to make a mess." She pulled the bottle from his precarious body hold, careful not to touch him.

At the hiss of released carbonation, he sneaked a look at her. Her legs were bare, panties showing below her shirt tail as she moved. She hadn't been in that big of a rush to go after all. His heart leaped. He wanted to pull the ridiculous plaid knickers down, finger her wetness, feel her smooth thighs around his ears as he made her moan. He ran a shaking hand down his face. Morning stubble scraped his palm. *Ach. Well then, hoo aboot anither go on the stool...* The cold bottle tapped his arm, jolting him out of the fantasy. He took the drink from her outstretched hand.

She raised an eyebrow, her eyes directed at his makeshift kilt. He looked down sharply, nearly spilling soda on his bare chest.

"Whit?" he demanded. He looked back down and realized the shirt's slogan was running between his legs. He was dressed in nothing but the shirt that was so awesome he didn't need pants.

Alice broke into one of her contagious laughs. Nick laughed partly from the relief that his thoughts hadn't been grassed up by his odd outfit, partly out of relief that she never stayed mad at him for long. They stood very close, very awkward.

"Good morning," she said softly.

"Moarnin," he whispered back hoarsely.

"Are you always as prickly as a hedgehog first thing in the morning?"

"Ah could ask ye the same." He quickly foundered ahead, worried he'd put his foot in it again. "Ah dinnae really think ye wis the sort ay lass tae dae somehin like the, um, ye ken, hit an' run thingmy byraway. Ah dain't ken whit ye see in me neither, but." He winced, waiting for the strike of anaphylaxis, or a divine lightning bolt from Saint Mungo for the blasphemy of his semi-apology. "Ah mean, Ah widnae blame ye if ye decided no' tae see me agin. Ye probably shouldnae."

Her fingertips rested feather-light on his chest for a moment before starting the slow glide down his flat stomach to rest along the line of black jersey.

"Ah-Ah'm gawn tae shut ma gub an' pit on some claes the noo," he stammered.

"Okay," she breathed.

"Gawn tae pit ma ginger doon," he warned.

She nodded slightly. He leaned past her to put his bottle on the island, dark eyes locked on hers, mesmerized. She moved with him, inches away. His hand found her neck, and he closed the small gap between their lips. A claymore earring tapped the back of his hand. Her fingers rasped on cheek stubble. He released his hold on the T-shirt and cupped her face in both hands. The shirt fell from his buttocks but remained caught in front. She lifted it free of his conspicuous erection.

He led her backwards with short, cautious steps. She gripped his hips and followed, kissing him hungrily. His calves bumped into the foot of the sofa bed, and he fell back onto his elbows with a grunt. She stripped off her clothes impatiently and crawled onto the bed, straddling him. Her wet hair tumbled down, cold as icicles. He gasped from the shock of it. Her nipples brushed his skin as she kissed him. He slid inside her. She sighed and sat back, and he felt her stretch to fit him. She rode him with slow intensity. As the tension peaked, she clutched the blanket in both hands and pushed hard onto him with a soft cry. She relaxed, lying on top of him. When their breathing slowed, she touched his face and smoothed the damp hair on his forehead. With shy fingers, he stroked her bare back.

"Christ on a bike, wumman. Ye go like the Glesga-Edinburrah Express," he murmured.

"Is that good or bad?"

"It's exhaustin. Ah'm jeeked an' Ah huvnae iven startit the day. Ah couldnae tackle a fish supper."

"But it's Sunday. Day of rest and all that," she said, playing with the few chest hairs he had.

"Ma point exactly. Were ye like this wey yer man?"

"No," she said emphatically. "I'm like this with you."

His hands paused on the smooth skin of her back. "It's no' me," he insisted.

"You started it every time," she retorted, rearing up from his chest.

"Ah dinnae," he said stubbornly, pushing the hair out of his eyes.

"So you didn't want me, just went along with it to spare my feelings?"

"Aye. Faked aw ma orgasms," he insisted.

"Very convincing," she answered, fighting a smile. "You deserve an Oscar for those performances." She kissed the flat medallions of his nipples. "Those *are* pretty spectacular, by the way." She sighed loudly and rolled off him. "But I need to go," she said reluctantly, "Or I'll be too sore to sit at my desk tomorrow."

She scooped her panties off the floor. He watched her pull them on and sashay to the kitchenette to fetch her jeans. As the denim closed around her lovely ass, he remembered his next tour of graveyard shift started tomorrow, just when he had found a good use for his nights. He bolted to the closet and crammed on scants and jeans. He noticed the tartan hanging neatly.

"Ur fur the dry cleaner's, pet," he whispered to it. "Cheers fur las' nicht." He stepped behind the protective fort of the island and pushed back his hair.

Alice's back still faced him. She straightened from tying her sneakers and shifted the small bag onto her hip. She squeezed its contents through the fabric, feeling a hot blush of shame. The camera cable and flash drive were safely hidden. She'd copied the files before his apology and making up. They could be wiped, sight unseen, as soon as she got home.

"Ah'm startin back shift themorra, ken," he said apologetically. "So ye dain't think Ah'm avoidin ye." *An' so ye dain't hook up wey ma fookin cousin.*

"Back shift? That's what, graveyard? I'm sure we can work something out. You don't work weekends, right?" She turned toward him and smiled fondly from the middle of the room.

"Nae. Tha's Mickey the grad student. Wahrks two twelves, poor bastart. Ye wullnae make me wait tha' long tae see ye agin, but? Ah'll huv evenins free."

"Call me, Lowlander." She gave him a long look, savoring him with her eyes. "I have to go. I'd kiss you goodbye, but I don't want you to get something started. Again."

She crossed to the door and stopped, hand resting on the doorknob. "I almost forgot. While you were sleeping, I downloaded the photos for you." It had been a good cover in case she got caught on his laptop, but he had slept through it. "You shouldn't leave your passwords just sitting around on a sticky note." She laughed at the expression on his face, so much like a kid caught with a hand in the cookie jar. "I don't have to look at your browser history to know you googled me. I don't mind. I'm flattered, really." She smiled as she wiggled her fingers in farewell, slipped out, and shut the door with a soft click.

24: Back Shift

The veterinary college was post-apocalyptic in its emptiness. Inside the fluorescent-humming concrete corridors, Nick found it easy to believe the normal world was obliterated. He had never really understood why a night caretaker was needed for birds that didn't move once you'd turned out the lights, but he didn't mind the solitude of the back shift. As long as he avoided the hospital wing's skeleton staff, he had the sprawling complex all to himself and his thoughts. He could be himself without consequences. The challenge was filling the time, not minding his deceptions. Dozing, reading, surfing the internet, working puzzles, circumnavigating the building like a mall walker, studying the specimens in anatomy lab, and always half-listening to the lab monitor for emergencies that never came.

The wide Commons was cave-like in the minimal night lighting. He climbed onto a table and zig-zagged around the room from tabletop to tabletop, making a game of it. Americans were such germophobes; if they only knew what he got up to in the wee hours... At the far end of the room, where the wall turned to windows, he sat on one of the long tables. He stared out at the empty courtyard and visualized one of Alice's hot chick zombies lumbering through, pressing her formerly firm body against the glass, licking the window until her tongue fell off with a wet plop. In his mind's eye, she was much of a muchness with Pavlov's Belle. Who was much of a muchness with Mary. He wondered what his brother had been playing at, planning to come all the way out here to be near their long-lost mother. He hoped he wouldn't have to play nice on a regular schedule.

The receiver in his lab coat pocket crackled with random static. He shook the dark thoughts from his mind and hopped off the table to begin the twilight-zone journey back into the bowels of the building. He considered calling Alice, despite the ungodly hour.

"She could keep ye busy, if ye get ma drift," the Nicktoon hinted with a leer and a rude gesture.

"Ach, ya dirty wee bastart," he scolded. His footfalls echoed in the industrial stairwell. "She wid think somehin awfy hud happened, an' lose the rag when the onerly emergency wis in ma troosers." He saw the empty building in a whole new light, an endless game of pornographic musical chairs. And couches. And tables. He shook his head to clear it.

His friend laughed. "Admit it. Ur a fookin sex addict."

"Piss aff an' find somehin tae dae wey yerself besides pesterin me, ya fookin numpty." Nick fell into a hard plastic chair. He ignored his roommate's particularly enthusiastic victory sign and opened an abandoned sudoku book to clock the rest of his shift with his mind safely out of the gutter.

The break area clock ticked off only fifteen minutes beyond his shift's end while he paced for what felt like two hours. Dave stumbled in at last, lab coat buttoned crookedly and coffee in hand. Nick was nearly vibrating with anger.

"It's the fookin backa eight!" he snarled, coat unbuttoned, hands on hips. "Whir the fook ye been, mate?"

Dave blinked, chastised and confused by the sudden outburst. He held up the extra-large coffee like an offering to an angry god. "Had to get coffee, man. Can't function without my cup of joe," he explained. "Not my fault the café lady likes to talk. I'm not going to be rude first thing in the morning, man, and tell her to shut the hell up so I won't be a few minutes late. I'd never be able to go back. Then I'd have to hit the Starbucks across town, and end up really late."

Nick glared for a moment more. He ground thumb and forefinger into his tired eyes to buy time for a mood shift before speaking again. "Awright, mate. Ma eyes ur hingin oot ma heid. First back shift's awyis the devil's erse, aye?"

Dave nodded slowly. "Been there." He thumped the large coffee onto the break table. "Don't really need that anymore, after that wake-up."

Nick patted the heavyset man on the shoulder in passing. Pausing in the open stairwell door, he offered, "If ye like, Ah kin gie ye a wakey-wakey bollocking themorra tae."

"I'll stick with 'my leetle friend.' " He gestured at the cup and grinned at his own Scarface impersonation. "Besides, I'll be back on middle shift tomorrow. Two out-of-cycle sub shifts in a row is my limit."

"Offer's open onie time, mate." Nick raced up the stairwell, leaving his fellow lab rat staring at the heavy metal fire door.

Dave shook his head. He muttered in a Spanish accent, "I'm the most interesting man in the world. I don't usually talk, but when I do, I'm fucking bipolar." He saluted the door with his coffee cup. "Stay thirsty, my friend."

Nick had his jacket off before he reached the kitchenette. He placed helmet and cell phone carefully on the counter and puffed out a long breath. He snatched up the phone and dialed before his courage gave out.

"Hi there, Lowlander. It took you a day longer than I expected." Alice looked guiltily at the flash drive protruding from her office computer. She'd spent most of Monday arguing with herself over reading the files, and had resorted to a coin toss first thing today.

"Be'er late than no' atall byraway. Ma teachers used tae say Ah wis a slow bastart. In fact, ma clan motto is 'late, but in earnest,' " he rambled. "Onie road, Ah hud a wee thoat, hen. Ah wis thinkin ye micht want tae get thegither an' that." It didn't sound nearly as smooth as it had in his mind.

"Telt ye it wis a dead stupit exercise, practicing a conversation," Nick Two remarked in passing, fresh from a raid on the refrigerator. He received a kick in appreciation of his opinion.

"I've never gotten a booty call at eight-thirty in the morning before."

"Nae, nae, when ye get oot at fiye. An' it's no' fur tha'. No' fur onerly tha'," he stammered. "Though tha' wid be brilliant. Ah meant tae get some scran. See Ah'll be wakin up aboot then." He was glad that she couldn't see his red face at least. It was odd to be so awkward after how easy it was to talk to her normally.

She snorted, and he pumped a fist in triumph. His roommate huffed in disgust.

"So what are you thinking? Pub?"

"Whitiver ye fancy, doll. Ah'm a bachelor, raised by a bachelor," he professed. "Lang as it's no' movin or foosty, it's fair gemm. An' sometimes iven then."

"Then I should definitely pick." She didn't want to brave Hutch's unsubtle staring or risk the lab coworker's reappearance. They needed somewhere new to meet. "How about the Tube. It's that small, dark hole on Main Street. You'll like it. It's supposed to be like a British pub. Not that I'd know."

"Ah ken the place. Nivver been in it."

"They have darts. Is that authentic?"

"Aye, Ah suppose. Dae ye throw darts tae?"

"Occasionally, and most of the time I even hit the board," she joked.

"Ach. Ah'll mind tha'. See ye err roond fiye then?" He immediately kicked himself for not allowing enough time to get cleaned up.

"Better make it five-thirty," she said. "Give me a chance to get there."

"Ah'll be err. Nae danger."

"Yeah, I was counting on that," she said, misunderstanding the expression. "Bye, Lowlander."

"Bye ya." He waited for the click before hanging up. "Gude luck tryin tae stack up zeds," he remarked to the now-empty room.

Alice leaned back and let out a long breath. Time to get to work. She felt guilty for downloading his browser history and favorites. Worse still about the e-mails. She'd save them for last, while she decided if that invasion of privacy was necessary. She didn't really want to know, but then again, she did. She had trust issues, unquestionably. It was a rare opportunity to investigate someone she was interested in. Of course, it could backfire quite nastily, but that might be a moot point anyway. She lowered her eyebrows, angry with herself for what she was about to do. " 'She generally gave herself very good advice, though she very seldom followed it,' " she muttered.

She grimaced and launched her internet browser.

25: Invasion of Privacy

She'd been right; he had googled her. It was all there, in the history. Instead of making her feel better about her own prying, it only reminded her of the huge difference between a standard search and lifting files off a personal computer. She hopped from site to site, unwilling for a rehash of what she'd lived through. Further back, the pages switched to work-related topics: the veterinary college staff pages, program information, abstracts on Hepatitis E research. Seemed legitimate.

She dove into the favorites pages, skipping the e-mail account link. University of Glasgow, Mapquest, Google Earth. Searching out good roads to ride, she guessed. She couldn't get user access to his Facebook account through the duplicated link. *Should have checked when you were there, on his saved login. But I didn't have much time. Would have, if you hadn't taken the shower. I needed the shower as a cover. He didn't know how long you'd been up; he was completely oblivious. Okay then, I needed it because I smelled like fried food, sweat, and sex. You didn't seem to mind that smell on him. Seriously, can we get to it or what, before I get busted for not working on real work?*

She waved her hands emphatically at the keyboard, nodded briskly to settle the argument with herself, and hopped through the rest of the history and favorites. There weren't many, and they were thin on social media; apparently he wasn't a big social networking guy. The only one that stood out was the Glasgow city webcam, refreshing every few seconds to make a jumpy, Keystone Kops movie out of ordinary city traffic. There, it was three in the afternoon, with fog and drizzle smearing the traffic lights into colored icicles, the honey-colored buildings glowing from hundreds of lit windows against the rainy dimness. Alice found herself mesmerized by the tiny, oblivious world of business people and sightseers, shoppers and loiterers, cars and buses, as if expecting to see something noteworthy happen while she watched.

The morning was slipping away, and she still needed to run through his e-mail. She skimmed over the messages for as little intrusion as possible while still intruding, looking only at senders, recipients, and subject lines, delving through inbox, outbox, deleted. She did her best to not read any content if she could help it. Several messages from his coworker sat in the deleted folder, most not even read. None to or from anyone in Glasgow. Some from the University of Glasgow alumni association, unopened, sitting in the inbox.

Basically a wasted exercise, she thought, soothing her conscience. Then she noticed the drafts folder had a lone message sitting in it. Addressed to someone named Rab, it dated all the way back to early June. She opened it.

All right? I'm dead sorry I didn't talk to you for so long. I shouldn't have gotten so bent, but you've always been a pure aggravating wee bastard, making such a muckle noise about being different from me. And there you were, in the thick of it, auditing classes and showing up at parties, trying it on. It wasn't so much that jimmies confused us. I'm the pure dead handsome one, by the way, and modest with it. What really ate at me was that maybe you were doing it because you weren't happy in your own skin. I know we haven't seen eye to eye on a number of things, but there's room enough in veterinary medicine for two Dr. Kerrs. I waited to send this until I'm safely in the States, far from the long arm of brotherly wrath. You should come visit but. See if you're interested in joining the Dark Side. Give old wounds a chance at healing instead of festering. Spit out your dummy and move on, before you become a sad old chancer.

It struck her as funny, his words and expressions without the accent attached to them, like he was subtitled. The unsent e-mail fit with what he'd already told her himself. The only new information was his brother's name. No need to pass on anything to Mary. That decision, along with wiping the flash drive, removed the possibility to pry any further and made her espionage almost palatable. She stowed the blank drive back in her purse and got back to her day job.

A low black railing hemmed in a wider area of sidewalk to make a patio. In front of a different venue, it would have been trendy *al fresco* seating; instead, it was a smoker's exile with resentful patrons and a cramped jumble of cheap resin lawn furniture. The miniscule storefront was misleading about the interior dimensions, if not the ambiance; it was much deeper than it was wide, with no space wasted. The front area was broad and open, housing six dart lanes edged with a row of freestanding tables at the ends of the lanes and another row of half-moon tabletops mounted into the wall beyond. Guinness posters and vintage London Underground maps and ads formed a rudimentary décor. The light from the dart lanes spilled over a touch-screen jukebox and the short end of the chest-high bar that ran perpendicular to the street. More tables pressed against the walls. Above the bar, multiple TVs broadcasted different sporting events, and above those hung flags: Welsh dragon, Irish tricolor, Saint Patrick's saltire, Saint George's cross, Union Jack, Scottish royal lion, Saint Andrew's saltire.

Nick peered into the dark. He was blinded by the bright glare of the narrow kitchen that shone at the end of the tunnel-like bar like the light one was supposed to head towards in an after-death experience. A red-faced man with receding ginger hair and sharp eyes nodded to him from the high, broad deck of the bar. As Nick stepped forward and opened his mouth to speak, the man pointed. He looked in the indicated direction to find Alice perched at a table in the near corner, sitting very upright, smiling brightly at the sight of him.

"Hoo'd ye ken?" Nick called to the bartender.

The man shrugged and paced down the rail to answer a silent signal like a skilled sheepdog. The few patrons were lined up along the bar in well-worn camaraderie. A pair of professor types with grey-streaked beards huddled at a table, their discussion quiet, but accented with hand motions and lots of drinking. There was no music, only the susurration of voices and clinking of glasses.

"Awright, hen?" He took in the curve-hugging dress, black with a pattern of raised green flocking like vintage wallpaper. The square-cut neck covered her cleavage and framed a jade-colored glass pendant in the shape of a leaf that echoed the dress and her eyes. A white rabbit-fur coat was slung across the chair back.

"Good morning," she said with a smile.

He brushed the hair off his forehead and smiled back. "Moarnin." He gestured at her dress. "Ye look bran' new. Whir Ah'm fae, the birds awyis get brammed up tae go oot, iven tae the pub."

"Sorry, I didn't get dressed up for you. I wore this to work," she lied. She pulled two dog-eared menus from behind the salt and pepper shakers, handing him one and hiding behind the other. After a few minutes, she placed the menu on the table. "I'm thinking the garlic personal pizza."

He narrowed his eyes. "Ah can go the 'Napalm' chili."

Right on cue, the bartender loped over to their table.

"I'll have the garlic personal pizza, please, and a diet cola." She grinned wickedly at Nick.

"Ah'm fur the dead hot chili an' a Tennent's, mate."

The bartender raised an eyebrow, but didn't look up from the order pad.

"Could I get the fish and chips instead?" she blurted suddenly. "And a Tennent's too?" She shot Nick an anxious look.

He returned her look calmly for a moment, watching her squirm. "Change mines tae the fish supper as well."

The ruddy man nodded once and returned to his perch. Alice collected the menus and slotted them back into place. She met his eyes and broke into a slow grin.

"Playing it safe, I see."

"So ur ye."

A pair of lagers appeared, and the bartender disappeared as silently as he'd arrived.

She eyed the pint he brought to his lips. "Don't you have to work tonight?"

"Dain't start on me," he growled, glaring over the glass.

She held up her hands in surrender. "Never mind. Forget I asked, Hedgehog Crisp. Guess it's none of my business if you aren't really on night shift. Or if you're a high-functioning alcoholic."

"Cannae huv a fish supper weyoot a pint," he said testily. "An' it's airly. Ah dain't heid in until midnicht. Yees Yanks ur a pure load ay nutters aboot the drinkin."

"No longer claiming that dual citizenship, huh?" she teased. "Yeah, this is what you get when your country is founded by religious extremists." She grinned and raised her glass. "To the breakfast of champions."

"*Slàinte*," he toasted in return.

"So your liver's not used to night shift?"

"Nut. Neither is the rest ay me," he agreed.

"That sounds dirty."

"Ye wid think tha'," he countered.

"Like you weren't," she argued.

"Nae, Ah wisnae," he insisted.

She slouched, so that her face occupied the place her chest had been, in order to meet his eyes. "If you say so, Lowlander."

He reddened. "Ah ken ma rights. Tha' wis entrapment."

She was about to retort when he was saved by the silent arrival of their food.

"Tha's a pure lovely sight the noo," he sighed happily as he seized the malt vinegar. "If onerly they hud HP sauce, it wid be a right taste ay Glesga."

They tucked in, letting other conversations wash over them.

"Couldn't do this every day, but it really hits the spot," she said after a bit. He nodded, awkward with a mouthful of fish. "I haven't been in here in a long time," she continued.

"It's like ma local at hame, but weyoot snooker tables. A right bearpit." He swallowed some lager. "We could go somewhir mair posh next time."

She raised an eyebrow. "Next time? Is that a threat or a promise?" she joked, then turned serious. "Only a little nicer, though. Really nice places make me feel..." She made a face.

"Skint?" he offered. "Ye ken, oot ay dosh. Nae money."

"I was going to say 'like a call girl.' "

At his sudden coughing fit, she sprang off her stool and leaped around the table. He waved her away and took a swig of his pint. "Ah'm awright. Gawn tae be trippin tae death wan day, on account ay ye, so Ah'm."

"I meant out of place," she explained. "Like the hooker in *Pretty Woman* when the rich guy takes her to the posh restaurant. She eats the garnish and launches snails everywhere."

"Ah could see tha'," he said, studying her and thinking about the Black Widow news photos. She slugged his arm but grinned.

"Agin wey the skelpin? Ur pure bloody minded, so ye ur."

The bartender appeared beside the table. He raised his eyebrows in a wordless question.

She nudged Nick's shoulder. "You want anything else? Another pint?"

He shook his head and bugged out his eyes for emphasis. "Tha'll dae me. Ah'm stowed oot."

"You sure? I promise not to slap a scarlet letter on you: 'A' for alcoholic. I'm a Revere girl after all, not a Salem witch hunter."

"Tha's fine, then. Ah dae fancy anither."

She turned to the bartender. "Another beer for him, Harv. Separate checks, please, and throw in a dart rental and two bucks in quarters on mine."

Harv gave a small frown as if he'd lost a wager with himself, and strode away to check on other tables.

"D'ye ken aw the bartenders in toon by name?" Nick asked incredulously. "An' ye act it like Ah'm the drunk."

She shrugged. "Only two places."

He checked that the ginger man was safely out of earshot behind the bar. "He's a wee queerie, byraway. Nivver a word. Ye dain't huv tae chin tha' yin, but."

"At least I know he's not gossiping behind my back." She gave Nick a knowing look.

"Ach. So ye ken aboot Hutch grassin ye up, dae ye?"

"Now I do," she said slyly. "I only suspected before."

"Ur sleekit. Ah'll huv tae keep an eye on ye."

Yes, you really should. "I thought that's what you were doing earlier?"

"Oh aye." He leaned forward. "Ah think Hutch wis tryin tae scunner the competition tha' nicht, ken."

She looked slightly nauseated. "I could have done without that insight, thanks."

"Nae bother, hen." He grinned with the small triumph of knocking back one more rival. The bar tabs slipped onto the table with the second round and extras. "Ah'm no' doon tae auld claes an' cauld porritch byraway. We dain't huv tae go haufers." He pushed both bills into a stack. "Let it be ma bell, hen."

"Another time. I really do appreciate the offer, though."

He was trying to do the right thing, and she wasn't having it. "Suit yerself. Ye kin be aw liberated an' buy ma brekwist then," he groused. He pushed the tabs in her direction.

"God, you're a pig," she said in mock disgust. "You're only one wicked sexy accent away from a slow, painful death." She froze, a haunted look in her eyes.

"Ah'm warnin ye, Ah'm pure difficult tae aff. Been malkied twicet," he said placidly, touching his ribs.

"You said yourself I was going to kill you with laughter." She smiled crookedly, pulling herself together.

He made a face. "Death by laughter wid be awright. By shaggin wid be pure magic, but."

"It's strange how often people joke about death and murder, isn't it?" she said thoughtfully.

He was wrong-footed by her lack of comment on the shagging bit. Did it mean it was a sure thing, or out of the question?

She swept up the quarters and rental darts. "Speaking of, I'm going to slaughter you at darts. And you can pay my tab after all." She headed for the lanes, leaving him to take care of the tabs, coats, and drinks.

He watched her sway through the pub. The dress was tantalizing yet revealed little. The demure neckline dropped lower in back, but her long hair formed a fringed curtain over the bare skin. The curve-hugging skirt ended just above the knee. She looked over her shoulder and waggled the dart flights at him, playfully chiding him for taking so long. He hurried after and dumped jackets and drinks on the low table nearest the lane she had chosen.

She handed him a dart to pitch for throwing order. She swung her arm in a couple of practice motions before letting fly. It thumped into the eleven near the middle of the pie. "Straight cricket, okay? 501 takes too long, like Monopoly with projectiles. Not to mention trying to do math while drinking."

He nodded, testing the dart weight. He seated the flights, aimed and threw, landing in the green ring of the bullseye. Alice bumped him out of the way with her hip.

"What, are you amazing at everything?" she said indignantly.

Nick grinned lasciviously at her, restraining himself from using a "that's what she said" comeback. She punched him lightly on the arm anyway.

"Ah'm no' really, haun tae God. Jist got sponny wey tha' yin, so Ah did," he lied. He hadn't spent every moment on the tables when he was hustling. He'd won a few straight wagers on the boards as well. "See ye, tha'll be me fur the bullseyes the nicht. Especially wey ye damagin ma throwin erm." He rotated it around.

She narrowed her eyes. "Uh huh. I'll believe that when I see it." She retrieved the darts and handed them over. "All yours, Lowlander."

He pushed his hair back and closed the twenty. He felt the green eyes all over him as he walked the length of the lane, marked his score, and came back for the hand-off. The Mona Lisa smile appeared as she slipped past him to make one twenty out of three throws. She strutted down the lane like it was a fashion runway, scrawled a slash on the chalkboard, and plucked out the darts. She turned with a pout and posed, hand on hip like a model. She tried strutting back, but broke down into laughter before she made it to the oche. She stopped toe to toe with him, holding the darts close to her chest. His fingers brushed hers as he gingerly pulled the shafts free.

"Ur tryin tae break ma concentration, urnae ye," he murmured.

"Trying to even the odds, dart shark. Is it working?"

"Nut," he lied. He leaned in for a kiss, heart racing.

She stepped sideways, leaving him hanging. "Crap. Well, there's always the Elle Woods bend and snap." Sweeping up the quarters, she weaved through the tables to the jukebox. She was getting paid well to hang out with someone she'd choose to be with anyway. She smiled and smoothed a curl behind her ear.

Nick surreptitiously checked around the pub to see if anyone had noticed his dropped pass. Reputation still intact, he remembered the darts in his hand and threw to the opening notes of Alice's first song selection. Returning from chalking his score, he caught sight of her dancing toward him to the sultry Latin rhythm. His feet shuffled to a stop. She undulated around him, all curves in motion. She pulled the darts from his frozen hand and threw in time to pauses in the music. Her performance was for his eyes only, but he noticed that the entire pub had turned its focus on her. She was the only woman in the room, and oblivious to the attention. He wondered if he was headed for the rammie of a lifetime.

She stepped in close to him, her green eyes shining with mischief, and ran the dart shafts down his chest. He snatched them from her hand, shoved his hair aside, and stepped purposefully around her to the line. He ignored her dancing as well as he could while remaining hyper-aware of her body behind him. On her next turn at the board, she leaned ridiculously far into the lane, one leg behind her for balance like a figure skater. The entire man-cave tried to sneak a glimpse upskirt, but only got an eyeful of dimly lit thigh in black tights.

"She's gettin on ma tits. Hoo am Ah supposed tae throw?" Nick muttered.

"Serves ye right," Nick Two heckled from the next table. He leaned so far sideways he had to grip the table to keep from falling from his seat, and raised his eyebrows at the view. "Hoo dae ye ken she's no' playin ye?"

Nick jostled the table hard, making his mate scramble for balance, but his throwing was shot. "Ah ken she's playin me tae scunner me at darts. Ah'm no' an eejit byraway," he snapped back. He gave up keeping track of what he was aiming for, instead going for the bullseye on each throw.

"Damn, you have amazing concentration. What's a girl gotta do to distract you?"

She stood in front of him, swaying to the acoustic version of Clapton's "Layla." The warmth of her hand settled on the nape of his neck. Her other hand lifted his left arm into the ballroom hold he'd taught her. He remained frozen, fighting his temper, until she nudged him into motion with her hip. He relented stiffly, moving on autopilot from long training in the farmhouse kitchen. She swayed him to the music, the familiar motions soothing his mood. His other hand settled lightly on her back. He relaxed into the gently loping music, then made her work to follow his lead. His girl laughed breathlessly up at him as she struggled to keep up with what she'd started. As the song wound down, he led her into a twirl, and reeled her into his arms. The crowd clapped and whistled. He gave them what they wanted, dipping her low and planting a self-conscious kiss on her lips.

She broke away and collected the forgotten darts from the end of the lane as he scanned the pub. Everyone had given up on an encore and was business as usual. Serious throwers occupied three of the lanes, and pockets of loud, intense discussions had sprung up. A few guys were arguing over the jukebox. One felt Nick's eyes and looked over, grinning furtively before hunching closer to the group. The Nicktoon was nowhere to be seen.

"Urnae ye dancin onie mair?"

Alice leaned against the table. "Nah. That's the end of my songs." She jerked her head in the direction of the jukebox. "We'll have to call an exterminator for all the Beatles that lot will put on."

"Ach. No' a fan ay the Merseybeat, then." He perched beside her.

"They get stuck in my head like glue. I prefer the rest of the British Invasion, including the most recent Scottish one." She grinned sideways at him.

He smiled back. "Gawn tae finish the gemm, then?" He cocked a thumb at the darts in her hand, hoping the answer was negative.

"I think you won two songs ago."

"Oh aye? An' ye let me keep throwin?"

She nodded, fighting a smile. "I tried to stop you, but you were very focused. Be right back."

He watched her through his hair as she set the darts on the wide bar, said something that made Harv smile briefly and utter a single word, and weaved back through the growing crowd. *Comin back tae me,* he marveled. He shrugged into his jacket to ensure a fast getaway to somewhere more private.

"Dae ye fancy anither blast?" he asked, pointing to her glass when she was alongside him.

She pulled on the fur jacket and slung her purse over a shoulder. "I'm not much of a drinker." She frowned to herself. Mainly because she needed to save her money to pay off her debt, but also to keep her wits about her in case of Black Widow fans or foes. And so she was available at a moment's notice to pick up any work the Booths offered.

As they stepped out into the night, she hooked an arm through his. He glanced back into the dim pub. Harv watched, leaning on the bar. He nodded once, then turned and disappeared into the flare of light from the kitchen. The jukebox lit the grinning faces of the group still hovering around it, now flashing Nick a mixture of thumbs-up and rock-on gestures.

"Have a nice night," called one of the patio smokers without a trace of sarcasm.

Alice looked back over her shoulder and waved. She squeezed Nick's arm and smiled.

"The hull pub wis starin at ye, ken. Wis dead awfy."

"What? No way." Her cheeks turned red. "Nobody saw anything back there with my...?" She recreated her figure-skater lean with her fingers.

He shook his head. "An' no' fae want ay tryin, neither."

"Did I throw off anyone else's concentration?"

"Ah think the wa's took mair darts than the boards."

She laughed and began walking backwards. "So where are we headed, exactly?"

He pointed. "Ma motorbike."

"And then where?" she asked impishly.

"Ah dain't ken. Tae airly tae go tae wahrk," he said, playing dumb.

She smiled expectantly but didn't help him out.

"Makin me wahrk fur it. Ma bit or yers, then?"

"Mine?" she suggested, eager to give the snooping a rest, and make this solely about spending time with him.

"Ah dae fancy anither keek at yer bones."

"I'll bet," she teased.

He thrust a helmet at her and pulled on his own. Eyeing her skirt, he swung a leg over the bike and waited for her to mount. She tilted forward, looking down herself.

"Oh dear. As if my performance in the bar wasn't bad enough. I'm going to make another spectacle of myself."

He grinned wickedly. "Serves ye right fur tryin tae throw ma gemm."

"For succeeding in messing up your game," she corrected. " 'It's all feasting and fun.' " She wedged on the oversized helmet. "Time to be spectacular," she said ruefully and threw a leg over the seat.

26: Bond, James Bond

The motorcycle glided through the portal of greenery and stopped outside her door. Nick held the bike upright as Alice dismounted. He followed her into the narrow kitchen. Her dress was slightly rucked up in back, revealing a little extra thigh.

"I've got cold drinks in the fridge, and tea bags are in that flowered tin on the counter," she offered. "Cups and stuff are in the cabinet to your left. Sorry there's no liquid Juicy Fruit."

"Later, mibbe." He leaned against the counter. "Whir's the wee cat?"

"Cheshire? Don't know. He just wanders, you know. Haven't seen him in a few days. I'm a little worried, but he's probably shacked up somewhere sweet."

All he could think was how older animals sometimes wandered off to die. Like the last member of his mother's cat colony. The mean-spirited old queen couldn't totter to the litter pan, but she managed to descend two flights of stairs and slip out the close door to expire two tenements down among the prize lilies in the neighbors' perfectly manicured front garden. It had cost Da quite a few rounds in the pub to smooth that over.

She slipped off the fur jacket. "You going to take off your coat and stay a while, or do you have to go already?"

In the brighter light of the kitchen, he could see her coat was separating in places between the pelts. He shrugged out of his heavy leather jacket and she took it from him, hanging both coats in a small closet off the kitchen.

He raised his voice to carry. "Ah huv tae go soon, but." He added, half-joking, "Kin onerly stay fur wan go, two at the maist."

She stalked toward him, hand on hip. "What makes you think you're going to get any at all?"

"On account ay Ah bought ye dinner?"

She shook her head.

"On account ay ye cannae resist ma accent?"

The Mona Lisa smile came closer. She shrugged.

"On account ay ye fancy hairy coos?"

She took his face in her hands and pulled it down to hers.

"Ya sick fook," he exclaimed before she shut him up.

"Jesusjohnny," he groaned and slumped to the back edge of the wide couch.

She scooted down and stretched out along him. He rested a hand on the soft curve of her lovely naked backside. They lay silent for a long time, curled together on the old couch like amorous sardines, until he thought she had fallen asleep. Her hair lay against his chest in a heavy mass. He stroked it gently, and when she didn't stir, he surreptitiously spread tendrils of it across his shirt to make a preposterous chest wig.

"Yesh. Tha' wull do nishely," he rumbled in an imitation of Sean Connery's distinctive burr.

"What are you doing back there?" Alice said languidly.

He froze, scunnered. She turned over, shifting one section of her body at a time and pulling her dress into place. The couch bounced and rolled, in danger of giving way completely after the evening's abuse.

He stuffed himself back into his scants and yanked his jeans up his hips. "Nuchin," he said guiltily.

"You were playing with my hair, weren't you? I could feel it." She stretched a tendril across his upper lip. "Diabolical mustache?" His eyes dropped shiftily, the eyelashes dark and long, as he breathed in her scent. "No? Amish beard?" She wrapped her curls around his face, her fingers spread into little points of pressure around his jawline.

A grin crept sheepishly across his face. "Nae, a wee lower doon."

She arched an eyebrow at him and let her eyes drop to his fly. He zipped it.

"My hair's not long enough to reach *that* far."

"Christ on a bike, wumman, is tha' aw ye think aboot?"

"You weren't complaining earlier, Lowlander. And you started it. Again."

He sighed loudly.

"So what, then? You have to tell me," she said eagerly.

"Ach. Makin up fur ma baldy chest," he admitted testily.

"Seriously?" With a throaty chuckle, she pulled his shirt up and spread the entire thick horsetail across his bare nipples. "You have a secret desire to be Magnum, P.I.?"

He patted the improvised chest wig vainly. "Mair like Bond, James Bond."

She leaned back slightly for a better look. He pressed the hair tight to keep it from falling off. She looked from the giant bush of hair to his pleased expression and back again.

"What is it with men and hair?" she said, bemused. She assumed a sexy villainess voice. "Vee hoff vays ov maykink you talk, Meester Bahnd." She rolled her hair away slowly while making a tearing noise.

He faked a low-pitched bellow of agony and covered his chest with both hands like a bashful virgin. She shook with laughter and pried at his fingers. He tightened his muscles and resisted full strength until she growled and gave up.

"You leaf me weeth no choices, Meester Bahnd," she said in a resigned voice, and dug her fingers into his ribcage and neck simultaneously.

He yelped and struck out involuntarily, sending her rolling off the sofa with a whoop. He grabbed for her as she fell and caught only a handful of hair.

"Ow!" she howled from the floor. "Are you trying to harvest my hair for your chest wig?"

He released it like it was on fire. He lurched to the front of the couch and leaned over the edge. "Ach! Ur ye awright…"

With a sudden predatory lunge that would have made a crocodile proud, she seized his upper body and hauled him down. He sprawled on top of her. Her laughter rang loud in his ears, and fingers dug into his neck again. He rolled to get clear, dragging her with him, her small wrists clasped in his hands. Her face hovered inches above his. The dark curls tickled his cheek and fell into his eyes, along with his own hair.

"Release me from your kung-fu grip," she demanded.

"Nut." He puffed the hair away from his cheek and eyes. It fell right back. "Ur right dangerous an' Ah dain't trust ye."

She wiggled her captive fingers at him, straining to reach. "You're hurting me."

He looked at her captured hands. "Shite. Ur ye keys? Ah'm keys if ye ur."

She nodded and he let go. She sat back into the space between his legs, unfolding hers behind him as he sat up to face her.

"You know, I'm starting to not mind a little manpower," she said, using a movie reference to test the waters for disclosing the other dark secret of her marriage.

He reared back and scolded, "Tha' is exactly whit Ah'm bangin on aboot. Ur awyis efter gettin me het up."

She decided not to ruin the mood. Let the secret stay dead with its perpetrator. All Nick's internet searching wouldn't have revealed the abuse. Ray had determined not to disclose because it would give her motive for murder and make her look more culpable in the civil case. She shrugged.

He was in a good position to look down the front of her dress, so he did. Her breasts rose and fell against a lacy black bra. The flocked dress fabric was velvety under his palms. The demure neckline sagged as she unzipped, the fabric slipping down her shoulders and chest to reveal the dark disks of nipples veiled in black lace. Her arms snaked free and into his shirt, warm and urgent. He pushed the dress down around her hips. On the way up, his hands cupped the small, firm breasts in their scratchy lace and pressed them together. He sank his face into them, feeling her laughing purr vibrate through the flesh. Her fingers trembled against his stomach, struggling with his jeans. He braced his arms around her back, fingers spread wide on smooth skin. She clung to him as he tipped her backwards onto the rough carpet.

While he unfastened his jeans, she lifted his shirt high. He ducked his head through and lifted each arm out in turn as he kept at the pants.

She helped him shove the denim down to his boots. One black bra strap rested loosely on her upper arm. He pulled the bra cup away from that breast, leaving the other in its black veil for tantalizing contrast. He savored the nipple, rolling it against his tongue. He rose, closing his mouth on hers, and she guided him inside her. She pushed her hips into his, panting eagerly. He sank to his forearms. Muscles contracted against each other, skin on skin. She sighed beneath him.

Her hands closed around his face, and she stared into the darkness of his eyes without blinking. His lips met hers, triggering a long post-coital make-out session. He reluctantly rolled off. The carpet prickled his bare ass, and his knees burned with the contact of air on raw skin. She leaned over him, sweeping her hair over one shoulder. She kissed his damp chest, one hand on his slightly concave stomach. His fingers traced along her neck.

"Tha's ma quota fur the nicht," he declared. "An' nae mair peggin on the flair, wumman. Ye huv a scratcher." He gestured at the futon. "Ay sorts. This kerpet's pure hell on the knees."

"It's not kind to the butt, either," she chided. "I'm going to have a scab. Right here."

She arched the pale moon high to point out a red patch the size of a quarter. He felt a laugh well up.

"It stings," she said huffily and sat back.

He pointed to the vibrant road rash on his knees. "Ah look like Ah crashed ma bike the noo. Ah'll be hobblin like an auldfaither at wahrk thenicht, byraway."

"Wow," she said, impressed. "You win. Or lose, depending on how you look at it." She straightened and stepped over him, lifting her bra back into place. The dress remained crumpled around her hips, the hem falling just past her pubic hair. "I think I have a cream for that. Be right back."

Nick eased his scants past his knees and back to his waist. He sat up and leaned his back against the couch, careful to keep his knees slightly bent to spare the tightening wounds.

She padded toward him, armed with a box of bandages and a tube of ointment. She had changed into what he guessed passed as her pajamas—shapeless drawstring pants in yellow plaid and a loose-fitting T-shirt. She sat cross-legged at his feet.

"Allow me to demonstrate my mad first aid skills," she said cheerfully.

"Whit the fook is on yer shirt?" he blurted. He stared at the design, a street scene in the woodcut style of the German Expressionists. A woman stared in horror with all twelve of her shocked blue eyes at a dissolute man smoking three cigarettes at once, one in his shark-toothed mouth, the others in identical mouths where his eyes should have been.

"It's a post-modern statement on the blinding nature of addiction and the voyeurism of the holier-than-thou bourgeoisie. Or just a weird band shirt, whichever explanation you like best." She bent over his knees. "I got it at the thrift store."

"Ah kin see hoo."

"I like it."

"Artists," he scoffed. "D'ye sleep in tha' thingmy? Hoo dis it no' gie ye nightmares?"

She patted a preposterously large amount of antibacterial ointment over the torn skin on his knees and covered it with oversized self-adhesive gauze pads. "I don't stare at my chest when I go to sleep." She leaned back to admire her work and barked a laugh. "Do you remember that episode on *All Creatures Great and Small* when Siegfried lectures James about wasting surgery supplies?"

He nodded, a grin spreading over his face.

"And then when James is using the tiniest bit of thread and a puff of antiseptic powder on a gypsy's horse, Siegfried shoves him out of the way…"

"An' he empties the hool can a pooder on it, an' stitches it wey a full yard ay suture thread." They grinned at each other over the expanse of gauze for a moment before he inspected the finished product. He turned serious, levering himself to his feet stiffly and self-consciously pulling up his jeans. "Ye dinnae huv tae bother yer shirt aboot it, but."

She glanced down at her chest, confused.

"Ah meant, ur no' ma mither or oniehin. Ye dain't huv tae take care ay me, hen. Ah've hud mich worse wey mich less care, byraway." He flopped back on the couch, letting his feet fly up to spare his knees.

She snorted. "If Mary took care of you, you'd be six feet under. Or needing Ray's legal services."

"Ah thoat ye dinnae ken ma mither?" he said sharply.

She busied herself with gathering the bandage wrappers. *Shit.* "I said I didn't know she was your mother. And that I didn't see them socially. That's true."

"Kin ye haun me tha' jumper?" He pointed to his shirt. He didn't know what to think, but he couldn't think clearly in the rubble of their lovemaking.

She pulled his shirt toward her and clutched it to her chest. "I owed them a lot of money. Ray was court-appointed for the murder charge, but he billed me out the ass for the civil case. Captive audience." Her eyes flicked up to his, desperate for him to believe. "Then he loaned me the money for the settlement. Said it was the least he could do, for not getting me out of it."

He stared back at her, nervously rubbing his thighs. He flicked the hair out of his eyes.

"I save up the best I can, pay it in installments. I do side jobs, too, to pay down the debt. Some things for Ray, but mostly tasks for Mary. It's a lot of money," she repeated. "*Was* a lot. I'm almost done. But she keeps finding ways to push the tab up, or finds fault to short me on the agreed payment, or sometimes even adds more charges."

"Soonds aboot right. She has a mean streak byraway."

She heard the mistrust in his voice relent a small amount. "Yeah. I guess so," she said cautiously, knowing from experience that jumping on the bandwagon could get even the most mother-bashing boy to turn on you without warning. "But I did not know she had sons. Especially not one as smart and charming and funny and wicked good in bed as you."

"The noo ur pushin yer luck wey tha' load ay mince," he growled, trying not to be swayed.

"Oh, and don't forget stubborn and aggravating." She lobbed his shirt at him.

He caught it just before it hit his face. "Tha's mair like it," he said with approval and pulled it on.

27: Quiet Evening In

Nick squinted at the shelves holding her skull collection and TV, trying to read the titles on DVDs and videotapes. "Ye got *Thunderbaw*? Or mibbe *Doactor Nae*?" he asked hopefully.

"In a Sean Connery mood tonight, I see. Sorry. Not even *Indiana Jones and the Last Crusade*."

"Whit am Ah lookin at? *Alice*?" he read.

"That's my name, don't wear it out," she sing-songed like a grade-schooler. "I'm kind of a big deal. I have a whole collection of Alice in Wonderland movies." She met his eyes and laughed. "Warped, I know. I didn't start it though. My father did. The Disney classic, Tim Burton, BBC, the SyFy Channel mini-series, Lou Bunin, musicals, you name it."

He looked at the shelf dubiously. "Ah'd raither watch the real Alice. Especially a repeat ay whit ye did at the pub thenicht."

"I thought you'd reached your quota for tonight."

"Ah wis talkin aboot the dancin. Huv tae wahrk the alcohol oot ma system somehoo."

She settled onto the opposite end of the sofa and tucked her feet between the cushions. "I'd rather sit and talk. I want to know more about you."

"Whit time is it, eh hen?" he asked in sudden alarm.

"About nine-thirty," she answered. "Why? Are you hiding secrets?"

He blinked. "Ah'm desperate. An' right starvin," he apologized. "Time fur ma dinner, byraway."

"You can help yourself to whatever's in the kitchen," she offered. "Ooh, unless that was a thinly veiled excuse to leave so you don't have to answer personal questions. In that case, I recommend faking a complicated food allergy. Or suddenly remembering an old, flammable appliance left plugged in at home," she added helpfully.

"Ah'm jist fur the lavvy," he said, raising an eyebrow and pointing in its direction.

She grinned. "I'm just messing with you, Lowlander. Knock yourself out."

He did a quick scan of the medicine cabinet, noting moisturizers, makeup, antiperspirant, first aid supplies, and the typical over-the-counter remedies. No antidepressants, sleeping pills, antipsychotics, or other pharmaceuticals that might serve as red flags. Or as murder weapons. He smoothed his hair in the mirrored cabinet door and stepped out.

Alice followed his movement through the room with her eyes. He felt a flare of guilt about his spying and slipped self-consciously into the kitchen.

"Wan mair wee meenit, hen."

He raided the refrigerator for sandwich ingredients. He paused in the middle of assembling and cursed to himself.

"Kin Ah make an extra piece tae take wey me?" he called.

"Piece of what?"

"A sangwidge," he explained. "Ah furgot tae pack oniehin fur thenicht."

"Yeah, of course. Help yourself." Her voice bounced with laughter.

"Ah'm at ma Auntie's, eh?" he paraphrased in Glaswegian, fishing for more laughs.

"Now who's a sick fuck?" she countered.

He returned to the couch, balancing a thick sandwich and a glass of juice. "It's onerly an expression. Ye look fook aw like ma auntie, byraway."

"Oh, that's a relief." She jabbed him with a foot. "Are you set?"

"Aye. Tha'll dae me till Ah get somehin tae eat," he joked.

He perched on the worn couch, balancing a plate on his legs. Her feet settled against his thigh. She rested a pad of drawing paper on her knee and watched him eat for a few minutes before lifting the pencil.

"Ur no' drawin me, ur ye? Some masterpiece tha' wull be: 'Malinky Scot, wellied in.' "

She shrugged. "Just a sketch. Would you rather I took your picture?"

"Kin Ah no' choose neither?"

She shook her head.

He sighed. "Huv at me, then."

"Try to be natural. Forget I'm drawing you," she scolded as he took mincing bites, staring at her out of the corner of his eye.

"Aisier said than done, byraway."

"What's Glasgow like?"

He squinted his eyes, thinking how to describe it as he chewed. "Ah dain't ken. It's a city. Sandstone tenements. Used tae be black wey coal, efter deindustrialization but, the city cleaned um aw tae the original golden hue. We huv ice skatin in the city center fur Christmas an' Hogmanay. An' a right muckle bagpipe festival in the summer. Got museums, an' culture, an' toaff shoppin in Sauchiehall Street, an' fitbaw an' that. An' ma neighborhood, tha's Maryhill, ken…"

"Maryhill? That's ironic. Mary of Maryhill."

"Ach. Ah suppose." He shrugged. " 'Mary fae Maryhill.' It's a chant fur oor oon footie team."

"Partick Thistle."

"Aye." He talked around a mouthful of sandwich. "Besides Thistle, Maryhill hus the canal walk, botanical gardens, murals ivrywhir, two libraries, an' loads ay pubs. The uni's right roond the corner. The city's no' bad, no' really. A wee rough roond the edges. Good people, but. Maist ay the time. No' pretentious, unlike Edinburrah." He took another bite.

She gave him a long look. "Like you."

"Hooch aye," he argued, but was pleased.

She thought of the webcam gazing longingly at a damp city square. "Sounds like you love Glasgow. Why did you leave?"

He finished the bite before answering. "Seemed like a gude opportunity tae travel." He smiled sadly. "Ah dinnae ken Ah'd miss it so mich."

"Seems like sort of a low-prestige job to travel that far. Did you come over here to be with anyone in particular?" she fished, thinking of Liam's warning. He shook his head. The pencil paused on the paper. "Did you leave behind one of those bad romances you said you're after?"

He choked and recovered quickly, his face red. "Nut." He held up the second half of his sandwich like a shield. "If ye want tae grill somehin, hoo no' this piece? Ah'd fancy tha' mair."

She narrowed her eyes.

"Ah ken whit ur efter, hen. Ur no' as sleekit as aw tha'." He waggled the sandwich at her. "Wid Ah be lettin ye pit yer hauns an' 'et cetera' aw over me if Ah hud some ither wumman somewhir?"

"Maybe. Some men would."

A strip of dill pickle slipped out of the bread and flopped onto the plate. "Ah'm no' the type whae lets hus pickle faw oot fur jist onieyin," he quipped.

She poked him with her foot and smiled despite herself. "Tell me about your brother. What's he like?"

"Ah'd rather no'." He felt her eyes on him as he stuffed the pickle back into the mix.

"You should have him come visit. Having someone to stay with, now that is a great opportunity to travel."

"Oh aye," he said simply.

She hadn't succeeded in digging up anything on why the e-mail remained unsent. She didn't dare push further.

"Tell me about your father."

He relaxed and started to ramble happily.

"Shite. Ah got tae go." He thought of Dave's hurt, startled face with a twinge of guilt. He hurried to the hall closet, finding his jacket hung neatly with other coats above a row of shoes. He shrugged into it.

"Don't forget your piece of sandwich," she reminded him.

He decided not to correct her. "Cheers. Ah'd be noshing nuchin but crisps oot the machine thenicht itherwise." He stowed it in one of his zip pockets.

"No big deal." She shrugged and gave him a crooked grin. "But I guess you owe me dinner now, huh?"

"Aye, awright then, hen. Onie time."

"We could meet tomorrow or Friday, but not Thursday. I have a work thing. A dinner."

"Wahrk wahrk or Mary Booth wahrk?"

She smiled sadly. "It's almost paid off."

"Aye right. Fingers crossed. Fain Ah dinnae get an invite."

"It could be for Ray's colleagues, and that's why you've been spared."

He nodded, glad to take the explanation. He leaned in for a quick peck, carefully leaving a space between them. She hooked a hand around his neck and held him in a long, passionate kiss. His arms closed around her on their own.

She pulled away, her fingers tracing the stubble down his cheeks. "I'm surprised she didn't insist you show up for cocktail hour, even if you do have to work after. But I'm glad. It would be wicked hard to keep my hands off you. Speaking of which, you'd better be going."

"Aye." He didn't move. His hands rested on her waist. "Ah dain't huv mich time…"

Her eyes were bright. "No, you don't," she whispered.

He lifted the tail of her distracting shirt. She pressed it back down with one hand while the other groped for the doorknob. He stepped toward her, hoping to win back the moment, but she pulled the door open between them.

"Ye dain't want tae huv tae admit ye start oniehin is aw. Ah'm away then." He flashed his feline grin and stepped through.

"I love you," she whispered suddenly. It had just slipped out. She wasn't sure if she meant it or not.

He stopped and turned, studying her face to see if he'd heard correctly. The green eyes looked worried, her cheeks reddening. If he told her he loved her too, she'd never believe it wasn't just a reflexive echo. He certainly wouldn't, if their roles were reversed.

"Ah know," he intoned gravely in his best Han Solo impression.

She barked a laugh. "I like nice men, not scruffy-looking nerf-herders."

He puffed out a breath to make the hair lift from his forehead and drop back into his eyes. "Whae ur ye cryin scruffy-lookin?" he replied. "If ye iver fancy a fast ship, yer hieness, Ah've got tha fastest in the galaxy."

"Okay, maybe this weekend," she said, breaking out of the dialogue. "I'm going to go count nerfs now," she yawned, "as soon as I figure out what they are."

He reluctantly crossed the dark yard. When the motorcycle rumbled to life, he looked back, but she was only a silhouette against the brightness. He raised a hand anyway and rolled the bike backward.

"Good night, Lowlander," she called over the idling motor.

The rectangle of light narrowed slowly to black. He opened the throttle and headed into the Tuesday night ghost town.

Nick wandered the concrete maze of the veterinary building, lost in thought. Every passing day meant more to miss when Alice got tired of him. Or found out.

He jogged hallways to shut off his mind. His torn knees throbbed, and the oversized gauze pads caught on the fabric of his scrubs. He rolled up his pants legs and pulled off the hanging bandages.

"Ur a doactor, deal wey it," he muttered through clenched teeth. "Aye, right."

For a moment, he saw his wee knobby knees sticking out above thick blue school socks, marked with scabs from the tenement steps. He yanked his pant legs back down and raced up and down stairs until his legs felt like jelly.

By the time Laura Beth arrived, he was reduced to staring blankly at a half-finished crossword, re-reading the cryptic clues with dry, scratchy eyes that kept drooping shut.

He pushed heavily to his feet as Pavlov's Belle rattled off instructions he couldn't act on until next shift, if he even remembered them. "Ah'm fur hame," he said through a yawn and shuffled past her.

She stopped mid-sentence, offended into silence. He sniffed at his underarms, making a note to shower before crashing.

"Ach, ma oxters ur howlin," he declared.

The lab door slammed behind the Belle's ramrod back. He grinned wickedly. Hauling himself up by the railing, he began the long trudge up the stairs against the protests of his legs.

28: Southern Business

Mary Booth brushed past the younger woman. "What is so secret it couldn't be said over the phone?"

Laura Beth closed the door and leaned against it.

"Make it fast," Mary snapped. She glanced at the sheet of paper the sharp-faced blonde thrust at her. "What? You've lost a cat?"

"This is why he won't talk to me. He's screwing her."

"The cat?" Mary played dumb intentionally to provoke her.

"No." The younger woman stabbed angrily at the flier with a shaking finger. "The person who owns this cat."

"Whose cat do you think it is?" Mary asked carefully.

"That Alice Bonner bitch." Her lip curled. "I saw it come out of her apartment. Late at night. When he was over there, for a 'house call' for this stupid cat!" She crumpled the paper and threw it. It skittered across the floor with the ineffete sound of a clumsy beetle.

"What makes you think they're sleeping together?"

"I've seen them together. At the pub. At her apartment. At the Highland Festival. At *his* apartment, *overnight*. You should see the way he looks at her. The way she acts. And to top it off, he doesn't have the faintest flicker of shame. So I kidnapped it. Cat-napped it."

"We are not criminals. We are the conscience." Mary was furious.

"Exactly. I'm not just sitting around watching him cheat on me with that whore. I'll make her life so miserable she'll back off," she snarled. "She's corrupted him. He wears leather. He eats meat!"

Mary grabbed the long ponytail and twisted. The petite blonde dropped to a crouch of pain, clutching at the hands in her hair. Her usually narrow eyes flew wide open, too angry to be frightened. She hissed like a cat herself. The older woman stared, her face a mask.

"Calm down. He was doing that before he met her. She's working for me, you idiot. Investigating Nick. Whatever it is you think they're doing, she's getting paid to do."

"You paid her to screw your own son?" she whispered, the shock reining in her fury.

"I paid her to investigate. What she does to get the information is her business."

"Why would you do that?"

"Finally the right question." She made a cluck of disgust. "Stay out of the way. You don't know what you're messing with. It's a family matter."

"Aren't I family?" The hurt came through in her voice.

"Not yet." Mary stared her down. "Alice is more family than you are. For God's sake, get rid of that cat. It's not even hers."

The younger woman nodded slightly, wincing at the pain the motion inflicted on her hair. "How?" she asked fawningly.

Mary released her with a small shove. "It's not rocket science. Call the owner and tell them you found it," she said disdainfully. "I used to understand what Nick saw in you, and I believed in it. Now I'm not sure what either of us was thinking. Maybe he's finally come to his senses." She smoothed her designer blouse. "Now get your head back in the game. I expect you to put personal agendas aside, just as I had to do. You will be at my house at six on Thursday, acting like you care about something greater than yourself."

She let herself out.

Alice backed through the kitchen door with a tray of used wine glasses held carefully in both hands. She let out a long sigh. She hadn't expected Nick's coworker to be one of the guests. It had been a long cocktail hour of avoiding stinkeye, filling obscure drink requests, and dodging accidental-on-purpose obstacles in her path, not to mention the pain of her own gnawing jealousy and doubt. Laura Beth was stunning. The expensive dress perfectly accented her figure. Her shoes were amazing, and matched exactly. Her jewelry was coordinated. Her bright blonde hair was swept up precisely. Everything about her was tailor-made to remind Alice how much she lacked and how much she didn't belong in the room. She was just a working-class girl, feeling almost morally opposed to ostentatious expense. Would family events with Nick be any different than the ones she'd endured while married into the Taylors?

When she turned, Liam was waiting for her, smiling his perfect smile. Not quite safely through the gauntlet after all. *"How cheerfully he seems to grin, how neatly spreads his claws, and welcomes little fishes in with gently smiling jaws!"* she thought suspiciously. She'd once wondered what her life would have been like if she's chosen him instead of Brad Taylor, but that time was long past. Now it would be like dating the boss's son. The power differential of her indenture trickled over. Liam had spent his childhood in Mary's care, under her influence, and was more son to her than Nick Kerr could ever be.

"You look beautiful." He devoured her with his gray eyes.

She lifted one eyebrow and looked down at her plain white blouse and black skirt. "Um, thanks. So do you."

He reached past her and turned the lock on the door. She put some distance and the tray between them.

"I assume you're in here to gather another debrief for your aunt."

He didn't respond to the cold shoulder. "Lucky for all of us you're serving," he flattered pointlessly. "I'm hopeless when it comes to wine. I always get bits of cork in it. Once I even tore the cork in half." His smile dipped into a brief grimace. "My father had to use his bronchial forceps to get the cork out. He was deadly serious, bent over it like he was in the operating room. He drilled a little hole, inserted them, and dragged the cork out."

He illustrated the painstaking process complete with a comically concentrated facial expression and pinching hand gestures. She gave a half-smile despite her annoyance with the roundabout conversation. He beamed at her. As he continued to talk, she unloaded the tray and set it with clean glasses. She pulled another bottle from the shipping box and uncorked it.

"Don't ask me why he had them at home. He swore they'd been autoclaved, but it still ruined it for everyone but him." He laughed. "I think of it every time someone serves wine. Off-putting, as you can imagine. That's why I'm avoiding it." He waggled his empty highball glass. "My father's an ear, nose, and throat surgeon. Still practicing, if you ever need your tonsils out, or ear tubes in. He had to do my ears three awful times. Maybe I should have had my uncle sue for malpractice."

Liam watched as she worked. He wondered why he still made an effort. Habit, perhaps. Maybe one day it would take. He couldn't perpetually be a reminder of his dead former friend. Former before he was dead, over her. He drummed his fingers on the counter, the tattoo of "Scotland the Brave." Smug, perfect Brad. He had never really liked that asshole. He always got the best girls, treated them like shit, and laughed when they came crawling back for more. Liam had attributed it to equal parts good looks, money, and power. With his father as head coach in a football-crazy college town, Brad was irresistible. Diabetes had kept him from becoming the star quarterback everyone had expected him to be, but he had acted with the same arrogance and entitlement anyway.

Liam had fallen under his spell in his own way. He had always had a nose for power. As wingman, he ran interference, keeping the jilted out of the way while Brad made his next play. There had been perks as well, he had to admit. Brad's shadow provided flattering light. Being a sympathetic shoulder to cry on for his friend's mistreatment demonstrated that he was sensitive and caring. It also got him a lot of rebound action. And he was always granted an easy out: the girl always broke it off herself because she felt guilty for using him to get back at Brad.

They had been an amazing team, until Alice. Liam had wanted to make the play for her himself. He'd tried hard and lost, and she was the only one Brad had kept. Liam was sure it had been out of spite for his loyal wingman daring to compete. Brad went so far as to isolate her from Liam, her friends, her family, everyone. He hadn't been allowed back in the game even when the golden boy died. Mary had refused to let him pursue Alice because of what it could do to the lawsuit, and then because of the debt and social stigma. He didn't care if she had killed Brad or not. God knows the bastard had it coming.

Now that the debt was nearly paid off, and thanks to his role in Mary's investigation scheme, he had the possibility for a comeback attempt.

"I'm joking, of course. I'd never sue my father. He'd spend all my inheritance money on legal expenses. Here. Why don't you join me? Mix a little pleasure with all the business. You work too much."

Alice set the empty bottle carefully on top of the others in the recycling bin. Turning toward him, she crossed her arms, clearly impatient to get the task over with and back into the gathering. "Frankly, Liam, I have a job to do, and I'd like to get back to it, before she docks my pay."

"And we are going to get back to it. She sent me in here, so you're fine. You Yankees and your rush-rush-down-to-business attitude. You need to relax, learn the fine art of Southern business." He pulled a long-necked bottle with a bulbous base from the cabinet. Flecks of gold swirled in the clear liquor like a snow globe blizzard. He raised his eyebrows pleadingly and smiled his beautiful smile. "Besides, we should celebrate your approaching freedom. With my favorite, Savannah Themes," he coaxed and set down two tall glasses. "Join me."

"Are they good?" She relented, leaning against the marble countertop. The way this evening was headed, she could definitely use a drink. She'd hated parties like this even when she'd been one of the guests. Being on the other side was only better because no one expected—or wanted—you to speak.

He handed her a glass. "You tell me."

The gray eyes studied her as she held up the mixed drink and watched the flakes move lazily at the bottom with the excess sugar of the sweet tea. She took a sip and pursed her lips thoughtfully.

"Not bad."

"Now you know what you've been missing," he said meaningfully. He chuckled and she tried to remember how many other drinks he'd already had. They drank in silence for a moment, leaning side by side on the counter. He cleared his throat and straightened reluctantly, setting his glass down.

"He's legit, you know," she said before he could start talking. "He knows cultural details. He's even homesick."

"You don't know what Mary wanted you to find. How do you know he passed the test?" He felt a flare of tenderness and pity that she could be so trusting after all she'd been through. "You didn't even uncover his engagement, did you?"

"There's no signs of one. I'd know," she insisted.

He smiled pityingly. "Bless your heart."

She avoided his eyes. He gave up, sighing deeply. She'd know soon enough. He'd make sure of it. Then she'd come looking for a shoulder to cry on, and he'd be there.

"I saw my cousin attack you at the ceilidh. He knocked you down, made you cry."

She started to correct him, but he cut her off.

"You don't have to keep doing this, you know. I don't like you alone with him. Forget about that assignment. Like you said, you found out plenty. You should have choices." He gave her a long look.

She wondered if he knew she'd slept with Nick. How could he? Lucky guess? Or did he and Mary assume she would?

"Please be my date for the Caledonian Society's masquerade next Friday on Halloween. I really enjoyed dancing with you at the festival. I'll even donate to your debt-elimination fund if you go. No strings attached."

But strings implied? She wasn't sure if his proposal was kind or indecent. "You're really into this heritage stuff, huh?" Her eyes caught a photograph of him, an action shot on the rugby field, magnetized to the stainless steel refrigerator. "At least it's not football."

He followed her gaze, pleased it was a flattering shot. "I'm not all tartans and bagpipes. I play on a local team, for fun and for the exercise. You should come out to our matches. We could use a cheerleader."

"Would you pay me for that, too?" She meant it to be funny, but it came out with an edge. She took another sip of her mixed drink to keep from saying anything else awful. When she put the glass down, the kiss took her by surprise. She jerked back.

Alice stepped quickly around the island to prevent him from shoving his tongue down her throat again. She wiped her mouth on the back of her hand. She felt light-headed and wondered if he had managed to slip something into her drink. She had barely touched it.

"Would it take that to get you to spend time with me?" His voice was soft.

She felt horrible. He was being nice, and she was being a bitch. "No, of course not. I'm not like that. I'm really sorry. We can talk later. I have to get back to work. No rest for the wicked." She picked up the loaded tray and moved to the door. He came up behind her, as if to follow her out. She turned partially toward him, and bobbed into a small curtsey to lighten the mood. "Could the gentleman get the door, please?"

He lifted the tray out of her hands.

"Liam, I need that. I still have to circulate."

"They'll have gone through to the dining room now. You can stay a little longer."

"I need to get back," she insisted. "You know she'll want me to pour at the table. And they'll notice you're not there." She reached for the tray. The glasses wobbled as he moved it farther away from her. She could see it now: he'd spill the tray, glasses would break, and the linoleum would get torn. She'd get the blame and owe the Booths more in damages than she'd make tonight. "Please put that down."

He placed the tray on the kitchen island with a rattle that made her cringe. She reached to turn the lock and get out of there before he asked her on another date.

He seized her wrist with his left hand and closed her in an embrace from behind, pulling her arm across her body, tight under her breasts. Her left arm was pinned against her side. He leaned into her and she tipped off balance. Her cheek pressed against the cold brass of the door's high handplate. She struggled to regain her footing as she fought back panic. A bra strap fell off her shoulder. He kissed her neck as he ran his other hand along her thigh, pushing up the hem of her black skirt.

"Liam, please," she said shakily, her breathing ragged.

He laughed breathily into her hair. "I know you want it," he said hoarsely, misinterpreting her words. "I love you. I'll always take care of you. I know what you need. We've waited a long time for this."

She stared blindly at the brass handplate and tried to pull her skirt hem down with a trembling, hobbled hand.

"Please…"

He laughed again and managed to get a hand into the waistband of her panties. He yanked both hose and underwear down her buttocks, jerking her like a ragdoll. She was stunned with fear and disbelief. Her breasts pressed into his restraining arm with every jerk, every gasp.

"God, this is hot." Brad's bragging hadn't been wrong yet about his women's sexual tastes.

It was as if her dead husband were alive all over again, angry and drunk on his own high blood sugar, taking it out on her. She heard the jingle of a belt buckle, the ragged sound of a zipper, the slithering of cloth, and the muffled thump of a leather belt hitting the floor. Some part of his flesh reached between her naked thighs.

"No!" She elbowed him in the gut fast and hard, once, twice, again.

He released her. He doubled over and staggered backwards. The pants around his ankles tripped him, and he fell onto his bare ass on the slick floor. Alice flicked the lock open and stumbled through the door. The skirt fell into place over her nakedness as she ran into the formal sitting room, her stride shortened by the mid-thigh web of hose.

"Wait!" he called after her. "We'll meet later! We can work something out!" She didn't look back.

He kicked the door. "Bitch! You'll screw that slut Brad and my incoherent two-timing Weegie thug cousin, but not me?" he muttered angrily as he pulled on his pants.

Alice yanked her clothes up on the fly. Outside the dining room, she paused to smooth her skirt and slow her breathing, composing herself with shaking hands to finish out the dinner party. She wiped her cheeks carefully. She entered the room, eyes lowered deferentially to the important company.

Liam hurried into the dining room and carefully took his seat, smiling his perfect smile to the people on either side. Laura Beth narrowed her eyes, looking between the two latecomers. The slut's hair and clothes were more disheveled than usual, giving it away. Alice blushed and hurried out of the room to get the wine for the salad course.

29: Family Reunion

Nick groaned from the warm cocoon of his bed. The knocking repeated. He lunged out of bed, only to fall flat on his face, the sheets tangled around his ankles like a snare. "Fook!" he roared, struggling to disentangle himself as the knocking continued.

"Haud the bus," he called at the door. He staggered across the carpet. The view through the peephole jolted him fully awake. "Fook me," he breathed. He brushed back his hair and rubbed at his teeth. He looked down at his plain white T-shirt and scants and shrugged. He opened the door a crack and wedged his thin frame into it.

The other man gave him a broad smile, his gray eyes bright. He held out a hand. "Liam MacAlister. Your cousin."

"Ah ken whae ye ur," he answered brusquely, ignoring the hand. "Fook ye want?" He made a show of looking up and down the hallway. "We huvin a wee clan gatherin or somehin?"

"Can I come in, please?" He ignored the belligerence.

"Ah wis stackin up zeds byraway. Awright, but."

Nick shrugged and stepped out of the doorframe. He sauntered to the kitchen island, leaving his guest standing outside. His casual gait contradicted the tension he felt. He settled onto a stool, planted an elbow on the island, and propped up his face.

"Whit kin Ah dae ye fur, Liam MacAlister, ma wee cousin?"

The other man hovered awkwardly on the opposite side of the island at the end closest to the door. He opened his mouth to speak, but was interrupted.

"Dain't ken aboot ye mate, Ah need a bevvy but." Nick slumped backwards to reach the refrigerator, dropping one foot to the floor for balance. He pulled out a wee heavy, shucked it open, and put it down on the island at arm's length. He pulled out a second for himself.

"It's only two in the afternoon," Liam said incredulously.

Nick took a long swallow. "Disnae matter tae me. Ah'm on swing shift. An' Ah wager ur no' plannin tae go back intae the office theday neither." He nodded encouragingly between cousin and bottle. "Gawn yerself." He held up his bottle and waited for the clink. "*Slàinte.*"

Liam repeated the toast and tipped up the bottle briefly. He came around the island and perched gingerly on the end stool, leaving an empty seat between them.

"Tae whit dae Ah owe the pleasure?"

"Can't cousins visit each other? I missed you at your parents' dinner party last night. I was concerned you weren't well. Or were trying to avoid an awkward situation." He smiled, a little too carnivorously for Nick's taste.

Nick stared, feeling inadequate and ugly. "Aye. So whit?"

"Well, I was talking to a mutual friend. And it seems that you forgot to tell her an inconvenient truth that would have made last night a lot more interesting." The gray eyes stared back at him angrily.

"Whit ur ye bletherin on aboot, ya bloody toaff?" The hairs on the back of his neck prickled. He took a drink to cover his unease. "It's nane ay yer affair," he said, now on guard.

"Interesting choice of words." The American smirked. "I can totally understand why you would fall for Alice. But you don't deserve her."

"An' Ah suppose ye think ye dae? Is tha' whit this is, ye warnin me aff? Nae chance. No' gawnae happen," he growled.

"I'd say that's up to her, wouldn't you? She does have some choice in this." He smiled his Bonnie Prince Charming smile, sensing the other man's unease. "But I have an advantage: I'm not already engaged. I didn't know you were keeping that on the down-low. Sorry. Guess I let that cat out of the bag." He tilted up his ale, giving his insufferable gloat a brief rest. "But there's a silver lining. Alice assured me that you were only a fling anyway, so Laura Beth may be willing to look past it and forgive you."

"Tha's pure mental." Nick tried to hide his repulsion and growing doubt. "Ur a rare patter merchant."

"I'd say you more so than me. You definitely have some explaining to do." He laughed, showing his white teeth. "Good luck with that. But while you're shoveling chicken shit, Alice will be where she was last night: on top of me, screaming with pleasure. All. Night. Long."

Nick exploded into action. His cousin yelped in pain and sprawled on the floor, holding his broken nose.

"Get fook oot ma hoose," he roared. "Afore Ah fookin kill ye!"

"Do it, then!" Liam bellowed back. His mouth twisted in pain as he struggled to his feet. "Come on! I've had worse on the rugby field. You're nothing but talk and a leather jacket!" He spread his arms wide, letting blood run down his face and drip onto the linoleum.

Nick grabbed two fistfuls of ruined shirt and bulldozed him through the kitchen. He freed one hand to yank the door open and shove the bloodied man out.

"Ye'd best haul yer bahookie tae emergency services if ye want tae rescue yer lovely face, ya fookin eejit."

"You'll be hearing from my lawyer!" bellowed the American, nasally, around his bloodied hand.

"Tha's a fine way tae treat faimly! Ah'll shoo ye hoo we dae it in Glesga!"

Nick lunged back inside and grabbed Liam's ale off the kitchen island by its neck. He rushed back out, causing his cousin to release his nose and raise his fists. He upturned the bottle and smashed it on the wall, soaking his bare legs and peppering them with shards of glass. He dropped to a crouch, threatening his cousin with the weapon. Liam shook his head and backed away. The Scot straightened and turned the broken stump against his own forearm. Blood flowed from the gash.

"Gawn then. Ah'll tell the polis hoo ye cut me in ma oon hoose!"

"You're fucking crazy!" Liam turned tail and ran.

"Aye, the noo ur gettin it!" Nick yelled after him.

He slammed the door. The pungent smell of ale followed him in. He held his arm up to keep from adding to the mess on the floor. He tossed the bloodied bottle stump in the sink.

"Cheers! Tha' wis pure dead mental," chuckled Nick Two, deeply impressed. "Shocker ye wasted the bevvy, but."

"Shut it. Wis fur a gude cause," muttered Nick absently, pressing a clean dishcloth over the cut and hurrying to grab crazy glue and butterfly bandages from the medicine cabinet. "Ah think Ah missed oniehin important in ma erm. Fook."

He pulled away the towel and dripped a ribbon of glue into the rapidly refilling cut and pulled it closed with the bandages. He waited until the glue set before carefully blotting away the remaining blood with a shaking hand. His head throbbed as the adrenalin rush subsided. Next, he checked his legs for glass splinters and cleaned up the small cuts. He'd been lucky not to get any shards in his bare feet. He was looking quite the worse for wear lately. Finally squared away, he paced, clutching his ale in his good hand and holding the other arm against his chest.

"Wis he sayin the fookin eejit is engaged? Tae *Pavlov's Belle?*" He ranted to himself. "Da would have telt me, as grandwean crazy as he is. Widnae he? Unless ma eejit brither got cauld feet, an' Ah get his dirty wahrk. Agin. Ah'm fooked. Christ on a bike, Ah need a fookin drink," he announced. "Ach." He noticed the bottle in his fist and drained it. "I need tae talk tae Alice."

He opened a third bottle of wee heavy and set it on the kitchen island so he could dial. His fingers fumbled through the wrong buttons again and again. He sucked in a long draft of ale and pressed each button with tedious precision.

"Hello?"

He hurried to swallow and halfway choked. "It's Nick, byraway." He muffled a cough and cleared his throat.

"I know. You're up early."

"Aye." He ran a hand over his hair, which fell back immediately.

"There's a movie playing downtown I wanted to see. You interested in fitting it in before your shift? It's at eight."

"Mibbe…" He took another swig of ale. "Uh, Alice—"

"Yes, Lowlander?" she said playfully.

"Ah'm no' engaged tae her," he blurted. "Tae ma cowahrker fae the lab. Ah mean, Ah ken ma cousin telt ye we ur. We're no', but." He hugged himself tight with the injured arm, subconsciously protecting his scarred ribs.

A long pause answered him. "Why do you think he would say that?" she said carefully.

"Ma cowahrker, Laura Beth. She mist huv been tellin people, Mary an' Liam an' that."

"Why would she do that?" She struggled to control her rising anger. That must be why she'd been offered the private investigation gig. A honey trap to find out how faithless a future husband was. And she'd fallen right into bed with him.

"She's pure mental. Ah've no' gied her the time ay day since Ah've been err."

"She showed me her ring." She felt sick to her stomach.

"We're no' thegither," he said desperately. "But we micht huv been. Afore Ah came tae the States, ken."

"You *think* you were engaged, but you don't know?" Her voice was angry, unbelieving. It all fit together. The woman's threatening tone and posturing. The ring. A new dent in the old Ford. Liam's warnings. "How wicked big of a drunk are you?"

"Ah'm no' a drunk," he protested, tossing his second empty ale bottle into the recycling bin, where it clinked against several others.

Nick Two raised an eyebrow.

"It's complicated. Ah dain't ken if Ah kin iven explain it."

"Well, I can think of a few ways. You're a liar or an asshole. Or a lying asshole. No wait…you were in an accident and have amnesia, is that it? But not all your memory is gone, just certain parts. Like your engagement!"

"It's no' like tha'. Haun tae God. Ah kin explain. Ah wull explain. But no' when ur huvin a wobbly at me!"

"You're surprised I'm 'having a wobbly,' Nick?" Her voice hit a warning note. "You made a fucking fool out of me. I didn't listen to Liam. I believed what I saw. I trusted you. I *slept* with you. You didn't think that being engaged was something you should share until now?"

"Ah dinnae ken aboot it!" The phone was slippery in his hand and his throat felt like sandpaper. "Gies a chance tae explain. Ye should trust me. Ah trusted ye, in spite ay the Black Widdy shite. Ah'm a novelty fur ye, a fookin accent, tha's aw. Nuchin but a tadger in a kilt. A hairy fookin coo. Ye wis onerly bidin time tae throw me over fur someyin else onie road. Like ma fookin cousin Liam. Ah'll wager tha's whae yer dinner wis wey, no' wahrk. Well go on. Dain't let me stoap ye. Ye awready did it wanst." His heart felt like it would burst.

"At least Liam can remember whether or not he gave someone an engagement ring."

"Alice? Alice!" He was only talking to himself. "Fookin hell!"

"Tha' went well," snickered Nick Two.

"Fook ye! This is aw yer fault!" Nick exploded, kicking his best friend in the gut and sending him crashing into the kitchen island.

"Ye sure aboot tha', ur ye, ya fookin chancer?" Nick Two gasped. They stared at each other, one crumpled in a heap on the kitchen floor, the other frozen in place.

"Ah dain't need ye or yer shite, Nicktoon," Nick growled.

"Oh aye? Then hoo am Ah err?" his roommate sneered back. "Ach. Tha's right. Ah'm no' err an' nivver huv been, cheers tae ye, ya numpty."

Nick looked away, ashamed.

"Ur bleedin, byraway." Nick Two gestured weakly and laughed.

He looked down at his arm. The cut and the small, crooked white bandages were unchanged from their Frankenstein appearance, but a fresh red stain spread on his white undershirt. He clutched his side in panic. When he looked back up, his mate was gone. On the dash to the bathroom, he grabbed the tube of crazy glue and yanked off his shirt. The mirror showed two overlapping scars, one newer than the other, but no blood.

30: Break Up Number Two and a Brilliant Plan

Nick shifted uneasily on the postage-stamp sized doorstep. The ticking of the cooling motorcycle engine was the only sound in the aftermath of his knock. She should have been home from work by now. He listened for footsteps either approaching the door or scuttling deeper. He knocked again. He was thankful of the bushes hiding his pitiable figure from the street. *Whit did ye dae this time, laddie?* Da's voice said from memory, patient and fond, tinged with disappointment. "Ach," he sighed. The word rose into the quickly darkening sky as steam. He retreated to the motorcycle, formulating a Plan B to fill the hours before his shift, and getting dead drunk was looking like the best option.

Alice heard the engine roar to life as she neared the corner. She could have stopped him before he walked the motorcycle to the street. Instead, she ran for the alley and ducked into the overgrown hedge, hoping the fur of her coat would blend with the skeletal gray branches. As the motorcycle flashed past the end of the alley, she felt the weight of the day come crashing down and sank to her knees. The damp soil exuded the pungent smell of stale tomcat urine. Engulfed in a sudden wave of exhaustion and loss, it took a monumental effort to crawl through the thin bottom branches, heave herself to her feet, and travel the remaining distance to the door. Tears blurred her vision. It took a long, fumbling minute to find her keys.

She stumbled into the living room and dropped her purse to the floor. She shed her coat and shoes beside it, not bothering to put them away. Falling onto the futon fully clothed, she hoped sleep would devour her quickly. She missed him. Did she really have a right to judge, to give up on him without letting him explain? The engagement had been a shock, but it was a way out of what the assignment had turned into. She shouldn't have become deeply involved. How could she have explained why she had sought him out? If only she hadn't been in league with the mother who'd let him down, it might have been different. This was what she got for thinking her life could change for the better.

For the first time since the Black Widow lawsuits, news stories, and hate calls had ended, she didn't care if she woke up again.

* * * * * * * *

"This nicht wid pit a beard on ye," Nick grumbled to himself. After reading the same paragraph four times and getting nothing from it, he gave up. He stowed the detective novel in his locker and took a roundabout route back. He ran all the stairwells, this time remembering to stretch out first. He sprawled across the lobby couch, staring blankly at the introductory slideshow in the reception area. After half an hour, he could recite it by heart as he paced. Adding different accents, voices, and inflections to it failed to lighten his mood, as did a version accompanied by every silly walk from the Monty Python "Ministry of Silly Walks" sketch.

One eternity and a nap later, he was struggling with the last sudoku in the book when Pavlov's Belle slammed in. Angry blue eyes narrowed even more than usual in her fine-boned face. His stomach writhed. He convinced himself this was for the greater good, not just his own.

"Ah, uh, aboot…" He pointed back and forth between the two of them. "It's me an' no ye."

She crossed her arms tightly. "You think?" she said scathingly and turned away.

"Ah should huv said somehin airlier byraway. Ah huv a lot ay doots. Self-doots. Ah feel like Ah'm no' the same pairson tha' Ah wis, back when we, uh….ye ken." He left it hanging, since he didn't actually know, but could guess. He grimaced, glad her back was still facing him. "Ah think we should take some time aff. Time fur me tae figure things oot, ken. See ither people an' that."

"Well, you got a head start there," she snapped in a tone that made him glad he didn't have a brand new pickup truck for her to reshape with a baseball bat.

"Fair enow. Ah kin tell Dave has some strong feelings fur ye. An' yees huv been wahrkin thegither lang afore Ah shooed up. Mibbe ye should resolve aw tha', onie road."

She spun around, ponytail swinging. "I need to resolve some loser's crush." She laughed bitterly.

"Ah jist need tae be sure," he said quietly, no longer thinking about the Belle. "Ma mither emigrated tae get marrit ontae ma da, an' they dinnae make it. Wis dead hard on ivrybody when she left." He hung his head and waited. He hated playing that card, but he meant it. He was surprised his brother had gone for an international relationship because of it. He always had been a bit daft.

She stared at him for a long time before answering. "You are making a big mistake, Nick Kerr. I may or may not be around when you get done sowing your wild oats with every lowlife in town. Just don't fuck up the research too. A lot went into it." She uncrossed her arms and walked away. The lab door slammed behind her.

"No' the first nor the last mistake," he muttered and heaved himself out of the hard plastic chair.

He rarely had a problem sleeping on swing shift, but today he lay awake with an unfamiliar hollow feeling gnawing at his insides. Alice hadn't answered her cell or work phones, and he'd left as many messages as he dared. The creaks and groans of the apartment served only to accentuate the emptiness. Conversations and canned TV laughter drifted through thin walls. The Nicktoon had pissed off as well. He actually missed the abuse; at least then he could take the good cop role and argue for a redeeming quality in himself. He downed a couple of wee heavies back to back. Instead of dulling his mood, they served only to aggravate it. A hot shower made him cleaner but no closer to sleep. Between the alcoholic buzz and the ambient noises, his only chance at rest was to wedge his head under the pillows. The soft lingering scent of summer heather from Alice's hair wafted out. He threw the pillow across the room.

He expected his friend to stick in the knife, but the Nicktoon remained absent. He took up the slack himself. "Ach, the lovely Alice. Ah bet rinoo she's aw over yer wee cousin like a cheap coat."

The weekend had been a blur of pacing, drinking, and checking the phone, followed by sleepless days after interminable back shifts struggling to keep his eyes open. Once sleep finally took hold, it required the gut-wrenching stench of the neighbors' cooking to rouse him. Feeling hungover from his instantaneous nausea and deep, disorienting sleep, he cracked open resentful eyes to an indeterminate gray light that could have been morning or late afternoon.

The Nicktoon was draped limply across the kitchen island, snoring softly. Nick lifted his head by a handful of hair, revealing a lopsided permanent marker mustache. "Numpty. Ye nivver could haud yer ale. Hope Ah did tha' tae ye."

The dark eyes fluttered open. Nick released his head, grinning at the sudden jerk as his friend resumed motor control. Nick Two gave him a baleful stare through bleary eyes.

"Whit's yer score, then? Two women bloody-minded at ma last coont."

"Since when dae ye care?" Nick cracked open a bottle of soda. "Ur a crabbit wee shite theday, urnae ye? 'Pricklier than a hedgehog crisp,' Alice wid say."

His mate stretched and scratched his balls leisurely to illustrate his disdain. "Alice wid say ur a fookin prick, haud the hedgehog an' the crisp."

"Ah wis pit in the frame fur tha', ken."

"Were ye the noo?" Nick Two stood up from his stool and inspected it. "Is this the wan whir yees..." He made a rude gesture involving a circle and a single digit. "Ye should mount an historic plaque, seein as ye wullnae be gettin onie mair ay tha'."

"Fook ye, ya numpty." Nick retreated to the closet and jabbed himself into some clothes. "Ye fund love, apparently. In questionable taste, but love onie road. Whit's so wrang wey the same fur me? The thoat ay nivver seein Alice agin is makin me pure mental. Ah want tae be wey her, if she'll iven huv me the noo, cheers tae yees."

"Ye want tae get marrit ontae her? The Black Widdy? Ya mad bastart."

"She's a lang sight be'er than yer wee doll," he responded stubbornly.

"Ye lied tae her, but. Aboot mair than an engagement. Hoo ur ye gawn tae explain tha' an' keep her fae offin ye?"

"First Ah huv tae get her talkin tae me agin." Nick stared at the poorly drawn mustache. "Ah got a brain wave." He ran back to the closet. "Whit day is it?"

"Christmas Day. The spirits huv done it aw in wan nicht," the Nicktoon snarked. In response to the dirty look and raised fist, he corrected, "Friday. Thirty-one October. Ye'd best turn supergrass," he scolded. "Ye cannae hide behind me onie mair an' use me as an excuse tae dae this shite. An' tae make yerself feel be'er aboot daein it, mind. Ah'm no' fur huvin it onie mair. Ah'm pure dead serious. Ah wullnae be err when ye get back. Or iver agin, byraway."

"A man kin dream," Nick retorted.

Alice eyed her midriff critically in the long mirror as she smoothed the slick black fabric of her fitted catsuit. Her figure was the same as always, but she imagined its imminent distortion. It had been so long since she'd considered sleeping with anyone that she'd forgotten about contraception. What was the point of going out tonight? She shouldn't drink, not as long as she was still considering keeping it. She loved the costumes though. It might even cheer her up to see how many coeds dressed up as the Black Widow murderer this year, wearing some sort of extremely inauthentic microskirted outfit with spider-themed accessories. She snorted at the thought. *You've been used and betrayed before and haven't died of it. But—"if he left off dreaming about you, where do you suppose you'd be? You'd go out—bang!—just like a candle."*

"Shut the fuck up," she growled at her reflection. "I do not need a man to exist." She patted her abdomen. "Right, little Nicky?" She gave herself a twisted smile, staring into her reflection's eyes as if subduing any disagreement.

"You're out drinking? Don't you have to work tonight?" Alice raised her voice to be heard in the crowded pub.

"Aye on baith coonts."

Juxtaposed with fire-red curls, her disapproving green eyes seemed to glow. She eyed him from the top of his tam o'shanter, down his awful fake orange beard, along the formal jacket and tartan, to the flashes and laced ghillie brogues. "Seriously? Now you break out the full deal, complete with stereotypical extras? You look ridonkulous." She fought a smile.

"See tha's hoo Ah dinnae wear it tae the festival. Pure ridonkulous."

"Is that a dead opossum under your arm?" She raised an eyebrow.

He squeezed the lump of fake fur protectively. "Tha's a haggis right oot the Hielands. Ah caught it maself."

"You're from the Lowlands. Unless that was a pile of shit too." She enjoyed his pained expression. "Why not bagpipes?"

"Ah dinnae huv time tae get onie or make um oot ay sticks an' an auld bunnit." While his mouth ran away with him, his eyes ran up and down her black bodysuit, tall black boots, wide belt, fake pistols strapped to her thighs, and bullet wrist cuffs.

"Well, a haggis is close enough, then, I guess."

"Cheers." He rocked back and forth in his ghillie brogues, admiring her. He gestured at her hair. "Is tha'…"

"Only temporary."

He stroked the bushy orange beard. "Awso temporary."

She barked a laugh. "No kidding. And you don't really look ridonkulous." *Wicked sexy, actually, but I'm not telling him that.* "Except for that clown wig on your face."

"Ach. Well then, on behauf ay centuries ay Scots, apology accepted." He gestured at the cat suit. "Ye sairtainly dain't look ridonkulous thenicht. Ah thoat ye wid be decked oot as Alice in Wunnerland, but."

She wrinkled her nose. "Why? Are you a pedophile?"

"Whit? Nut! Whit aboot the Tim Burton version? She wisnae a wee lass."

She shrugged and made a half-hearted raspberry.

"So ye ur…" *Pure magic.*

"The Black Widow, of course. From *The Avengers.*" She struck a wide-legged action-heroine pose with a fake gun.

"Pure dead brilliant. Boattle isnae in it."

"Thank you, Lowlander. Or should I say Highlander?"

"Thenicht onerly." He nodded at the room as she reholstered the plastic pistol. "Ah'm no' keepin ye fae oniehin, am Ah? Ye ken, Black Widdy shite. Defendin justice an' seducin an' assassinatin an' that."

She gave him a sharp look. He grimaced. "Ach. Ah'm in ma oon road. Ah dinnae mean oniehin by it, hen."

"I'll let you slide. Costume contest is at midnight. Cash prize. Nothing else going on but some serious drinking and people-watching until then." She found herself falling for him again. She craned to look around behind him. "Where's your fiancée?"

"Dain't ken, dain't care. Fur tha record, Ah broke it aff officially, as we hudnae been thegither since before Ah came tae the States." All of which was true.

"Like that makes it all better." She shook her head, hand on hip. "As if I can believe anything you say."

"Ye kin ask ma mate Dave. Ah spottit hum airlier…" He searched the room. "Tha's hum. 'Moan then."

Balancing haggis and drink, he took her hand and pulled her into the crowd. He clapped a disco king on the back, making the man's afro wig wobble precariously. Dave Barrows turned, holding a beer out away from a polyester shirt with a pattern so loud it could be heard over the roar of the crowded bar.

"Hey, man! Holy shit. Dude, you are hilarious." He took Alice's hand during the introductions and nodded distractedly. "Can you hand me some of those?" He gestured at a napkin dispenser. "Nick made me spill my drink, and I nearly lost my hair. Again." He grinned. Several large gold medallions jingled together as he toweled his abundant chest hair dry, oblivious to Nick's covetous look.

"Urnae wahrkin thenicht? Hoo'd ye manage tha'?"

Dave tossed the wad of damp napkins onto a passing tray. "I finally got a sub for a change. Had to ask the weekend guy, Mickey Patel. Laura Beth wouldn't do it. Can you believe that? After all the times I've switched for her."

"Ah'll vouch fur tha'. He's awyis hauf-asleep fae stoatin aroond on random shifts," he said as an apology to Dave for his past outburst.

"You still go in at midnight, or is that why Laura Beth wouldn't sub for me?" Dave eyed Alice's costume.

"Ah'm still on. Takin it aisy, but." He saluted with his glass.

"I hear you. Though no one would know the difference on graveyard anyway. Am I right?"

"Oh aye." He turned to Alice, catching the frizzy beard on the epaulets of his jacket, and gestured her closer. "Hayonya Dave, fur tha record, wis Ah engaged tae Laura Beth?"

"Sutphin? Fucking what the what?" Dave clutched his forehead and spread his fingers in a burst, making an explosion sound. "Mind blown. There's no fucking way. She totally hates you, man. And the feeling is mutual. Besides, she knows better than to compromise the research by dating coworkers. That's why I'm out of luck. Not that I don't keep trying."

"See? Proof tha' Ah wisnae a complete lyin, cheatin bastart."

"Operative word being 'complete.' I'm not sure that really covers it. She probably hates you because you forgot you were engaged." She turned to Dave. "He paid you to say that, didn't he?"

"No, I swear. Though he probably should, since it seems I'm bailing him out of some shit." He leaned over to stage-whisper in Nick's ear. "Damn, man. If you're juggling that many hotties, the least you can do is throw me a bone."

"Nae danger. Ah put in a gude word fur ye wey the Third Wheel."

"Thanks man. Fucking beautiful." He wiped a fake tear.

"Ma bell, mate. Gie ye anither?"

Dave nodded. Alice waved her soda in answer to Nick's request. He held out the blob of fur to her.

"Haud tha' fur me, aye? Take gude care, he's the rare anticlockwise kind."

"You're presumptuous, expecting me to take care of your hairy ball." She held it doubtfully, as if expecting it to pee on her like an excited puppy.

"It's a sure sign that 'he'll be back'," Dave chipped in helpfully, doing a Shwarzenegger impersonation.

"Whit he said." No one seemed to notice Nick anymore.

"Especially since I've got him by the ball." She grinned and settled it in the crook of her arm.

"What the hell is it, anyway?" Dave asked the blob's current handler, leaning in close to check both it and her out.

"He said it's a haggis. I think it's basically a Scottish jackalope," Alice explained. "You know, a taxidermy prank. Though this one looks more like a tribble."

Nick hovered like a third wheel himself, wondering if she was making him pay by flirting with his coworker, or if she really was oblivious to the effect her costume and conversation were having. He absently scratched at the scab on his forearm through his jacket.

Dave laughed. "Sweet. You know, the vet school used to have a jackalope in the anatomy lab just to mess with the first-years. God, I wanted to put it out at open house the year I worked it, but nobody else had a sense of humor."

"That would have been awesome," she said with enthusiasm. "I'd love to get my camera lens on that."

Dave beamed, waving a finger at her. "Wait. I remember you. The red hair threw me off. You were there that year! You wanted to take photographs, but they told us we couldn't allow it. Some crazy shit about someone putting pictures from the previous year's open house online and PETA went nuts over it." He shook his head. "Unbelievable. I thought our whole point was to get people excited about it, right? Not let the terrorists win."

She nodded eagerly. Nick desperately wedged himself into the conversation. "Ah could gie ye access. Thenicht if ye like." He raised his eyebrows encouragingly.

Her eyes lit up, this time for him. "Really? You would do that? Is that allowed?"

"It's a gray area," Dave shrugged, categorizing the technique for potential future use. "Besides, I'm on for Mickey on Saturday morning, and I'm cool with it."

"I'd be long gone before the end of your shift," Alice agreed.

"It could work," Dave insisted.

"It wull wahrk. Ah promise."

Alice gave Nick a brief, awkward hug and kissed his cheek above the fake beard. She could feel his muscles through the thin jacket, but the effect was ruined by the strong chemical smell of his prosthetic beard. He winked at Dave over her shoulder.

"Fucker. I'll get the drinks, but you're still paying." He held out his hand and Nick slapped a bill into it. Dave began singing The Kinks and dancing as much as the crowd allowed. "He'll end up blowing all his wages for the week, all for a cuddle and a peck on the cheek..."

He turned to wedge himself into the throng, and tangled himself in a long dress. "Sorry, sorry, sorry," he rattled. "Whoa! So that's why you wouldn't sub for me!"

He loomed over Laura Beth in a Cinderella dress. "Can I buy you a drink?" She shook her head, causing the tiara on top of her updo to wobble. "C'mon, it's on Nick's dime." He waved the paper money.

She looked around, trying to find a way through the crowd that would take her away from him.

"I'll forgive you for the subbing thing if you have a drink with me," Dave coaxed.

"I have to go." The crowd squashed her against his beer-damp shirt. She cringed.

"It's not even midnight yet. The magic won't wear off for hours!" he joked, waggling his eyebrows suggestively.

"Stop making fun of me. I feel stupid enough as it is." She glanced in Alice's direction and fought to gather her full skirt.

He noticed her look. "I'm not making fun of you. Scout's honor." He held up his hand in a three-fingered salute. "I think you look amazing."

"Okay," she said grudgingly. "One drink."

"Yes! Thank you Lord!" He dipped his knees and raised his arms in triumph. His grin threatened to split his moon face in two. "Hang on to my shoulders for a wild ride."

He turned around and she gripped his shoulders hesitantly. He pressed into the crowd and bulldozed their way to the bar. Once they were securely taking up barfront property, he turned and sized her up.

"You look like you want to watch the world burn." She narrowed her eyes at him and nodded slightly. "I have just the thing. He leaned in, held up two fingers to the bartender, and ordered something she couldn't overhear.

Laura Beth crossed her arms as she waited. She chewed on her bottom lip as the bartender set up two half glasses of stout and poured mixed shots.

"What did you order?" She looked at the collection of glassware with distrust.

"Irish car bombs. You take the shot—"

"What's in there?" She wrinkled her nose at the cloudy glass.

"Irish whiskey and Irish cream. Okay so far?" He asked solicitously. She nodded. "Okay. Now comes the fun part. You drop it into the big glass and chug-a-lug." At her look, he said, "If you don't, it'll go everywhere. And taste nasty. Trust me." He smiled reassuringly. He lifted his shot and nodded at her to do the same. "We'll go together. Ready?"

"I don't know about this," she backpedaled. "I'll watch you do it first."

"Okay. On three. One...two...three...go!" He dropped his shot into her pint glass.

"What!" she shrieked.

He waved frantically as the bubbling mess surged in the glass. "Go! Go! Go!"

She grabbed the glass and drank. Dave dropped the remaining shot in his own glass and tipped it up. Voices sprang up around them, chanting, "Bomb! Bomb!" A lopsided idea formed in her mind as she choked down the drink. Near the bottom of the glass, her tiara slipped in her blonde hair. She clutched it, pressed it back in cockeyed, and slammed the glass on the bar.

His empty glass landed beside hers. He hooted, impressed. "What did you think?"

She fanned her face like a beauty queen trying not to cry.

"Want another?" He bent his knees so he could look into her eyes.

"Oh my God! I hate you for that!" She covered her mouth and belched, trying not to gag. "But it was just what the doctor ordered." She grabbed a handful of chest hair and planted a quick peck on his lips, silencing his squeak of discomfort. "Now be good, you hear," she drawled and shoved him out of her way.

"Wait! Um…okay. Catch you later!" He called after her. His smile spread from ear to ear. He started singing again. "I'll end up blowing all my wages for the week, all for a cuddle and a peck on the LIPS! Come dancing!"

31: Gray Area

"Don't forget your haggis." Alice handed it over as they left the pub with an hour to spare before his shift. "So, Lowlander," she crooned, "did you go traditional tonight?"

"Ah'm decked oot in ma tartan, Prince Charlie jaiket, ghillie shirt, ghillie brogues, flashes, a stupit tartan bunnit, an' an orange bush on ma coupon."

"And you brought a pet haggis."

"Aye." He settled it on his hip and patted it. "It disnae get mich mair traditional."

"You didn't answer the question, Dr. Kahhrrr," she purred.

He held up a hand to fend her off. She advanced, wiggling her fingers and eyebrows at him. He tossed the haggis at her as a distraction. As she fumbled it, he sprinted down the sidewalk, dodging clusters of costumed people. She yelled and pursued.

"I'm going to find out any moment now, if you keep that up!" she called after him.

He turned and ran backward for a moment. Grinning broadly, he flipped up the back of his kilt. She roared and put on a burst of speed. He spun forward again, laughing and whooping.

She caught him by the arm and jostled into him, her cheeks pink and dyed hair wild.

"Ah huv a confession tae make," he said softly.

The smile faded from her face. "What, another forgotten fiancée?" she joked stiffly.

"Nae." He dropped his voice to a conspiratorial level. "Ah'm wearin scants."

He dodged her fist and sprinted down the street. *An' hopefully no' fur lang.*

*   *   *   *   *   *   *   *

"He didn't even notice me," Laura Beth complained to the kilted teddy bear. "He's taking her into the building tonight. 'To take pictures.' " She waved finger quotes. "Photograph me like one of your French girls, Nick," she snarled.

She balled up the Cinderella dress and threw it deep into her closet, pitching the tiara after it. A handful of bobby pins tumbled onto the dresser like pine needles after Christmas sags into the new year. She shook out her hair and angrily bundled it into a ponytail. She yanked on jeans and a long-sleeved t-shirt. She needed to get her head in the game, not forget anything important. She grabbed pen and scratch paper and began her list. *Costume. Rubber gloves. Siphon. Gift bag. Gelatin. Lighter. Fireworks*—fingers crossed they were still available for football game celebrations. She finished her list with *recycling bin*. She tapped the pen against her lip, then added *wine*. It would be backup in case the recycling had already been collected. Or she could drink it.

Nick stopped in the doorframe and leaned his head into the bedroom, thankful he'd been forgiven enough to be invited in. The small windows were covered with blackout shades so that the only light came from a dim overhead fixture. A large metal device stood on a work table against the far wall. A cocoon-like sack hung from the ceiling, and a crude handmade drying rack hung next to it with a few prints clipped to it. The room would have barely contained a double bed, but it made a sizeable darkroom.

"So this is whir the magic happens?"

She glanced up from packing a camera bag with a look that clearly said to cut the crap.

"Aye, tha' wis pure dead awfy. Ah'm no' iven gawn tae make like Ah wis jawin aboot tha photies, byraway. Dis it mean Ah'm oot ay luck err?"

She shrugged. "Admitting you have a problem is the first step to recovery. So there's still hope for you."

He leaned far into the room as she came toward him, and reached an arm around her waist to pull her close. She pinched his thumb and lifted his hand away. "Not that much hope."

"Hoo kin ye say nae tae this coupon?" He cocked his head and fluttered his eyelashes. "Ach, jist a wee meenit." He took off the tam o'shanter and clutched it under his chin, shook his hair down over his forehead, and fluttered his eyelashes again.

She rolled her eyes and gently pushed him aside. "Are you sure this is okay?"

"Aye. Right as rain." His eyes were stuck on the curve-hugging suit.

She punched his arm. "Not my costume. Me going with you tonight."

"Ooyah! Ye been wahrkin oot, huv ye?" He rubbed his arm dramatically. "As lang as we pit ivryhing back the way it wis. Ah'm thinkin of quittin soon onie road. Tae mich baggage." He lifted the bag's strap from her shoulder. "Speakin ay which, let me take tha'."

"Thanks. You don't have to…"

"Nae bother. Whit dae ye huv in err? Weighs a right ton, so it dis." He hefted the bag over his head and settled the strap across his chest.

"Just my camera and different lenses and lots of film." She eyed his wiry form straddled by the bulky bag.

He tossed the hair out of his eyes, crammed his cap back on, and bounced to settle the weight better.

"Do I have time to change?" She looked down at herself dubiously.

"Nut," he said definitively, and gestured for her to lead.

Laura Beth placed the full wine bottle into the seasonal gift bag. The makeshift cork was secured with electrical tape. She placed the package carefully by the apartment door and removed the dishwashing gloves in order to change into her second costume of the night.

"Who are they going to blame? The one who looks like he escaped from a motorcycle gang, that's who. And his criminal girlfriend." Smiling at herself in the full-length mirror, she smoothed the black catsuit and adjusted the cheap plastic accessories. She tucked a lighter into the flimsy pouch and snapped it shut. She tucked her hair into a tight swim cap, then carefully fitted the long wig over it. She secured the edges with bobby pins and arranged the red curls over her shoulders.

She turned side to side in front of the mirror to see all the angles. Not perfect. But close enough to tell whomever would be reviewing the security footage whose fingerprints they'd find on her little present. If anything would be left of it. She was unsure on that part of her plan, but better to have more arrows pointing in a certain direction than not enough. She checked her cell phone for the time and added it to the pouch. Time to get this party started.

"Let me clock in an' huv a wee blether wey Mickey. Then Ah'll get changed afore Ah get ye set up wey the bones, awright hen?" Nick smoothed his kilt, wanting to touch Alice but not sure of the reception. He looked through the windshield at the recessed courtyard that opened onto the Commons. "Anatomy is in the basement, opposite side fae ma lab. Ah think it's best if ye drive roond back." He looked at her through his falling hair. "Erras a door across fae the midden. Ah'll let ye in over err." He opened the car door and stepped out. He leaned down to add, "Gies aboot twenty minutes, awright?"

"Sounds like a plan." She smiled and gestured for him to come closer. He leaned into the car expectantly. She reached for the fake beard.

He reared back out of reach and hid his disappointment with a grin.

"Ah've got remover in ma sporran. Wullnae come aff weyoot it. Ah'm fur the aff."

She nodded. "Okay. I'll be in the back. Near the middle."

"Nae, the midden. 'S closer tae the far end." He corrected. At her confused look, he elaborated. "Whir we pit the garbage, ken. The middens bin."

"The dumpster?"

He pointed at her. "Aye, tha's it."

She gave him a thumbs-up. "Got it. The door across from the midden."

He closed the door and gave a little wave. She waved back and he headed across the parking lot, kilt slapping his thighs.

She started to drive, then stopped and rolled down the driver's side window. "Nick," she called, but he didn't stop. "Lowlander?"

"Aye?" He stopped short and turned.

She lowered her camera. "Thanks."

"Ach. Ma eyes wis probably shut an' ma gub hingin open," he fussed. "Worse, ye snap me when Ah look a fookin teuchter an' no' a self-respectin Weegie. An' wey this 'ridonkulous' beard, as ye pit it. Fantastic." He struck his Monarch of the Glens pose. "Gawn yerself. Onerly the wan mair, but."

She raised the camera and continued to shoot as he dashed for the courtyard.

"Ach! Ye'll nivver take me alive!" he shouted and screamed out a battle cry.

She laughed as he disappeared out of sight. She rolled up the window and eased the car into a slow circle back the way she had come in.

There should be an access drive running behind the building for trash trucks to access the dumpster, and for deliveries by tractor-trailer. She was partially right. A road led behind the left end of the building, but instead of running straight through to the other side, it opened out into a paved area broad enough for a large truck to back up to the loading dock. Woods closed off the end of the road and edged the pavement.

She parked near the dumpster so she was out of the way, in case of an early morning delivery or trash pickup. The door was across the pavement from her, with a wall-mounted light shining above it. From here, she could see the orange glow of the brightly lit commuter student lot through a patch of trees. A packed-earth path, wide enough for two people to walk abreast, led into the tree-shaped darkness toward the hidden lot. The blue light of a police call box gleamed somewhere along the path, the bioluminescent lure of a deep-sea fish in black ocean.

"That's not creepy," Alice muttered to herself. She reached under her seat and pulled the release to give herself more leg room. Now that she'd stopped rushing around, she felt exhausted. She slumped against the door and wedged her elbow on the door frame to hold up her head. A twenty-minute nap might give her a second wind.

From the corner of her eye, she saw light bobbing in the trees. She lifted her head off her hand and stared hard as it became larger. Soon she could tell it was a cell phone used as a flashlight to navigate the path. The glow stopped at the tree line and turned upwards for a moment before disappearing. The face it had illuminated briefly was distinctive: narrow eyes, small upturned nose.

"What the hell?" Alice's stomach flipped. " 'Large as life, and twice as natural,' " she whispered and slumped low in the seat.

The figure looked around before crossing briskly to the door. Alongside the thigh holster of her cat suit, the other woman held a wine gift bag stiffly. Long red acrylic hair hung down her back. She pulled on the front edge of the hair, keeping her face tilted down. A twist of the wrist, and she pushed the door open and stepped inside. The door settled slowly into place with a muffled clack.

"Shit shit shit," Alice muttered as she struggled out of the driver's seat. She ran over to the door and looked up, searching for security cameras. A lone one was mounted just above the doorframe. She turned to face it fully.

The plain gray metal door opened from the inside. Alice stayed still, crouched low in the seat until she recognized the person in lab coat and scrubs leaning out of the opening. She stepped from the car.

"Took langer than Ah thoat tae get ma beard aff," Nick called. "Ah'm aw but mad fae the fumes." He headed across the pavement, letting the door thump closed behind him. He met her at the back of the car. "Let me carry tha' elephant fur ye." He hefted the camera bag from the open hatch. "Mickey wis pefter-efter gettin oot fur the festivities. He dinnae mind gettin loused airly. 'Moan, then. Let's gies set in anatomy lab afore the nicht is pure gawn," he rattled. He gave her a smile over his shoulder and finally seemed to notice her reticence. "Awright?"

"Just a little tired." She forced herself to smile back until it felt natural. She decided not to tell him about her double. She had no idea what it meant anyway, but just in case, she had done some ass-covering. She looked up into the camera again as they entered the building.

He led the way. Alice was glad she had him for a guide through the convoluted passages. He stopped and swiped his ID, opening a door wide for her. The fluorescent light stuttered to life over skeletons of a horse, steer, sheep, and hog parading around the perimeter of the room. Steel tables with stools stood in neat rows. He set her camera bag down on one of the tables and crossed to the back of the room. Floor-to-ceiling metal cabinets framed a large service sink and a huge plastic reservoir of preserving fluid. He flung the doors wide with a grandiose gesture, then dashed to the wooden cabinets above the work counters and did the same with each. "Pick yer pushion, doll," he said with a mad grin on his face. "Urnae they belter?"

She hurried to his side, amazed by the extensive collection of mounted skeletons and preserved animals. Some floated in jars of fluid. Others sat lifelike and rubbery on the shelves as if in an enchanted sleep. Several had fleshy doors carved into their abdomens for viewing organs. "I've never seen most of these," she breathed.

He climbed up on a stool and pulled out a specimen. "Hedgehog. Ma favorite."

"Let me get up there and take a look," she said eagerly.

"Ah'm no' ready tae come doon." He grinned wickedly from his vantage point above her Black Widow costume. She punched him in the shin. "Mind tha'!" he scolded. "Wan, ye nearly made me drap auld Tiggywinkle err, an' two, ye'll knock me doon an' then splat, sure as guns ur irn, ye'll huv tae preserve me in tha' vat ay formaldehyde an' stow me in the cabinet next tae the sea turtle."

She laid a latex exam glove over the cleavage he had been eyeballing and made a face at him. "Now can I get up there?"

He grimaced back. "Shite. Looks like the invisible man is feelin ye up byraway." She rubbed the glove up and down, making an orgasmic face and moaning. He jumped down and shoved the hedgehog at her. "Kin Ah watch fur a wee bit?"

"You just were."

"No' tha', ya perv." He nodded at the camera. "Tha'."

"Only if I can use you too."

"Aye. The noo Ah dain't look ridonkulous, ye kin use me." He slung an arm around the human skeleton model. "An' ma mate Nigel err. Ye dain't mind, dae ye, Nigel?" He made the skeleton wave and moved its jaw, adding in a falsetto, "Nae bother, hen."

The glove fell to the floor as she dashed to grab her camera and get him in the frame. She was a whirlwind of motion, running from cabinet to cabinet, getting ideas.

"And then you can hold the flaps open on the meaty ones. Then whale's baleen for hair. And intestine mustache!"

"Heart on ma sleeve?" He held a heartworm-ravaged organ against his arm, its preserved parasites dangling like dirty, tangled string.

"Yes!" She turned the camera on him. "It also looks like something out of a zombie." He moved it to his chest and make a heartbeat noise.

"Ah could awso gies dog biscuits fae the hospital. Ah could haud wan fur the beggin dog skeleton. Ye want me tae go ask the noo?" he said eagerly.

"No, no. It would be better to use a bone from another skeleton, if we can." She flashed him a wide smile, the encounter with her double forgotten. "I hope I brought enough film."

32: Best Laid Plans Do What is Expected

The lighter caught on the third try. Laura Beth lifted the lamp-oil-soaked tail hanging out of the gift bag and applied the flame to its end. She turned from the break room table to the lab door and pounded on the reinforced glass. A flurry of wings and startled clucks answered back. She raced into the stairwell and headed back through the maze the way she had come in. She hoped Nick would get there in time.

Nick's distorted face peered into Alice's lens through the fluid surrounding a two-headed fetal pig. They both jumped when the lab monitor in his pocket exploded to life with dull thumps, followed by cackling and whirring wings. He straightened and reached in his lab coat. He set the monitor on the table and turned up the volume.

"Tha's ferrlie. Dae ye think Ah should go check?" he asked her, reluctant to leave.

Alice thought of her twin. She rested the camera against her chest and fidgeted with the advance lever. "Probably. I saw your coworker go into the building while I was waiting out back."

"Pavlov's Belle?" He pushed the hair out of his eyes. "Hoo dinnae ye tell me? Whit the fook wid she be daein err?"

She shrugged. "She was carrying some kind of present. You know, like one of those skinny gift bags for a wine bottle."

"Ah doot she wis bringin champagne tae celebrate the holiday wey me." He hurried to the door. "Wait err."

"Okay. Be careful."

He paused at her worried look. " 'Hell hath nae fury like a wumman scorned,' aye?" He smiled reassuringly. "Nae bother, hen. Ah'll be awright."

The anatomy door closed behind him. He set off at a quick jog. The last thing he needed was some crisis while he was away from the lab. He sped up, suddenly concerned. He reached the final stairwell and burst into the break room. He looked around the cramped space. Dead center on the table was a narrow gift bag. On it, a lone skeleton held a cocktail glass, with the words "evil spirits" running vertically along the bag's side. The pungent smell of gasoline struck his nose. He noticed the short white tail projecting from the top of the bag.

He leaped for the heavy steel door and yanked it open. He stepped through and tucked into a duck and cover. The three firecrackers wedged into the bottle's neck exploded, triggering the next cluster of three hanging just above the gasoline mixture inside. Glass and liquid splattered the small space. Sharp hornet stings flared along Nick's back. The door slammed into its frame, shutting out the growing fire.

Searing heat burned into his back. He tore at the placket of his lab coat, forcing the buttons to give way. He threw the burning cloth onto the floor and stomped on it. Flames stuck to his trainer sole. Spluttering curses, he leaped up the stairs to the next landing and jerked the fire extinguisher from its bracket. He held the heavy red cylinder up and tried reading the directions as he stamped his smoldering foot on the floor tiles. The warmth on his foot grew. The stench of burning shoe rubber made him cough. He gave up, ripped out the pin, and squeezed the handle. The hose jerked as the dry chemical burst out. He grabbed it and pointed it at his foot, covering it completely, then ran down and sprayed what was left of his lab coat. He kicked it into a corner of the stairwell and gave it another blast of powder.

He heaved a long breath and peered through the diamond grid of the reinforced glass. The table was a donut with a still-flaming hole melted into the center. Discolored water rained from the lone sprinkler head, but a patchwork of small, stubborn fires raged in odd places. Flames licked out of the gap between the vending machines. Campfires burned under chairs. A small table wedged in the corner was a bonfire of old newspapers and crossword digests. "Fookin hell," he breathed. He dropped the extinguisher with a loud thunk and dashed back up the stairs two at a time. He shot out onto the first floor and launched himself at the nearest pull alarm. He raced down the hall, dodged into the next stairwell, and down a few stairs back to another section of the basement.

"Whit mad bastart designed this fookin mess?" he muttered as he sprinted through the maze, alarm shrieking around him.

*　　*　　*　　*　　*　　*　　*　　*

The concussion crackled through the monitor Nick had left behind. Startled, Alice yelped, then held her breath as she listened to flutters of startled, clumsy flight and distressed croaking groans from the chickens. Her ears strained for human screaming. She pulled the strap from around her neck and placed her camera on the metal table next to a preserved iguana. She ran to the lab door and leaned out. "Nick?" she called into the empty corridor. "Where are you, Lowlander?"

She ducked back inside and grabbed a lab coat from a row of hooks along the wall. Easing the anatomy door closed against a doorstop, she left a small crack for reentry without an access card. She headed in the direction she'd seen him go, slipping into the lab coat as she went. If she ran into anyone else, at a glance she'd look legit. She stopped at the first set of reinforced fire doors and looked through the glass at the branching hallway, unsure which way to go. The alarm split the air, making her jump. She ran back to the anatomy room.

Camera, lenses, and film were hurriedly jammed into the bag's compartments. Alice slung the strap across her body and lifted the bag off the table. She jogged to the door and seized the handle. She paused, turning to look around at the specimens strewn on the metal tables. She couldn't leave them like that. She ran back, grabbing animals and stacking them in her arms. As the alarm drilled into her skull, she rushed to the cabinets and jammed them inside. She headed back for another load, then hesitated. The alarm's shrill sound unnerved her. She turned between the door and the tables, taking uncertain steps in each direction.

Footfalls rang out in the corridor, thudding to a stop outside. She turned toward the sound, grabbing the hedgehog by its base and swinging it so the quills faced out like a weapon. Nick hauled open the door and stuck his head in. A dark stripe of soot was smeared across his forehead.

"We huv tae go," he yelled over the alarm. His eyes dropped to the defensive hedgehog. "Lee it!" He grabbed her hand and pulled her through the door.

She dropped the taxidermied animal and stumbled behind him. She turned the way he had come from, but he pulled her in the opposite direction. "Nut. This way." He released her and fumbled out his phone as he ran down the corridor. He dialed, held it to his ear, cursed, and pulled it away, jabbing the end call button.

"Whit's the fookin number fur emergency services?"

"Seriously? 911." Alice stopped for a moment to rearrange the heavy camera bag.

"Move, wumman!" He seized her wrist.

She clutched the bag against her body and ran harder to keep from being pulled off her feet. Her eyes dropped to his tattered scrubs shirt. "You're bleeding!"

He twisted, lifting an arm to try to see his back as he ran. "Ach. No' the first time, hen. No' likely the last, neither." He grinned at her. "At least it's in a new place."

He dragged her up a stairwell, then slammed open the Commons door. They dodged tables and ran through the outer doors at last. Stumbling over roots and rough ground in the dark, he dragged her into the old growth trees of the park-like lawn. He slowed to a stop at the sidewalk that led to the main entrance. The alarm was muffled enough to make his call.

He dialed, then thrust his phone at her. "Ah, uh. Err. Ye tell her."

"What? Tell who what?"

"Shite." He put the phone to his ear again and shoved the hair off his forehead. "Erras a Molotov cocktail in the basement ay the veterinary college…nae, a Mol-o-tov cocktail! Ken, a boattle ay petrol wey a rag stuffed doon it an' that. Ye light it an' lamp it at the man. Kablooie! Flames ivrywhir." His free hand illustrated wildly like he was playing charades. "Aye! Tha's it!" he crowed. "A bomb." He turned to Alice, who hugged the camera bag. Her face looked pale in the glow of the streetlights. "It went aff! Erras fire ivrywhir doon err. The sprinklers ur huvin a hard go ay it… Ah dain't ken whae pit it err. It wisnae me, jen up!

"…Ma name? Uh, Nick Kerr. Ah wahrk err…Ah set aff the alarm an' that. Tae get ivryyin oot, ken. Erras a skeleton staff in the animaw hospital. Ah kin see um oot err."

Alice twisted to look.

"Aye. Ah'll no' be gawin onie place. We'll be oot front ay the buildin… Awright. Cheers." He turned to Alice as he dropped his phone into his lab coat pocket. "Ah think they unnerstood whit Ah telt thum.

We'll find oot in a wee meenit." He took her cold hand in his. "Sorry aboot aw the runnin an' kung-fu grip an' that. Ah'm no' used tae bombs, byraway." He felt the chill now they had stopped moving. Dew had soaked through his trainers, cleaning off most of the chemical powder. "Nichts ur fair drawin in. Fain Ah hud ma jaiket the noo. Iven tha' teuchter wan."

He sat down on the curb to wait. She settled next to him, resting the weight of the camera bag beside her. She shivered, partly from the cold, partly from nerves.

"Turn around," she instructed. He obediently shifted. She eased his shirt up, uncertain what she would find. Her stomach twisted at the multiple gashes on his back. Still clutching the torn shirt up away from the blood, she guided him so the parking lot lights shone on the wounds. She bit her lip. "It looks like something's in there. Does it hurt?"

Nick craned over his shoulder to look. He flinched and stopped short as the compression shifted the glass shards embedded in the muscle. "Ach. Burns a bit, aye. Kin ye pull oot whitiver is in err?"

The howl of sirens grew louder.

She shook her head. "I don't think I should try. I'd be worried I wouldn't get it all. Or it would start bleeding again. We should wait for an ambulance."

"Awright then. Ah'll thole through."

He gestured for her to come around to his left side. She scuttled over. He wrapped an arm around her shoulders and held her against his unhurt side for the mutual warmth. She curled against him. Nick worried about the hens in the research lab. The fire door should keep out the flames. Could it keep out smoke? Then there was heat buildup. Maybe the fires were already out. Then there was the job.

"Shite. Hoo am Ah gawn tae explain ye bein err?" He pulled his arm away. "Mibbe ye should dae a bunk. Naeb'dy kens ye wis err. Ah'll be awright."

Alice took his hand. "No. I'm not going anywhere. So you have a visitor at a weird time. I was escorted, except during the emergency. It's a gray area. You'll probably get a slap on the wrist."

He shoved the hair out of his eyes. "Ah dain't ken…"

"It'll look a lot worse if I run and they find out. They'll think I did it. That *we* did it," she insisted.

"Ah suppose," he agreed doubtfully. "Disnae matter the noo, onie road."

They stood as a fire engine blared past them, tailed by an ambulance. Firefighters jumped down and jogged to the main entrance. One entered a pass code into a keypad next to the swipe access. He stepped through to the inner foyer and opened a fire control panel with a key to locate activated sprinklers and pinpoint the fire.

"Ah suppose tha's me redundant," Nick joked.

Alice patted his arm. "It's in good hands," she reassured him as the firefighters disappeared into the main building, heavy wrenches in hand to open the hydrant system and attach hoses. "We should have the EMTs check you out." She hooked her right arm through his left and began leading him toward the emergency vehicles.

Three police cruisers turned into the lot in succession, cutting their sirens. Nick and Alice cringed as the headlights and strobing blue lights raked across them. He heard the shriek of tires as the cars stopped abruptly. Officers stepped out, crouched behind open car doors, weapons drawn. A spotlight blazed in their faces.

"Hands on the back of your heads. Now!" barked an officer.

Nick pulled away and looked around to see who they were yelling at. Alice was trembling, her hands locked on the back of her head. He looked at her, lifting his hands slowly, and realized what the officers were seeing. The white lab coat was too short to cover the thigh holsters. All he could think about was all the news stories of police shootings.

"Shite! They're no' real! Thum's fake! Haun tae God! 'S onerly a fookin costume!" he yelped. Alice's eyes were wide but unfocused. A tear ran down her cheek. "We dinnae dae nuchin!"

Two cops covered them with drawn guns from behind their cruisers.

"Ah ca'ed aboot the bomb in the buildin." He squinted into the light and rambled on as a third officer, a man no taller than he was, but twice as wide, approached cautiously with a gun trained on Alice.

"She's the Black Widdy, Ah mean, dressed as the Black Widdy. Ken, fae tha' Avengers movie byraway. Ah'm dressed as maself, the noo, tha' is. Afore Ah wis heid tae fit in heuchter-teuchter Hieland shite, in ma clan tartan an' that. Fur Halloween, byraway."

"Shut up and don't move!" an officer screamed.

Nick shut up. The stocky officer crept closer. He lifted one pistol out of Alice's thigh holster as she shivered, tossed it aside, then took the other. He holstered his gun and patted her down and did the same to Nick. He took the camera case and prodded through it with his baton. Up close, his prominent eyes and stocky figure gave him the appearance of a bullfrog. He gave the Scotsman an exasperated glare no doubt given much use on loud, obnoxious drunks.

"Stand down," Officer Bullfrog called to the other officers. "They're clean." He kicked Alice's pistols. "This shit is plastic. This is why you don't paint your plastic toy guns to look real. Even for Halloween. Especially not for Halloween. You know how much bullshit goes down tonight? It's wall-to-wall crazy."

The searchlight cut out. One officer left his vehicle blocking the drive and stood on guard. The other officer joined Bullfrog.

"This the guy who called it in?"

"He talks a lot, and I can barely understand him, but that's the gist," Officer Bullfrog replied. "You two can put your arms down now." He turned back to Nick and gestured at his bloodied shirt. "That happen during the incident?"

"Aye. Ah think Ah felt somehin. Ah wis a bit preoccupied wey some fire an' shite."

The police officer nodded. "Are you hurt, honey?" he asked Alice solicitously. She shook her head adamantly. "All right. I'm sorry about all that, but we have to assume the worst until we get it checked out." She nodded. "I'm going to take this one over for treatment and get his statement," he said to his partner. "You stay here with her and get hers."

"Can't I go with Nick?" Alice asked, her voice trembling.

"You can join him in a few minutes, okay? Right now, I need you to tell Officer Clark here everything you know about tonight. Including why you're here." Bullfrog gripped Nick's left arm and steered him toward the ambulance.

He had no sense of how much time passed before Alice ran over to where he sat on the ambulance's bumper. The firefighters had emerged. The research lab was intact and unharmed, but the break area was a scorched mess. The fire chief had gone in to begin an arson investigation. A fourth patrol car had arrived, with a yellow Labrador running from window to window in the back seat, panting with excitement. The bomb dog had gone in to sweep the building. A portable crime lab van had squeezed into the drive behind the K-9 car.

"How bad is it?" She lifted up the clean t-shirt to look at the bandages.

"Anither clean shirt an' tha's me," he joked. "Speakin ay which, dae ye like ma new tap?"

She smoothed the black volunteer fire department T-shirt down gingerly and smiled. "At least it's in your color."

"They got some glass bits oot ma back. Telt me they're evidence or some sich shite. Same wey ma ither tap. Soonds like they think Ah hud a haun in it. Wid take a stupit crim tae blow humself up. Ah guess Ah look the part." He pushed the hair out of his eyes angrily.

"They're just being thorough." She rubbed away the soot on his forehead with her thumb and a little spit. "So it was a wine bottle with gasoline in it?"

"An' somehin else tae. Erras a loud bang, mibbe two, whit startit it aw." He repeated the details Officer Bullfrog had carefully recorded. "An' it wis like the petrol stuck tae things. See when Ah tried tae stamp oot ma jaiket, it startit anither fire on ma fit."

"Did you tell them all that?" She looked worriedly into his dark eyes.

"Oh aye. Did ye tell thum aboot seein Pavlov's Belle?" She nodded. "Ye saw her wey a gift bag? Black, wey a skeleton on it?"

"It was on the side away from me, most of the time. But it was dark with some white on it." She put her head in her hands. "This is crazy."

"Hoo wid she dae somehin like tha'?" he wondered. "Torch the break room. Disnae make onie sense. At least the research an' the birds ur safe. Tha' part Ah get."

"It's all my fault."

Nick tried to look at her, but she hid in her hair. "Hoo dae ye figger tha', hen?"

She tossed her head back. "She was dressed like me. The catsuit. The accessories." She slapped at herself angrily and grabbed a hank of dyed curls. "She even had on a wig. It's about me. She tried to frame me for it."

"Fookin hell. Ma brither kens hoo tae pick the mad bints, disnae he jist!" He swore angrily, glaring at the lights and confusion around them.

"What did you say?" Alice said sharply.

His eyes met hers, for a moment showing something startled, pained, and raw, before changing into an unreadable expression. "Ah said, ma brither warned me aboot her an' Ah dinnae listen." He turned away.

Alice stared at him, now unsure of what she'd heard. A police officer walked past with a spool of yellow plastic crime scene tape. Nick shot up and headed after him.

"Where are you going?" She hurried after him.

"They're markin the break area as a crime scene. It's the onerly way tae get in tae care fur the birds, ken." He started to jog. "They cannae make it aff limits. Ah huv tae tell thum."

Alice let him go. She waited on the walkway above the recessed courtyard, watching him plead with the uniformed officer, then chase down Officer Bullfrog. After a heated conversation, they seemed to come to an agreement. Nick looked up and around until he spotted her, arms crossed, watching him. He jogged over to her.

"Ah've convinced the polis no' tae add animaw neglect tae the list ay crimes. Ah dain't need tae go intae the lab thenicht. Dave wull in a wee bit, but. They wullnae let me ca' hum neither." He noticed the heavy camera bag still slung across her chest. He patted it. "Haun over tha' ton weight." She lifted it off and let him take it. "Ah'll gie ye a buttie tae yer motor. Ah huv tae hing aboot until the end ay ma shift, ye dain't need tae be err, but."

"Can't I stay here with you?" she pleaded. "I'm a little afraid to go home. And I feel like I should put away all the stuff we used in the anatomy lab."

He looked back at the building. "We huv tae wait fur thum tae check the hull thingmy fur mair bombs first. Ah kin take care ay it byraway. Ur ye sure ye want tae bide wey me?"

She nodded. "Maybe we can take a walk while we wait for the all-clear."

"Awright. Kin we park this beast in yer motor first?" He hugged the camera bag.

"Of course."

He was relieved to see her smile for the first time since he'd left her alone in the anatomy lab.

"What the hell did you do, man?" Dave stage-whispered. He lifted the sunglasses off his puffy eyes. He watched a police officer beeline for him. "Lord, I am too hungover for this. I may actually be still hammered. That's why I took the bus instead of driving," he added loudly for the officer's benefit and took a long swallow of his oversized coffee.

"Wheesht," Nick shushed, gesturing to Alice's head in his lap.

She sat up, appearing from under the table, and pushed the red curls out of her face. "Um, hi."

"What the fuck?" Dave mouthed at them as the uniformed officer handed him two large plastic bags with blue and white bundles inside. He held them reluctantly. "What is this?"

"Somehin pure dead awfy happened whilst we wis away fae the research lab byraway." At Dave's expression, he added, "Anatomy lab's awright. Birds ur awright. Research is awright. Break room's fooked."

"It's toast," Alice chipped in. She raised her hands. "Not our fault."

"What happened?" He turned a bag back and forth, eyeing the folded disposable jumpsuit, booties, face mask, and gloves.

"You are required to wear one set of protective clothing to access the research lab, and another set to come back out," instructed the officer. "You will be going through an active crime scene. You must wear a sterile suit to prevent contaminating the scene with evidence."

Dave's eyes widened. "You mean, contaminate it with any more evidence than is already in there, because I walk through there several times every day, not to mention eat my lunch in there!" His voice rose. "Just like him—" he gestured at Nick with the sterile suit bags. "And Laura Beth, and Mickey! This is insane!"

"Calm down, sir!" The officer rested a hand on his taser. His dark mustache pulled back into a snarl.

Nick stood and stepped between Dave and the cop. " 'S okay, Dave. They urnae pointin fingers at ye."

"Good. Because I have an alibi," he said over Nick's shoulder at the cop. "I was at the Irish pub until two a.m. Half the town was in there. The bartender will remember me—I was the guy in the afro wig and gold medallions doing car bombs. Then I went home and crashed. My roommates can verify that! Even though they were trashed, too."

"What did you say about bombs?" The officer surged forward.

"What?" Dave yelped. "I didn't say bombs!"

"You did, sir. Get your hands up!" the cop ordered.

"Aye, ye did," Nick said apologetically to Dave. "Tha' is a four-le'er word roond err theday."

"Sir, I need you to step aside," he growled at the Scot blocking his way.

He read the cop's name tag. "Officer Cox, Ah believe whit ma esteemed colleague wis tryin tae communicate is tha' he wis doon the pub, huvin thum shots ye drap intae ither beverages an' mist drink wey aw haste. Awso kent as 'bomb shots.' Fur instance, the perrly named Irish car bomb. Am Ah right?"

Dave nodded vigorously. "What he said. I swear."

Cox grudgingly accepted the explanation, but patted Dave down anyway.

"Can't a man just phase into his shift quietly any more?" Dave grumbled. He slumped into a chair and tossed the packaged protective gear on the table. "I am definitely finishing my coffee first. Especially since I have to put on this spacesuit." He cupped a hand over his mouth and breathed like Darth Vader. "This isn't the evidence you're looking for," he said in a deep voice. "Okay, I know that line was Obi-Wan instead of Darth, but you know, the suit…"

He closed his eyes and drank his coffee, worn out already. Officer Cox scribbled down his alibi while the others sat in silence. A sudden thought made Dave straighten.

"Does Dr. Riesen know?"

"Ah huvnae telt hum."

Dave glanced over at Alice. "Oh, man. This is so bad."

"Ah dinnae think ay it, actually," Nick said sheepishly.

Cox slapped his notepad shut. "You are not to discuss this ongoing investigation with anyone."

"An' then err's tha'," he added. He grinned crazily. Alice burst into nervous giggles.

Dave's face cracked into a smile despite himself. "This is strictly need to know, Mr. Bond. And you do not need to know," he said in a terrible British accent and laughed.

33: Call Backs

It wasn't his first time in a police station, but at least it was his first time in an American one. Nick swiveled idly back and forth in a worn office chair, curiously cataloging the differences, which were few. He and Alice waited in what was apparently a break room, at least part of the time, based on the table, jumble of mismatched chairs, oversized white bakery box of assorted donuts, and vending machines. They had been given an offer of cop coffee or money to get a drink from the machines. They both opted for the drink machines. She passed on the pastry, but he dove into a classic glazed and immediately regretted the sugary film it left in his mouth that even the acid in his soda couldn't wash away.

Alice toyed with her bottle cap. They could hear voices in an adjoining room, jovial and unconcerned. Her investigation hadn't turned up anything criminal on Nick, but that didn't mean theirs wouldn't. She reached out with a foot and stopped his chair.

"Lowlander."

"Aye?" He looked at her expectantly, twisting the chair back and forth slightly against the brake of her foot.

"I don't know how they do it in the U.K., but here, you can plead the Fifth Amendment. That means you don't have to tell them shit if you don't want to. 'You have the right to remain silent,' " she said seriously. " 'Anything you say can and will be used against you in a court of law.' Do you understand?"

He nodded. "They cannae possibly think we hud oniehin tae dae wey it but."

"Just in case," she implored him. "They won't tell you your rights unless they actually arrest you and interrogate. But your rights are still in play whether they read them to you or not. Or whether it's an interrogation or 'followup questions.' " She made air quotes with her fingers. "That's their loophole. They won't tell you about choosing not to answer until it's an actual interrogation."

"Is tha' knowledge lairned the hard way fae las' time?" he asked quietly.

"Yes and no. I've done paralegal work for your stepfather." She glanced toward the door as the voices grew louder. "Another thing. You can play the lawyer card at any time. You have the right to a lawyer. Ask for one and they have to stop asking you questions."

"Dae ye think Ah'll need it, hen?" He tried to keep the indignation from his voice.

"I hope not. And I hope Ray Booth doesn't charge family if you do." She smiled crookedly. "But no one else is going to protect you in there if you don't."

"Dis tha' mean ye'll no' huv ma back?" he snapped. His hair fell into his eyes, and he shoved it out. "Dae ye think Ah hud somehin tae dae wey the bomb?"

"No! Of course not. They won't let me..."

She was cut off by two officers entering the break room. Officer Bullfrog called for Alice to go with him. At the doorway, she turned back toward Nick. She held up her hand, fingers spread wide into a five, and mouthed, "Plead the Fifth." A second officer came in for him. He was young, tall, and thin, with an eager, unblinking stare. It made him look like some kind of long-legged wading bird hunting for dinner.

"Is this normal, chiefie? We awready telt ye ivryhin," he protested as he was led down the hall to a different room.

"Just a few followup questions." He pointed to the drink in Nick's hand. "Everything to your liking?"

"Oh aye." *Awright, gude cop. Folleyup questions. Aye, right.*

The officer left him in a room that held nothing more than two uncomfortable-looking folding metal chairs, a slightly more forgiving wooden one, and a plain metal table. The officer gestured for him to sit in one of the metal chairs and set a piece of paper on the table.

"Release form. This gives us permission to take your fingerprints and a DNA sample and compare them to anything found at the scene."

"Awright. Nae bother." He should be fine. He read the cop's nametag. Byers. He skimmed over the paper and signed with an illegible flourish. "Officer Byers. Aboot Alice?"

"We're asking her to do the same. Simply procedure."

"Ye dain't huv tae trouble her. Ye ought tae huv hers on file, byraway. Fae a few years back. Nae need tae upset her an' get her hauns aw dirty."

Byers gave him a long look.

"Whit? Erras enow cop shoos on the telly. Ye lairn some things."

"I've watched a lot of cop shows. They're not very accurate. And I have not seen a single episode that shows how damn hard it is to get fingerprint ink off a suspect's fingers."

He shrugged. "Hoo about detective fiction? Dain't tell me ye've read aw the American books in print, let alane aw the Scoattish wans."

"You have me there, Scotty. Sit tight. I'll be back with the kit." Byers took the sheet with a little more snap than was absolutely necessary and closed the door behind him.

He scrubbed at the leftover ink on his fingers, shredding the paper towel into ragged black crumbs. He paced the room to get the blood circulation back into his legs from sitting in the hard chair for so long. He peered into the one-way mirror, shading his eyes in a futile hope to see into the adjoining observation room.

"Christ on a bike, this is worse than back shift," he groaned.

As if on cue, a plainclothes detective came in carrying a thin manila folder. He sat and gestured for Nick to do the same. "Nicholas Robert Kerr?"

"Kahrrr," he corrected automatically, his r's rolling musically.

The detective nodded and repeated it back. He held out his hand. "Special Agent Terry Lance, ATF. Bureau of Alcohol, Tobacco, Firearms, and Explosives."

"Ach." Nick instantly had the "Secret Agent Man" theme running through his head, substituting "special" instead of "secret." He shook hands hesitantly, expecting a power squeeze but not getting one. "Shouldnae tha' be ATFE, special agent man? Hoo special ur ye?" He softened it with a ferrety grin.

"I guess you'll find out." Lance allowed a smile to flicker across his mouth. It left no trace evidence of its passing. "Because of the destructive device, this is a federal investigation. We called you in because I have a few additional questions that the police didn't cover."

"Nae bother, chiefie. Gawn yerself."

"You work at the veterinary college, is that right?"

"Aye. Research assistant. Ah'm on rotatin shifts. Ah've jist come aff back shift, midnicht tae eight."

"Does Alice Bonner work there too?"

"Nae, she wahrks fur the café, alang wey the ither cafeterias on campus, she disnae wahrk fur the veterinary school directly but." He didn't like where this was going. "It wis ma idea, tae huv her shoot photies in anatomy lab on ma shift. She said they wullnae let her dae it onie mair at the open days an' that, an' Ah thought it widnae dae onie harm."

"I'm sure there's a good reason it's not allowed." Lance stared him down. His military buzz cut seemed to crackle with electricity.

"Aye, Ah suppose. Somehin tae dae wey animaw rights nutters." He rolled his eyes. "Ah ken hoo some ay thum kin be. Alice, but. She widnae dae oniehin tae harm onieyin or oniehin." He pushed his hair out of his eyes. From his experience it was true, though her reputation said otherwise.

"Was she with you the whole time?"

He shifted in the hard seat. "Maist ay it. Ah escorted her through the buildin, an' we wis thegither until Ah went tae check oot noises in the lab. An' got blown up." He anticipated where the agent's train of thought was headed. "See hoo the idea jist came up ma humph thenicht. She wis wey me the hale time efter Ah came up wey it. She widnae huv hud time tae plan an' get a bomb pit thegither an' that. Ah watched her pack the camera bag. Nuchin but lenses an' a right big camera an' lots ay fillum. Err wisnae room fur a boattle. Especially no' wan like tha', no' iven on its side. It wid huv spilled. An' Ah'd huv smelled the petrol onie road. Ah smelled petrol the meenit Ah stepped intae the break room, no' a moment afore, but. She let me carry the bag, ken. An' she hud nae time tae pit oniehin oniewhir. See, ye need a swipe card or a key tae get intae the buildin. So she couldnae enter weyoot me."

"Or someone else. How many other people have access?" Lance asked sharply.

"Hoo should Ah ken? Ye need tae ask the vet school tha' wan. If ye kin access the buildin, ye kin access the break room." He pushed at his hair and felt the sweat beaded on his forehead. He hated the scoobies. He snapped his fingers and sat up straight. "Hayonya. Hoo urnae err two ay yees? Ye cannae use oniehin Ah say weyout corraboration by anither polis."

Lance squinted his eyes. "No, son. This is the United States of America, not Scotland. And it's being recorded to make sure everyone behaves himself. Just calm down. No one is accusing you of anything at this point. I'm just asking you a few questions to get a full picture. Seems a little unusual to bring your lady friend in after hours. Did you leave her unattended at any other time?" Lance insisted.

"Onerly when we first got err. She waited fur me in her motor roond back. Tha's when she saw ma cowahrker fae the lab, Laura Beth Sutphin, go intae the buildin, up tae nae gude. Ye kin ask Alice."

"You're sure there was no other time she had access, or left your sight."

"Aye," he said irritably. "Erras a wee window ay time tae pit the bomb in the lab an' licht the fuse. An' she wis wey me. Hoo?"

"I don't know how. That's why I'm asking you."

"Nae. Hoo ur ye still askin?"

Lance stared at him for a moment. "*Why* am I still asking?"

Nick nodded impatiently. "Tha's whit Ah said. Ah'm no' speakin Gaelic or nuchin byraway."

Lance raised an eyebrow. "Because her fingerprints were found on the bottle." He sized up the subject's reaction.

Nick was struck dumb, his mind racing. "On the boattle? Hoo wis err onie boattle left tae find fingerprints on? Soonds like a fit-up tae me." He shoved his hair off his forehead and leaned back in the chair. "Ye should check the security fitage."

"Thanks for the insight, Taggart."

"Ah, gude wan." He narrowed his eyes. The long-running TV show revolved around police detectives in Maryhill and greater Glasgow.

Based on the agitation, the news was a surprise. So the Scot wasn't covering for her, no matter how well he'd anticipated the usual questions. Lance changed direction with his interview. "I'd like to talk about your proximity to the incident. I find it very interesting how you heard a disruption, ran all the way across the building, and arrived just in time for it to go off."

Nick shrugged. "Ah'm a dead lucky bastart." He didn't like the special agent's special tone. "Ur ye tryin tae say Ah set the bomb, an' then wis sich a muppet tha' Ah dinnae get ma bahookie oot the way afore it went aff?" He raised up out of the chair, just about done with cooperating. "Ye think Ah did this tae ma oon self?" He lifted up his shirt and gestured awkwardly at his bandaged back. "Hoo the fook wid Ah bomb ma oon joab? Ye think Ah wid liven up a slow nicht wey some anarchy? See Ah'm nae mad skull wantin tae watch the wirld burn, mate! See Ah'm onerly a keelie fae Glesga daein ma joab the best Ah kin." He leaned on the table, mixing a little intimidation with his indignation. "So Ah hud ma bird wey me on ma shift. Tha's ma onerly crime err—Ah wantit tae impress a wumman."

Lance leaned backwards to stare up at him. "I believe that you didn't plant the bomb or set it off." Nick nodded briskly and straightened. "You're right. It's not a crime to bring some bimbo to work with you. Poor judgment, certainly. But we don't care about that."

Nick bristled, but sat back down. "Dain't ca' her tha'."

"However. The fact remains that a destructive device was used in a research facility that employs foreign nationals." Lance tapped the manila folder in front of him.

"Mickey Patel's idea ay a superhero is Gandhi, an' he volunteers fur Oxfam," Nick interjected hotly. "An' Ah've got dual citizenship, so Ah'm no' iven furrin."

His outburst was ignored. "So we rechecked credentials for everyone on the project. More in depth, this time. Apparently human resources did a cursory statewide check instead of a full national or *international* check." He carefully emphasized the word and watched for a reaction. "Mr. Patel is not a concern."

Nick nodded absently, eyes on the folder. He should be fine, international check or not. Nicholas Robert Kerr's record was white as the driven snow.

"So my real question for you is this." The agent's blue eyes were hard and cold as he opened the manila folder and pushed a sheet of paper across the table. "Why do you look so damn good for someone who died about five months ago?"

The Scotsman looked down at a fax of his own death certificate, dated the day after his university commencement. His stomach tightened. He fought the donut and soda back down from their efforts to escape.

"Ah plead the Fifth."

"Alice Bonner?" She nodded. The ATF agent closed the door. He held out a hand and showed his badge. "Special Agent Terry Lance. I was hoping you could help me out with my investigation into the veterinary college bombing." He smiled and set a manila folder on the table. "I understand you don't actually work for the vet school." She shook her head. "Do you have access to the building?"

"No. But I have clearance to be unescorted, once I check in with the main office and get a visitor's pass." Her eyes met his and skittered away. "The main office was closed long before I got there that night, though. Nick Kerr had to let me in."

"Okay. Why were you there?"

"We were taking photographs in the anatomy lab. Well, I was, and Nick was helping me and being one of my subjects." She smiled nervously.

"That's not exactly normal procedure, is it, to have visitors in the middle of the night."

Her smile faded. "No."

Lance leaned in. "So why then?"

"Because that's when he was working," she said weakly. His blue eyes drilled into her. She sat back and crossed her arms. "And because the veterinary college doesn't let anyone photograph the specimens any more. So it had to be done when no one was around."

"Was this your idea?"

"That's not relevant."

"You should let me decide what's relevant, Miss Bonner. Especially in a possible terrorism investigation. Whose idea was it?"

She was silent for a moment. "Nick's, I guess. It just came up naturally in conversation. We were talking about it—his coworker Dave and I—and Nick suggested it. Is that the problem here? I knew it was probably frowned on, if not actually breaking the rules, but I really wanted to do it."

"Thank you for your candor. I'll let the veterinary school worry about that infraction." He watched her. "Was there any time that night when you were alone?"

"Nick was with me the whole time I was in there. Except when we heard noises on the monitor thing he carries. He left to check on the lab. I had a bad feeling, because when I was waiting for him to let me in the building, I'd seen somebody else go in. Someone who really shouldn't have been there either." She saw the special agent's eyebrows move slightly. She didn't want to throw anyone under the bus, not without knowing for sure. Especially when pointing a finger could mean several pointing back at herself. He didn't ask her to elaborate, so she finished her report. "I heard this boom over the monitor while he was gone. It must have been that thing going off. He came back all freaked out, told me we had to go right away. Then he dragged me out of the building."

She looked the detective directly in the eyes. "He was lucky he wasn't hurt worse. What kind of person would do something like that, Special Agent Lance?"

"I've arrested all sorts of people, for a variety of reasons." He watched her intently to see which words would get a reaction. "Pranks. Vandalism. Activism. Terrorism. Personal revenge."

She breathed in sharply and held her breath. Bingo.

"But maybe you can tell me what it was in this case, Miss Bonner, since the main component of the bomb was a cabernet bottle with your fingerprints all over it."

"What?" She searched the room, unseeing. "Oh my God. The dinner party. She was there. I was framed! Please. You have to believe me. I'm not a terrorist. There's no way I could have even gotten in to do it! Did you watch the security tape for the back door?"

He watched her panic. "Funny how you're not the only one to bring that up." He opened the folder and took out several still images, spreading them out on the table. "Why don't you explain your unusual behavior on that tape."

She looked at the ATF agent and then at the pictures. The first clearly showed her face staring into the camera. Another showed her holding out a key ring, all the keys spread, pointing to the bulky, distinctive shape of the state-issued key. Then a still of her inserting the key in the door, her body to the side, so the camera could catch that it didn't fit. Then an exaggerated shot of Alice pulling on the door, to no effect. The next to last image showed her holding her driver's license beside her face for the camera's benefit. She seemed to relax visibly.

"That is me covering my ass." She lined up all of the images but one. "I was proving that my key doesn't fit." She reached into her pocket and pulled out the ring, arranging it to match. "You can have somebody check. That door is set to stay locked. You can only unlock it as long as the key is in it and turned. You can check that too." She pulled two still frames out and turned them so they were right-side up for the agent. She looked intently into his face. "Did you watch the video yourself? First *she* came to the door, unlocked it, and went in. Then I got out of the car, and showed my face and identity to the camera." She tapped the time stamps on the images.

She leaned back in the chair. "I saw her walk up to the back of the building along the commuter lot path, using her cell phone as a light. She must not have known I was there. I saw her face when she looked at the phone." She tapped at the image again. "She was careful to keep her face hidden, but she's dressed like me. In a costume like the one I wore that night. The Black Widow character from the Avengers. I dyed my hair for it." She lifted up a lock of hair. "But she had to wear a wig. She pulled on it a few times. The camera might have caught that."

Special Agent Lance pulled the photo in closer. He could make out a narrow rectangular shape beside the figure's leg. He pulled the image of Alice's full face shot next to it. He looked between the two images.

There were small differences in the clothes, hair, and bodies. Cleavage didn't lie. The stills showed two women.

34: Pulling the Switch

Glasgow, June

"Come on, ye daftie! Whit wis ye thinkin, wearin tha' shite doon the pub!" Rab shook his head in wonder, a bad idea, as it threw them both off balance. "Ye changed oot the full kit, ye hud tae keep the bloody robe, but?" The brothers held each other up, staggering along the sidewalk, bumping into other revellers out enjoying the nice weather. He could feel the warm wet blood on his side.

"Claes hud nuchin tae dae wey it. The neighborhood hus gawn dead dangerous since Ah been away," Nick panted back. He had assumed the humpback posture of the very drunk. "It burns like the devil's erse efter a burrito binge, mate."

Frustrated with his whining, Rab used his grip on the back of the black robe to give his brother a shake. "It's onerly a couple ay cracked ribs. Ah've hud worse." He pulled him around the corner into an alley and pressed him against the wall. "Ah've hud worse protectin yer malinky erse an' yer stupit causes." Grabbing him by both arms, he bent down to look into his twin's face where it drooped at the end of his neck. "Nick. Ah'm gawn tae take ye hame. Ye huv tae sleep it aff so ye kin catch yer flight in the moarnin. Ye huv tae go tae the States an' tha' research joab."

Nick raised his head reluctantly, as if fighting passing out. His face was pale and damp, eyes unfocused. He leaned sideways and heaved.

Rab recoiled, barely keeping his grip. "Christ on a bike, ye cannae haud yer ale. Ye awmoast hueyed on me, ya dime bar."

"Fook ye," he said thickly.

"Let's try agin, ya tossbag. Whir ur we gawn the noo?"

Nick panted out the address.

"Jesusjohnny. We'll huv tae take the bus. Ye couldnae get far enow away fae us, could ye?"

Nick stabbed a long finger into the chest of his mirror image. "Dain't steal nuchin when we get err."

Rab jerked like he'd been shocked. He winced and touched his gashed side automatically. "Fook. Ur a right piece ay wahrk." He shoved the hair off his forehead, leaving a bloody smudge.

"Ye've smeared blood on yer coupon fussin wey yer fringe like a wee lass, ya fuckwit."

Rab studied his wee brother. Nick leaned crookedly against the dirty brick wall, his eyes slits. The only thing keeping him upright was his brother's fist clutching a wad of his commencement robe.

He looks aboot a hunnert years auld, Rab thought. *He deserves be'er than this. An' the hale fookin alley stinks ay auld pish, keelie desperation, an' the fookin shipyard irn smell ay blood.*

"Ach. Ur full ay it." He shifted his grip and steered his brother to the nearest bus stop. "Pure lucky Da's no' drivin thenicht. If he got wan look at the sorry state ay ye, he wid marder us baith."

He dug clumsily in his brother's pocket for the keys. They tottered through the narrow door of the bedsit flat. Rab eased his twin onto the bed, where he sprawled loosely, his robe spread beneath him like a cape. Rab watched him breathe for a while as he panted from the exertion of dragging him up three flights of stairs.

"Sleep it aff, ya mad skull." Rab patted his leg affectionately and turned his attention to his own needs.

He opened the leather jacket and looked at his slashed, bloodied shirt. "No' agin," he sighed. He shrugged out of the jacket. He didn't want to go down the hall to the shared lavvy.

"Really, Nick? This is the best ye kin dae? Ur livin like a ten-quid hooer."

He stepped over to the small handwashing sink and ran the water until it was hot before filling the basin. He gingerly peeled shirt from skin, teasing it away from the fresh clot with warm water. He carefully stripped off the ruined shirt and tossed it in the bin. He held a clean-enough looking towel in place as he looked around the small, sparse room. Bed, chest of drawers, small table with a hot plate and electric kettle, a rickety shelf. A small mirror hung over the chest of drawers. A pair of cardboard boxes sat on the floor, waiting for a pick-up later in the week for storage. A large rolling suitcase was poised next to the door like a patient butler.

Rab knelt carefully and opened the nearest box. Nothing useful. He opened the second and rummaged, pulling out a very long knitted scarf in earthtone stripes. He smiled. Nanna had made it for Nick when he was in his Doctor Who phase. He wound it carefully around the towel several times and tucked in the ends. He reached back into the box and pulled out a T-shirt with an animal clinic's logo on it. He pulled on the shirt and arranged it over the makeshift bandage. He felt like a street-corner Father Christmas with that much padding on his middle, but he definitely wouldn't bleed through. He eased himself back into his leather jacket and took the few steps over to the mirror.

He rubbed the dried blood off his forehead and flicked at his hair. He glanced down at the suitcase. The front compartment was open so that he could see the corner of a wad of bills. He knelt and unzipped it all the way. A fat bundle of American dollars tumbled out, along with a passport, plane ticket, and cell phone. He looked guiltily over at his brother, who hadn't moved. He stuffed everything back in and zipped the compartment closed. He straightened and studied his reflection for a long time. He stepped over to the bed and looked down at his twin, listening to the ragged snoring. For the first time, he noticed his brother was getting a potbelly on his otherwise lean frame. Rab rolled him gently onto his side to prevent aspiration if he were sick again. Nick moaned but didn't wake. He stooped and kissed his twin's sweat-damp hair.

"Fat bastard," he whispered affectionately, satisfied with his brother's condition. "Ur doonright disgustin."

Holding the makeshift bandage, Rab settled into the corner made by the bed and wall. He crossed his arms and rested his head against the edge of the mattress. "Ah'll wait tae see ye aff in the moarnin. An' make sairtain ye get on the plane."

Rab woke curled up on the floor beside the bed. After struggling to sit up, he ground the crusty residue out of his eyes and shoved his hair back roughly. He ran his tongue over his teeth, grimaced, and rubbed a finger back and forth across them. He reached backwards and slapped at the mattress. "Wakey, wakey, ya wee bastart." No response.

" 'Moan then. Ye kin nurse tha' hangover in the airport wey a bacon roll." Rab straightened up and stretched, catching himself at the pull on his wound.

Nick was flat on his back, the robe tangled around him. Rab grabbed his shoulder and gave him a good shake. His head flopped around. Rab leaned over his twin and slapped his cheek three quick times. The skin felt unnaturally cold. He bent over the still form and pressed an ear to his chest. He poked two fingers under the jawline like he'd seen people do on the telly. Nothing. He checked the location of the pulse in his own neck and tried again. Still nothing.

"Shite! Wake up, ya eejit!" Rab wedged a knee next to his brother on the narrow bed, the opposite foot levered against the floor. He cupped one fist in the other hand and leaned into his motionless brother with short, quick thrusts. He tilted the pale face back and pinched the nose shut, a nose identical to what his own had been before it was broken and healed. He breathed and pushed, breathed and pushed.

Finally he sat back beside Nick. He lurched forward and screamed into the pale face, "Wake up!" He reached out to slap him, but stopped and let his arm sink to rest uselessly against his leg. Rab slumped off the bed onto the floor, tears streaming down his cheeks, chest heaving. He pressed the bandage against his reopened side and rested his head back against the mattress. He shut his eyes tight against this waking nightmare. *Whit am Ah gawn tae tell Da? Nanna? Granda?*

"Ach. Should huv been me, no' ye," he moaned. "Wis ma fault. Should huv been me…"

Rab's eyes flew open. He jerked to his feet. He bent over his brother, patting him down until he found what he was looking for. It would have been much simpler if Nick had still been in kilt and sporran. He grimaced as the body wobbled from the clumsy motions of having its pocket picked post mortem. Rab pulled out his own wallet and forced himself to put it into his brother's trousers. He closed his eyes and turned away from the bed, taking a moment to pull himself together.

He strode purposefully across the small room. On the way out the door, he grabbed the suitcase's handle. Dr. Nick Kerr was going to the States.

35: Chickens Come Home to Roost

Special Agent Lance stood up and shook Alice's hand. He was anxious to have the new person of interest brought in. The case was coming together, but he needed to understand motivations. Especially with a stolen identity surfacing in a critical witness who was exercising his constitutional rights against self-incrimination. How involved was he? And who was he? It was time to shake the tree and see what fell out.

He pulled a permission-to-search form out of the folder and placed it and a pen in front of her. He watched her sign, then collected the document. "Officer Byers will take you to a waiting room." He slipped a second paper from the folder and placed it face-down. "This is for you."

Byers rushed out of the observation room to meet Special Agent Lance in the hall.

"Give her about five minutes to read it and let it sink in, and another five to get pissed off. Then put her in there with bagpipe boy," Lance said grimly.

"Why? What did you leave?" Byers' eagerness made him look even more like a bird than before.

Lance gave him a long look. "The second bomb in this case."

"We need you to wait in here while we check on a few things," Byers said kindly. He smiled at her. She looked like shit and wouldn't meet his eyes. He didn't always like his tactics, but he had to admit that when Special Agent Lance led the task force, it always got results.

She stepped into the room with the resignation of an inmate while the gangly officer closed the door behind her. She stayed just inside the room, fighting fear and anger and an unprecedented sense of violation. It was hard for her to look at the hunched figure in the far corner. The man she'd known as Dr. Nick Kerr sat with elbows on knees, his face hidden in his hands. She wanted to punch him. Real punches, ones that would hurt him as much as she was hurting right now.

"What does it mean, Lowlander?" She threw the wadded copy of his death certificate at his head. It ricocheted off with a pop.

"Lowlander, right? Because it's not Nick, is it." She shook her head and angrily swiped at a tear. "Whoever the fuck you are. At least fucking look at me!"

Moment of truth, the one Da had warned him about. He had to lay it all out and hope she didn't walk. He tilted his head up slowly, his hands dragging across his features. His eyes were red. He wiped his face on the tail of his shirt. He took a long, ragged breath and dove in.

"Ah lied tae ye. Ah pretended tae be someyin Ah'm no'. Ah used the wrang papers tae come err. Ah'm no' a veterinarian, and Ah'm no' Nick. Ah'm a fookin wee shite."

"Quit dicking around!" she yelled. "Who the fuck are you?"

"Rab. Rabert Nicholas Kerr. Nick wis ma wee brither. Ma twin brither. Isnae the first time twins huv changed places, byraway," he added defensively.

"Spare me the Parent Trap crap!"

He met her eyes steadily, pained at the anger, hurt, and mistrust he saw. "Ah'm aulder by three meenits. He wis oor mither's favorite. The maist bawheidit, aggravatin, dull wanker. An' stuck on humself wey it." He sadly waved a nearly empty soda bottle. "Some wake." He drained it and held the empty bottle loosely on his leg as he continued. "Awyis bangin on aboot animaw rights. Well, Ah hud tae be the brawn ay the ootfit, mind, awyis gettin intae rammies tae protect his malinky erse, an' he hated me fur it. Ah hud tae be the hard man. Worse, eejits couldnae tell us apart, except by whit we wis wearin. Ah'm the dead fit yin, byraway." His attempt at humor fell flat, weighed down with pain.

"The graduation photo. In the mortarboard, laughing. That was you," she said so softly he almost didn't hear.

"Oh, aye. Aye, an' it wis me hingin aboot, gawn tae the uni parties. He dinnae fancy tha'. Ah nivver telt onieyin Ah wis hum, but. When people fund oot err wis two ay us, they cried me Nick Wan an' hum Nick Two, like thum blue-haired Thingmies in Dr. Seuss, ken. Like he wis the copycat. He's been a fookin wanker since. Actin it like he dinnae ken me. Like Ah wis a numpty. Efter aw Ah'd done fur hum, he wantit tae pretend Ah dinnae exist. Wantit tae pretend he wisnae a keelie, same as me an' Da." He felt the need to qualify his underachievement. "It's on account ay hum Ah dinnae huv tha marks fur the free uni tuition. He wis awyis startin rammies tha' Ah hud tae finish, an'Ah took tha blame."

He shifted nervously and flapped the tail of his shirt, which now showed darker rings in the armpits. "Ah took a different career path. Wisnae exactly legal. Made a fair number ay enemies." He appealed to Alice's silent form. "Ye ken. Hustlin snooker. See Ah hud a character. A uni toaff, scoobied, moderate skill, maistly lucky, an' arrogant enow tae make the punters want tae pit hum in hus place. A right chancer. The punters couldnae resist." He couldn't help grinning. "Wahrked a right treat fur a gude while, until wan sore loser took it a wee far an' malkied me. Ah stoapped then. Tae dangerous." He hugged his ribs tight. "Kin ye credit it? Nick an' Ah dinnae speak fur years. Fookin twins, an' no' speakin fur years. Ah ken whit the ersehole is thinkin afore he dis, an' he wullnae speak tae me."

Alice slipped into the other hard metal chair, sitting sideways to face him. She should have walked out, but she couldn't make herself go. Besides, the Feds had told her to wait here.

"Until uni graduation. No' the undergrad. Fur his doactorate. Ye nivver clapped eyes on sich a fookin event. Hale clan wis oot fu' force, tartans ivrywhir, pure dead proud, byraway. See Ah kent hoo mich it meant tae hum, tae Da an' Nanna an' Granda. See Ah buried the hatchet. Ah wis dead proud ay hum maself, jen up." His eyes were bright but inwardly focused. "Ah got hum tae come doon the pub wey me tae celebrate, jist us two, auld lang syne an' that."

He felt her eyes on him. "Eejit hud tae kit oot in the dead stupit black robe, dinnae he jist. See some nugwatt thinks he's me, or tha' is, ma character fae when Ah wis hustlin, onerly right rippin the pish on account ay the gear. See Nick patterin away tae defuse things, sayin it's oor bell an' that. Free bevvy usually wahrks. This punter isnae huvin it but. Gaws pure mental. Fookin bastart toe-enders hum in the chest like ma wee brither is a fitbaw, an' tha's Nick flyin across the room intae a table. Huge crash. Ah jump the bastart and he malkies me, in the same fookin place as afore, whilst Ah lamp hum a gude wan." He left off the inconvenient part that he hadn't put down his pint mug before taking the swing.

"Ah got us the fook oot ay err. Ah thoat he wis onerly dead pished." Rab shook his head heavily. "Turns oot the bastart burst his spleen."

He raised his pained eyes to hers and held them. "Ye wid think Ah wid ken. Ah should huv felt it like a great fookin disturbance in the Force or somehin." His eyes fell away. Maybe he had known all along. Maybe he'd known and not called emergency services so he could step into his shoes. He thought of the arguments and banter with Nick Two since he'd been in the States. He swiped at his hair and decided to keep the insanity to himself.

"But why did you pretend to be him? I don't understand." She put her head in her hands, struggling with the information.

He shrugged. "Ah dinnae mean onie harm," he pleaded.

"You must have wanted to get back at him pretty bad, Rab, to steal your brother's identity." She wondered what kind of vengeful psycho she had involved herself with. She put a hand on her abdomen protectively.

"It's no' like tha'." He rubbed damp hands on his jeans. "Ah wisnae thinkin straight. Jen up, it made mair sense at the time."

"And yet here you are. Living in your brother's apartment. Working his job. I'm surprised you didn't hook up with his fiancée."

"She's no' ma type! Ah widnae huv done it if Ah'd kent aboot her!" He turned to her like a trapped animal.

"What about me?" She crossed her arms.

"Ye wis an accident, hen."

Her eyebrows shot up. *Not the only one in this room.* "Oh right. The bad romance," she said bitterly.

"Ah dinnae plan tae fa' fur onieyin. Ah wis layin low. Tryin tae. Ah wis gawn tae tell ye." She leaned forward. He knew that look in her eyes. He could feel the nervous sweat trickle down his forehead.

"When?"

"Ah…Ah dain't ken. Ah wis wahrkin up the boattle." He hunched his shoulders. " 'S hard tae explain hoo Ah did it. Ah dain't rightly ken maself." He pushed the hair off his forehead.

"You weren't going to tell me." Her eyes drilled into him. She felt a pang of guilt about her own secrets, but squashed it under her indignation. No wonder Mary had him investigated; she'd guessed he wasn't the real Nick Kerr. "When the grant was up, you were going to dump me, if not earlier."

"Ah'd hoped it widnae matter, in the end."

"Because you were always going to dump me," she snapped. "What did I expect?" She flew out of the chair and started pacing.

"Nae. On account ay erras somehin between us."

She stopped and stared at him. "Yes. A big fat lie."

The damp hair failed to hide the desperation in his eyes. "I gied ye hints aboot ma situation," he finished lamely.

"Hints? You didn't even admit to being a twin," she retorted angrily. "Asking me if I thought I'd be able to tell you two apart doesn't exactly count as a revelation that you were posing as someone else! I trusted you. I wasn't playing 'find the differences' between someone who lied to me from the start, and someone I've never met. You're a sick fuck, Rab, you know that?" She turned away from him to face the wall.

" 'Moan, hen!"

Alice leaned her forehead on the one-way glass. A tear ran down her face. On the other side, Byers shifted uneasily. Lance crossed his arms.

"Interesting," said the detective.

"But not helpful," groused Byers, feeling like a voyeur.

"I wouldn't say that. Sounds like he didn't plan the bombing with the other woman to frame Bonner. And it explains why Sutphin would want to get rid of them both, through either a frame or an explosion. I wonder if she suspected he wasn't who he claimed to be?" Lance raised a hand to head off a response as Alice turned back to the miserable Scot.

Rab was folded in on himself, forehead on the table with his unruly hair spread out.

"Why did you do it?" she asked softly.

"Tae keep hum alive, the onerly way Ah could," he said to the table. "Soonds dead stupit when Ah say it aloud. Tha' moarnin Ah became hum, he wis awready gone. Ah hud nae idea it wis so serious when Ah pit hum tae bed. He wis the yin wey the bright future. He deserved tae live, no' me. So Ah made it happen." He raised his head reluctantly. "Jen up, itherwise Ah wis maist likely gawn tae the Bar-L."

"What's the Bar-L?" she asked suspiciously. "Some pub?"

"Barlinnie. A prison in Glesga."

"Why would you be going to prison?" She shook her head in disbelief. "You think they'd arrest you for your brother's death?"

"No' fur tha'." He pushed his damp hair back only to have it fall again immediately. "Mair like fur daein in the bastart whae killed ma brither. Ah lamped hus thick skull wey a pint mug."

"Jesus Christ, Lowlander." She slumped into a chair. "You think you killed somebody? Holy shit. You eejit!" She straightened and punched him on the arm. "Fuck!" She punched him again. "Well, that explains why you got over my reputation so damn well. Fuck!" She punched him a third time for good measure. "Shit. You disturb me." She crossed her arms. "I don't know squat about British law, but maybe that could be ruled self-defense. Especially if you use your brother's identity in court."

He raised his hands in surrender. "Wee harsh, pet."

"Shut it," she said bluntly. She fought to keep her voice calm and steady. "I need to get this straight. What parts of the guy I knew were actually you? Okay, the hustling. But did your grandmother teach you to dance? Did you try to save hedgehogs by eating potato chips? Did you even like James Herriott and want to be a vet? Do you even know the first damn thing about the poor birds you've been experimenting on?" She made a move to smack him and stopped herself. "Have you been acting like your brother? Dressing like him? Are those his movies in your apartment?"

He didn't seem to have heard her. Part of him had wanted to know how the other half of the Kerr twins lived, wanted to know what it would have been like to be the good twin, the one who went to university and lived his dream of becoming a vet. It was a relief, no longer living in his brother's shadow, cleaning up his messes. No longer hearing his voice in his head, hallucinating him everywhere he went. He was free of his twin at last. The Nicktoon was gone. Time to learn how to be Rab, just Rab, not the lesser brother. No more evil twin.

He looked into the angry green eyes and held them. "Oor Nanna taught us the dancin when we wis on their farm fur the summer holidays. Ah wis awyis be'er at it than he wis, byraway. Summers on the farm ur awso hoo Ah kent aw aboot hens an' the ither farm animaws. The joab's so aisy a monkey could dae it. 'S jist raisin chickens, an' the necropsy is jist butcherin, except ye weigh ivryhin an' take notes." He spread his hands placatingly. "Aw tha' aboot the Hedgehog Crisps wis me too. We baith liked *Aw Creatures Great an' Sma'* an' wantit tae be vets, but Ah couldnae. Ah wouldnae. On account ay hum, an' ma mither. Dinnae want tae be like thum. They're animaw rights nutters. Ah used tae huv tae rescue ma daft brither fae shite he started wey people over it. Mary used tae be like tha' too. She left us fur tha'. Dain't ken if she still is intae the activism. Ah fookin hope she is, or Ah'd feel iven worse aboot her walkin oot."

He took a deep breath, encouraged by the change in her eyes. "See, Ah dain't want tae be hum, an' Ah dinnae try tae look like hum onie mair than Ah kin help. Ah've been wearin the uniform fur wahrk, an' Ah hud tae wear his claes until Ah could get ma oon. Except fur the kilt an' that, which ye insisted Ah wear tae the festival, mind ye. Tha' wis a gift tae oor Nick fur his commencement, an' happened tae be in his valise, fookin teuchter an' pure boaky favorite tha' he wis." He took her hands in his. "Ah'm onerly a lorry driver."

She stiffened. "And a liar. And an identity thief."

"Aye. There's tha'." He kept his eyes on hers.

"And maybe a manslaughterer! Or however you say it!" She raised a fist to smack him again.

He caught it and pulled her arm around his neck. She didn't resist. He rested his forehead on hers. "Ah widnae blame ye if ye walked away. Ye probably should."

"Yes, I should. You know, special agent man is probably watching all of this."

"Ach. The noo she warns me. Be'er make it gude then." Their lips met.

She pulled away. "Seriously, I think you should lawyer up."

"Rinoo?" he murmured.

She smiled and ran her fingers into his hair. "In a moment. Give me a few minutes alone with the suspect."

36: Lawyering Up and Coming Clean

Alice had been allowed to go hours ago, leaving him with Raphael Booth's cell phone number, the reassurance that he would be in good hands, and a last lingering kiss. Rab fidgeted with the scrap of paper, folding and refolding it into different shapes until it was limp. He'd already read the one thin cop trade magazine the front desk officer had kindly dug up for him, along with a hunting and fishing magazine that had been the man's personal reading material.

It was late Saturday afternoon when a tall, broad-shouldered man with distinguished silver temples and a tailored gray suit entered the room with a confident, take-charge air. He looked to Nick like a Hollywood interpretation of Rabbie Kerr, bigger, broader, more dashingly handsome, more well-educated and sophisticated. Only the man's crooked teeth, white as they were, seemed natural. *Probably calculated tae gie hum a dod ay humanity a jury kin cling tae*, Rab thought cynically. Again, the Americans were making him feel inadequate. The lawyer extended a hand formally, and the Scotsman rose to take it.

"Raphael Booth. Your attorney and stepfather." He smiled warmly and motioned for Rab to follow him down the hall.

"Cheers fur this. Pure dead shame tae be meetin this way."

"It is what it is. But don't be a stranger, and I do not mean that you should get into more trouble with the law." Booth gave him a stern look that dissolved into a smile. "I apologize for taking so long. You caught me golfing, so I had to clean up. I did a little background work, and then when I heard the Feds were involved, I made sure to look as intimidating as possible." He pushed open the door to a small conference room. "Have a seat." He noticed Rab's indignant expression at the tidy room with comfortable chairs. "It would seem our boys in blue have been using some intimidation on you. Let me guess: they kept you in that ratty break room, when you weren't in an even more bleak interrogation room."

"Ach. Nuchin like a hard seat on yer bahookie tae get ye tae the truth faster." Rab flashed his ferrety grin.

Booth unbuttoned the jacket of his suit, revealing a slight paunch, and placed a plain black leather briefcase on the table. He pulled a pair of reading glasses from the inner pocket and put them on. "Don't worry. They're not watching or listening in on this room." He winked over the frames of his glasses. From the briefcase, he lifted out a portfolio and an expensive-looking pen. He thumbed open the portfolio to a page of notes on a yellow legal pad. He tapped it briskly with the pen. "All right. Let's figure this out."

"Am Ah gawn tae be charged wey identity theft?" He wound his fingers together under the table. That would be the kiss of death for his newly patched relationship, and could mean months, maybe years, before he was free to go home.

"The good news is that this does not fall under that designation." He smiled reassuringly. "Unlike felony identity theft, you did not pose as someone else to defraud banks, take out credit cards, run up debt you had no intention of paying, and ruin innocent lives. Your intent was not criminal *per se.*" He looked over his glasses at his client for acknowledgment.

Rab nodded. "Oh aye."

"We also don't have to concern ourselves with the university pursuing charges. They're too busy dealing with the fallout of Miss Sutphin's alleged actions, as well as revamping their protocol for screening applicants."

His stepson grimaced and swiped hair out of his face.

"However," Booth cautioned, "we do have to deal with the State Department." He poised his pen over the notepad. "Which passport did you travel on?"

"Nick's."

Booth looked over his glasses. "Obviously. But you boys have dual citizenship, correct?"

"Aye," Rab said patiently.

"So which passport, American or British? I need to know how many governments you're in trouble with."

"Ach."

"Now he gets it." His smile softened the words.

"The American wan. Is tha' bad?" He squinted his eyes as if expecting a blow.

"I presume you also used the American passport as identification for your I-9?" At Rab's blank look, he clarified. "When you were hired. They have you fill out proof of employment eligibility."

"Aye, Ah did. Ah left ma oon wey ma brither."

"So two counts of false documentation."

"Hoo bad?" He shoved his hair back into place, even though it didn't need it.

"Since you used an American passport, I can represent you. So, false documents, first offense, that's a fine. Anywhere from a few hundred to a few thousand." He studied his stepson. "Identical twins...and your names..." He looked back a page in his notes until he found what he was looking for. "Your names are very similar. First and middle reversed." He held up two fingers, twisting his wrist back and forth to make a flip-flop gesture. He rested his elbows on the table and tented his fingers in front of his face as Rab tried not to fidget.

"We can claim you grabbed the wrong passport on accident, in your state of grief and confusion." His eyes unfocused as he thought aloud. "When you realized the error, you panicked and didn't know what to do except continue to use it. Maybe we should imply a dissociative fugue state—disorientation, sudden travel, amnesia, assuming a new identity. You came out of it when you saw the death certificate."

He refocused on his stepson, whose raised eyebrows had retreated under the falling hair at the proposed defense. "Special Agent Lance did us a couple of favors, saving us some time and money. Don't worry, this is *pro bono*." He smiled reassuringly and continued, "He verified your identity using the fingerprints you so generously provided to his investigation."

"Hoo? Dinnae we huv the same prints?"

Booth leaned forward personably. "You would think so. It's a common misconception. They are very similar, but each identical twin has unique fingerprints. Same DNA, different prints. God, in his infinite wisdom, right?" He leaned back and smiled broadly. "Protecting the innocent by design."

"Oh aye," Rab answered, at a loss for anything to add. He wasn't sure what to make of his legal counsel.

"Special Agent Lance also checked that you have no outstanding warrants on either side of the pond. So whatever happened in Glasgow, stayed in Glasgow." He shut the portfolio and stood to repack the briefcase. "So I'm able to get you released on your own recognizance, ironically enough."

"Ah kin go hame?" he sighed in relief.

"You can go back to your current living arrangements," he clarified, shaking a finger at him. "You are not to leave the country. Not that you could, with Nick's passport confiscated and the State Department aware of your situation. We'll know when your hearing will be after I confer with them on Monday, but probably no sooner than twenty-eight days out, based on their usual schedule. We'll make an appointment with the closest passport branch to speed things up on your own U.S. passport as soon as you get the necessary documents sent over from Scotland—birth certificate and driver's license. British passport won't hurt either. Then you can choose whether to stay with us or go back." He clapped Rab on the shoulder. "You're welcome at our house any time, Rob. You're family." He scribbled the address on the back of a business card. "How about coming over for dinner tonight?"

Rab's smile wilted into a rictus of dismay. "Thenicht? 'S been a lang day. Ah need tae process, ken."

"How about tomorrow? Sunday dinner. It's tradition." His stepfather steamrolled over his reluctance. "Please don't disappoint your mother."

Pure dead late fur tha', Rab thought bitterly.

Rab placed the helmet on the kitchen island and rubbed a hand roughly through his hair. The stench of police station permeated his skin and clothes. He wanted a shower desperately, but needed to finish facing the music. He sat deliberately on a stool, his phone on the counter staring balefully at him. He inhaled and exhaled carefully before seizing it and dialing in a rush. He tapped his fingers while he listened to the ring.

"Awright, son?" Da's voice was a welcome sound, despite the unpleasant conversation ahead.

"Nut," he blurted. "Ah been nicked."

"Ach. Ah wis hopin ye wid stay oot trouble wey the polis over err," Rabbie Kerr's voice lilted soothingly. "Whit did ye dae this time, laddie?"

"Used Nick's passport."

"Hoo, son? Ye huv yer oon. Ye dinnae need tae dae tha'." His voice shifted with a sudden insight. "Ach. Urnae wahrkin hus joab, ur ye?" Guilty silence answered him. "Ye telt thum ye wis hum. Shite, son." He was struck with a sudden concern. "Dis yer bird ken?"

"Da! Ah'm in the shite an' aw ye kin think aboot is tha'?"

"Ye dinnae tell her, did ye. She fund oot on her oon." His voice was heavy with sadness.

"Fae the polis. Starin doon Nick's fookin death certificate!" He snatched a drink from the refrigerator and slammed the door. "Then Ah hud ma wee tell-aw."

"Fookin hell, son. Ah'm dead sorry." Rabbie sighed.

"Me tae. Wis fine until a wee kerfuffle wey a bomb made thum look a smidge harder," he said sheepishly. "Nae bother, wisnae mich," he reassured his father. "Ah got aff lichter than Ah usually did wey the hustlin." He looked at the soda, recapped it, and switched it for the last ale.

"Did ye travel on hus papers?"

"Aye."

"Ach. Tha's ye stuck, is it no'?"

"Fur a wee. Ah huv a hearing comin up on usin the wrang papers. Ma lawyer disnae think it wull be tae serious. Onerly a fine, fingers crossed. Ah need tae get ma oon American passport in the meantime. Kin ye send ma Scots passport an' documents?" He fidgeted with the bottle cap.

"Ay course." Da's voice was kind. After a thoughtful silence, he said carefully, "Whit aboot yer wee hen?"

"She wis dead furious. Less than when she thoat Ah wis engaged tae someyin else, but." He grinned despite himself. "Ye dinnae tell me Nick hud humself someyin tae gie ye grandweans. Pure sleekit."

"Ah dinnae ken aboot it. Maist likely on account ay he kent Ah wid be pesterin hum like Ah'm daein tae ye," he admitted.

"Nae doot." He laughed. "Well, me an' Alice kissed an' made up. She's been a real doll. She helped me wey a lawyer, the same mintit lawyer ma mither marrit ontae."

"Thank the dear Laird fur tha'. Ye made me sweat it oot, dinnae ye jist?" he teased. "Ah micht get some grandweans efter aw. Ur ma onerly chance the noo, ken."

"Fook, Da. Ah need her tae be sairtain she's over it, no' gawn tae dae a bunk on me or onie weans we micht huv." He shook his head in frustration. "Kin ye lay aff the weans fur a wee? Ah need tae fix aw this shite first."

"Fair enow," he said apologetically. He continued cautiously. "Rab. In the morgue, Ah dinnae ken if Ah should say it wis ye dead, since ye sheeped it. Ah awmoast telt a porkpie. Ah kent ye wid tell me yerself in yer oon time whit happened an' hoo ye did it. So ur ye gawn tae tell me or no'?"

He rubbed his scarred ribs. "We got in a rammie. No' wey each ither, mind. Some eejit thoat Nick wis The Uni. An' Ah wis malkied."

"Ach. Agin?"

"Same fookin spot. Kin ye credit it?"

His father made a sympathetic noise.

"Aye. Tha' wis nuchin. The bastart toe-endered Nick dead hard intae a table, but. Wis ma las' rammie defendin hum."

"Ah think he let ye dae aw the fightin, so ye wid feel important," Da said gently.

"Fook tha'. Ah dinnae need ma ego fluffed." He pushed his hair back. "He wis aw talk, oor Nick. If Ah hud a pound fur ivry time he gied some punter a right bollocking on the subject ay veal cutlets…"

"Fair enow," Rabbie said to placate his son. "Hoo take hus gear, pretend tae be hum?"

"Ah couldnae let it end like tha'. Err he wis, aboot tae start his grand new life, dead on account ay me. Ah dinnae realize he hud mair than cracked ribs tha' nicht, so Ah dinnae dae nuchin. Tha's whit kilt hum. He could huv made it in hospital wey a burst spleen. Ah tried tae bring hum back. First wey the CPR. Then tha ither way." He hid his face in his hand. "An' Ah thoat Ah wid get done fur the chancer whae started it. See Ah wis slashed dentin his skull wey a pint mug. See Ah micht huv killed the bastart." He half-chuckled, half-sobbed, "Ah thoat Ah wid dae the wirld a service by keepin the best Kerr brither alive."

"Ah nivver thoat ay ye as onie less, laddie," Da said gently.

"Nae, she awyis did, but." He let the years of hurt come through in his voice.

"Ach." Rabbie knew it wasn't his place to argue that point. "The thick-skulled chancer lived, byraway. He's daein time fur yer brither. Jimmies in the pub grassed him up. So nae danger ay the Bar-L. When ur ye comin hame then, son?"

"Aboot a month. Efter the hearing."

"Ay course, son. A month, but. Tha' lang?" Da asked anxiously.

"Aye." Rab couldn't help the smile in his voice. At least he knew he was still wanted at the tenement with pink doors on Clouston Street. "Ah huv a few threads tae tie up, onie road."

"Ye soond like a mystery novel. Ah hope some ay those threads ur yer hen…"

His son sighed with exasperation.

"An' yer mither." At the angry silence, he gently added, "Pairfect time tae come tae peace wey her."

"Hoo is ivryyin tryin tae make me come tae peace wey her?" he raged. "Burden is on her, no' me."

"Fur yer sake, no' hers. Please, laddie."

"Awright, Da," he promised reluctantly.

37: Black Widow's Final Web

Rab answered the soft knock to find Alice at his door.

"Hi, Rab," she said shyly.

"Hey ya," he said back. He was glad she was here, after everything. He thought for certain she would have used the rest of the day to come to her senses and have nothing else to do with him.

She kissed him gently. "Best ye come through," he whispered and pulled her inside. "Nae mair free shoos theday," he announced to the empty stairwell.

He settled onto a stool with a long sigh. She stood between his legs and took his hands in hers.

"How did it go?"

"Gude, Ah suppose. Ma stepfaither says Ah'll huv a hearing wey the State Department in aboot a month." She squeezed his hands. "Nae bother. He thinks I'll onerly huv tae pay a fine. A few thoosand."

Her green eyes were worried. "What are you going to do?"

"Ah huv some dosh pit away. An' Ah huv tae sell ma motorbike onie road." He smiled reassuringly. "Dain't bother yer shirt aboot it. Ah'm no' takin oot a loan, faimly or no'."

"What did you think of your stepfather?"

He pulled a hand free to brush his hair off his forehead. "Ah dain't ken whit tae make ay hum. Awright, Ah suppose. Gude as lawyers go. Ah think he's daein right by me, onie road."

She laughed. "Fair enough."

"He wants me tae come tae dinner roond err themorrow but."

"You're a doctor. You can deal with it," she joked. "I'll go with, if you want. I'm still your 'hauner,' right?"

"Aye." He grimaced. "Ivryyin is tryin tae make me go. Least if Ah dae Ah'll get a yap nap."

"Good idea," she said distractedly. She moved away and took off the rabbit fur jacket. He motioned for her to lay it across the island. "Rab, there's something I need to tell you."

"Oh aye?" he said cautiously. *Err it comes, the big letdoon.*

"A confession." She smiled crookedly at him and crossed her arms defensively.

"Ah'm no' a priest, mind." She didn't relent from her posture. "Confession, is it. Tha's serious, then." He stepped off the stool and into his kitchen area, not meeting her eyes. "Calls fur a cuppa." He waved the small saucepan that served as a kettle and pulled out a tin of loose tea.

She hesitated, then nodded. At least it would give her something to occupy her hands, though she wasn't sure she wanted him armed with hot liquids. She moved to the end of the island, just in case.

"I haven't been completely honest with you," she said to his back, trying not to remember what it looked like bare.

He half-turned, looking at her through his hair. "Ach. Breengin straight intae it. Cannae it wait fur the tea?" *Or nivver?*

She opened her mouth, then closed it and shifted from foot to foot. "Actually, I'm afraid I won't be able to say it to your face." He turned his beautiful dark eyes on her again. She motioned for him to turn around, smiling wryly.

"Cannae be worse than mines." He kept his eyes on her. *Look away, an' tha's yer heart malkied pure through,* he warned himself.

"It's pretty bad."

"Ur really Alice Bonner, aye?" he joked. She nodded. He narrowed his eyes. "Ur no' gawn tae say ur engaged tae ma cousin ur ye? Or someyin else?" She shook her head adamantly. He studied her a while longer. "Awright, then," he said resolutely. He turned back to the tea. "Ah'll make it aisier fur ye tae crush ma soul intae mince." He expected a playful punch, but got none. So it was serious, then. He said carefully, "Ah awready heard aboot ye an' ma cousin byraway."

"Liam? There's nothing to tell."

"Ah widnae cry peggin hum nuchin," he insisted, unable to fully subdue the flare of temper.

"I didn't sleep with him," she said softly, her voice trembling. "Did he tell you that?" She gripped the edge of the kitchen island tightly.

"Tha' porkpie isnae gawn tae wahrk." He crossed his arms tightly and glared. "Hoo'd ye dae it? On account ay thinkin Ah wis engaged?"

"I didn't sleep with him," she repeated. "He tried to force me, but I fought him off."

He gave her a fierce stare. Her expression doused his anger. He wanted to hold her, but when he started to come around the island, she flinched. "Fookin hell. Did he hurt ye? Ah'll find hum an' add mair tae the list ay broken bones than his fookin nose."

"You broke his nose?" Her eyebrows went up.

"Aye, when he telt me he'd hud ye," he admitted reluctantly. "Ah'm no' usually like tha', ken."

"It's okay. I think I broke a couple of his ribs," she said placatingly.

"Brilliant." He swiped at his hair. "Proves Da wis the gude hauf ay the gene pool, disnae it jist. Ur ye huvin ma cousin nicked?"

She shook her head.

"Dain't haud back on ma account."

"Ray Booth would only bargain it away with the commonwealth's attorney. And I don't want to go through another media circus." She looked away, waving a hand dismissively. "I'm okay, really. I just want to forget about it. But that's not what I wanted to tell you."

"Awright." He nodded and turned back to making the tea. "Whit is yer confession, then?"

"The Black Widow thing."

"Ach. Disnae matter tae me, hen. We're nane ay us pairfect."

She smiled sadly. "Tell me that afterwards, if you still feel the same way."

He looked over his shoulder at her briefly. "Ye dain't huv tae tell me, mind. Ah'm no' feart fur ma life." He spooned loose tea into an infuser.

"I did it," she blurted. "It was assisted suicide."

He fumbled, scattering tea leaves into the sink. "Is tha' hoo ye swerved charges then?" he lilted.

"No. I lied," she said bluntly.

"Hoo dae tha' if ye wis…" he struggled for a euphemism. "Helpin hum oot?"

"Because there wasn't real proof of his intention. No suicide note." She shrugged, even though he couldn't see it. "I just knew."

He looked at the wasted tea leaves, imagining portentous shapes. He scraped them into a heap. "Hoo did ye ken?"

"He'd injected two full syringes of insulin and had a third ready to go." She stared at the island's countertop, seeing them again in her memory. Two empty needles jabbed deep into the mattress, as if trying to kill it. The orange plungers were pulled back up part way, making the plastic tubes into a sword, or a cross for the dead. "And he let his emergency rescue kit expire. A whole year out of date."

"Ach." He closed the infuser he'd forgotten about and dropped it into the boiling water. He shifted the pot to a cold stove eye.

"But the facts are that I gave a hypoglycemic man a glucagon shot that purged his liver of any glucose he might have left in his body to keep him alive. Then I gave him a very large dose of insulin. He was already unconscious. He couldn't tell me what he wanted." She let out a long, ragged breath. "He might have been beyond saving before I did anything. No way to know. I never told a soul about the three syringes, and I got rid of them in a hospital waste bin so no one would ever find out."

Rab watched the dark color spread from the infuser like blood in water. "Cheers fur tellin me."

She swept a strand of hair behind one ear. "You're welcome," she said uncertainly. "I just wanted you to know the truth."

"Tha' wisnae so bad. Be'er than Ah expected." He flashed an uncertain smile. "Can Ah turn roond the noo?"

"Almost. I'm not done confessing."

"Haun tae God? 'Ma engines cannae take mich mair ay this,' " he joked, struggling not to get upset. "Ah'm gettin whiplash fae this conversation, an' the tea is awmoast ready. Kin Ah please jist turn roond?"

"No!"

"Ach! Nae need fur the heid-nippin."

She took a deep breath and plunged in. "It wasn't a coincidence that I was there in the pub, all those nights in a row before we spoke. Or that I was at the veterinary college when the false alarm went off. Actually, I set it off to get you out of the building, so I could see you."

"Ye wantit tae get thegither wey me tha' mich?" He smiled at the saucepan of brewing tea.

"I was told where to find you. Your mother paid me to find out personal stuff about you."

He turned toward her, tea infuser dripping from his hand onto the floor, the smile twisting into a rictus of horror.

She continued in a rush of words. "She suspected something off about you. I was paid to learn personal details about you and report back, through Liam."

"An' whit did ye lairn?" he growled.

"That I'm terrible at investigation. I got personally involved with the subject." She shifted more fully behind the island for safety. Her eyes pleaded with him.

"Oh aye. A big mistake."

He noticed the drips and threw the infuser hard into the sink. She winced. It skittered and clattered, breaking open and spewing soggy tea leaves.

"Ye wis fookin paid tae peg me. By ma oon mental mither. Ah kent it wis tae gude tae be true."

"No," she said firmly, her eyes watching his hands for signs of an imminent attack. "The job was only the catalyst. Everything that happened between us was real, was my free will. My choice. It wasn't an assignment any more. I was getting paid to spend time with a smart, funny, handsome man."

"Hoo fookin fantastic fur ye." He leaned heavily on the sink, hiding his face from her, caught in a whirlwind of fury and loss. He'd lost her, won her back, and lost her again. He'd lost what he'd thought he had with her. Had she ever existed, this person he'd thought she was?

Everything his mother had a hand in was poisoned. "Dae ye seriously expect me tae believe tha' load ay shite?"

"Yes. No. Yes," she floundered. "I want you to. I need you to."

His muscles ached from gripping the sink.

"We might never have met without that assignment. But it was always me, not an act. From the beginning, from the moment we spoke. There was something special between us. Not the job," she anticipated his retort. "Something else. Chemistry. I know you felt it too."

"Get oot ma hoose." He said it so quietly she almost didn't hear it.

She stayed still, wanting to pretend for a moment longer that the world didn't hurt. "I wouldn't be here, after everything, if I didn't believe it."

He ducked his head down and bellowed, "GET OOT!"

The door slammed. Rab sank to his haunches. His fingers still held on to the sink edge for life, for sanity. He locked his forearms together and sank his face into them. He stayed in that position until his cramped muscles gave way and he landed on his rear. He hugged his knees tightly.

Rab woke in a fetal position on the linoleum. He lay there, too indifferent to move. He thought about Alice's genuine anger over the engagement. If it had been only a job, the engagement was a perfect out. She'd taken it, but then forgiven him. There had been no need for that. She'd even forgiven him for not being what he'd claimed to be. Why? Out of guilt for her own deception? Then there was the way she looked at him. The way she was with him. If that was an act, she deserved an award. She was probably the only person who could fully understand and forgive his choices. After all these years, would his mother be able to perceive that? If his brother had been keeping in touch, filling her in on all Rab's missteps, it was possible. But why would she bother with him? Why would Mary indulge in twisted matchmaking to crush his spirit—find his perfect girl and set it up so that they meet, fall in love, and betray each other? Because he'd impersonated Nick, her favorite? But she hadn't made him pretend to be someone he wasn't, pretend to have an education and qualifications. Or had she? Had his entire childhood led to this inevitable charade, of Rab himself destroying everything he wanted, because he was too stubborn to let go of old wounds inflicted at her hands? Was it chance, or fate, or design?

He needed to believe he'd always had a choice, every step of the way. He wouldn't let his bint of a mother have that much power over him. He wouldn't lay the blame on her doorstep.

He tried to stand, but rubbery legs refused to support him. He caught the edge of the island as he went down and hung on like a drowning sailor as he cursed and rubbed the circulation back. Gritting his teeth through a massive case of pins and needles, he perched on a stool to weather them out. His eyes wandered the small apartment, imagining his few belongings back in the rolling suitcase. One call and Goodwill would haul off the rest, as if he had never been here. Then he spotted her coat. It sprawled at the base of the island, lying where it had fallen. She'd gone in a hurry, too upset to notice the loss. A few hours ago? A day? It felt like weeks.

His legs held as he tottered over. The yellowish fur was soft against his skin as he gathered it off the floor. He smiled. She'd given his stubborn, proud self an excuse to come see her if he wanted to do so.

38: Sympathy for the Devil

Rab pushed hair out of his eyes and tried to think about his mother from Nick's view. Nick the favorite. Nick who had loved his mother and kept in touch. He peered through the oval cut glass panel and leaned on the doorbell, uncomfortably reminded of a November evening in Glasgow twenty-five years ago.

Unlike then, Mary opened the door. He forced his face into a smile. She stepped back and he followed, half-expecting the threshold to magically block his entrance as if he were an uninvited vampire.

"Ray told me you were coming." She gave him the inverted smile over her shoulder as she led the way to a formal sitting room that looked like a photo in a home magazine.

Booth greeted him with a half-handshake, half-hug. "Glad you could make it. Your mother's been beside herself, knowing one of her sons was here in town, and not getting to see you."

Rab perched awkwardly in an expensive but uncomfortable chair. "Ur ye sure it's me ye want tae see?"

Booth looked between mother and son. "Of course it is. I'll let you two get caught up." He disappeared into the adjoining kitchen.

Mary moved alongside Rab and placed a hand on his leather-clad shoulder. The dark nails made a faint scratching sound.

"You're still dressed in this obscene cow skin." Her hand dropped away. "Let me get a good look at you."

He obediently raised his head, but had to work to meet her eyes. She reached out again, and he stiffened. She smoothed the hair back from his forehead. Memories tumbled into his mind of watching his brother get this kind of attention, not himself.

"Ah ken Nick wis awyis yer favorite."

"Is that what you thought?" The blue eyes stared him down. "Why?"

"Ye wis awyis daein things fur hum. Ah wis awyis a disappointment. Ma hair wisnae pairfect. Ma claes wis a right mess. Ye wis awyis on me aboot the shoelaces." He felt foolish for it being so important. "Ye dinnae hauf go through me for the laces."

"Rabbie never told you?" At his indignant look, she continued. "Of course he wouldn't have. He didn't want you to ever think you weren't as good as anyone else." She sighed and took a step back. "Today, they would call it mild dyspraxia. Back then, all we knew was that you were a little clumsy and had trouble with your hands." She pulled up another chair to face him. "We argued about how to cope with it. He said you needed to struggle, work it out for yourself or it would never get better. I couldn't bear to watch the fumbling." This close, she looked old and fragile.

He thought about himself as a wee lad. Everything had taken longer for him than for others. Tying shoes. Cutting with scissors. Always a slow bastard. Always the messy one. Stuck between the goal posts, out of the way. He'd often given up on getting his hair right. Comparing himself to the other kids hadn't made him feel slow and stupid; comparing himself to Nick had. The old anger flared.

"You didn't even want the help. You wanted to do everything for yourself. It was nerve-racking. I thought your father was cruel to just watch you fail over and over. We were experimenting on our own child." She twisted the prominent diamond on her finger. "Gave me a distaste for experiments of any kind."

"So ye hooked up wey thum animaw rights nutters." He crossed his arms and leaned back, not completely buying the explanation.

"BUAV. Yes." She was oblivious to his incredulity.

"Hoo dinnae ye come hame fae the protest?" he asked sharply. "Couldnae haunle the burden ay a handicapped wean onie mair?"

She stood up and put her vacated chair between them. "I was arrested. The BUAV paid my fine. But I decided your father was right, about everything. I was putting you both at risk of being taken away." She gripped the chair back tightly, as if she would use it to fight off an angry lion at any moment. "A clumsy boy in foster care? You would have been abused. I left Scotland and came back here." She reached for a picture frame on a side table. "I had your Uncle Malcolm's girlfriend Maureen send me some of my things, including this."

She handed him an old photograph of two identical dark-eyed, dark-haired boys crowded together like puppies, caught in the middle of rough housing. One looked serious, the other was mugging for the camera. Both were equally disheveled. Rab wasn't even sure which one he was.

"It was the hardest decision I ever had to make." She turned the photograph back to herself and stroked the glass. "I chose to keep you two together. What kind of mother divides her children down the middle like dealing cards? That's what the divorce lawyer suggested. I gave up both of you so you could have each other. Rabbie raised you well. Better than I could have. Better than I did, before I left." She dabbed at a tear to keep her mascara from running.

Rab watched the performance skeptically. "Ye nivver ca'ed or wrote, but. Ur no' gawn tae say ye did, an' ma faither kept it fae us?"

She put the framed photograph down. "I thought it would only hurt more. I preferred to have you hate me rather than follow in my footsteps. Even though Nick did become an activist too." She smiled her downwards smile. "If you boys wanted me in your life, I knew you would be able to find me here."

"Ah wis a wee lad! Wisnae ma joab tae find ma deadbeat mither."

Her hand shot out and closed tightly on a large hank of dark hair. She jerked hard, dragging his head down to her hip. He felt like a ram for the slaughter, held by the horn, neck twisted to expose the arteries. He glared unrepentantly into her angry blue eyes. She smiled her anti-smile down at him and released him with a little shove.

"You always were a fighter. Even if the fight was only against the people who loved you the most." She took a step backward and turned partially toward the kitchen as Booth pushed through, carrying a bottle of wine and three glasses.

Rab looked warily between the two as he accepted a glass. His eyes shifted to the bottle. Wine bottles all looked pretty much alike to him. No way to know for certain if it was the same kind as the one that left shards in his back, since that one had been inside the black skeleton gift bag. Alice's fingerprints, Nick's fiancée—all they had in common was Rab and his mother. His eyes shot up to Booth, who was watching him carefully. No doubt he'd already made the same connection.

Booth held up his glass. "To family," he toasted.

"*Slàinte*," he murmured. He smoothed his hair down from Mary's rough handling.

"Rab, your mother's pleased with your work at the veterinary school," Booth said over-enthusiastically. "It's not how she planned it…"

"I wanted to nail Riesen red-handed." Mary smiled her inverted smile. "I'd been watching him for years."

"But he was forced to resign in all the fallout. So it had a happy ending. She can set her sights on another ethics-impaired researcher playing God." He smiled indulgently at her.

Mary looked up at her husband. "Riesen knows how to bring in grant money. You know he'll simply get hired somewhere else, become another institution's problem."

"And one day you'll catch him out, if he isn't humbled by the whole experience," Booth added proudly.

Rab took a healthy swallow from his glass.

Mary turned to him. "Now that you're at loose ends, would you be willing to take your brother's place? Not pretending to be him, of course, but doing what he did. Being a mole in research facilities to catch animal rights violations." She took a sip of wine as she waited for his response.

"We'd pay for your education," Booth interjected. "Veterinary technician, or all the way to DVM."

Mary gave him a sharp glance. "That could take six years for the doctorate. He doesn't have any prerequisities."

"Ye dain't think Ah could dae it?" Rab challenged. "If Nick could, Ah kin. We're basically the same pairson byraway."

"As you amply demonstrated. No training, and able to fool everyone on the research project. What do you say, son?" His stepfather beamed at him.

"Ah dain't want tae go intae research. Pure dead boring. An' morally questionable at times."

"That's why I dedicated my life to being its conscience," his mother asserted with missionary zeal.

"Thanks, but nae thanks." He emptied his glass and set it down on the side table next to the photograph of the wee twin boys. "Ah'm fur the aff."

"I won't take that as your final answer. Think it over. You've got about a month before you can leave us." Booth put his arm around his wife. "Won't you stay for dinner?"

Rab shifted nervously on the doorstep, wondering if he should knock again. Alice opened the door hesitantly. She was wearing a gray sweatshirt, and her hair was pulled back. The red dye had nearly shampooed out, leaving her with more highlights than usual.

"Lowlander!" She leaped on him, hugging him tight.

He buried his nose in her hair and breathed in the high lonesome smell of heather. Her skin seemed more radiant than ever. He swung her around the small yard until he was dizzy, and set her down gently. He kissed her neck, sending a little shiver through her. "Moarnin," he whispered in her ear. He couldn't wipe the grin off his face. "Ah brought ye somehin."

They moved apart. He handed over her worn fur coat with a little bow.

She snorted a laugh. "Thank you, kind sir." He helped her into it.

"So...dinner with the Booths. How did it go?" She searched his face.

"Ach. Breengin right intae it." He pushed the hair off his forehead. "Ah dinnae make it aw the way tae dinner."

"Well, baby steps." She squeezed his arm. "I'm proud of you for doing it. You know I would have gone with you."

"Went be'er than Ah expected, jen up. Ye wid be dead proud. Ah wis a gennleman." She smiled at him. "Ah onerly ca'ed her wan name."

She slapped him on the arm. "Rab!"

"Ooyah! Aisy wey me! Ah'm a wounded man, mind. Ah left on gude terms, haun tae God." He looked around at the tree tops that were rapidly being stripped of their colors for bare branches. Glasgow would be dark by this time of day, even if this were local time.

"So what's next for you, Rab?" she asked finally.

His dark eyes rested on hers. "Ah like it when ye cry me tha'."

"I'm still getting used to it. But I like it much better than Nick or Knickers."

"Me tae. Ye huv nae idea hoo mich trouble tha' caused us."

"I can imagine. Can you blame your mother or your father for that?" She cocked her head.

"Ah dain't ken. Ah wullnae make the same mistake, Ah promise."

She gave him a startled look, then her eyes dropped as she realized he was speaking in far-off generalities. "Golden. You never did answer my question, Rab Kerr. What's next for you?"

"Well, Ah wis hopin tae make wild, passionate love tae ma wumman a few times in a row."

She looked over his shoulder. "Really? Where is she?"

"C'moan, hen." He swiped the hair out of his eyes.

"The last time we were together, you threw me out of your apartment." She turned serious eyes on him. "And now you're being squirrelly about your future plans." She tried to pull away.

"Ah'm pure dead sorry aboot tha'." He cupped her elbows to keep her from going away. "Ah've decided ye wis right. Ah dain't care whit brought us thegither. An' efter Ah sort things err? Go hame, see ma Da. Say ma farewell at Nick's grave."

She nodded. "I'm sorry about your brother."

"Me tae. He wid still be roond if it wisnae fur me." He let go of her arms.

"You can't think like that. It wasn't your fault."

He shrugged. She stared up at the swirling gray sky. Silence stretched between them again, sad and heavy. She reached out and touched his hand, a kiss of skin on skin. He was surprised the distance was so much smaller than it felt. Her eyes said she knew he wasn't coming back.

"Come wey me," he said suddenly. "Ye kin get an expedited passport wey me. We kin bide wey ma da. He wullnae mind. He's got an empty room."

She looked away. "I'm not sure I even know you."

He side-stepped into her line of vision. "Ye ken me be'er than onieyin."

She studied his face. "Even if I did go with you, I could only stay six months on a tourist visa, at the most, before I got kicked out. If I could afford it. Then what?"

"Ah dain't ken. Ye could huv a fresh start oniewhir ye want."

She turned her back on him and headed for the apartment.

He grabbed her arm. "Ye cannae want tae stay err, alane. No' efter ivryhin. Come away wey me."

She looked at his fingers digging into the fur of her jacket. He released her.

"Erras options, hen. Us thegither past the six months. Ah dinnae want tae assume, efter aw Ah've pit ye through. Ah'm fur it if ye ur, but. Ah mean it," he pleaded. "Ah'll be pure dead respectable. Dull, iven. Ah wis thinkin aboot gawn tae the uni when Ah get hame, fur veterinary technician. Mibbe iven large animaw doactor. Ah could huv a practice in the Borderlands. Or Ah could go sma' animaws an' stay in the city. Whiriver ye want tae be."

She blinked back tears.

"Ye could be dead sick ay me lang afore the six months run oot, or mibbe no'. Ah huv ma fears, too. Bein Scoats isnae unique in Scoatland, mind. Ah cannae promise ye'll love Glesga, or maself. Aw Ah ask is tha' ye dain't walk away fae this rinoo." He searched her face for some sign of encouragement. "Please say somehin. Oniehin."

She gave him a long look, seeming to come to a decision. She reached under her coat to the kangaroo pocket of her sweatshirt, pulled out a thin booklet, and tossed it to him.

He caught it. An American passport. He looked at her. She mimed turning the pages. Inside the cover was her photo.

"Ach! Ya dancer!"

" 'I'll believe in you if you believe in me.' "

"Ye'll pure fancy George Square decked oot fur Christmas." He kissed the top of her heather-scented head.

"Are there any beaches near Glasgow? I miss the ocean wicked bad." She squinted up at him, hopeful but afraid of the answer.

"Oh, aye. Loads. Seventeen weyin aboot thirty kilometers, an' mair iven farther oot. 'S an island, ken." He grimaced. "In the North Atlantic, but. A wee Baltic maist ay the time."

"Golden. That just means it won't be crowded." She smiled and gestured toward the door. "Are you coming in? The Glasgow-Edinburgh Express is about to leave the station for all parts south."

"Err ye go—startin it, as awyis." He pretended to be offended. "Ye'd best go through wey tha' threat, hen."

She laughed and disappeared into the apartment.

"Folley the White Rabbit," he said softly and ran after her.

www.ingramcontent.com/pod-product-compliance
Lightning Source LLC
Chambersburg PA
CBHW031113030726
47496CB00002BA/531